SHADOW

BOUND

L.A. MCGINNIS

FATE · LIES

SECRETS

BOOKS BY L.A. MCGINNIS

WICKED REALMS SERIES
Savage Is My Kingdom
Cruel Is My Court
Merciless Is My Crown
Vicious Is My Throne
Dark Is My Exile

DARKFELL VAMPIRE CLAN SERIES
Night Marked
Shadow Bound
Lost Kingdom
Iron Queen

BLACKSTONE VAMPIRE CLAN SERIES
Immortal Inheritance
Immortal Betrayal
Immortal Vendetta
Immortal Secrets

SHADOWSEND VAMPIRE CLAN SERIES
Blood Claimed
Ruthless Liege
Dark Redemption
Eternal Legacy

NOCTURNE VAMPIRE CLAN SERIES
Fated In Blood
Fated In Secrets
Fated In Ruin
Fated In Forever

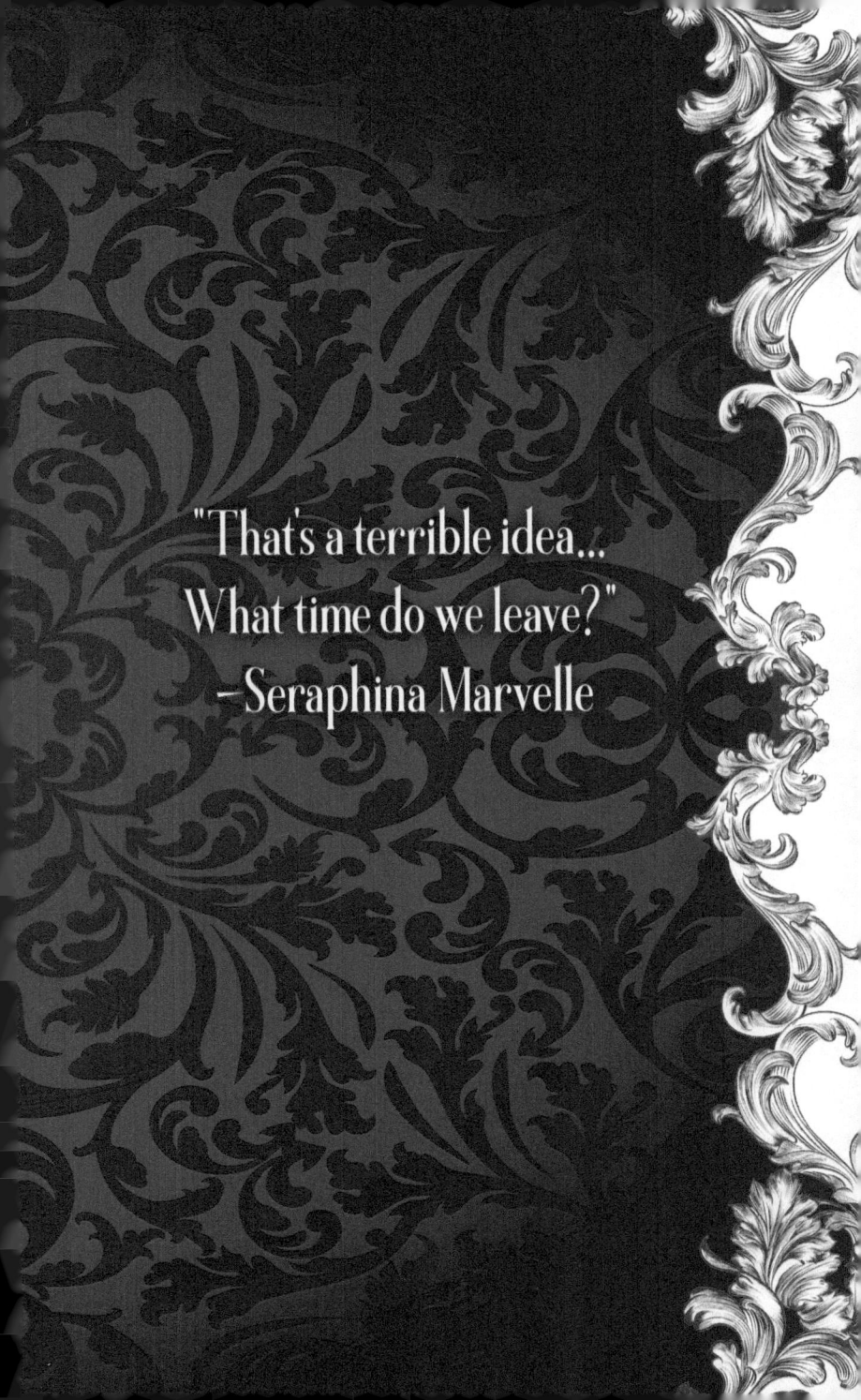

"That's a terrible idea...
What time do we leave?"
—Seraphina Marvelle

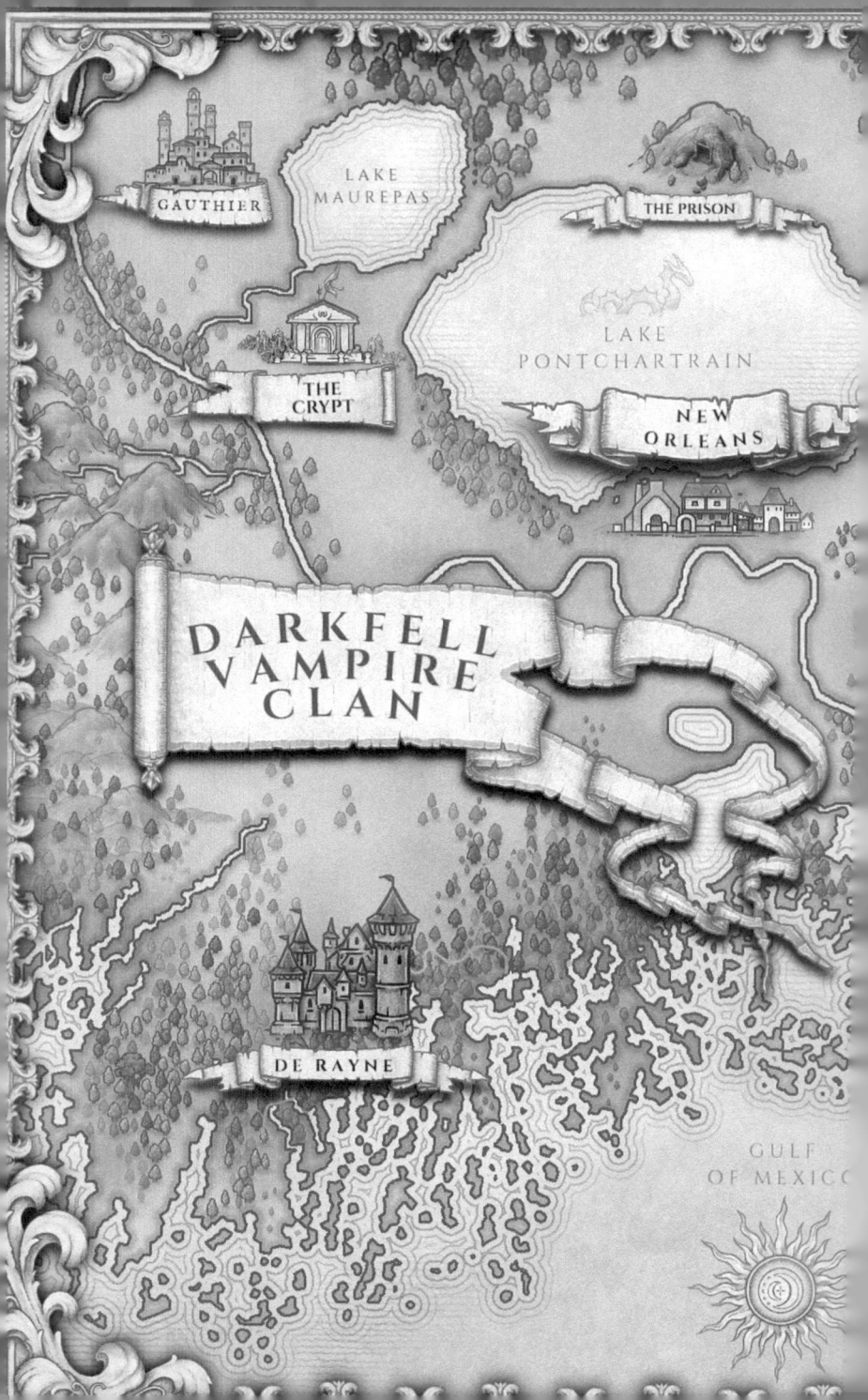

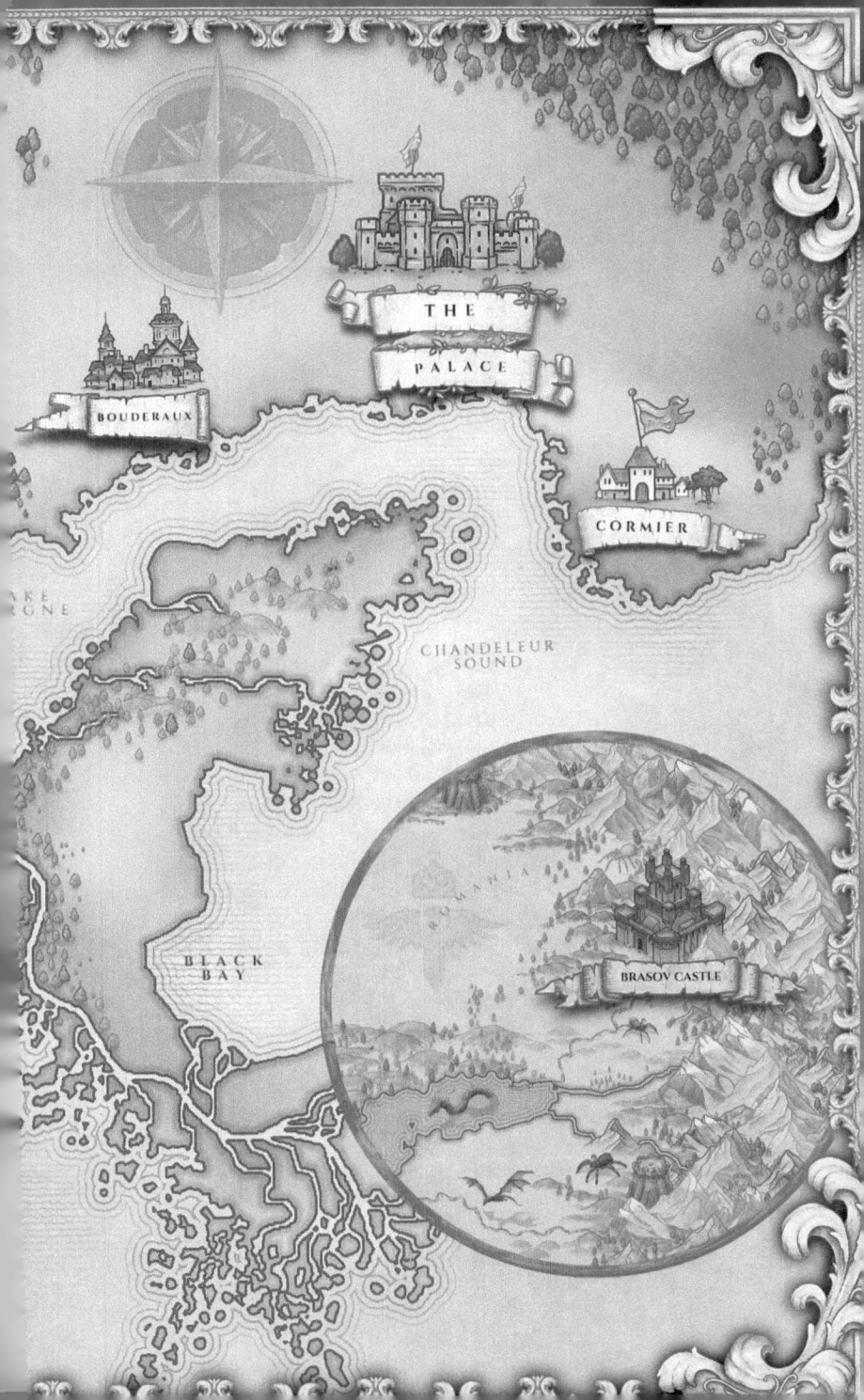

ISBN-13: 978-1-970112-38-2
ISBN-13: 978-1-970112-40-5

Published in the United States of America by Fools Journey Press, 2021

Chapter 1
Seraphina

When the third revenant stuck its hideous head around the corner, my lungs stopped working, my palms turning sweaty as I retreated.

"Could you even *be* more of an asshole," I muttered, magic and shadows spilling unchecked from my hands, a sad little side effect of my current full-blown panic attack. "This is supposed to be a lesson, not an execution. Three against one isn't *fair*."

"What is that saying the humans have?" Deston's deep, mocking voice echoed through the long chamber. "*Life isn't fair*. Stop dithering and get on with the lesson, Seraphina."

"Dickhead." I muttered, reaffirming all the ways I hated that bastard.

The first thing I was going to do—providing I survived today's test—was knock Lord Deston de Rayne on his admittedly fine ass. If I was lucky, in front of Cyrus, so we could laugh about the whole thing later.

The largest creature in the middle pinned those hungry, beady eyes on me, nose flaps slapping open and shut with a wet, sticky sound. Out of all the horrible things in my new, generally fucked up existence, I hated revenants the most. These creatures used to be vampires, corrupted with the king's foul magic and turned into monsters. Mindless killing machines, answering only to him.

Deston knew I hated these beasts. *Loathed* them with the force of a thousand suns.

Deston was also a certified sadist with a habit of torturing me in the name of teaching.

Honestly, he sucked at the latter, but was expert-level at the former.

The revenants closed ranks, their heads low to the ground, mouths drawn wide to show off their double rows of needle-sharp teeth, spindly legs moving unnaturally as they crept along like spiders, deadly claws digging chunks out of the parquet floor with every step.

Added to their terrifying appearances was the overwhelmingly foul stench. Black bog water and putrefying flesh, mixed into one malodorous combination.

My eyes watered as I retreated, keeping all three in my sights.

If I lost track of even one of them...

Well, I didn't know what they'd do, given that they were illusionary monsters conjured up by Deston to make my training session seem *more real*. But Deston's illusions had a habit of drawing blood, so I couldn't drop my guard for a moment or I'd be dragging my beat-to-shit self back to my room after today's lesson was over.

Another cautious step back and I froze, the hair on the back of my neck prickling.

Okay, so there were four revenants and one was directly behind me.

You clever fucking bastard. You're really trying to punish me today. My heart hammered so hard, every panicked breath hurt.

"Anytime now, Seraphina. I don't have all day." Deston's ghostly voice floated through the frescoed hall of mirrors that reflected the prowling beasts, increasing their numbers tenfold.

All of a sudden, I was surrounded by a whole pack of these things, and adrenaline flooded my body in a rush of panic and primal terror. Four were bad enough...forty sent my body straight into fight or flight mode.

But there was nowhere *to* go.

Deston had locked me in.

Surrounded by priceless gilt and crystal, I wondered why Deston had chosen this room for today's carnage. Monsters and ornamental finery seemed at odds, but maybe I was missing the irony. Every day he came up with some new horrific test, every one of them created with his strange, transmutative magic.

Most days, I passed.

Let's hope today was one of those days.

Bad enough there were three revenants in front and another right behind me; even worse, two broke off to flank me on the right. I hated the way these things moved, that creepy scuttle-slide gait they had. They were aberrations of nature, although they were usually faster than this.

And they usually only hunted in pairs.

"They only hunt in pairs, you know." My voice echoed through the chamber. "There are four of them, so you didn't even get the illusion right."

"I'm impressed, you can count. Most days, I have my doubts."

Motherfucker. Magic gathered at my hands, and with a twist of my wrist, I threw out a small stream of flame. My necromancer magic resembled white-hot plasma and was twice as deadly, providing I hit my target.

Predictably, I completely missed the revenant but shattered a handful of mirrors, sending glass showering down over the creature. The shards bounced off the tough hide and scattered across the floor like ice.

I used a two-handed approach for the next one, yet only managed to sear a long burn down its leather-like torso. The monster threw its head up and howled, the sound echoing off the gold-embossed frescoed ceiling as I spooled up more power.

They skittered closer, talons scraping on the floor.

So close, their damp fetid breath skimmed across my face with expended breath; so close, I saw the blood and gore caked into their curved claws.

I held my ground, unable to maneuver for a better position, moisture washing over my shoulders, the stench making me gag.

Jesus Christ, it's right behind me, isn't it?

Even though I knew this move was against every rule of engagement, I spun, completely turning my back on the three approaching revenants. The single attacker was barely four feet away. Surely, I couldn't miss from this distance?

I used both hands to cast. My magic did some weird jerky-hop thing, skittering toward the lone revenant like an errant rubber ball.

Thankfully, the monster launched off the floor at the same time my plasma bounced up. The blast caught the revenant squarely in the stomach. Within a blink, a thousand-pound creature became nothing but drifting ash.

I pivoted quickly, threw another ball of magic, and ashed the smaller one on the left.

Treading carefully, I retreated step after step, glass crunching beneath my tennis shoes, matching their movements while they advanced, pushing my magic down through my arms into my hands. But instead of blistering heat, all I got was a tingle. I shook my hands to reset them.

You'd think after three months of practice, I would be better at this.

Twenty feet beyond the revenants, Lord Deston de Rayne—all six-foot-two of him—materialized into the room.

His smile was brittle, not a shred of warmth. One hand rested firmly on his ever-present silver cane, and his black hair seemed to absorb—rather than reflect—the warm light. In his black, bespoke suit, the elder vampire was handsome, I'd give him that, but all I wanted was to wipe that arrogant smile off his face.

I half-wondered if he'd let these things tear me to pieces, just to watch the show.

"Stop dithering, Seraphina." Deston's velvety soft voice turned into a rough purr. "Hands up and cast. Hesitation will get you killed."

I threw everything I had at the burned revenant, smoke rolling off its charred flesh, the stench of cooking meat replacing dirty bog water. Still howling in pain, my magic went straight down its throat before the thing shuddered and burst into a cloud of ash, blotting out most of the room.

I choked, waving a hand in front of my face to clear the air.

Fuck. Now I couldn't see the other one. I backed up, then one foot slipped on a shard of glass and went out from under me.

I course corrected, but too quickly, and lurched forward, arms pinwheeling. A dark shadow shifted furtively within that smoke. Tumbling onto my knees, I cast everything I had into the cloud, praying the sloppy ball would be enough. The creature was still moving when it disintegrated, and ash washed across my feet like a wave on a beach.

Relief swept through me; my eyes blurring with tears as I wiped the grit off my face. Across the chamber, Deston rubbed his chest as if *he* were the one who'd just faced down four revenants. Still, this was better than yesterday. I was still bruised from our last session, which had been an unqualified disaster.

"There. I killed them. Are you happy?"

One minute, Deston was twenty feet away, leaning on his cane.

The next, he had my arm in a vice-like grip, those obsidian eyes glittering with rage.

"No, I am not *happy*. That was the sloppiest display of magic I've ever seen. *Merde*, one would think you are a youngling, not a blooded vampire Queen who's practiced every day for three months under the tutelage of a master."

A master, my ass. But I pinched my mouth together. Arguing with Deston never got me anywhere because in his mind, 'the master' was always right.

"*Tu es une telle déception.* If those creatures had been real, you would've been dead."

"Gee, guess who's nothing but a pile of ash on the floor?" I countered sarcastically, pointing at the destruction around us. "Hint, it's not me."

He pushed me away as if I wasn't even worth his time. "They were moving at the speed of sloths." He sneered down his nose. "And even then, you barely succeeded."

Okay, so they had been slower than usual. But I was still standing, which meant today's training session was a definite success in a sea of failures.

"Why did you pick this place?" I asked curiously, changing the subject. "Pretty fancy room, if you ask me, for a revenant showdown. Honestly, I hated to destroy it." Not only that, but this room looked vaguely familiar, as if I'd seen it somewhere before.

"Why don't you turn around, Seraphina?"

Turning your back on an enemy was a huge mistake, and Lord de Rayne was deadlier than any revenant pack. Still, curiosity would, most likely, be the death of me.

I spun slowly, broken glass crunching underfoot, using the mirrors to keep him in my sights.

Ah, now I knew why we were here. "Did you really recreate the throne room in the royal palace?" I asked, walking toward the raised dais at the head of the room.

"No, it's a coffee shop on Bourbon Street," he said caustically. "Of course, it's Viktor's throne room. Why else would there be a throne?"

I ignored him and his fouler-than-usual mood, because I knew when to pick my battles. I'd never seen King Viktor's throne room in person, but knowing Deston's attention to detail, this was likely a perfect replica.

A dark throne perched on a raised platform, and I climbed the five steps leading up. Soft, dark red carpet muffled my footfalls, my old battered tennis shoes outlined against the plush surface. When I reached the top, I turned and looked down the long, mirrored concourse.

Somehow, even though this was only an illusion, standing up here made me feel powerful.

This was what Viktor saw every day.

The throne was crafted from black, riveted metal, with a high back and ornate arms forged into the bodies of fantastical beasts. The ironwork—*I assumed it was iron*—was intricate, covered in runes and raised designs, some of it so delicate, the filigree no wider than a hair.

Deston hadn't moved from the center of the windowless room. There wasn't a shred of natural light, yet the entire space was suffused with a golden glow, every unbroken mirror reflecting the ancient incandescent bulbs glowing in crystal chandeliers.

"I bet you used to stand up here, didn't you? How many times, I wonder, did you dream about sitting in this thing?" I was only trying to piss him off, and sure enough, his narrowed gaze skimmed from me to the throne before a wicked smile twisted his lips. My instincts went on high alert.

"As the future ruler, perhaps you should try it out for yourself," Deston crooned. "In fact, I insist." He paused before adding, *"My Queen,"* turning my title into an insult.

I glanced over at the throne. "Yeah, I'm not sitting in that hideous thing until I'm forced to." On cue, a wave of dark power shoved me forward a step. I glared back at him, bracing my feet on the carpet, resisting with all my might.

"One would think you don't even *want* to be Queen." His mockery echoed through the cavernous space. "What's the matter, Seraphina?" Another smile flit across his face, this one tinged with malevolence, and I was pushed another step closer. "Aren't you curious to see what real power feels like?"

I shook my head. "Stop fucking around, Deston."

I wasn't ready for this. I didn't even want to be queen, not when I didn't have a choice in the matter. Not when the decision was being forced on me. I didn't want power, or influence or the crushing responsibility of ruling over an entire kingdom. Three months ago, I'd been a college student.

Now I had fangs. I drank blood.

I was—*technically*—undead, though I felt as alive as ever.

Supposedly I was some mythical, unkillable vampire queen, but what I'd learned these past three months... mostly, I sucked at magic and everything vampire.

My ever-constant failure was a real ego crusher, especially since most of my mishaps occurred in front of this gloating asshole. And when everyone's lives depended on *me,* the time was fast approaching when failure would no longer be an option.

"What if I offered you better motivation? If you can stop me, *ma cherie,* I shall release you from our bargain." Deston's challenge rang out softly, "Think of it. I shall be gone from your life, forevermore. You would never see me again."

Now that *was* proper motivation.

I'd love to get rid of his backstabbing ass, no matter how fine it was.

I dug my heels in, pulled up my magic, surrounding myself with an impenetrable barrier, one even this douchebag couldn't get through. Deston lifted a hand and I slid across the dais sideways until I slammed into the throne.

"Fuck you, Deston." I braced my hands on the arm of the throne, fingers gripping desperately, every muscle straining against his magic trying to force me into that fucking chair. Then my feet left the ground, and I twisted midair, my ass landing in the seat.

Hard.

Deston leaned on his wolf's head cane, a mocking smile on his face, daring me to stop him.

But I couldn't. I was stuck in this chair, trapped in this fate. I was smothering, and I couldn't breathe and...

Just like that, Deston released his magic, and I sagged forward, pulling in breath after ragged breath. My hands gripped the arms of the throne and I pushed myself upright, every muscle groaning from the effort of resisting Deston's overwhelming power.

"You can't keep me here." The words came out in short bursts, my magic skittering through my body like errant lightning. "And this isn't funny anymore."

"Then do something about it, Seraphina." He prowled closer, a primal predator cloaked in shadows and Saville Row. "*Stop me.*"

How could somebody so hauntingly beautiful be so menacing?

How could someone so old be such *a child*?

"Fine, I will." My arms strained to the limit, I managed to push myself out of the throne, take one shaking step forward, body aching from the effort, until I reached the top of the steps, and raised my hands.

This time, I let my magic go, not caring if I leveled this entire castle. The white, glittering wave carved through the walls of mirrors like a scythe, spewing glass everywhere, sending shards of glass spinning straight toward Deston, standing unbothered in the center of the chaos.

He shot me a mocking, disgusted smile, then flicked them straight toward me. The entire room turned into a sea of deadly projectiles, every gleaming edge a razor, every point sharper than a knife, as that wall of glass sped in my direction.

"Stop them, Seraphina. Stop them or die."

I threw up a shield of magic in front of me. White hot plasma charred the wooden parquet floor between us, heated the air to a glowing red.

The mirrored shards hit my wall and melted, dripping down like water. I was able to stop most of them, except for the ones that got through, peppering my skin with a hundred fine, burning cuts.

Something warm and coppery trickled into my mouth as I kept my shield in place.

Blood trickled down the side of my face, more and more glass slivers crashed against the shimmering wall, my barrier failing by the second beneath the unending assault.

Death by a thousand cuts, I thought desperately.

Was Deston planning to kill me today? Then the onslaught was over, nothing left except a puddle of cooling, melted glass on the floor in front of me, the beautiful parquet singed to black.

For a second, we stared at each other over the carnage, the air reeking of spent magic, dead revenants and charred wood. *And blood.*

One sniff and Deston's eyes changed, glowing like banked embers. He prowled closer; my heart thumped faster. I didn't know the last time he'd fed. Hell, I didn't know *if* he fed, but he was looking at me like a linebacker eyed a juicy steak.

"Careful there, de Rayne." Luthor's deep voice rang through the chamber, stopping Deston in his tracks, his hungry gaze devouring me as I blew out a shaky breath, swiping the blood off my face as he stalked toward us.

Luthor always had the most perfect timing.

The ancient warrior stepped between us, his cold blue eyes fixed on Deston, his broad shoulders taut with purpose as he studied my cut-up arms. The scar down his face only made him look more dangerous, and if he wanted, he'd snap Deston's neck without a second thought.

Right now, I wouldn't stop him.

"*Je suis en contrôle*, Fontaine. *Va te faire foutre*," Deston cursed. In French, of course, because he knew I couldn't understand. But he stayed put, his eyes dark and empty once more. My heart beat normally again.

"We're finished here." I drew myself up to my full height, still nearly a foot shorter than the two males below me. "I'm done for the day. I've had enough of your shit and my hands are blistered now."

Deston muttered something else in French, and Luthor replied in the same.

"I'm sure that was properly foul, but it still doesn't change the fact that I'm leaving." I descended the steps, advanced into Deston's personal space, my nose nearly touching his silk tie. After a second's hesitation, he stepped back out of my way, eyes flashing.

"You lost, Seraphina," Deston hissed as I pushed by him, my feet crunching through glass. "You *owe* me that advisory position." He barked out a harsh laugh. "If you even survive long enough to become queen."

"Looks like we're stuck with each other, then," I told him sweetly, even though I was tired of his never-ending arrogance. Weary of wondering when he'd sell us out to the king. Exhausted by his constant bullying.

I turned before I reached the doors, found him still staring after me.

"But remember this, Deston. I won't need you forever. And if I were you, I would worry about what happens the day you're no longer useful."

Chapter 2
Seraphina

That evening, I was in the library reading a particularly boring account of the settlement of New Orleans, when Deston strolled in like he owned the place.

Which he did, but that didn't give him the right to interrupt my evening ritual. Two precious hours of tea and books and complete utter silence were the only things keeping me sane at the moment and *how dare this asshole ruin my night?*

He cleared his throat.

I ignored him.

Everybody knew mortal enemies didn't speak to each other. *Especially* when one of them was buried in a book. You had to be a special kind of arrogant to interrupt someone when they were reading, but that was Lord de Rayne.

A swaggering, backstabbing pain in my ass.

Three months ago, I was a medical student, meandering my way through a bland, safe life like an obedient little human. I'd had a crochety grandmother, a messy studio apartment in the Garden District, and dreams of changing the world.

These days I lived in a beautiful mansion—actually, a medieval castle—plunked into the middle of the Louisiana bayou, built from magic, and protected by spells. Gram was gone, my apartment was a distant memory and my dreams... well, those dreams were as dead as my long-lost humanity.

Instead of Gram, three gorgeous, ancient vampires watched over me.

Two I was in love with. The third...I despised with every piece of my being.

To further complicate matters, I was the long-lost Queen of the Darkfell clan, but I knew nothing about being a vampire queen. Hell, I didn't know anything about being a vampire.

So, here I was, teaching myself how to be an undead bloodsucking regent. I'd tried the internet, but online sources, while plentiful, were understandably unreliable.

Deston, however, possessed the library of my dreams. This place was better than a museum, he even had all the original works of Shakespeare, including all four Folios and an assortment of Quartos. I resolved to read his dog-eared copy of Cymbeline cover to cover once I got a handle on this queen stuff.

But though Deston's library went back centuries, there was nothing here on vampire queens, hence, I was reading the driest possible book imaginable—*A History of New Orleans Through the Ages.*

Ugh, I'd read IKEA manuals with more conflict and tension.

"Seraphina." Deston was growing impatient, and out of habit, I pulled the sleeve of my sweater down to hide the ugly scar on my arm.

"Go away. I'm busy." With a thought, I threw up a shadowy wall of magic between us, hoping he'd take the freaking hint and disappear.

Instead, he tore a hole in my barrier and stepped

straight through, nose in the air, like he was so much better than me. For a moment, I toyed with blasting him through the doorway, but I'd only wreck the library, my favorite room in this whole miserable place.

"Personal space, Lord Asshole." I snapped. "Luthor and Cyrus both warned you to steer clear, and I still have an hour to go." My fingers clenched the book tighter. Every single time Deston was this close, my jittery nerves went on edge, fight or flight instincts unanimously voting to run.

And I would have, except those same instincts warned me...*he might chase.*

"*Seraphina.*" He hissed my name with that seductive, French lilt. Another one of his clever disguises, a veneer of civility over the predator lurking beneath. "*Ma petite.* We must talk."

"We don't have anything to talk about, you traitorous bastard." I didn't look up from the page, even though I had long since stopped reading. "I have work to do. I'm not wasting any more time on your lies."

One of his eyebrows went up. "Why are you reading that pitifully boring tome?"

"Because I have to learn to be a queen," I gestured around me at the shelves of leatherbound books. "And there's no Darkfell Clan for Dummies laying around."

His brows rose. "*That's* what you're doing in here every night?"

"It is, in fact. Nice collection of vintage vampire novels, by the way. Is that a signed copy of Dracula I saw?"

He tipped his head to the side, curiosity gilding his gaze. "I find the human's view of us... interesting."

"Bull-fucking-shit. You collect those books because you're the biggest narcissist alive. Or dead, in this instance. Having Stoker on your shelves strokes your impossibly huge ego. It's probably even better than posing in front of a mirror in that gothic getup of yours." I waved him off. "Unless you can teach me to be queen, leave."

"What would you like to know?"

He inched closer, that focused, predatory intensity making the hairs on my neck go up. It irked me that I smelled him so intensely—his lush, erotic scent stirring up something inside me—my new vampire senses far superior to my human ones.

And I couldn't help sneaking peeks at him over the top of my book, cursing every stolen glance.

But there was no denying Lord de Rayne was vampire crack cocaine, one hundred percent pure and uncut. With his perfect cheekbones and silky black hair, he was predatory, powerful, disturbingly carnal, and every time he was around me, I had to deal with this terrible juxtaposition of hate and lust warring inside me.

Every rake of those dark, pitiless eyes, had that forbidden urge inside me growing stronger, more demanding, and I wondered if he'd come here purposely to torment me. Good thing I hated Deston de Rayne far more than I could ever desire him.

"Everything, since none of you will tell me anything useful about the clan or being queen. All I want to know is what I'm up against."

"Sometimes, knowledge muddies the waters." I rolled my eyes at his predictably unhelpful answer.

"Usually, knowledge helps you stay alive." I countered. "With Viktor hunting me, I figure I'd better learn as much as possible, but since you're unwilling to contribute anything except your usual vague, worthless tripe, you can leave now."

"I cannot tell you...." Black eyes flashed with sudden

anger, his handsome face tightening. "But what if I could show you? Would that be satisfactory?"

I picked his seemingly innocent offer apart, looking for the catch. In addition to being a traitor, Deston was also a self-serving prick, which meant he was only helping me because there was something in this for him. Not so much for me.

Maybe a thirty-seventy split, at best.

Still...

"Okay, sure, tell me everything you know about the clan and being queen of said clan." Deston was the king of hollow promises, but to my eternal surprise, an enormous book dropped into my lap, open to page one.

I flipped the cover over to see what, exactly, he'd conjured for me. *History of the Darkfell Queens* was embossed in bright gold on the calfskin cover. "This thing's like a thousand pages long," I complained.

"You were not specific in your request, *ma cherie*, so that is a short history of every queen, all the way back to the first."

His gleaming eyes never left my face, as if searching for a reaction. When he didn't get one, he sighed. "It includes all royal houses and protocol, ancient feuds and ever-changing alliances, as well as which royal houses swore fealty to each queen during her rule. I was...trying to be helpful."

"Is there anything shorter?" I asked hopefully. "Like something with bullet points? Or just the highlight reel? Maybe a pamphlet?"

Deston's expression darkened, and in that moment, I wished I could hear his thoughts behind his impenetrable mask. "If you are quite done sniveling, we need to talk."

"So talk, I'm not stopping you."

"I have located the source of Viktor's power." He glided closer; magic heated my fingertips, in case he decided not to play nice.

"I've heard this story before." I reminded him. "Your intel didn't pan out last time, remember?" Not only that, we'd wasted precious time chasing down his tip. "Luthor and Cyrus were nearly killed on that little excursion, and we all decided that you were not to be trusted."

"I know I *j'ai fait une erreur*... made a mistake before, in not bringing you... what did you call it? *Hard evidence*. But this afternoon, I followed Viktor to the closed-off section of the castle. He disappeared for over an hour, then returned to the throne room."

Still not biting but definitely listening.

"When he returned," Deston continued, "Magic rolled off him in waves, more than he could comfortably contain, which means he'd accessed the source of his power. That source is close, inside the castle itself, somewhere in the restricted section."

"Any time now, you can explain how this information helps us defeat him."

"It is but a breadcrumb on the journey to illumination, Sera... *my Queen*. Piece enough of them together, and you shall have your answer."

"At what point does stringing me along get old? Because breadcrumbs won't defeat Viktor. You're his advisor, for fuck's sake, part of his inner circle. The most solid lead you've brought us is... *he keeps his source close*."

"This discovery is important, my Queen, though I cannot yet explain how." Deston inched closer, his eyes never leaving my face. So close, I leaned back to keep him in my sights, baring my neck. His pupils dilated, breath coming fast.

"Explaining is why you're still alive and useful to us." I willed my voice to remain steady. "That is the only reason, Deston. You sold us out, betrayed us, and we should have killed you for it. Do better."

His hand tensed reflexively, knuckles whitening as he gripped the wolf's head cane. For one long, shuddering moment I waited for him to attack. Then tension leached from the air, as the sound of soft, prowling footsteps grew closer.

"I'd listen to her, Cousin."

Cyrus—Deston's *actual* cousin—leaned in the doorway, his tight black designer jeans and a bright purple V-neck highlighting every gorgeous line of his muscular body. The sweater all but shone a spotlight on the bite mark on his neck, and I flushed, reliving last night's escapades. "She's not buying into your bullshit."

Cyrus took a casual step into the library, controlled aggression radiating off him. His long, blond hair was pulled back; his green eyes flashed silver when he measured Deston's proximity to me and decided he was too close. There was a menacing glide to his quiet steps, his wide shoulders braced for violence.

"Luthor has warned you to stay away from Seraphina, except during training. When he or I can monitor you." Cyrus flexed beneath the cashmere, sending a clear message. "I think it's time you started listening."

Cyrus was a warrior. A warrior that liked nice clothes—especially anything in pink and purple—but a warrior, just the same. Besides my teeth marks on his neck, there was a wide, white scar that went nearly all the way around his throat, and I shuddered at the sight.

Viktor had nearly cut off his head.

Cyrus had survived through sheer determination.

Just like the rest of us. Viktor had marked us all in his own way. Luthor, Cyrus, and I had physical scars to show for crossing him, but Deston's wounds remained invisible and ran deeper.

Much, much deeper.

The longer the two males stared at each other, Deston's too-handsome face tightened as sparks swirled in his dark eyes, his calm, collected façade beginning to fray as he gripped his ever-present cane tighter. There was a dangerous aura to him, as if he was debating violence. Then his face smoothed back into an unreadable mask. Emotionless. *Empty.*

He bowed his head in false submission. "Understood, *mon amie.*"

This had been his modus operandi lately. He'd been *tractable*, as Luthor called it, *cooperative*, though I'd caught glimpses of resentment boiling below the surface. His anger, perhaps, was understandable. We all had to rely on each other, and none of us liked it.

We had one hard and fast rule—no one was allowed outside the protective wards, except for Deston. The directive worked because, so far, Viktor hadn't come back to finish the job of killing me.

But I'd been stuck here for three months.

Over four thousand hours, my entire existence completely dependent on a vampire I distrusted with every fiber of my being. "Truthfully, I don't know how much more of this I can take," I muttered, the book long forgotten. "I can't trust you, and truthfully, *your one job*—teaching me to control my power—is a failure."

"You came to me, *cherie*, let us never forget that."

Translation: Don't blame me because you suck.

"You maneuvered the situation to your advantage, and

you know it." Cyrus perked up as our argument escalated. The male lived on drama, and there was never a shortage around here.

Deston wanted to talk? Fine, we'd talk. I'd been stewing about my shitty situation for too long. Maybe it *was* time we hashed this out.

"Give me real information we can use to defeat Viktor and for once, leave out your patronizing little French asides. I'm so over them."

Deston's face tightened with frustration. "Before he took the throne, Viktor had no natural abilities except his death magic, which was weak, at best. Yet after he ascended to the throne, he became the most powerful vampire in America. The most destructive necromancer I've ever seen." Deston moved to the fireplace, and even with the cane, somehow managing to move with lithe, deadly grace.

"That power is what makes the King invincible. Discover where he draws his magic from... and you can kill him." His dark gaze drilled through me, sharp as a razor. "Fail to find his power source, and he will destroy you."

His hand tightened on the silver-topped cane again, and I realized it was a nervous habit he wasn't aware of. *Deston de Rayne had a weakness. How about that?* "I am searching for the source of that power, and in the interim, I am weakening his court. Thanks to me, Viktor has lost three courtiers in the last two weeks. *Trusted* advisors."

There was a malevolent twist to his lips as he added, "I shall remove another two before month's end."

"That was not the plan," I countered evenly as my mind rushed through potential problems-slash-benefits of this new development. "Your job is to bring us new information."

He shrugged. "I saw an opportunity and took it. I'm sure you would have done the same." *Clever bastard, lumping me in with him so I couldn't argue the point.* "The moment Viktor is at his weakest, you will take back the throne."

I set the heavy book on the side table, my palms instantly sweaty. *I wasn't ready.* Not to take on a vampire king, certainly not to ascend as Queen when I didn't even know the rules. No, I needed more time...

"*Seraphina.*" Cyrus warned, and I looked down.

Shadows pooled at my feet, the tendrils wrapping around Deston's ankles. Instinctively, I recalled my magic too quickly, yanking the shadows toward me and jerking Deston off his feet. He crashed onto the stone floor, cane flying.

"Oops." I shook my hands, and the shadows dissipated into errant smoke puffs.

"Nice move." Cyrus's mouth quirked up into that devilish smile I loved so much. Partly why he had teeth marks on his neck at the moment.

"Total accident," I said innocently, only half-lying.

Sometimes magic really did work in the most wonderful ways.

Deston sprang back on his feet—he was quick for a four-hundred-year-old vampire—brushing dust off his tailored suit jacket and picking up his cane.

"That was so no accident, *ma petite.*" His voice was perfectly even, but those obsidian eyes promised pain, and I belatedly remembered we had another training session tomorrow.

"Here is a lesson for you. I removed Viktor's court members far too easily. Which is why you shall choose strong members for your own court. Instead of relying on your... *feelings*, my queen."

"I've already told you that I'm not building my court solely based on strength and power. I will assemble my court based on trust. And right now, you are definitely not on that list."

"*Putain de merde*. I'm doing this *for you*, Seraphina." He spat bitterly. "I've done *everything* for you. I don't know how else to prove my worth to you. Why can't you trust me?"

"Well, for one thing, selling me out to Viktor was a bad start to our relationship. For another, I know you're only helping us for your own gain and I see right through your blind ambition and fake French insults." I tapped my finger on the book cover.

"Your endgame is to be in power once more. Everything else is secondary to that motive, and you would sell us all to the devil if you thought our deaths would benefit you."

"My endgame is none of your concern as our objectives are momentarily aligned. Since my methods bother you, I shall cease all non-sanctioned removals of court members and focus on discovering the source of Viktor's power."

He glared at Cyrus, eyes flashing in warning. "And next time, I shall bring you the proof you obviously require. Perhaps then you will trust me." His lip curled. "*Cousin*. My Queen."

Chapter 3
Deston de Rayne

S *he was gone.*

I crept like a thief into my own library, cursing Seraphina, yet unable to stop myself from running a finger along the cover of the book she'd been reading moments ago, sinking into the leather chair, still warm from her body.

Just feeling her residual heat made my body turn to butter, my heart rate slowing back to normal.

She'd tried to hide her scar from me tonight. She'd tried to hide the fact she was attracted to me, though her scent told me otherwise.

I'd nearly broken earlier, itching to wind my fingers into her dark, silken curls, to taste her full, soft lips, to see her gold-amber eyes look up at me with desire, not disgust.

I might have succeeded if Cyrus had not interrupted us.

Over these past months, I'd watched Seraphina's soft curves harden with muscle, her expressive, oval face become more secretive as she learned this new world was not as forgiving as her human one.

I'd learned every nuanced expression, every small curve of her lips, every sigh and scornful sneer, and gods help me, I'd only fallen deeper in love. The harder she tried to hide her feelings from me, the more I ferreted out every quick-silver emotion that flushed her cheeks and brightened her eyes.

I smelled her in every corner of this castle that had once been my prison and was now hers. She was everywhere I looked. She was the only thing I thought of.

Seraphina Marvelle was all I dreamed of, in my lustful wicked fantasies that had me waking in a sweat, my hand on my cock, her name on my lips as I burst apart.

I was going mad, caught between the mating bond and trying to keep my distance.

Between patiently teaching her and wanting to lock her up, so she'd be safe.

But Seraphina was never meant for cages. She was made for wide open places, for great things, for power. She was made for the throne. My mate would become the most powerful queen in vampire history, and if I played this right, I would be right by her side.

If she survived Viktor.

The mating bond rejected that thought with a burst of fiery pain, like a knife disappearing into my heart, tearing the organ to bloody shreds. No, if anything happened to Seraphina, I might as well die, right alongside her.

Her magic was there, waiting beneath the surface. A power I could practically touch. *Taste.*

Like a thunderstorm building and building, ready to explode. I'd tried fear, outright terror. I'd tried pleading, then gently coaxing her power into being. I'd tried every trick I knew and she was right. I was an *instructeur de très mauvaise qualité.*

Something was stopping Seraphina from accessing her power. From finding the control she so desperately needed. And until she succeeded, she'd remain locked up here, safe from that fuck Viktor. *In a cage.* Every part of me rebelled against that idea.

I wanted her strong.

I wanted her safe.

But mostly, I just fucking wanted her.

The idea that I'd never have her, that she'd spend the rest of her life despising me...was a curse that haunted me night and day. I sank back into the chair, let her scent envelop me like an embrace.

Surely, I was going mad.

Chapter 4
Seraphina

The next day, I was back in my most hated place doing my most hated activity.

And bonus, I was with my most hated person.

Could my life possibly suck any worse?

Under different circumstances, the walled garden would be my favorite refuge. Today, it was filled with beds of white, fragrant flowers that surrounded the flat, grassy center. Even the air smelled delicious today; the stone wall was covered in cascading roses that looked like they'd been painted by a master.

Somehow, every night, Deston managed to repair my destruction with a wave of his hand.

I swore, the male never slept.

A blast of pure power rippled the air around me, and I smelled burning hair. At this rate, I'd be bald by dinner. "Please pay attention, *mon amie*." Deston ordered calmly, his flat, pinched lips telling me that was no accident but payback for what happened in the library last night.

"Stick your fake concern up your tight ass, Lord de Rayne." I patted the back of my head, coming away with a handful of frizzled, charred strands.

"Fine," I grumbled. "Take *this*."

I gathered magic at my core, pushing it down my arms, then out through my hands. Power turned the air around us liquid, waves undulating out from me like ripples on a flat, smooth pond. The walls around us shook, the wave built and built until it was twice as tall as me. I *shoved*, sending a wall of pure darkness straight toward him.

Deston lifted a hand and the wave parted in two before the darkness struck him, passing by harmlessly, taking down a statue, crushing the roses into a smear of green.

"Gah. What am I doing wrong?"

"Three months ago, my queen, you couldn't have done that. You're getting better every day," Luthor called from where he was curled on top of the wall. His big body was as boneless as a cat, yet his fierce blue gaze followed Deston's every move, sparks glittering in their depths. He was my biggest cheerleader, and I loved him for it.

He was also right. I had more control these days, even though I wasn't getting better fast enough for my liking. When I'd started, I was all power, no control. Now I had a little control, but my power...seemed somehow out of reach.

Deston strode over, circled behind me, and grasped my elbows, pulling my arms out wide, positioning my hands at chest-level.

"A wider stance, Seraphina," he instructed quietly while Luthor eased off the wall, ready to intervene. "Hands right here." He cupped my elbows. "When you push your magic with your hands in this position, you will have more control over where the strike goes."

I didn't like having Deston this close, but I wanted this session over. My back was aching, and my shoulders hurt. Having magic race through my body took a heavy toll on my muscles, and I was looking forward to a long bath tonight.

Hot, with lots of bubbles. *And Luthor and Cyrus. And their mouths and fingers and...*

Behind me, Deston shuddered, his hand slipping off my arms before he stepped away.

"Now try, *ma petite*," he said gruffly. "Push the magic to your hands but concentrate on the space between your palms, focus everything on that empty spot, let the power build, and when you have gathered enough for a blow, release it."

I followed his instructions to the letter and this time, magic formed a ball between my palms, as if the power became amplified, somehow. My palms heated, skin crackling, then I pushed, the air bending upon itself as the ball roared across the garden, shredding delicate flowers as is passed. Luthor vaulted over the wall and ducked when the wave passed over his head, taking a few stones with it.

"Better. Practice that, five more times." Deston grasped my shoulders and turned me toward the other end of the garden. His fingers slid slowly over my shoulders, trailing down my arms before his thumb rubbed along the horrible scar on my arm, tenderly tracing every gnarled bump.

I stepped away, thrown completely off-balance. He'd never touched me before, at least, not like this.

That was a lover's caress, and he and I were very much enemies.

"Hands off, Rayne." Luthor growled as he limped toward us, his silver-flecked hair gathered at his nape. The watery sun accentuated the sharp planes of his face, his gaze fixed with murderous intent on Deston. "Or do you need a reminder of the rules?"

"Just making sure she masters today's lesson before nightfall." Deston sneered, his disgust clear. "Or shall we have her face Viktor with no hope of success?"

"Teach and don't touch," Luthor reminded him, menace coloring his threat. He towered over me and Deston, a formidable, powerful presence as he took up a closer spot near the arched wall.

"Arms apart," Deston instructed, completely ignoring Luthor. "Focus on that empty spot... good... *now push*."

Again, the wave became a tangible thing, spreading through the air like a thunderstorm, flattening everything in front of it. Internally, I wept for the shredded flowers, even though I knew by tomorrow Deston would make them whole.

He circled me like a wolf, then stalked away, pulling off his suit jacket. He tossed that and his cane onto a bench, rolled up his sleeves, then planted himself dead in front of me, legs spread wide, hands folded behind his back. "Again."

I glanced at Luthor. Then the flowers. Then Deston.

"Get out of the way."

I hated this male, but every single part of me balked at hurting him.

"Let me give you some incentive." With a mocking smile, Deston swept his hand across the garden and a dark whip of shadow knocked Luthor to his knees in the grass, opening a gash on his forehead, blood streaming down over his scar. "*Again*."

Fury turned my magic incendiary, power burning my fingers as white lava flowed out, then gathered into a ball of fire that blistered my palms, made my lips crack. I let that energy build and build, bigger and bigger, then sent it crashing toward Deston. Plasma blackened the grass, incinerated the flowers, charred the stone walls black.

I didn't know what I expected.

Not for Deston's handsome face to be flayed apart before me, as if enormous, cruel claws raked across his cheeks, his smooth chest, his lightly muscled arms. Blood bloomed, turning his white shirt red. I managed two faltering steps toward him, horrified, before Luthor tugged me back.

Something flickered deep in Deston's eyes, something long hidden, something that almost looked like pride. That burst of emotion *transformed* him, making his flat, cold visage come alive. I'd never glimpsed this side of him. My breath hung in my lungs as I realized just how beautiful he was.

And just how treacherous.

"Ah. There she is." His cunning purr stroked down my spine, made the hairs on my arms rise. "Finally. The Darkfell Queen has made her appearance. It's about time."

Deston wiped his face with what remained of his shirt and smiled faintly. "Twice more and then you may quit for the day. See to it she finishes, Fontaine."

Then he picked up his wolf's head cane, his jacket and limped out of the garden.

Since Luthor always kept his word, I cast my magic twice more, my stomach churning every time I sent that horrible power hurtling across the garden. This was dangerous. *I* was dangerous.

I didn't like hurting people.

Except for Viktor, and only because I'd do everything in my power to protect Luthor and Cyrus. They were all I had, and I'd die—I'd kill—to save them. My family, the one I'd found, and now would fight to keep.

That night I soaked in the bath longer than usual, and not only because my hands were burned, and my body aching.

Something happened when Deston touched me today.

I couldn't describe the feeling, other than a fleeting sense of...completeness. As if his touch somehow filled me, where I hadn't known I was empty. Which was crazy, because he was a backstabbing liar, and I despised him.

Feeling *anything* for Deston was perilous.

Besides, I had everything I wanted. I had Luthor and Cyrus, two good males I trusted and loved more than anything on this earth. Nothing would ever jeopardize our bond. *Nothing.*

I slid under the water, letting the room blur.

Why, then, couldn't I make this feeling go away?

Chapter 5
Seraphina

The water was cold by the time I got out and wrapped my robe around me.

I didn't know why that one moment—seconds, really—bothered me so much. And because I was obsessive, this would bother me until I figured this out. However, I had two handsome vampires waiting in my bed, and I intended to spend my night reminding myself exactly how much we loved each other.

Cyrus was glued to the flatscreen—he was positively obsessed with cartoons—while Luthor's appreciative gaze ignited the second I emerged, steam following me through the doorway like a misty ghost.

For a long second, I drank him in, leaned back on the bed, stripped to the waist. His beautiful face was set off by high cheekbones and a strong, cut jaw, densely muscled shoulders were flecked with scars. His toned torso tapered down to a ribbed abdomen, topped by wide pecs. Luthor was a work of art, but his gentle compassion was what had stolen my heart.

He searched my face before patting the empty spot on the bed.

"Feel better?" he asked quietly as Cyrus threw his head back and roared, the coyote slamming into the side of the cliff. "I know you had a rough day, even though the lesson was a success." He turned my hands over, inspected my healing palms.

"A little." I snuggled in beside him, relaxing as his fingers dug into my tense muscles. "I hate what I did today. I don't like hurting people. Not even Deston."

"I know, love. But we must unlock the full potential of your power. And you are not quite there yet." He smoothed his hand up my arm. "Close, though. Closer than last week. And the week before. You can do this, Seraphina, you just have to keep trying."

I curled myself into him, smiling slightly as Cyrus laughed uproariously, then fell backwards onto the bed. "Any tips for getting over this *not wanting to hurt people* thing? Because I know I have to be ruthless when I face Viktor. I thought I was ready, but after today..."

Watching blood bloom all over Deston had shaken me to my core, and I couldn't figure out why.

"You have a soft, kind heart, Seraphina. We both love that about you." Luthor bent his head to nuzzle my hair. "But Deston is right, when it comes to the King..." His body tensed up. "When you fight Viktor, you cannot hesitate, you cannot afford doubts. You must strike and strike hard. Then hope he never gets back up, after you knock him down."

The television shut off, then Cyrus pressed into me from behind, taking over massaging my neck, and more of my tension ebbed away. "I'm tired of this talk of killing. Of Viktor. Of what I'm supposed to do. I can't wait for this to be over so we can stop running and start living."

"Me, either." Cyrus nibbled his way up to my ear, his soft lips in sharp contrast to the nip of his fangs. "But I believe I still owe you from this morning."

His bite marks had long since healed, but I shivered beneath his hands and his mouth, remembering how good he'd tasted. He was delicious, and I was starving again, after using so much magic today.

"Last night," I corrected him softly, leaning into him. "Not quite midnight, as I recall."

"Details, details." He laughed, turning me so he could capture my lips with his. Our tongues tangled lazily, familiar and soft, my entire body relaxing.

I broke away, breathless. "How can it be..." I raised my hands so Cyrus could pull my shirt over my head, "I still want you both this badly?"

"We're amazing, that's why," Cyrus teased while Luthor pressed me flat to the bed. "And we're going to *keep* being amazing so you keep wanting us."

Cyrus recaptured my lips, pressing my hands up over my head with just the right amount of pressure. Luthor grasped my knees, forced my legs wide as he settled between them, his fingers skating up the insides of my thighs. I loved them both touching me.

Loved how they were completely different, Cyrus with his wickedly sharp teeth and clever tongue, and Luthor, who handled me with such gentleness and control.

I sighed, every worry sliding away beneath their touch.

I had the best of both worlds.

With no hesitation, Luthor buried his mouth between my legs, his tongue licking through my folds, pausing to suck my already-swollen clit into his mouth. That warm, wet suction nearly did me in, and I moaned, loud enough that Cyrus chuckled. "Do that again, Luthor, I think our Queen needs more."

"Shut up." The order was more of a squeak, but I was already arching up, eager for exactly that.

"You are so beautiful, Fina," Cyrus coasted his hand slowly down my body, fingers lightly trailing over my sensitive skin. "So fucking beautiful, I ask myself every day how the fuck we got so lucky." He kneaded my breast, shot me a wicked grin, dipped his head, and my mind went blank, his warm, clever mouth fastening around my taut nipple the only thing that mattered.

Luthor gently squeezed my thighs as he suckled, and my entire world narrowing down to the press of his tongue dancing across my sensitive bud, flicking and flicking before he pulled it into his mouth and gently bit down.

My hips rocketed off the bed, and Luthor was still laughing when he prowled up my body, sliding the head of his thick cock through the slickness where his mouth had been. His kiss tasted salty, his rumbled groan vibrating against my chest while he pressed into me, my core clenching as he pushed in, inch after delicious inch, never stopping until he bottomed out.

Luthor released my lips, gazing down at me, beautiful face framed by a tangle of brown and silver hair, long enough for Cyrus to fasten his mouth to my throat and bite down, the sharp jolt of pain tangling with the surge of heated pressure coiling between my legs.

Euphoria swept in, and I made a desperate, keening sound, writhing between them, impaled by Luthor's cock, pinned down by Cyrus's bite, until they were all that mattered. Them, and the pleasure wracking my body.

God, they knew me so well, knew how to work me in tandem, knew exactly what I liked. What I needed. How hard. How fast. When to be gentle, when to be rough. They played my body like a symphony until my stomach quivered with need and my fingers were tangled in Cyrus's long hair, dragging him closer.

"You are beautiful, my queen." Luthor murmured, pulling out and slamming back in. "Powerful and kind."

Another long, slow withdrawal, another hard thrust that sent my eyes rolling back in my head. "You are going to change this world, like a force of nature." His eyes glowed, his big body moving like a wave of muscle over me, his cock slamming into me, hitting just the right spot to make me bite my bottom lip. "You are a goddess, the most beautiful creature I have ever seen."

Then Luthor slid a strong arm under my leg and lifted my hips so he could go even deeper.

This was...every single time was a revelation of how easily my body turned to honey, how fast my pleasure rose. Embarrassing, really, that I became putty in their hands, so desperate for their mouths, for every demanding thrust of Luthor's cock, for every hard pull of Cyrus's mouth against my throat.

"Come for us, Seraphina." Luthor's whispered order tickled my ear, and that fast, I was cresting the rise of that wave, bliss rushing in my veins, my ears pounding as I splintered to pieces, a million shattered pleasures, flying in different directions as the entire world ground to a halt. Another wave rose and rose, then broke apart.

Then another. *Oh God, I was going to...*

That's it. One more my Queen. Give me just one more.

Luthor kept up his leisurely pace, his strokes perfectly matching Cyrus's greedy draws, his hands cupping my breasts, tracing down my sides, my stomach, petting me tenderly while he drank his fill. *We are all part of each other*, I thought hazily, my hips moving to meet Luthor's. *All of us inside one another in some way. Partners. Lovers. Friends.*

God, this was dangerous, how much we loved each other.

How easily we could be broken apart.

The second the thought came into my head, I pushed it away.

"More," I told them. "Give me more. Make the entire world disappear."

"Gladly, my Queen." In the bedroom, I'd decided I didn't mind the title so much, especially when he said it in that lust-ravaged voice. Luthor pumped into me hard, and another orgasm shattered me, rocketing through my body. I trembled as Luthor and Cyrus traded places, Cyrus's thick cock sliding into me, stretching me even wider, his green eyes hazy from feeding as he slid in to the hilt.

He paused, pressed into me so deep, I could feel every ridge, every vein, even without him moving.

And then he pulled out, so slow I moaned, my core clenching, as if I could keep him inside me forever. With a wicked grin, he thrust back in, hips pressed tight to mine as he swiveled, my eyes rolling back in my head from the sheer pleasure of having him inside me.

I'd never get tired of them, these two males who had stolen my heart. When Cyrus finally came, I came with him before we fell into sleep, tangled together so tightly, I didn't know where I ended and they began.

Chapter 6
Deston

I paused my reconstruction of the destroyed garden, long enough to glare up at the arched window where the light still burned, even though it was well past midnight. Fontaine and my cousin were up there.

Up there with my mate. My *fucking true mate*.

While I was stuck down here, cleaning up the day's mess, as usual.

Despite centuries of control, I didn't know how much longer I could keep my mouth shut, my feelings hidden, while they enjoyed what was rightfully mine. Putting aside the fact I'd betrayed Seraphina—*to save her damned life*—I honestly couldn't understand why she still hated me so much.

After all, I'd done everything she'd asked. I'd infiltrated Viktor's court. Spied on the King, killed off members of his corrupt court, weakened his Knightsguard. Everything I did was for her. I fucking *existed* for her.

I undermined the bastard more every day, and he hardly even noticed. Viktor was too caught up in orgies and hunting parties, imported cars and week-long parties. He'd turned into a foppish caricature of our species and not for the first time, I wondered how he'd managed to usurp the throne in the first place.

And I hadn't been lying to Seraphina.

As far as Viktor's seemingly limitless magic, I knew I'd

finally narrowed down the source. It *had* to be there, behind the formidable wards that guarded the closed down section of the castle.

No one had been in that wing since Lyra herself had been queen, and I'd tried myself to circumvent the wards, but they were too powerful to be undone quickly, and the constantly rotating patrols of guards were a nuisance as well.

But the source was there, I just had to find it.

Then, when I brought Seraphina her *hard evidence*, she'd finally see me for who I really was. Perhaps instead of distrust in her eyes, I'd see the affection she was always lavishing on my cousin and Fontaine. Then all I'd have to do was convince her that she was my true mate.

And once I convinced her, Luthor and my cousin would be shown the door. Because while they had no problem with their little arrangement—I looked again to that window while a low growl built in my throat.

I didn't fucking share.

Chapter 7
Seraphina

The darkness in this place didn't seem to have an end, my footfalls loud as gunshots in the cavernous throne room, no matter how quiet I kept my steps. All around us, those enormous gilt mirrors reflected our progress, the stillness amplifying my hitched breathing.

Luthor was to my right, Cyrus to my left, and Deston...

I looked around, but he was gone, disappearing into the shadows.

Up ahead of us, the Darkfell throne sat empty, though something dark puddled at the base of the dais. Another echoing step, and I cringed.

Too loud.

We were too loud, and Viktor would hear us and swoop out of the darkness and kill us all—or worse—turn us into mindless monsters. My pace slowed, despite Luthor and Cyrus tugging me along, marching me forward as if we were heading to my execution.

Why was I here again? I looked wildly around. I tried to speak, but no words came out, I tried to stop, but Luthor's big hand just clamped down tighter, propelling me forward.

When we got closer to the throne, the dark puddle took shape.

A body, sprawled out grotesquely, as if death had no

respect for the flesh. Blood surrounded the corpse, the macabre scene reflected in the ornate mirrors, the heavy scent of copper tinging the air, old death turning sickly sweet.

Look at what you have wrought, Seraphina

I don't want to see. I wanted to go back to bed, I wanted to be anywhere but here, except Luthor dragged me forward, giving me no choice but to look.

The body had a face. *Viktor.*

The King was dead, his body horribly mutilated, his bloody, empty eye sockets staring blankly up at the vaulted ceiling. What kind of monster would do this?

I clawed at the hands banded around my arms, but they were unmovable. We were almost there when Deston swept out of the shadows, a predatory glow in his eyes. He smiled that cold, hateful smile before he took his place to the left of the throne as my advisor.

I kicked; I screamed. I cried as Luthor and Cyrus—these males I loved with all my heart—dragged me toward the dais.

They were going to put me on that throne. Once I was seated up there, I'd never get away. This would be my future and all my choices would be gone. I would have to kill, I would have to be ruthless and cruel and heartless and...

I didn't want to be Queen.

My feet bumped over Viktor's cold body on my way up the steps, and I didn't stop fighting until Luthor pressed my back flat against the cold metal, colder even than the other day in Deston's illusion. I stared into the shadowed hall, that seemed to stretch forever.

I couldn't do this.

I couldn't do this and...

Viktor rose from the floor, his empty sockets fixing on me, and he snarled, baring huge fangs. I threw up my hands but not before his teeth sank into my throat, so deep I thought he'd tear my head off. Luthor and Cyrus kept me pinned down, Deston laughing softly while Viktor drained me, the obscene gilded room fading away as I died.

I woke screaming, grasping my neck, my feet still kicking. Cyrus snored lightly beside me. Luthor instinctively banded his arm around me and pulled me closer. For a second, I froze, still half-stuck in the dream before I remembered what was real.

"S'all right, Seraphina. I've got you," Luthor mumbled sleepily, tucking me tighter. Heat radiated from him, but my freezing body couldn't absorb enough of his warmth, no matter how much I pressed against him.

It wasn't all right. This was the third time I'd dreamed this exact scene, every nightmare identical, down to how Viktor's teeth felt when they pierced my flesh.

The more I went back through the dream, the more I became convinced...

The day I faced down Viktor was the day I'd die.

Chapter 8
Seraphina

I was shaky the next morning, waiting in the newly restored garden for Deston.

It was barely past dawn, the air tinged with a hint of rain.

The flower beds were white perfection again, except for the addition of one deep red rose, climbing over the top of the wall, like drops of freshly spilled blood. I brushed a petal on my way past, unable to keep from touching its water-dropped perfection.

They smelled heavenly, deeply perfumed, tinged with a scent I couldn't place. Cloves, maybe, or something equally exotic. The grass was cold and wet, heavy with the dew from last night. Luthor and Cyrus were already up, scouting the perimeter, their morning activity. They'd only left once I reassured them I was perfectly safe with Deston.

I wasn't a hundred percent on that, but I had to shake off the fear of last night's dream, and destroying something seemed a good start.

"You are early, *ma cherie*." Deston leaned heavily on his wolf's head cane, his face inscrutable in the pale light.

"I couldn't sleep." I rubbed my hands on my jean-covered thighs to fend off the chill. "So I figured we might as well get on with today's disaster."

His dark gaze raked over me with a hint of disdain, and I sighed. Deston was the picture of perfection this morning in his Saville Row suit, his perfectly groomed hair, his unfairly high cheekbones. In fact, the male looked as sleek as any runway model at a Tom Ford show.

Me, on the other hand, had outrageous bedhead paired with old jeans and an oversized sweatshirt thrown on for warmth. Not exactly runway material, but I didn't care.

I just wanted to survive this morning without catching on fire.

"You are not sleeping?" His troubled expression was visible for a second before disappearing beneath his usual, cold mask. "Is the bed not to your liking?" Something broody and almost malevolent flashed across his face, the barest darkening of his eyes, a muscle flexing in his jaw.

"The bed is perfectly fine." I sighed. "Can we get started? I'm freezing."

"You remember the stance?" He asked quietly, searching my face for a too-long, impossibly awkward moment. "Hands a foot apart, brace your feet, unlock your knees."

I mimicked my pose from yesterday, Deston coming up behind me and making a slight adjustment, his fingers brushing my elbow. Barely touched me and yet, I couldn't stop the shiver that traveled up my spine.

"Now gather the magic... hands a bit farther apart... plant your feet firmly... now push, Seraphina."

Magic flowed out of me like half-frozen water, heavy and reluctant, not at all like the fire from yesterday. I rubbed my hands together and resumed the stance. "Let me try that again."

"*Ma cherie*, what is wrong?"

"Nothing. I'm just cold and tired of being a failure at this magic stuff."

His eyes narrowed. "Then stop failing and try again." I

felt his gaze on me the entire time. Through my failed second try. My third. My fourth.

"Enough, *cherie*, enough." He grasped my cold hands tightly, sandwiched them between his own. "Why did you not sleep last night?"

"Bad dreams," I muttered. "I don't want to talk about them." I'd decided the worst part of it was Luthor and Cyrus throwing me onto the throne like I was a rag doll.

To my shock, Deston reached up and smoothed my hair back, his fingers gently tracing my forehead, finally resting behind my ear. The longer he stared into my eyes, the tighter his face became until there was no doubt in my mind what I was seeing.

Anger. Bitterness. Then regret.

"I should not have pushed you so hard yesterday. And I should have chosen a different setting for your session. I had no desire to give you nightmares, *ma cherie*."

I froze. *He'd seen my dream.* "Stay out of my fucking head." I snapped, yanking away. "Consider that an order, from a queen to her advisor." Outrage spiked, then fizzled as my shoulders slumped from sheer exhaustion

I couldn't figure out my magic.

I was afraid of becoming queen—this was not going to work.

"That was not the first time. You should have told me about the dreams sooner, *mon amour*." He cupped my chin, and I blinked away my tears. "Hide nothing from me."

Confused, I batted his hand away, retreated from the genuine concern on his face. I didn't want to notice the pity sparking in his depthless eyes. Nor did I care for the way Deston peered straight into me, like he saw my deepest, darkest secrets.

We were *enemies*. I needed him aloof and distant.

He was far less dangerous that way.

He followed me step for step, his hands catching my elbows when I stopped at the edge of the garden. "They're nothing. I hardly remember them."

"They are not nothing." His whisper was quietly angry. "They frightened you."

"They woke me up, yes, but they're only dreams."

"Are they?" he asked tightly. "If that's all they are, why are you still scared?"

"I'm not scared. I'm frustrated. There's a difference."

"You are frightened and rightly so." Deston's palms were so warm against my skin, a shiver of something going through me at where our bodies made contact. "Being shown your death each night is enough to unsettle even someone as strong as yourself."

After all his bullying, after all his taunting...Deston thought I was strong? I clenched my hands into fists. "Like I told you before. This is none of your business. Stay out of my head."

"Tell me the truth, *mon amour*, and I will not have to pry. Lie to me and I will do what I must to protect you."

"Get your goddamned hands off of her. *Right the fuck now, de Rayne.*" Luthor's voice rang across the enclosed space, and this time when I stepped away, Deston stayed put, his jaw clenching as an enraged Luthor bore down on us like a bull.

Before I even knew what I was doing, I stepped between them. "He's just... teaching me to duplicate what I did yesterday. That's all."

For the life of me, I didn't know why I'd just straight up lied to Luthor.

To protect Deston.

What the hell was I thinking? But I couldn't take the words back, not now that they were out there.

Luthor stopped in his tracks, looking between us, trying to figure out what was going on. "From the state of the garden, I'd guess you've not been successful," he said carefully. "You're tired, Seraphina. You didn't sleep much last night."

Deston muttered something foul in French, then shot me a look that clearly said *we were so not finished.*

In the next instant, the air changed; it grew charged, as if an electrical storm was brewing.

"Those are the wards activating. Something's trying to breach the south side," Deston warned, his gaze shooting to the edge of the grounds. The ward was still intact. I could see the rainbow shimmer from here.

"Nothing will get through," Deston assured me softly, closing his eyes before adding, "but there are ten revenants, perhaps more, prowling the bayou." He nodded beyond the castle. "They cannot breach the ward, but you should be inside where it is safer."

"He's right. Keep our Queen safe," Luthor ordered Deston, pointing us toward the castle. "Cyrus and I will handle the monsters."

"They are just sniffing around," Deston warned Luthor, tugging me closer, nonetheless. "There is no possible way Viktor knows you are here."

"I mean to ensure that." Luthor growled.

"What if you're wrong?" My voice rose another octave. "What if he is out there?" The last time Viktor had sent his revenants to kill me, he'd shown up to gloat, then he'd killed Gram out of spite, what if...

Viktor's not anywhere close to us, Seraphina, but there are revenants in the bayou, Cyrus explained patiently in my head.

And you know this how?

48

Because I'm outside, keeping an eye on them. No sign of the Knightsguard or the King so far, but I'll report if that situation changes. For now, listen to Luthor, he'll keep you safe.

"Why is Cyrus alone, outside the wards with ten revenants on the loose?" I demanded. "He should be inside with us, where it's safe. Isn't that the rule?"

Deston and Luthor exchanged a long look and I threw up my hands. "Oh, wait, let me guess. That rule only applies to me?"

"We've been taking turns patrolling the perimeter every day." Luthor didn't look nearly sheepish enough for my liking. "Seraphina, we *had* to keep you safe."

"That's bullshit. I thought you were patrolling *inside* the wards. And I am safe. I haven't been anywhere in three months."

"Seraphina." Deston's patient tone had me grinding my teeth. "The castle has an extra layer of protection, powerful enough the creatures cannot set foot inside without turning to ash. Let us wait inside until the danger is past."

He turned to Luthor. "If you kill them," Deston said carefully, "Viktor will come to investigate. Better to allow them to go on their way. Don't provoke them, and they will pass by, *mon ami*."

"Yeah, no shit," Luthor scoffed. "Not the first time I've done this." His back muscles bunched as he gathered his shadows around him and disappeared.

"Damn it, Deston, that's two against ten." I bounced on the balls of my feet, my magic sparking at my fingertips. Deston took one look at my face and shook his head.

"You'll only be a distraction, and besides, the revenants have been keyed to your scent. One step outside the ward, and Viktor knows where you are. That quickly, you've lost your refuge and your element of surprise, all in one fell swoop."

Now that this place was about to be compromised, I realized how lucky we'd been to have not only a roof over our heads, but food in our stomachs, and a place to sleep. Honestly, life with Gram had been so hard, I should know when to count my blessings.

Deston opened his arms, and I stepped inside them, beyond pissed that I was choosing safety over helping my males. "This seems cowardly," I muttered before he landed us in the castle's foyer. "We should be out there with them."

Deston's expression softened. "You are very brave, but Luthor and Cyrus have been doing this a long time, *ma cherie*. They can handle themselves and they'll let the beasts pass by and not raise an alarm."

"Okay." I pressed my fingers into my aching temples. "Okay, you're right."

Deston's low chuckle nearly made me stumble. "*Mon Dieu*, she agreed with me. May miracles never cease." The foyer stayed tomb-silent while I imagined a million terrible things outside in the swamp. Deston's hand tightened around my arm, and I realized he'd never let me go.

"Although..." His entire body tightened, his face darkening with something that looked like anger. "This could be the perfect opportunity to teach the king a valuable lesson." I opened my mouth to ask what that lesson might be, but he laid his finger over my lips.

For one fraught moment, we stayed like that, inches apart, his fingertips on my mouth, then he backed away.

"Quiet, my Queen," he shushed. "Stay quiet, and I shall return momentarily."

He disappeared, and I paced back and forth in the

grand entrance, wanting to fly across the field to join my males in the fight, while my head warned me to listen to Deston.

Shit, I hadn't even listened to Gram, and I *loved* her.

Why would I listen to Deston?

I sagged with relief when Luthor and Cyrus materialized in, both of them wet and stinking like bog water, but unharmed. "Where's Deston?"

"He's *taking care of things*, or *reste hors de mon chemin*, as he put it," Cyrus grumbled. "None of Viktor's creatures passed beyond the ward, and Luthor and I left them alone." He didn't look happy about being denied a little violence, but relief washed through me.

He could easily kill a revenant—I'd watched him myself —but caution was the smart play. If we killed one of Viktor's little pets, sooner or later the king would come, and I wasn't ready for another confrontation.

"Good," I murmured, running my hand down Cyrus's arm, finding him wired tight as a drum. "This is the sensible move right now. As much as you would have enjoyed killing them, we stay off Viktor's radar until I'm strong enough to face him."

Luthor didn't look any happier about the situation. "Deston's laying out a scent trail leading deeper into the bayou. This will keep them away from the other royal families... and humans."

"Was Viktor with them?"

"*No*," Deston snapped, cold air sweeping through the foyer when he reappeared, making his grand entrance. "But the King and I will be having words about his misplaced suspicions."

"And how will you placate Viktor?" I asked. "By selling us out again, perhaps?" The moment the accusation left my lips I regretted it. But it was too late to take it back, too late to stop the hurt that flashed across his face.

His eyes never left me, but they changed.

From glowing embers to cold, glittering diamonds, just that quickly.

"No, my Queen," he said smoothly, a hint of menace in his voice. "I shall tell the King if I catch his revenants on my lands ever again, I'll dump their steaming corpses in front of his throne."

Chapter 9
Seraphina

In the end, Deston decided a lesson was, indeed, in order.

He disappeared for hours and returned, splattered in foul smelling blood, and in an even fouler mood and I had a feeling Viktor was down a few monsters. As it turned out, the revenant drama spared me a few hours of training, nothing more.

Now Luthor and Cyrus were back on perimeter duty and I was alone with Deston.

Apparently, when it came down to who was more untrustworthy—a grotesque abomination of nature or Lord de Rayne—Deston came out slightly ahead.

I shivered with déjà vu when I stepped through the arched stone doorway and into the center of the flower-lined grass. It was midday, and the red roses were fully opened, their thick, soft petals begging to be touched. I took a deeper breath of the clove scent, mixed with the sweeter smell of the lilies.

"Maybe we should take the afternoon off," I hedged.

"Stance," Deston barked, and I bent my knees, my tight calves screaming.

"Hands."

I opened my palms farther, and a small ball of magic gathered between them. "Aim for the doorway."

I hesitated. I mean, how many times could I destroy the

garden before this charade became ridiculous? By my count, we were already there.

"Pay attention, my Queen. Stop daydreaming and focus on the arch. *Pour l'amour de Dieu*, try not to destroy everything in your path."

One deep breath and I cast my magic, intending to thread it neatly through the doorway.

My magic hit the opening off center, slicing through one side of the stone arch, which tumbled into a pile of dust and stone. But one half still stood. That was something, right?

A muscle worked in his jaw. "*Putain d'enfer.* What was that?"

I shrugged. "Me, trying to do magic."

"You are an utter disaster." Deston bore down on me, hands clenched in anger. "*Je ne comprends pas*...how you can be this incompetent? Your very survival depends on learning this magic."

"Spare me your outrage." I tipped my chin higher. "I told you I couldn't do this today."

"You want to die, is that it, Seraphina?" He was so close his breath heated my cheek, rage vibrated off him in waves. "Because that's what will happen if you are not ready. You do not have the will to control your magic, much less the skill to cast it."

He flung his hand toward the once-beautiful arch. "Death is outside, sniffing at your heels, and still, you do not take this seriously. If Viktor had been standing *right there*, you would have missed him completely. You will forfeit your one opportunity, and then he will kill you." His hand grasped my shirt, pulled me close enough I saw the banked heat in his eyes.

A thrill of fear—and something forbidden—streaked through me.

"*One.* That's how many chances you will get to kill the King. Let that chance get past you, and there will be no other. He will kill you, or worse... turn you. Either way, *you will be gone.*"

The last part shuddered out of him while I searched his face for some clue to why he was losing his shit right now.

"You possess more raw power than any queen I've ever known." He yanked me even closer, my body pressed against his while I braced my hands on his arms. "Yet you refuse to use your magic, you refuse to *fight.*"

I shoved against him, my magic rose and rose, a tsunami of power thundering up through me. The onslaught was so fast stars danced in my vision, and I threw out a hand, intending to grab on to Deston but instead, magic exploded out of me.

The consuming wave tore through the beds like a thresher, churning up dirt and grass before roaring through all four stone walls, leaving us exposed in a sea of utter destruction.

"And now she has a temper tantrum." Deston glared at me in disgust, releasing my shirt. "You will die, Seraphina." His voice was too quiet. Too certain.

I got all tangled up, for a minute, in that unwavering certainty.

"You will die, and there is nothing I can do to prevent that from happening." A breath shuddered out of him while he held my gaze. "All because you do not *want to be Queen.* All these failures, because you cannot embrace your destiny."

I could barely breathe.

There. He'd said it. The thing that kept me up at night, gave me nightmares.

Scared the shit out of me.

I shoved him away. "Don't be ridiculous. I most certainly do not want to die," I snapped. "And I *do* want to be Queen. *I do*."

He threw back his head and laughed, the sound wild and reckless, his hair coming loose around his face, color blooming on his pale cheeks. I swallowed, taking a step back. Deston had never looked as alive—or as unhinged— as he did right now. "Now who's the liar?" he hissed, advancing on me while I retreated.

"You lie to Luthor. You lie to my cousin. You lie to *yourself*. And you can lie all you want, Seraphina. Tell yourself what you must so you can sleep at night." My back hit something hard, and I stopped.

Deston didn't. He kept coming, voice narrowing to the barest hiss, then leaned in until our lips touched and I tasted the barest hint of spice.

"But don't you ever, ever lie to me, *mon amour*. Not when I know every part of you, down to your very soul."

Something written in his face made me go still, some change in his expression, a touch of sadness, maybe.

I shoved him away. "*How dare you?* You're the one who lies so often, you don't even know what the truth is anymore." I shoved my hands into my pockets so I didn't do something foolish, like blast him to kingdom come. *Or fucking pull him closer.*

"Trust me, I want to control my power, but *it does not want to be controlled*. It fights me at every turn."

"Of course, it does," he snapped. "It's exactly like you."

With those words—so obvious, so simple—logic clicked into place. "What do you mean?" All this time, I'd been looking for ways to force my magic to obey. For some way to force my control over it. Except...force...wasn't the answer.

Because I hated being controlled.

What if my magic did too?

"Ah, she's finally figuring it out," Deston mocked softly. "It took you long enough, Seraphina." The twist to his lips was clear. *I was a disappointment.* There was nothing I could ever do to make him look at me as anything other than a failure.

I didn't mean to hurt anyone.

I was frustrated. Off-balance. Pissed he'd seen right through me. Angry the solution had been right in front of me this whole time.

My palms burned as magic burst out of me, hitting Deston hard, opening a long gash on his cheek.

Good.

I *hated* his fucking perfect face, his mocking eyes. His wicked tongue that spoke my truth *when he had no right to say a thing*.

He shot me a dark look, then brushed himself off. "Again. *If* you're capable."

I roared, this time spearing my power toward an ancient oak tree, splitting the trunk cleanly in two. I was sure Deston could regrow a replacement tonight, however his transmuting magic worked. I threw up my arm to shield my face from the flying leaves and bark as the trunk hit the ground with a satisfyingly reverberating thump, then turned to him.

His face was slack, eyes wide in horror while my heart sank as low as my soaking wet tennis shoes. "That was... *mon Dieu*, my grandsire planted that tree five hundred years ago." I swear, he teared up.

"Oh my God, I am so sorry. I thought it was like every-thing else here, you know, created by magic." I looked between the smoking, cracked trunk and Deston. "Please tell me you can fix this?"

"That tree was irreplaceable," he whispered hoarsely. "Not to mention the showpiece of my gardens." His expression fell, from shock into sorrow. I'd expected the anger, but this crushing show of vulnerability... my stomach curled in on itself.

His skin was cold when I set my hand on his arm. "Oh, Deston, I didn't mean to ruin it. Is there no way to fix this, then?"

When he raised his chin, his black eyes sparkled. No, not sparkled. Laughed. *At me.*

"You are terribly naive, my Queen." He waved to the gardens, the trees and castle that loomed over them. "Of course, I created that tree, and there shall be another just like it by tomorrow. all of this is my creation, and my grand-sire...never saw this place."

Oh. My. God. He'd completely played me.

"You..." Magic welled from the pit of my stomach, fueled by anger and something a bit darker. "You are *such an asshole.*" I would wipe this place clean. Give him a perfectly empty slate. I hoped it took the fucker all night to fix the destruction I was about to wreak.

The blast rocketed out from me in all directions. Even Deston stumbled back a step, throwing up a shield to protect himself from the worst of the damage.

I could have stopped the wave heading for the castle.

Could have. And didn't.

A harsh cracking sound thundered, followed by a deeper rumble, then in slow motion, one entire section of the castle crumbled into smoke and dust.

Deston stared at me incredulously, a hint of rage coloring his beautiful face. "Those were my rooms you ruined. *Mine*."

"Good thing you have the magic to fix them, *my lord*," I told him.

I walked over, picked up one of the red roses, so ruined, the crushed petals stained my fingers red. I dropped it between us, a red flag of war.

"There." I surveyed the wreckage approvingly.

"*That's* a proper temper tantrum, since you seem to be confused."

Chapter 10
Seraphina

Thank God, I hadn't wrecked the entire castle.

If I had, we wouldn't have had anywhere to sleep tonight.

As for Deston, I didn't give a good goddamn where he laid his head tonight. Out in the bayou with the revenants and the alligators, for all I cared.

I was so done with this stupid vampire turf war. Maybe it was time I took my two knights and hightailed it to some exotic land. Somewhere Viktor would never find us. There had to be somewhere, right?

I peeked out the window and watched Deston carefully raise a statue's severed head back onto her neck, the crack healing over like it had never been there. Guiltily, I lowered the shade.

I regretted my little temper tantrum because that's exactly what it was.

I'd gotten pissed off, and now... I felt bad.

Somehow, Deston saw the truth I'd been trying to evade for months. He knew I didn't want to be Queen. He knew fear was holding me back. But I couldn't make myself want a future that had been forced on me, from the moment they dragged me into Viktor's dungeons.

Maybe I didn't have to focus on being Queen and running an entire kingdom, which scared the hell out of me.

Maybe I needed to start small.

Experimentally, I sent a tendril spiraling through the air and pushed a pile of clothes off the end of the bed. Drew it back to me, curling my hand into a fist. I'd felt the clothing distinctly, especially the velvety softness of the sweater on top of the pile.

Over and over again, I pushed a tiny bit of my power out, then called it back, letting the tendril explore a bit farther every time. By the time I'd finished, my arms were shaking, but I had a newfound sense of confidence.

I could do this. I'd planned to be a doctor, to change the world. Maybe...maybe this was just a different way of changing the world. Maybe magic was something to learn, not fear.

And *I had to do this.*

The cracking sound as the huge dresser mirror shattered pulled me from my daydreams. Shards flew across the room, covering the bed, the floor.

"Fuck." I yanked back too quickly and dragged my resistant magic across the dresser top, wiping the entire surface clean of brushes, hair ties, and...

"Oh, shit." Mom's painting hit the ground hard, tumbling across the floor before spinning beneath the armoire. I gingerly crawled through the glass, knelt, found the painting, and pulled it out of the wreckage. The picture was ruined.

"No, no, you can't be broken. You can't be."

I carried the painting to a table, set it atop the huge book Deston had conjured and turned up the lamp. I'd cracked the frame on one corner, but that could be fixed, right? Maybe Deston could repair it with his magic if he wasn't too angry with me for wrecking his gardens.

And his castle.

Trying to wedge the diagonal crack back together only seemed to make things worse. My heart sank as the halves slipped apart, tearing the brown paper—scrawled with mom's signature and the date, January 4th—across the back.

No, no, no. I wanted to scream. *Please don't take this away from me. This is all I have to remember her by, it can't be ruined.*

I fumbled the halves back together and only managed to tear her signature completely in half. "Goddamn it." Cursing and half crying, I nearly missed the key that fell out and clinked onto the wood floor, coming to rest in the shards of the splintered mirror.

I tiptoed into the middle of the mess and picked the key up, my head swimming with curiosity.

The key was gold, about the length of my finger with a thin chain wound around the shaft, and the links caked with years of grime. I ran my finger over the key, something like dread tightening my chest. At the top were a pair of intertwined snakes, their eyes glinting green as I turned it this way and that, looking for any distinguishing markings.

There were none, but I was pretty sure this key was solid gold.

Unwrapping the chain, I loosened the dirt, slipped it over my head and turned back to the painting, discovering I'd completely ripped one side of the canvas from the frame. I set the whole mess carefully onto the dresser.

I'd glue the frame back together, later. I'd fix this, some-how. Maybe I'd ask Deston for a favor, even though that was sure to be a shitshow.

But this picture was the only tangible thing I had left of Mom. Gram had given this to me before Viktor killed her and now look at it. I glanced from the ruined painting to the key at the end of the chain.

Why was there a key in the back of a painting?

There were only two possibilities. Gram or Mom had hidden it there. I didn't like the implications of either of them possessing something like a solid gold key. Even worse, *hiding* something like this.

I turned the thing over in my hand.

The key was not only heavy, the workmanship was incredible. I made out every scale on the serpent's bodies and their gemstone eyes had to be real emeralds. I let the chain fall back between my breasts and inspected the painting closer, questions racing through my head.

I wormed my fingers along the inside of the frame. Wedged between the torn paper backing and the canvas I found a rolled piece of paper, the edges worn, but saw enough of the writing to know it was from Mom, and fear like I'd never known gripped me.

You're a goddamned vampire, Seraphina, grow some balls. Open it up and find out what your mother wanted to tell you.

I unrolled the small missive with shaking hands, her tight, precise printing—because she never wrote in cursive —covering the entire surface.

My dearest Fina,

If you have found this, then Claire and I are dead. Mother and I disagreed on many things, but one thing we always agreed on was shielding you from the clan as long as possible. I hope you will remember us both fondly, despite our many mistakes.

You have been my greatest treasure. Embrace your new life with the same fearlessness you face every day. You were always meant to change the world, but more than that, I know you can.

If you are reading this, know that some things in life are inevitable, and you ending up with the key is one of them.

This key unlocks a secret that will bring the King to his knees. We tried to use it, but we were not strong enough to face him. You are. Be stronger, be fearless, and make Viktor pay for what he's done.

All my love,

Isabelle

Despite being dead for years, Mom knew. That I was a vampire. About Viktor, and the Darkfell Clan. About everything. And yet, she'd spent most of my childhood trying to make life as normal as possible.

Emotion became a hard knot in my throat as I reread the letter. Once. Twice.

"Normal." I chuckled through my tears. "Yeah, that's a crock of shit."

"What's a crock of shit?" Cyrus asked, leaning in the doorway. Having no idea how long he'd been there, I slid the key beneath my shirt. "Besides the fact that our sleeping quarters look like they've been hit by an earthquake?"

"My life, pretty much," I said, tucking the note into my pocket. "Practice didn't exactly go as planned," I waved to the broken mirror. "Neither did my second practice."

I didn't know why I didn't want Cyrus to find out about the note and the key. Maybe because my heart hurt so badly right now. Maybe because this secret was too new for me to share, even with him. Maybe because it was time for me to start figuring things out on my own, instead of letting everyone else fix my problems for me.

Whatever the reason, I didn't tell him.

Instead, I didn't argue when Cyrus offered to get Deston to clean up my mess.

But all night, all I thought about was that key.

Chapter 11
Seraphina

I spent the next five days snooping, testing the key in every lock of every door in the castle.

Not only did it not fit, I knew why it didn't fit, since I'd spent hours online educating myself on the arcane art of skeleton keys. Unlike being a vampire queen, there was plenty of how-to information on keys.

They'd been invented to work on warded locks—not the magical sort—by clearing a corresponding set of notches in the lock and releasing a sliding lever.

Life became a game of sorts, destroying the gardens during the day, then sleuthing around Deston's castle by night, searching for the right door to unlock.

Luthor and Cyrus usually bought my excuse that I had research to do in the library, and while I felt bad about my white lies, I became increasingly determined to figure this mystery out for myself.

I didn't expect my key to open any of the doors in Deston's castle—they were, after all, created by him—but I was hoping I would discover what type of lock it fit, and where such a lock might be found. According to my internet searches, warded locks were used in monasteries and churches, usually in the UK or Ireland.

After the first few nights, though, my curiosity turned into obsession, and now... all I could picture was sliding that mysterious key into a lock and seeing what it revealed.

Every room in the castle had a different mechanism. Every lock was a work of art covered in intricate ironwork or brass, copper, or gold. Eventually, I discovered Deston actually had a key room and sat until dawn, comparing my key with the hundreds hanging in the key box.

None of them were close.

Except for one.

And that's where Deston found me, holding the bent, broken key—twin to the one around my neck—cross-legged on the floor of the tiny room.

Chapter 12
Seraphina

"What are you doing up at this hour, my Queen?" Deston snapped off the end of my title, much like I'd snapped his oak tree in half. Since that day, I hadn't seen so much as a flare of temper from him. No mockery, or disdain, either.

He'd been cold as ice and just as unreachable.

As he reached down and yanked me up off the floor, I figured that situation was about to change.

"We have training in the morning, and if I may be so bold, you need your rest in order for tomorrow not to be a complete disaster."

"Oh, trust me, it'll be a disaster whether I get any sleep or not."

His eyes flickered in agreement, but he said nothing. I ran a finger over the broken tooth of the mutilated key, feeling the twisted, sharp edge cut into my skin as I debated my next move.

Deston knew what this key was for. Had nearly broken the thing in half, trying to make it work.

But if I asked him, he'd lie. Deception was in his blood, and I needed this truth, more than anything.

"Do you ever feel like you're keeping the world's biggest secret?" I asked curiously. "Like something that will change the world, but you can't tell a soul?"

"What secret are you keeping, my Queen?" There was no mistaking the way his dark eyes gleamed when he focused on the key box and noticed what was missing, his gaze dropping to my closed fist.

"On a scale of one to ten, from the look on your face, I'd say this one's about an eleven."

"Stop playing games, Seraphina. You are a guest here, and even for my Queen, some areas of my life are off limits." In a flash, he closed the distance between us. "Did Claire not explain the rules of hospitality to you?" His mouth twisted into something ugly. "Or perhaps your mother died too early to teach you?"

"That's right, Deston. Deflection through anger, just like always," I chided, though my hand tightened over the ruined key at his insult. He was *such* an asshole.

"Well, your methods of redirection won't work, not this time. Since you're so fond of counting off my options, we can do this a couple different ways. One, you can tell me the truth. An odd request, I know, as it's something you are unfamiliar with." Instead of retreating, I took a step closer, his eyes widening.

"Two, I can involve Luthor and Cyrus, and they'll get the truth out of you by other means." My smile was all tooth. "I don't care which approach works because, for the first time since we met, you have something I want, and I mean to get it."

I revealed the bent key. "Tell me what this goes to."

"One of the doors in the castle. I shall show you which one." He lied so easily, so smoothly, like deception was second nature. If I hadn't already tried my own key in every single lock, I would have bought the falsehood.

"Try again." He opened his mouth, and I smiled. "And

consider this before you lie a second time. I already know what this goes to. I just want to hear you say it."

I wasn't nearly as good a liar as Deston, but I did have one thing going for me. He didn't know that. Luthor and Cyrus did, but Deston didn't know me well enough to know I was terrible at deception.

But Cyrus had been teaching me to shield my mind, and I was a fast learner.

Malice drenched the air. His mouth twisted as he expanded on his lie. "As I explained, one of the doors in the castle. Give me the key, and I shall show you which one." I closed my hand around the broken key and slipped it into my jean pocket, his dark eyes flashing in fury when it disappeared.

"Fine. I'll let Luthor sort this out." I lied right back. "Be a good boy and stay here, will you, while I go and fetch him. He'll be most displeased to be woken in the middle of the night. I sure hope you've fed. You'll need your stamina."

Deston snagged my arm, I yanked out of his grasp. "One more chance. What does this unlock? Or should I ask around until I find out? I expect Cyrus and Luthor still have some contacts, and I've been dying to get back out in the world after being locked up for so long."

"Do not do that, Seraphina." Deston spoke too quickly. "That key...this is not something the rest of the clan... we cannot call undue attention to ourselves, especially not now."

"Nobody can know about a bent-up key hidden in the bottom of an old key box, for what looks like about a hundred years? Tell me why."

"It is... *compliqué*... complicated."

"Yeah, secrets usually are. Now tell me what it's for."

"Your best course of action would be to put that back

where you found it and forget you ever saw it. The key is ruined, so this conversation is pointless." Every word seemed to reverberate, as if he was attempting to hypnotize me.

Was he seriously trying to glamour me right now?

"Let's pretend we argued about this for a while, and I politely refused to forget about it, and we've now moved onto the part where you tell me what's really going on."

"I... my Queen, I beg of you, do not pursue this path." His voice turned cajoling, underscored with a hint of menace. "Such curiosity leads to dangerous places. Better we redouble our efforts during training. If you simply concentrate, you will make great strides in—"

I cut off his lies with a hard press of magic against his throat. He fought me, fangs descending.

"As you can tell, my magic is getting stronger every day. Also, I'm pretty determined to get a straight answer from you. Frankly, I think Luthor..."

"No." Deston gasped, and I eased off. I had no real wish to involve Luthor or Cyrus, who would be like two mother hens up in my business about the key and the letter and me creeping around the house all hours of the night. No, I'd rather do this in secret, and once I got my answer, I'd figure out what my next move was.

"*Mon Dieu*, I will tell you." He rubbed his neck, red from the pressure. "But *cherie*, once you know... you shall wish you didn't."

Chapter 13
Seraphina

I didn't tell Deston the twin key—undamaged and perfectly usable—hung around my neck.

Better he believed I possessed nothing but a worthless relic because, once I discovered what these things unlocked, I had every intention of opening that door and marching straight through.

"*Ma cherie...*" He stepped closer, voice thrumming with seduction, and I wondered at this new tactic. He'd never tried to enthrall me before, and no lie, my traitorous body responded like a goddamned tuning fork. "Please, listen to me. This is not anything important. You should worry about Viktor, and what you must do when you face him."

He sighed dramatically, ran his fingers down my arm. I was immune to his glamour, but his light, seductive touch woke something deep inside me, sent waves of pleasure humming through my body.

"Forget the key. It's nothing," he soothed in that same hypnotic tone. "Forget what you saw tonight and go back to sleep."

Funny thing.

A couple months ago, his glamour would have actually worked. I'd have wandered back upstairs, slept the night away, and never remembered a key. He was so old and powerful, I might have even believed the one around my neck was just a worthless pendant and forgotten all about Mom's letter, urging me to fulfill my destiny.

But that was plain old, human Seraphina.

Every night, Cyrus had been teaching me to erect a barrier around my mind, and I was a quick learner. He was also a very, very good teacher.

Kick-butt vampire Seraphina wanted answers, and after Deston's whole—*you don't want to know this big, huge secret anyways*—routine, I was simply *dying* to know.

I reached the broken key out to him, like I was sleep-walking, even though the whole time I itched to rip that self-satisfied, arrogant smile off his face. "You're right, I want to forget. Make me forget, Deston."

His eyes were indecipherable when he lifted the broken key from my open palm and disappeared it into his pocket. "Now go to bed, Seraphina," he ordered softly before he lightly brushed my cheek with his knuckles, leaving a spark of heat behind. "Sleep well, have no nightmares and we shall speak first thing in the morning."

No doubt to make sure I really had forgotten.

"What does the key go to?" I asked dreamily. "If I'll forget anyways, just tell me, so I can finally stop dreaming about this."

"A chamber in the palace where no one should ever visit. Now go back to your warm bed." His dark gaze searched my face, as if committing it to memory. "And your lovers."

All the way back upstairs, I wondered if I'd imagined the venom in Deston's last words.

Because to me, he'd sounded almost jealous.

Chapter 14
Deston

The second Seraphina turned away, I slid the fucking key into my pocket, resolving right then and there to melt it down to nothing.

Until tonight, I'd forgotten all about this damned thing.

I'd kept this relic for decades, ever since the last time I'd used it—ruined it—on that bastard of a lock. I'd believed—in a moment of complete madness—Lyra might still be alive, locked in a room in the palace. Though I'd neutralized the witch spell keeping the chamber sealed, the key had snapped the moment I'd pushed it into the lock.

Viktor's guards had swooped in moments later and I'd barely escaped with my life.

But how could she know...

I turned the thing over in my hand, replaying our conversation. This key—impossibly—meant something to Seraphina. "But how could you possibly recognize this?" I mused softly as I headed back to my chamber.

I regretted using mind control on my Queen, but just the thought of her getting anywhere close to the palace—or worse, close to Viktor—shook me to my core. I'd never allow Seraphina anywhere near the palace. Not so long as I lived.

True mates were an oddity in the vampire world, and I'd heard all the cautionary tales before.

How the bond took over your life, how true mates could

barely function without each other, but I'd never expected my existence to hang by a thread, reliant on Seraphina's moods and questionable actions. Every time she lost control of her magic, fear coursed through my veins.

Every time she disappeared upstairs to her shared bed, jealousy consumed me.

In truth, I was grateful for her decimating my gardens, because repairing the damage took my mind off what she and Luthor and Cyrus were doing. If I didn't keep busy, I'd materialize into that bedroom and kill them both, so I could have her to myself.

But killing her lovers wouldn't win Seraphina to my side.

No, I'd bollocked that chance by selling her out to Viktor, despite everything turning out in the end. A slow and steady road to winning back her trust was my only option, no matter how long this process took.

I watched her meander down the hall toward the staircase, relief making my knees weak.

But how could she know...

My hand closed around the key, my thoughts trailing off into nothingness as realization struck me. The door this key opened was in the same section of the palace I'd seen Viktor disappear to the other day. I'd already determined the source of his power was there; the secret we needed in order to weaken him.

My chest ached as I watched Seraphina take the steps, jealousy churning like acid in my veins. Somehow—perhaps on that damned internet she was always talking about—she'd seen a picture of something similar. I hadn't misinterpreted that flash of recognition in her golden eyes, nor her claim that she already knew what this went to.

Better she forgot all about the key.

She had enough challenges at the moment. *We all did.*

My list of allies was shorter than I would have liked. Luthor and Cyrus would never be on my side, not with Seraphina between us. It was clear Viktor had his doubts about me, and there were rumors floating around the court that he meant to kill Seraphina properly the next time he caught her.

I shuddered at the thought.

Viktor's means of meting out death were inhumane and archaic. If I failed to protect Seraphina and Viktor got his claws into her...

No, better she woke up in the morning and forgot all about this key business, though the next time I visited the palace, I'd search every square inch of that wing. If I couldn't discover the source of Viktor's unnatural power, then I'd focus on molding Seraphina into a weapon strong enough to take him down.

"Dieu, donne-moi la force pour ce qui est à venir."

Somehow, I highly doubted God would hear my plea.

B ack in my bedroom, I snuggled deeply into the delicious warmth between Luthor and Cyrus, my thoughts whirling as I pulled the covers over us.

How could Mom have a key to a door in the royal palace?

In her letter, she claimed *we tried using the key*, which indicated she or Gram had been there.

But I couldn't imagine Claire—much less my sweet mother—being at the royal palace for any other reason than as Viktor's captives. Being hunted your whole life meant never going into enemy territory. I mean, that was the number one rule of survival.

And yet... if this key opened a door at the palace, then my assumptions were all wrong.

But Mom said the key unlocked a secret that would bring the king to his knees.

What secret? And how could I use that to my advantage? And what good was the intact key, if I didn't know what door it unlocked or even where the palace was?

I needed information.

I knew next to nothing about how this whole vampire world operated. I knew I had fangs, and magic, and royal lineage, but because I'd been stuck in the middle of a swamp for months, because the three experienced vampires were more interested in protecting me than explaining how things worked, I didn't know shit.

I had to find out where the palace was.

My gaze drifted over to the book Deston had conjured up for me. Chances were, the answer was somewhere in there, but I didn't have time to read a thousand pages of history.

I needed a more...direct source of intel.

Once my eyes adjusted to the darkness, I ran a finger down the key, looking for clues. This key tied everything together; I just didn't understand how.

Deston had one. I had one.

Mom left me the damn thing, along with a cryptic warning. Then there was Deston, who wanted me to forget everything, which meant this key led to something big.

But if Luthor or Cyrus found out, they'd have questions, and I didn't have any answers. I slipped the chain off my neck and tucked the key into the nightstand, beneath the huge book that constituted my entire to-be-read pile.

"Fina, stop moving around. I can't sleep." Cyrus reached over and cupped my ass. Fire shot through me, flaring low in my belly.

"Mmmm," I said, turning into him, my fingernails digging into his chest. "You're awake." Cyrus groaned dramatically, but his fingers were already trailing around the curve of my thigh, dipping in between. His thumb brushed my clit, and I jumped.

"Easy, my queen."

Then I opened my thighs to let him worm his entire hand in between. Cyrus's clever fingers danced between my folds with the expertise of a male who knew exactly what he was doing, and my bones turned to liquid. Dragging his thumb across my clit, I whimpered softly, and he stopped instantly.

"Too much?" Cyrus asked softly.

"Not enough," I tell him truthfully. "More. Harder."

"I was so hoping you'd say that, Fina. And I live to serve." Those magic fingers delved in deeper with a featherlight touch that had me jerking with need. With a chuckle, he pressed his thumb to my clit, and I disappeared inside the chasm of pleasure pulsing inside me.

Between his soothing magic turning my brain to sludge, and his knowing strokes that were *just so*, I forgot all about the key, and Mom, and mysteries that needed to be solved.

No, I became a bundle of writhing nerves, waiting for release. Also, I was hungry.

Reading my mind, he tipped his head, offering me his throat, and I bit down gently, careful to avoid the scar. I drank as gently as I could, running my tongue over the punctures when I was finished, planting a kiss on the wide, white band around his neck. Then another one.

Then another.

Overcome with emotion, I reached up, touched his beautiful face. "Cyrus..." My voice turned ragged. He'd been wounded so badly. I wanted to promise he'd never be hurt again. I wanted to tell him I'd never let anyone hurt him, but I knew I couldn't make those kinds of promises.

Not yet.

"Enough of that, Seraphina," he said gruffly. "Don't you *ever* let him come between us, *especially* not in our bed."

He was right. Viktor had stolen too much from us already, he didn't deserve anything more. I yanked him down to me, kissed him as hard as I could, branding myself onto his lips, leaving a sparkle of magic behind. My canines nipped his lip; I tasted blood.

With a harsh laugh, he rolled me on my back, teeth tightening on my nipple, his fingers stroking and stroking as I grew wetter and wetter. "Come for me, my Queen."

God help me, I did, my body unfurling beneath his hands, my hips moving fast as he plunged one finger, then two into me, keeping time with the press of his teeth on my breast. I came apart, my scream muffled by Cyrus's tongue darting into my mouth, his warm lips moving against mine. Possessively enough heat rushed through my blood like a bolt of lightning.

This was exactly what I needed, connection and safety and the simplicity of being loved while I loved them back. Then Luthor was there, sucking my other nipple into his mouth, nudging Cyrus out of the way before mounting me, his cock sliding in slowly, stretching me as he went deeper and deeper.

Cyrus took over kissing me, his tongue every bit as clever as his fingers, tracing my teeth with a featherlight touch, teasing a moan out of me, while Luthor filled me up. I tightened around him, my core already coiling, ready for another release. My skin felt superheated where they touched me, yet cold where the air hit my naked flesh. A yin-yang of opposing sensation, much like Cyrus's teasing kisses and Luthor's cock sliding in and out, his knees pushing me wider with every stroke.

He slid his hand beneath my ass, raised me higher, angling his cock in even deeper.

"Oh fuck." I moaned into Cyrus's mouth. He laughed, gripping my face and kissing me even deeper. Between his tongue dancing in my mouth and Luthor's cock, I climaxed, a spiral of pleasure spearing through me, my entire body going rigid as Cyrus swallowed my scream.

One more stroke and Luthor came, his rough growl

muffled by the pillow my head lay on. He collapsed, rolling off me at the last second, his chest heaving.

"Out of the way, Commander," Cyrus ordered, "before I move you."

"My ass you can," Luthor muttered, but he settled heavily beside me, eyes hooded, lips pressed against my cheek.

"Drink from me," I told him softly. "I want your teeth in me while Cyrus is fucking me."

"Now that's the way to give an order, my Queen." Luthor tenderly turned my head to the side, bit in just as gently, so careful not to hurt me. Cyrus thrust in, filling me up with one stroke, his fingers digging onto my hips, holding me still while he pummeled into me, faster and faster. With a groan he came. "Sorry, that was fast."

He crawled off me, curled into my side.

"Well, I already came twice, so I think I'm way ahead," I whispered, my words already fading away as darkness swept in. Luthor licked the bite closed, then went limp, his head nestled into the curve of my neck.

I fell asleep with my arms around them both, holding them tight.

Chapter 16
Seraphina

S tepping back, I shook my numb hands, wisps of smoke trailing off my fingers.

"*Très bon*, Seraphina, much improved."

I shook off Deston's faint praise and zipped up my hoodie. Gram had always counseled against complacency and while I was steadily getting better at this *magic stuff*, I was still nowhere competent enough to face Viktor, which was really all that mattered.

Twice, he'd sent revenants sniffing around the bayou.

Another week had passed, and every day, my magic grew by leaps and bounds.

Once I'd stopped forcing my power to obey, my magic had expanded, and now I spent all my energy trying to contain it inside me.

Not even Luthor, who knew me down to my soul, knew how deep my pool of magic went, like a well without a bottom. The knowledge that my magic could be limitless was both frightening and exhilarating. The more I expended, the more I seemed to have at my fingertips, and I was becoming more and more adept at wielding.

Deston's garden was stunning today under the bright blue sky. There wasn't a shred of white in the explosion of color, where deep red and purple blossoms tumbled from the beds, stretched over the walls in untamed arcs of sensual, rich texture.

Part of me wondered if he'd taken my declaration of war seriously and replied with one of his own. Red roses abounded throughout the garden, their fragrance heady, huge blooms hanging low from the weight.

Best of all, everything was still intact, including the arch. Despite me threading enormous plumes of super-heated magic through the opening, I hadn't dislodged a single pebble.

There was a slight pressure on my arm, and then Deston was staring down at me. "*M'as-tu entendu?*" He actually looked... happy. Pleased.

"I'm fine." I realized I'd been daydreaming and pulled out of his grasp. "I'd like to try the arch one more time."

Deston's eyebrows furrowed, and I thought he'd argue, point out that I should cut my losses while I was still ahead, but then he stepped back with a curt nod.

"Once more, then."

Magic, I'd discovered, not only had a mind of its own, but required a light, delicate touch. Like I'd once hoped to wield a scalpel, I now wielded my power. Funneling it into a thin spiral, I threaded a stream of molten plasma neatly through the arch, then drew it back to me without so much as a stone out of place.

"*Très, très bon, ma chère.*"

"Still needs work, but I'm getting a feel for this."

"I visited the palace late last night," Deston offered casually. "I believe I am quite close to discovering where Viktor draws his magic. And he is down one more court member. A most annoying hanger on, always going on about his Florida beach house and his cars. One Lord Simon Emmett."

"You didn't eat Simon, did you?" I teased softly, letting a curl of magic twine around my arm.

"Don't be ridiculous." He snorted. "Can you imagine how he'd taste?"

"Like shrimp and margaritas?"

"More like old leather shoes and hair grease."

I snorted out a laugh, covering my mouth while I realized Deston's smile had transformed his entire face, turning him impossibly handsome. For a second, I lost my breath, not able to take my eyes off him.

When had I started joking around about people eating each other, and it only half-being a joke?

When had Deston and I gone from hating each other to... this? *I need him, is all. Need him to finish my training so I can kill Viktor, then all of us can go back to our regularly scheduled lives.*

Well, except for me because I'll be stuck being Queen forever.

"Be that as it may, I thought we'd decided not to kill any more court members, so we don't call attention to ourselves?"

His mouth quirked upwards as his gaze met mine. "No one will miss that blowhard. But since you are worried, my Queen, Viktor himself requested Emmett disappear. You could say I was acting in my role as advisor to the King." He sketched a bow.

"Well, I guess that's fine, then." Jeez, how my life had changed. Now, murder and mayhem and regicide were every day events. "What's the royal palace like? I've heard you and Luthor talk about that place, and it sounds horrible."

If I was going to find answers about the key, I had to do this now, while Deston's guard was down. And I'd only get one chance.

I double-checked my mental barrier and found the shield intact.

"The palace is ugly grandeur, Seraphina." Deston's smile faded slightly, leaving him pensive. "The most beautiful building in the world, filled with bloated, deadly creatures who do not deserve to draw air."

I gestured to his grand castle. "More beautiful than yours?" I felt bad maneuvering him like this, but I was determined to find the truth, even if I had to lie to get it.

"Very much," he murmured, regarding me intently, like he was trying to figure out my motives for this line of questioning. "The royal palace was modeled after Versailles, naturally, given our French roots. There is even a Hall of Mirrors."

"Modeled after Versailles, huh?" I widened my eyes. "That has to be pretty fancy."

Of course. I *knew* I'd seen the throne room from my training session before. It looked exactly like pictures I'd seen of the Hall of Mirrors, right down to the frescoed ceiling and the crystal chandeliers.

I should have figured that out before, but now all I had to do was find a blueprint of Versailles online, and I'd have a diagram of the royal palace. Including the layout of all the doors, corridors and wings. How hard could it possibly be to sneak in, especially now that my magic was so powerful?

I'd reread Mom's note a hundred times and she and Gram weren't strong enough. *But Mom thought I was.* I *had* to be stronger, I *had* to kill Viktor and finish this. There was no one else but me.

I batted my eyes at Deston, hoping he'd keep talking. "Versailles is close to Paris, right? I've never been to Paris. Or anywhere in Europe, for that matter. What's it like?"

A hint of suspicion sparked in his dark eyes. "Paris is a beautiful city. Or was, the last time I was there."

"I'd love to see it someday. When were you there last? Recently??"

"Well before your time." His smile grew bitter before he shook his head, his mouth twisting into a snarl. "Are you manipulating me right now, Seraphina?" A burst of cold emanated from him, shadows swirling in his eyes.

I shrugged, not surprised he'd seen through me, given he was about a million years old.

He'd revealed a valuable clue, which made my play-acting completely worthwhile.

"Now that I know where to look, I can figure out the layout of the palace. Once I do, I imagine it will simply be a matter of me finding the correct locked door before the guards find me."

His face darkened in anger as he realized his glamour hadn't worked.

I matched his frosty smile with ice. "Pro tip. You can't compel me anymore."

"You were feigning compulsion the other night?"

"Yep, totally faking." I snorted. "I warned you to never try to compel me again, and you couldn't even honor that simple request. Maybe now you'll learn your lesson."

"You played me?" Deston asked slowly, as if not believing that, yes, I was capable of treachery and perfectly willing to manipulate him to get what I wanted.

"I did. You went into my head to steal my memories, after I specifically asked you not to. If anyone should be apologizing, here's a clue. *It won't be me.*"

"Ah." His face cleared as he figured out why his glamour wasn't working. "My dear cousin has taught you to shield your mind. It appears you are good at something, after all."

His jab missed the mark. "It appears I easily played a four-hundred-year-old vampire who should know better."

"You forget, *ma cherie.*" Every soft word promised reprisal. "I am in possession of the key, which I have already destroyed. Without it, there is no mystery, no reason to go to the palace. Forget about the key, it is nothing."

"Trying to compel me won't work, I thought I just explained that."

"*Obviously,* it won't work. I'm not compelling you. I'm using logic to convince you not to commit suicide." He gestured to the wall where Luthor usually sat. "Let me tell you about the palace, *mon coeur,* since you seem to be under the impression that you can stroll right in and explore at will.

"Firstly, you will never find the location because it's warded with magic more ancient and powerful than mine. Three hundred years of magic that has been reinforced and strengthened by every queen, as well as Viktor. If you did make it through the wards, the grounds are patrolled by packs of revenants, and trust me, Viktor keeps them hungry. The second you appeared on the other side of the ward they would rip you apart."

"Go on," I said, wondering whether he was aware he was giving me a blueprint for breaking in.

"If you accomplish the impossible and make it through the ward and the revenants, you must still enter the palace, itself. There are guards posted at every door, trained as well as Luthor and Cyrus, instructed to kill intruders on sight."

"And what comes after that? Because knowing Viktor as I do, I imagine he has a thousand ways to torture anyone who makes it inside."

"You'd never even make it that far because you'd be dead before you set foot inside the building." He shook his head. "Don't forget about the innumerable doors and wings and corridors and floors. You would never find the lock you're looking for, Seraphina. Your best choice right now is to continue training until I deem you ready."

"See, that's what I don't like about this whole plan. Everybody else decides what's best for me. How about this? Consider my training over until you tell me the truth about that damn key. Once you do, I'm back on board with the plan." I crossed my arms over my chest. "Until then, consider your wizard school shut down."

"Seraphina." Deston's eyes narrowed in frustration, and I could practically see what he was considering.

"Try it," I spat. "Just try to compel me again and see what happens."

"*I'm not going to compel you*," he snapped right back. "I regret the other night, but I deemed it the best approach until I knew what you were up to. Now I'm trying to use logic to make you see reason."

"I'm not seeing anything until I find out what deep, dark secret that key leads to," I insisted. "You know what it's for, so just tell me already."

"Some secrets..." he murmured softly, "are never meant to see the light of day. And this may well be one of them."

Wait, he didn't know what was behind the door?

"Fine." I turned on my heel. "I'll discover the truth for myself."

He cursed softly in French beneath his breath. "What has come over you? You saw that key one time, Seraphina, *once*. The thing is nothing, means nothing. Why will you not listen to me?"

I didn't plan on doing it, but I pulled my key out from beneath my sweatshirt. The snake's emerald eyes glittered in the dim sunlight.

"Because my mother left this for me. The fact that yours is broken tells me you've already tried to use it. So, let's just cut to the chase, shall we? Tell me what this key unlocks, then explain down to the last little detail why it's so important I leave this alone."

The second Deston saw that key, he went preternaturally still as he studied the key, my face, the key again. *Where did you get that?* his dark eyes seemed to ask.

"That is not my key, Seraphina."

"No, it is not," I retorted, already regretting my decision. I should have kept mine a secret, especially when Deston's face was impossible to read, but impulsivity got the better of me and now my secret was out.

"Tell me what this unlocks and I'll stay here where it's nice and safe. I'll practice. I'll learn how to kill Viktor. And I won't go to the palace by myself."

I tucked the key back between my breasts, his gaze tracking the movement, my heart rate picking up. "Other than that, all bets are off. And good luck keeping me inside this prison of yours for a moment longer. I'm itching to get outside these wards." My voice turned frosty. "*Explore on my own.*"

I couldn't decipher Deston's expression as he stared me down. Nor the sudden intense quiet that took him over. Nor the tightness that invaded my body, the longer he looked at me like that.

"And if I tell you everything, you'll stay here? In the castle? You will not attempt to leave?"

"Yes," I said with no hesitation.

"Liar," he hissed vehemently. "You're lying to me, and you're lying to yourself, Seraphina. Give me the key. Hand it over before you get yourself killed."

I didn't budge. "I've got news for you. Everything in this

new world wants to kill me. Viktor, revenants, you name it, I might as well paint a giant target on my back. But I'll tell you this. I'd rather go out doing what I want, instead of blindly doing what everyone else wants me to do. At least then, I have some say in the matter."

His face grew inscrutable again as he stared down at me.

"You have a say in the matter."

"No," I told him quietly. "I don't. All I have is three males who tell me I must kill the King to become the Queen. That I have to use my magic to become a weapon. But that's your dream, not mine. Nobody has *ever* asked me what I want. No one ever asked if I regret giving up my old dreams, for a future I never even asked for."

I looked down at my hands. "I was going to be a doctor. I was going to save lives. I was going to be *good* at something. Now...now I'm not good at anything, no matter how hard I try."

His dark eyes gleamed, but his demeanor changed, as if he was considering my point of view.

"Let me decide." He pushed up on his cane. "In the meantime, try not to destroy my garden. I consider this my favorite version so far."

"No," I called out to his retreating back. "I told you, no wizard school until I know the truth."

"No truth until you manage one day without destroying my gardens," he counter-offered, knowing I'd take that deal in a heartbeat.

As it turned out, I only *slightly* wrecked the garden, so maybe today would count in my favor. By the time I trudged back to the castle for a quick shower and lunch, just one of the beds was ruined, flattened by a swirl of errant magic that got away from me.

Even if Deston wouldn't tell me the whole truth, I was confident I could get inside the palace. And while I figured his *innumerable locks* comment was an exaggeration, there probably were hundreds of doors.

Wait, my logical side urged. *Wait and see what Deston's version of the truth is.* Then I'd determine what my next move would be.

Today's good news? I'd practiced for nearly three hours, and the arch was intact. My magic felt more like a sleeping volcano, rather than a pressurized boiler ready to explode. I was growing more powerful, my control was getting better, and my confidence was improving.

As in, I was confident that should revenants appear, I could ash them with a thought.

Deston had been overly protective today. Usually, he was perfectly happy to put me in harm's way by blasting magical plasma at me, but he seemed determined to keep me out of the palace.

And away from whatever secret this key revealed.

Which meant he already knew what was behind the door. He *was* trying to protect me.

You mean protect his investment? I reminded myself. After all, I was his tool to remove Viktor from not only the throne, but from this Earth.

The one thing that remained unchanged was Deston's unwavering hatred of Viktor. That, I could count on.

He was the master of manipulating a corrupt, jaded royal court. I was the neophyte who didn't know what the court was, much less the rules.

But I didn't need to know everything about the Darkfell Clan, I just had to learn to maneuver people as easily as Deston. That was power, and once I mastered the art of deception, Deston could shove it.

"Who's going to shove what?" Cyrus strolled into the garden looking around with approval. "Hardly a flower out of place." He only grinned when I indicated the ruined corner.

"Well, nobody's perfect, and you're getting much better, Seraphina. Are you hungry?"

"As a matter of fact"—I eyed his neck, saliva filling my mouth—"I am." I stopped him with a hand in the middle of his chest, then pressed a kiss at the bottom of his throat. He was slightly salty, and there was a brief pressure-pain before my fangs elongated.

He slipped his arms around me, and just like that, all my worries melted away. "I do like your particular brand of magic, Cyrus. It's kind of like taking a whole-body Xanax."

"I don't know what that is, but I'm glad you like it." He led me out of the garden and pulled me into his lap beneath the newly restored oak tree.

"Drink, love, you were studying late last night," he chided gently. "You have to get more sleep, there are dark circles under your beautiful eyes." I ignored the twinge of guilt and pretended white lies didn't matter.

There was something about being cradled in his lap, feeding, that was impossibly intimate. Almost more than sex, this bonded us together. I couldn't believe I'd once found it distasteful. I licked the punctures closed and settled against Cyrus's chest. I hadn't lied; he was like a muscle relaxant, and my entire body was relaxed, my head logy from the feeding.

"Wouldn't it be nice if this was our life?" I asked dreamily. Between the feeding and the fact that I hadn't slept more than a couple of hours last night, I couldn't have walked if I'd wanted to. "If we could just enjoy life without all this other bullshit?"

Cyrus tucked me in tighter. "That will be our life, after Viktor is gone. Removing him from our world will only make it a better place. You'll be doing our kind a favor, Seraphina. Sires won't have to worry about their daughters disappearing, revenants hunting them, the constant threats and cruelty. You have a chance very few of us have, to change things and actually make them better."

He was right.

I *wanted* to do all these things, even killing Viktor.

There were people I'd never even met, depending on me to fix things.

"I'll do everything I can to help them," I promised, even though tears pricked my eyes. "It just seems like I'm at the bottom of a mountain, and somehow, I have to move the whole thing out of my way. Everything seems impossible when it's so big, and I'm so small."

"You're the strongest person I know." I felt Cyrus's lips in my hair, his arm banded around my back. "You'll change the world. Not many people can say that. Think of your bragging rights when you succeed."

"Put her down," Deston snapped. "She should be practicing." I blinked dreamily at him, caught up in the lovely fuzziness of post feeding.

"I was practicing, and then I ate, and now I'm resting. That's an accounting of the last three hours of my life. Hopefully, it's satisfactory."

Deston jerked his head at Cyrus. "Leave. Seraphina and I have matters to discuss."

Cyrus's body went loose, like he always did, right before he attacked. "That's a bold statement coming from you, Cousin. Seraphina does whatever she wishes, and you are in no position to command her."

Now Cyrus did set me aside, rising to face his cousin.

Cyrus was unrecognizable from the emaciated vampire I first met in the dungeons. He'd filled out, his smooth, golden skin stretched over bulging muscles. His legs were powerful, his abs perfectly cut. He'd embraced the internet and was dressed in the finest clothes money could buy.

His magic was far stronger now, as well. One touch of his fingers and every bone in my body went loose. If he wanted, I didn't doubt he could do some serious damage with that power. But beyond all of his physical attributes, Cyrus always took the time to listen, he always supported me, and he never played games or lied to me.

Unlike Deston, who'd done both those things. And more.

Everybody needs a Cyrus in their life, I decided. *Someone they could rely on forever.*

"Speak to Seraphina again in that tone, Cousin, and I'll rip your head right off, whether Luthor thinks we need you or not." Cyrus was almost scary, with this casual air of menace about him. He never got angry, never raised his voice, but I knew from experience, he would have Deston flat on his back in a heartbeat.

I put my hand on his arm and blinked hazily up at him. "There will be no ripping off heads today, I'm afraid. Deston and I have some business to discuss. Once we're done, I'll come back inside. We can have dinner together."

"Are you sure?" His green eyes measured me up, then he stepped back. "Mind your manners, Cousin. Or you'll answer to me."

Then he shot me a lopsided grin, tucked his hands in his pockets, and strolled away.

"One of these days, I will teach *him* some manners." Deston growled at Cyrus's retreating back, just before he dematerialized back to the house.

"If anyone around here needs to learn manners, it's you," I countered. "You've had time to think, what's your decision?"

"Explain where you found that key. Then I will decide how much to tell you."

"That's a pretty shitty deal. There's no way I'm going first."

Deston looked skyward. "I swear on my life, if you tell me where you got the key, I will tell you what it goes to." I peeked at his fingers, which weren't crossed.

"And what's behind it, and where it's located," I added, well aware of the dangers of making deals with supernatural beings. At least, that's what I'd read in books.

"That only works on the Fae, and we are the same species now. Since you are not a human making a bargain with a superior being, this is an agreement between equals." His face twitched, as if he was trying not to roll his eyes.

"The key came from my mother, that's all I know."

"After you master your magic, we shall work on your lying. Somehow, I fear that will take you longer to figure out."

"All right, Mom left me the key *and* a note. Which doesn't tell me anything except the key unlocks a very dangerous secret."

"I need to see that note."

"I've already read it like a hundred times, and there's nothing that's helpful."

"You've had this key all along?" he asked, not a hint of emotion in his voice.

"No, I just found it four days ago."

"Where exactly did you find it?" He moved closer until we were touching, and I resisted the urge to take a step back. Maybe a step forward, but that could be this post feeding haze.

"It was hidden in the back of one of her paintings. I accidentally broke it the other day and found the key and her note."

"How long has this painting been in your possession?

"My entire life, I guess. As far back as I can remember, it always hung on the wall of whatever bedroom of whatever rundown house we lived in."

"And you never noticed it before a couple days ago?"

"No, I did not," I insisted, confused to why he was so hung up on this. "And why the twenty questions? If you don't believe me, I'll show you. Would that convince you I'm telling the truth?"

"You're the one who's always yammering on about *hard evidence*. Perhaps I would like to see the same." Since I still didn't know how to materialize and refused to get toted through the air like a sack of garbage, we walked to the castle, where Deston lingered awkwardly in the doorway of our disorganized bedroom while I retrieved the picture.

"This is it." I handed him the painting. "The painting was ruined when I accidently broke the mirror. Try not to destroy the frame any more than it already is."

"*This* is your mother's hiding spot? Unbelievable." I ground my teeth at his feigned outrage. He was such a sanctimonious bastard.

"Such a prize could have been lost so easily."

"Well, not really, since that painting is my most valuable possession in the entire world, and I take it everywhere I go." I didn't know why Mom hid the key there either, but that painting had kept the secret for all those years, right under my nose.

He straightened it, stared hard at the seascape, then at Mom's signature on the back. He ran a finger across the bold strokes of the cliffs. "Where did your mother get this?" His voice went from benign to dangerously soft.

"She painted it." I surveyed the mess of canvas and wood that had once been lovely. "I can't believe I ruined the only thing I have left of her."

His voice gentled, lost that edge of arrogance. "When... do you know when this was painted, by chance?"

"I don't." There was no year on the back, only the month and day. "Gram once said Mom went to an art school in Paris, but Mom never talked much about her past. Even though I asked a few times."

I should have asked more. I should have pushed harder, made her talk about her childhood, learned more about her. Instead, I knew next to nothing about the only parent I'd ever had.

"No, I suppose Isabelle would want to forget that part

of her past," Deston said thoughtfully, running his fingers around the edge of the painting.

Before my eyes the frame straightened out, the painting once again taut. I flipped it over, and even the torn paper with her ripped signature was flawlessly mended.

Emotion welled up inside of me so fast, my throat tightened, the whole room went blurry. "Thank you." The words came out hoarse, so I reached out, brushed his arm. "You don't know how much I..."

I dropped my head and squeezed my eyes shut before I made a complete fool out of myself. "Anyways, thank you. This is the only thing I have that belonged to her. Everything else was lost when Gram's house burned down."

Deston rubbed his arm where I'd touched him.

"That's not exactly true," Deston murmured. Then his hand slid around mine, and before I knew it, he was pulling me down one hallway, then another, until we reached a section of the castle I'd never been in before. We ended up in a miniature art gallery, with paintings hung on every wall, from the chair rail up to the ceiling. My feet froze to the floor, my mouth hanging open. "Is that...a Gauguin?"

"From one of his first shows." I could only stare as Deston shrugged. "I liked to get in on the ground floor, and the late 1800s were a thrilling time in the art world."

I shook my head. "Why am I not surprised?"

Now that I was really looking, most of the works were impressionistic, and while I didn't recognize every piece, they were all beautiful. I leaned in to get a closer look at a tiny watercolor, signed *Degas*.

"Come. This is what I want you to see, Seraphina." Deston's hands were featherlight on my shoulders, turning me until I faced a beautifully rugged seascape, infused with chaos. There is no doubt in my mind who had painted this, whose gentle hand had made every vicious stroke.

"How...how did you get this?" I wanted to scream the words, but they came out a whisper. I swept his hands off my shoulders and spun around. "Where did you get this?"

Had Deston known my mother? He lied about everything. Was this simply another way to manipulate me?

"Your mother was the most promising painter the Beaux-Arts de Paris had ever produced." His voice was nearly as rough as mine, his expression every bit as haunted as my tangled, twisting emotions. "From what I know, your mother hung her final show, and that was the last anyone ever saw of Isabelle Smith."

He had our family alias right, which lent some credence to the rest of his story.

"You knew my mother." I jabbed my finger in his chest. "You've been lying to me all along, haven't you?"

"I swear to you, Seraphina, I am not." There was an intense desperation to him, as if me believing him meant everything right now. Which only made me distrust him even more.

"Then why didn't you ever say you knew my mother?"

"Because I never met Isabelle in person. And before you accuse me of hiding things from you, I only recognized your painting by the style and the signature, and put two and two together." He kept rubbing his chest in circles, as if his heart hurt.

But that was *my* heart, breaking over and over and over again, the pain too much to endure.

"I bought these paintings years after your mother disappeared. The Beaux-Arts director at the time held on to her work. I bought everything he had, and have another twenty of her pieces in storage. But this one..." His voice trailed off, and he gazed the painting, his expression softening. "This one was always my favorite."

I snuck a glance at his face.

Deston didn't look like someone who was playing me, but then again, did he ever?

"I don't know what magic your mother had, but every time I look at this, I feel... transported. She had a gift, and it shows."

"Yeah." I settled down a little, staring at her canvas, the vastness of emotion contained in such a tiny square. *She'd really been a painter in Paris*, I thought, caught between amazement and sorrow. *And a good one.* "I just never thought there could be more artwork out there. I thought Mom only painted one thing."

"This is yours, Seraphina. All of them are yours. When you become Queen, you can decorate the walls of the palace with your mother's work, so you'll see her, everywhere you look." He brushed a finger against my hand, and after a pause, I reached out and brushed mine against his.

His dark gaze never left the painting, and there was so much emotion in his voice—*in me*—that I lay my head against his arm, wondering if maybe, he saw the same things I did.

Wildness. Wanting. Loneliness and happiness mixed together in a tangle of paint and furious brushstrokes that were so at odds with the quiet, gentle woman I remembered.

"She was really good, wasn't she?" I leaned closer to run my finger along an especially aggressive ridge of paint. "Thank you for this. It's the best gift anyone's given me... well, in forever."

Maybe...*maybe I'd misjudged Deston.*

Maybe he wasn't quite the villain I'd made him out to be.

I reached for his hand, but Deston stepped away, the air in the room turning charged, tinged with the faint scent of ozone. "I will take you to the palace." He said softly, still staring at the painting. "I will show you what's behind the door."

"Why the change in attitude?" I asked suspiciously.

"Because after all this time, I think we both deserve to know the truth." He slid me a sideways look. "Because maybe it's time we trusted each other, since we're going to be working together for a long, long time."

I mulled that reason over and found it acceptable.

"You broke the first key trying to unlock that door," I pointed out. "What makes you think mine will work?"

"The last time I was careless." He muttered. "Clearly, I did not remove all the layers of magic, which meant the key did not work as designed, and yes, I tried to rip it out of the lock before I was discovered."

"That's a pretty defensive-sounding explanation."

"The stakes were high. It was not my finest moment."

"Deston de Rayne, willing to show a little weakness." I smiled. "May miracles never cease."

Besides the mystery of the whole thing, there was something else at play—an idea—that had been growing larger in my mind, ever since I'd found the key. This idea didn't make sense on a logical level, and I'd spent as much time trying to talk myself out of it as imagining it might be true.

The Idea was the impetus behind my seemingly mad obsession with finding the door, uncovering the secret that lay behind it. Call it madness, but in my defense, I liked to call it hope.

Finding these paintings... I took this as a sign I was on the right path.

Mom hadn't been what you'd call a proper vampire. She'd been, by all accounts, human.

No magic, no fangs, and a helluva lot of artistic ability.

But there was one thing that held true. Isabelle had been a Marvelle by blood. And even though I'd watched her die in front of my horrified, teenage eyes...dead by Viktor's hand...

Marvelles could rise from the dead.

So, despite all logic, every time I imagined myself unlocking that door and revealing what lay behind it... for these past three days...I'd seen my mother waiting.

My head knew this was a ridiculous fantasy, but my heart hoped I'd get her back, and I wouldn't be so alone anymore.

Or maybe I just wanted to stop feeling so guilty about my part in her death.

Chapter 18
Seraphina

T wo nights later, I stepped out of Deston's embrace and realized, for once, he hadn't lied about a single thing.

We'd landed in the middle of nowhere, an unsettled tract of wild Louisiana that looked like nothing but boggy bayou and tangled brush. My breath turned to fog beneath the full moon.

A shimmering wall of magic stretched as high as I could see, turning everything behind it wavy. Even beyond the illusion, I saw more bayou, still, dank water reflecting cypresses dripping in moss. I wondered if we were in the right place.

"The royal ward has been keyed to my magic," Deston explained quietly. "I can neutralize the magical protections long enough to smuggle you through, but it will only work for a few seconds each time. Any more and I'll trigger the spell and alert the Knightsguard."

Despite the cold and the fact that we were walking straight into danger, I squared my shoulders. "Just get me inside. Then we'll worry about the rest."

In truth, I was plenty worried, and feeling more than a little guilty. Luthor and Cyrus were fast asleep, a bottle of wine and a big dinner taking their toll. I was supposed to be in the library. *Studying.*

Nonsense, I reassured myself, *I'll be back in an hour and they'll be none the wiser.*

I'd decided to strip this quest of mine down to a one-step-at-a-time approach. I figured every little victory put me one step closer to discovering the truth, and I wouldn't allow myself to get caught up on all the ways this little adventure could go wrong.

Easier said than done, especially looking at these wards.

Deston held out his hand and I took it reluctantly. I'd just spent five minutes wrapped in his arms, and just that small period left me feeling strangely off-balance and flushed with heat.

"This ward is infused with enough necromantic magic to kill all intruders. This shield will not behave like the wards around my castle," he warned, searching my face before his hand tightened around mine. "Passing through this one... will hurt, Seraphina."

The other thing I'd decided was I was willing to risk anything to figure out this mystery. What was a little pain along the way?

Deston set his hand against the nearly imperceptible wall, and beneath his palm, the magic slithered away like so many snakes. A hole opened, and I ducked through the narrow opening. Crossing over mixed cold with pain, the magic leaching the warmth from my flesh, stripping the bones from my body, and turning them brittle.

But once I passed through the shimmer, the pain, along with the empty bayou and skeletal trees, disappeared. My mouth dropped open.

In their place were perfectly manicured grounds, a wide-open field that ended in a wall of dark woods. A small, overgrown building perched on the distant forest's edge, covered in vines. The enormous palace loomed like a shadow in the distance, lights glowing in the windows.

I wrapped my shadows around the both of us, eyeing the sheer width of the field we'd have to cross. If there really were revenants here, those grounds would become a nightmarish gauntlet meant to cull the weak and unsuspecting. From far off in the woods, something howled, and shivers crept down my spine.

"This is just lovely. Let's hope we don't end up running for our lives."

"I tried to warn you," Deston murmured, his lips brushing my ear. "I still don't understand why you are so determined in this, Seraphina. If you applied yourself half as hard to your magic, Viktor would already be dead."

"Or you, if you keep talking," I countered, sticking close in case monsters came creeping out of the fog. I hoped the combination of my shadows and Deston's magic kept us off their radar. But damn, was that field wide open.

We'd be completely exposed until we reached the castle in the distance.

"Or me," he agreed easily. "Although I feel the need to point out that killing me at this juncture would be counter-productive to your plans." He shot me a wolfish grin. "Also, Viktor deserves to die far more than myself. And if you succeed, you'll get to sit on the throne."

"Thank you, Mr. Motivational Speaker, I'll keep that in mind."

"Now hush, we'll be out in the open for a few minutes, and we don't want to call any attention to ourselves."

"No shit, Sherlock." I'd watched Deston rebuild a castle, mend broken walls, and restore an antique mirror, but I'd never actually seen him kill anything and wondered if he was any good in a fight. Kind of late for that issue to pop up.

The grass was sopping wet, and my tennis shoes were already soaked. But fear, excitement, and anticipation roared through me. The trifecta of making bad decisions, I decided as the castle grew closer and closer.

"In and out," Deston counseled again, as if I couldn't remember simple instructions. As much as I was desperate to find out what the key was for, now that we were here, I was more anxious to get out. Preferably alive.

Because every single inch of this place was steeped in dread.

A strange, dark sense of foreboding filled me with every step, like there was some horrid, magical compulsion in the air, but there was no denying I was scared shitless right now.

"Stay steady, Seraphina." Deston's quiet warning didn't do diddly squat to ease my growing fear. "Viktor's gone, as are most of his guards, I made sure the castle was empty tonight. This is our best chance to find your answers. Once we are back at home, then you are free to... how do you say it? Freak out."

"Thanks for getting Viktor out of the way. I appreciate it."

He looked affronted, as only Deston could. "I wouldn't allow you within ten miles of the palace if I couldn't guarantee your safety."

"Well, thanks anyway. I know you went to a good bit of trouble to set this up."

He'd gone to more than a *good bit of trouble*.

Deston had manufactured a *rogue queen sighting* by whisking me up to Ohio and back. Viktor had responded by mobilizing the troops and heading north with half his Knightsguard. I didn't know how Deston managed to be so convincing, but with several vampires

105

corroborating the story, Viktor hadn't asked any questions.

Which gave us our opening.

We'd almost reached the entrance when Deston braced his hand against the small of my back and hurried me toward the front doors. Two shapes loped jerkily out of the forest, oddly rounded heads held high.

"They can't see us yet, but they've scented you." Deston pushed me through, and the doors snicked shut behind us, locking us together in darkness. "But we'll be safe inside. The outer ward keeps them from escaping, and Viktor doesn't allow them too close to the palace."

"Thank God for small favors," I muttered.

"Don't thank me yet. Not until we're safely back to Ravenswood."

I snorted. "I still think it's funny you named your castle."

He did his best Deston-is-affronted face. "Every proper castle must have a name. That's how things are done."

"So says the male who takes an hour to dress every morning."

"Seraphina. How do you know how long it takes me to dress?" He scolded. "Quiet, now."

He didn't have to tell me twice.

I'd never been to a haunted house, but this place was scarier than anything I could have conjured up in a nightmare. This monstrosity stank of limestone, and there must have been a leak, given the steady drip-drip-drip sound echoing from somewhere up ahead of us.

Magic stained the air, and from the smell, it wasn't the good kind.

I wrapped my shadows more tightly around us, as if I

could fend off the dread. Despite the air of corruption, I couldn't stop my mouth from falling open.

As big as Ravenswood was, this place was ten times bigger.

But Deston's castle had a different feel. Ravenswood was brighter and airier, less mildew and mustiness. I didn't know how old this place was, but the tapestries were frayed at the bottoms, the rugs worn through in spots. I kept looking for rats and skirting dark stains on the floor.

My feet stopped moving when I realized where the dripping sound came from.

Viktor was a monster, and he had to die, I vowed as I tried to keep going. But my feet wouldn't move, my gaze remained glued to the wall opposite the throne, the bodies nailed there, and I might have stopped breathing. Deston hooked his cane over his arm, wound his strong arm around my waist.

"You must keep walking, my Queen," he murmured. "Though you do not see them, there are eyes everywhere. My shadows will hide us for only so long."

We were in that macabre Hall of Mirrors, every surface reflecting my white face, my dark, wide eyes.

I managed a halting step, then another, my gaze riveted to the wall we'd have to pass beneath.

Three vampires were nailed to wood beams, blood still dripping from one of them, the other two wholly desiccated, their empty eye sockets fixed on the mirrors around them. From what I knew about decomposition, they had to be months old.

Deston pressed his body into mine as we proceeded to the hallway leading away from the mirrored room and the putrid stench. The brush of his arm against mine nearly made me go limp with relief. *Any port in a storm, Seraphina*, I reminded myself, carefully avoiding the pool of goo below Viktor's latest victim.

How did anyone—even a complete sociopath—treat his fellow vampires this way? I mean, I knew they—*we*—were ruthless creatures, but this kind of cruelty eluded me. How could someone behave like this?

There wasn't a guard in sight, but Deston had warned me about this as well.

Just because I didn't see them, didn't mean they weren't there.

We didn't make a sound as we moved through the enormous palace, my heart pounding in my throat. Every hall was lit by ancient incandescent bulbs, mounted on mock-iron wall sconces, while high windows let in moonlight.

We finally stopped, and Deston brushed my arm, which was my signal to slip him the key.

Yesterday, I'd insisted I didn't trust him as far as I could throw him, and I'd only give it to him once he got us inside the palace. Well, Deston had kept his word, and I kept mine, slipping the chain over my head and pressing the key into his hand.

The moment of truth was here, and I wasn't close to being ready.

I took Seraphina's key with equal amounts of regret and fear.

If my suspicions were correct, neither one of us wanted to see what lay behind this door. Then again, if my suspicions were correct, we could now stop Viktor's reign of terror.

Seraphina's face was paper white, her golden eyes wide, pupils blown from fear, but her jaw was set in that determined way I knew not to challenge. I didn't much believe in fate, but right now, I couldn't help but feel the universe was watching over the two of us.

How her mother had managed to steal the only other key to Viktor's secret chamber, I didn't know, but there was a story there.

I never thought I'd get a second chance to unlock this door, but here we were. The stars had aligned, and if I was right—though I hoped I was wrong—what lay behind this door would be what we needed to defeat Viktor for good.

I scanned the empty hallway. Even if we were discovered, I would glamour the guards, who were barely out of their first century. The revenants were a different story. They were created with necromancy and blood magic, and my own power was useless in compelling them.

They answered to one master, and that wasn't me. But

if this went wrong, I would keep her safe, no matter the cost.

"Are you ready, my Queen?"

Seraphina gave me a wide-eyed nod, and while she wasn't prepared for this, a rush of admiration warmed my belly at her determination to see this through. The mating bond tingled between us, and she pressed a hand to her stomach. I was encouraged she sensed *something* between us, even if she didn't know what.

"I will not leave your side," I assured her, even though I wanted to ghost her away this very second. But she'd only return alone because, knowing Seraphina, she wouldn't be able to live with unanswered questions. Truly, her curiosity was her most dangerous quality.

I took account of her high color, her racing heart and dropped my hand. "If you wish to leave immediately, we shall do so. But you must decide right now, my Queen."

Every fiber of my being screamed for her to agree. Seraphina was in danger. This entire escapade was against my better judgement, and yet, I'd been incapable of refusing her. If I was correct, she'd most likely be traumatized by what lay behind this door. Worse yet, once we were done here, she'd run back to Luthor and Cyrus for comfort.

Not me.

No, never me.

I shut my eyes, reached out a hand, and unbound the first spell that sealed the door. Then the next. They were all intertwined and took me longer than I liked to untangle, but I'd been sloppy the last time.

I couldn't afford any mistakes tonight.

I murmured, "*Lignum et ferrum solvite, et veritatem celat.*" There was a groan as the final spell unbound the ancient door, the wood creaking, a shower of dust cascading to the floor.

I pushed the key into the lock and immediately the inserted end liquified, filling the chamber with molten gold. Skeleton keys were old fashioned and easily duplicated, but this key was blessed with a special magic. The entwined snakes symbolized the planet Mercury, and like the liquid metal, the device melted to fill the chamber and turn more than a thousand mechanisms, some so small they couldn't be seen.

Seraphina blinked as if she couldn't believe what she was seeing, and I half-hoped she would turn and run. But her face cleared when the lock unlatched.

Seraphina squared her shoulders beneath one of the ghastly hooded sweatshirts she was always wearing. Even without reading her mind, I recognized that look on her face. *Hope*.

"Open the door, Deston. I'm ready for whatever's behind it."

Chapter 20
Deston

I'd envisioned a hundred scenarios of what lay behind the door.

A stranger was not one of them.

Deston stayed true to his word and didn't leave my side as I approached a granite altar draped in white cloth. Smoldering sconces painted the chamber with golden light and filled the space with the scent of charcoal and something far more pungent.

The flickering light made the woman on the altar look like she was moving. Or, at least, breathing until I got closer and realized she was doing neither.

Her coarse hair trailed to the floor, black and curly on the ends, white-gray at the roots, while her fingernails were badly splintered, as if someone had recently sawed them off. One hand hung free, the sight of those horridly mangled nails making me wince.

Her face and lips were bloodless white, and she appeared dead, yet some innate vampire instinct told me she was not.

"Who is this?" I whispered, feeling we'd stepped into a holy place or a burial crypt. One glance told me Deston had shut himself down completely. Instead, he'd gone eerily calm, as if he'd expected this macabre scene.

"That is Queen Lyra Marvelle... she was your grandmother's cousin."

"This can't be her." I scanned the unmoving woman, then our surroundings for answers. Found none. "Gram and Luthor and Cyrus, they all told me she was dead."

"In human terms, she is." Deston walked up to the woman, stared intently at her serene face, his own remaining impassive. "In vampire terms... she's in deep stasis and has been for a long time."

"I don't know what that is."

I'd been a med student for two years, and stasis... I knew reptiles and turtles were capable of deep hibernation, but nothing warm-blooded was meant to shut down for a season. Except bears, I guess, they did. But they ate a lot beforehand, and Lyra looked positively gaunt.

But from a clinical point of view, I agreed with Deston. Going by the hair and nails, she'd been this way for a long time.

"Vampires can shut themselves down until they have just the barest functions to keep them alive. It's useful in certain situations, like when you need time to rehabilitate from injuries."

"But for a hundred years?"

His lips pinched. "It's not unheard of...but I didn't want to think it could be true."

"You knew she'd be in here," I observed flatly, noting he wasn't shocked by what we'd found. My awareness quickly turned to disgust. "Why am I not surprised? You know, every time I think I can trust you, you prove me wrong."

"I had my suspicions," he admitted, leaving my side to lift her dangling hand and place it gently on her chest. "But no, my Queen. I did not know for sure Lyra still lived, not until I opened the door."

I mulled his explanation over and decided maybe this once, he was telling the truth, or his version of it.

"Why is she here, Deston? Why did Viktor keep her... like this?"

Because there had to be a reason. "Is she even breathing?"

"Barely. Ten breaths a day, give or take, enough to keep the blood oxygenated. Her heart is beating about the same number of times." I must have looked surprised, and he smiled secretly. "I see things you cannot, Seraphina. Not yet, but someday, you will be able to sense another vampire's functions as easily as your own."

"Huh." I looked at him, slightly horrified, as my brain pinged with realization. "Does that mean..." I shook my head. "Never mind, don't answer that. I don't want to know."

His wolfish smile told me everything I didn't want to know.

Note to self: *Work on masking bodily functions from this creeper.*

"Okay, let's say I've come to grips with the physiology part of this. It doesn't explain why she's in the royal palace on an altar like some weird sacrifice."

"It does, actually, explain everything," Deston muttered, brushing her white hair away from her face, which had once been beautiful but was little more than skin stretched taut over bone. She was so tiny now, shrunken, diminished.

A twinge went through me when Deston touched her sunken cheek tenderly, and it took me a moment to recognize the feeling as jealousy. Which was utterly ridiculous.

"Lyra is still alive because she is the source of Viktor's power." Deston waved his hand, his fingers bent unnaturally, and ozone stung my nose. Tiny white sparks traveled up Lyra's body and disappeared.

"Her stasis isn't naturally induced. A powerful binding spell cast a hundred years ago, reinforced many times since." He passed his hand over her face, then frowned. "I don't sense any brain activity."

My mind was still struggling to keep up, to figure out where science ended and magic began, to make sense of this act of cruelty, and my rising anger over seeing someone so helpless.

"Viktor's keeping her like this and stealing her power? How does that even work?"

"Lyra was one of the clan's strongest queens, but the whole point of stasis is to conserve energy. But she can't expend any magic, either." A feral-sounding growl came from his mouth, his fangs fully descended. "All that power is trapped inside her."

I rubbed my arms. "It's a relief to expel my magic first thing in the morning." I said quietly. "Not that I was good at it, but otherwise, all that power just...boils over. If all that was trapped inside of me..."

Our eyes met and I didn't think I'd ever seen Deston as angry as he was right now.

"Lyra isn't even vampire anymore. She is a pure magic being, and Viktor's been siphoning power from her, like a succubus."

"That can't work, not the way you're describing. I can't take magic from another...." My voice trailed off as I realized it *was* possible for Luthor, Cyrus, and I to share magic between us. If it could be given, then it could be stolen.

Deston held out a hand over Lyra, and while I watched, magic trickled from her into his open palm. He closed his hand, shuddering, his beautiful face suffused with pain.

"I'm what some call an abjurist." He opened his hand

again, and magic streamed back into Lyra while I watched, fascinated. "I can take power... and give it back."

"That's how you settle my magic, isn't it? When you touch me sometimes?"

"I siphon a bit off occasionally, enough to ease the burden." His face darkened when he looked down at me. "This creates a problem, Seraphina. Lyra is now a *purmagicae*, a being made purely of magic, she exists only in an astral state, not a physical one."

"Why are you telling me this?" I asked, sure there was some deeper meaning, looking between the ghost of a female on the altar, and Deston's ravaged expression.

"Because we have to kill her."

Chapter 21
Deston

Seraphina looked up at me, horror etched across her beautiful face.

"What do you mean, *kill her*?" She asked slowly, even while I saw horrified understanding dawn in her eyes, the frantic way they kept bouncing between Lyra and me.

I hated that she'd seen this part of our evil, corrupted world. The lengths vampires would go to for power. What they would do to keep the throne.

And there were others out there, worse than Viktor. Far worse.

"Deston, what are you talking about?" Her voice went higher, her face was flushed from her heart pounding. These walls were thick, but the guards had noses, and she smelled delectable.

"We should go."

I glanced at my old queen. I thought I'd reached my limit of guilt over what happened that day. I was wrong. I'd failed Lyra twice—once when I'd betrayed her to the Carpathians—and again by abandoning her to this fate.

I had no intention of history repeating itself. I'd sold Seraphina out to Viktor in order to save her, but I'd never let her down again. "The longer we stay, the harder it will be to get out unnoticed."

"But we can't just leave Lyra. Can't we take her with us?" she protested, while I cursed the mating bond between

117

us. The one that made it impossible for me to refuse her. *Merde,* I'd brought her here against my better judgement, knowing what we might find. Now I'd have to lay out some hard truths.

"You can't save her, my Queen." Neither could I, but I'd come back alone, later tonight, and finish this myself. I wrapped my hand around Seraphina's arm, determined to drag her out of here if I had to.

"She's been like this for too long. Her magic is all she has left, and..." I sighed at the savage look on Seraphina's lovely face. "Lyra will never wake up. And while I admire you wanting to help her, the best thing would be to end her life as gently as possible."

"*You will not so much as think about doing that.*" She growled. "And don't you dare tell me we can't save her. She's still breathing, so she's not dead."

Could I tell her what happened to vampires too long in stasis? Did I even know?

I glanced at Lyra's desiccated form.

I could end this right now.

Had Seraphina not been here, I wouldn't have hesitated to kill Lyra. But there was no way I would end her life in front of my mate. If I did, Seraphina would never trust me again. I'd never claim her as mine. I'd lose everything.

And yet, while Lyra lived, Seraphina was in danger.

"Seraphina. As long as he can draw magic from Lyra, Viktor is invincible." Damn it, I *would* do this. Leaving Lyra alive was too great a risk for my mate. I held my hand over her prone body and bit back a curse as raw, uncut power flowed up into me, cold as ice in my veins.

"Stop it, Deston." Her voice turned pleading, and she tugged my hand away. "Please, you can't kill her."

My hand wavered in midair, as if she commanded my

very being. "Leaving her alive is a mistake, Seraphina. We could end all of this right now." I pulled, and magic flowed into me again. But there was so much of it. Too much, and frost turned my fingers blue.

"Killing Lyra won't end anything. You and I both know that."

Lyra's magic turned to ice in my veins as I weighed my decision. Showing mercy toward Lyra would win Seraphina to my side. Which was my end goal, but first we had to survive this incursion into enemy territory.

"I won't just leave her," she said, that defiant little smile on her lips that told me hours of arguing lay ahead.

She stepped toward Lyra and, before I could stop her, was a pace away from the altar. Fear roared through me, and I dropped my hand, reached out, and caught her before she took another step.

"Don't get too close, Sera," I warned. "Her magic will sense a competitor. Her power will, perhaps, strike out."

I was pulling her away when a thin lash of energy flicked out and slashed across Seraphina's throat. If I hadn't stopped her, if I'd hesitated, her jugular would have been laid open. As it was, her hand went up and caught the blood sluicing down from the cut on her neck.

"Holy hell, that hurts." She gasped, wide eyes finding mine.

I covered her hand with mine, sent a jolt of magic into her, stopping the bleeding.

But I was too late. The entire chamber was perfumed with her blood, the pungency of the scent making my vision dim; my fangs punched out so fast it was painful. Even with the door shut, the guards would soon come circling, like sharks in the water.

Added to that, Lyra's power crackled in the room like

rampant electricity. It was said a queen's magic could sense another's, though I'd never seen anything like this before.

"That is it." I dragged her toward the door and away from the altar. "We cannot save Lyra. She's too far gone. You, on the other hand, I *can* save."

"Damn it, there has to be something we can do," she hissed, eyes flashing angry gold. "How do I know you're not playing me, somehow?"

"I'm not," I assured her, pissed she'd even consider tonight some sort of ploy.

She snorted softly as I urged her toward the door. "If that was me up there, you'd kill me right this minute, wouldn't you, just so you could watch Viktor die? You hate him that much, don't you?"

That question froze my immortal blood. Just the thought of Seraphina—my fucking mate—in this state made me pant. Between the scent of her blood pounding in my head and Lyra's poisonous magic in my veins, my ancient body felt like it was finally coming alive.

Or finally dying, it was hard to tell.

And right then, I realized that for the first time in a hundred years, I wanted something even more than revenge.

Slow, deliberate footsteps approached the door.

"Use your shadows. Hide yourself, Seraphina. Quickly."

I might be jealous of Luthor, but I had to admire the way Seraphina wrapped his shadows around herself, the illusion nearly seamless. She disappeared into the ether seconds before the nameless guard lunged into the room, his magical attack bouncing off me harmlessly.

He dropped to one knee. "Sire... apologies... I didn't know..."

He sniffed the blood in the air, the magic dancing in the air, a look of confusion on his face.

His gaze wandered from me, to Lyra sleeping on the plinth, then back to me. The recognition that dawned on his face would have been a death sentence had I been alone. As it was, he was perfectly safe since Seraphina was here, a witness to how I'd handle our newest problem.

"Of course, today is the day you decide to play the hero," I muttered. Killing him and feeding him to the revenants would be the cleanest, simplest solution, and require the least amount of effort on my part.

She must have read my mind, because beside me, still thankfully invisible, Seraphina muttered something foul. The guard looked alarmed.

"Forget what you saw," I whispered, plucking the last hour's memories from his head. "Turn around. Go back and take your post and remain there until the end of your shift."

The moment he was gone, Seraphina reappeared, her suspicious gaze narrowed on me. "Somehow, I expected you to kill him."

"Normally, I would have." I shrugged, stymied by my newly developed conscious. Frustrated by my inability to mete out justice but strangely satisfied when I saw the expression on her face. I'd finally made the correct decision, after a run of disastrous calls. Maybe there was hope for us yet.

"But dead bodies lead to questions."

"And this is an in and out kind of operation." She laughed softly. Her smile, simple in its joy, made my heart beat faster, my pulse race.

I caught her hand and guided her toward the door, my cane over my arm so we didn't make any undue noise.

"Sera, if there was the slightest chance to save Lyra, I would."

There were ways, but I wasn't Viktor.

I refused to create a monster.

"I know, I see it in your face." She sighed, her shoulders slumping. "I do, in this rare instance, agree with you. If she's been unconscious for that long, her mind... I can't imagine she'd be able to function." Her gaze flicked over to Lyra, then back to me. "She'd have extensive brain damage, I would assume."

I tried to work out how she knew the first thing about vampire physiology, and then I remembered. She'd been studying some sort of human medicine, not that I'd paid attention to the information at the time.

"She's existed in a dream state for a century. I've heard of elder vampires going into stasis for months, even a handful of years, and even so, they were never the same again." I used my heightened senses to search the empty hallway outside, then the next. They were empty.

"Then what do we do?"

"I will take care of Lyra. Later." She shivered, and I left it at that because there was no reason for her to know more. She already had seen enough.

I'd get her back to the castle, then return with the key and end this.

Releasing Lyra from her prison was the least I could do.

I relocked the door and the molten end of the key solidified. I recreated the ancient spells that guarded the door. No one, not even Viktor would be able to tell the difference, which was one benefit of being older than dirt.

She wordlessly held out her hand, and I pressed the key into it. "Amazing." She touched the now-restored end gingerly. I tilted her head to get a better look at the cut on her neck and found it was little more than a pink stripe of new skin.

"Maybe, someday, you'll tell me how your mother managed to get that key."

"If I knew, I would. But my guess is, Gram stole it."

"A mystery, then," I said lightly, determined to figure out how Viktor's missing key ended up around his enemy's neck.

"It is," she agreed, her arm still laced with mine as we made our way through the grand entrance that stank of putrefaction. "I have to admit I thought I'd find something different behind that door."

"It must have been a shock, seeing Lyra." I knew I'd been shocked to the core, and I'd been half-expecting it.

"More than you know." Her sad whisper had me turning, but I had to get her out of here, and one hesitation could mean the difference between us strolling out, or fighting our way out. I would much prefer the former.

We stopped a few feet from the huge doors. There was nothing on the other side. According to my senses, the revenants had returned to the forest. The guards were all still at their stations. We were safe inside the castle, and we'd be safe again, once we reached the other side of the protective ward.

Everything in between was a threat.

I relaxed. I knew this palace like the back of my hand.

I knew every protective spell, every trick, every booby trap in this place. I even knew the female who'd laid the basis for the wards, hundreds of years ago.

Once we stepped through the door, I'd transport Seraphina to the ward, a few seconds at most. Once we were safely outside, I'd return her to Ravenswood. Then I'd come back here and do the unspeakable, and once

Viktor was out of the way, I would hand Seraphina her kingdom.

Everything I'd ever wanted was within my reach.

I held out my arms, and she stepped into my embrace with no hesitation, and for a few precious seconds, my mate was pressed up against me. "I thought..." she whispered while she slipped her arms beneath my coat. "You know, never mind, it's ridiculous."

"Tell me, Sera," I urged, my lips an inch from her cheek. One move and I could taste her, but instead, she looked sadly back the way we'd come.

"I thought Mom might be there. I know it sounds impossible, but somehow, between the key and the letter and our Marvelle blood, I thought she was sending me a message." She hiccupped against my chest, and I realized she was crying.

"I guess I just thought I'd get to see her again."

I hugged Seraphina close, marveling at this stubborn, beautiful, complicated woman who was not only my mate but who had somehow stolen my heart.

At the same time, the first of the revenants crept over the rise, raised their heads to the moon and bayed for blood.

I gathered her close and dematerialized.

Chapter 22
Seraphina

Deston cursed against my cheek, his arms crushing me tight as he tried to dematerialize again. *And again.* We hadn't moved, even though I'd sensed Deston's magic gather, ready to transport us out of here.

"I can't...my magic isn't working." He muttered, "Do not turn around, Seraphina. Not so much as a blink, do you understand?"

The boggy-dirt smell of revenants blew on the wind, and my whole body tensed when I realized they were getting closer. The pounding I thought was my heart was the ground beneath our feet, and my eyes flew up to Deston's.

Then the world became a jumbled mess when Deston tossed me over his shoulder and ran. Being carried like a sack was disorienting, humiliating, and painful as his shoulder bumped up into my hips, but this was better—so much freaking better—than getting eaten alive.

We were thrown sideways when one of the creatures hit us full force, my world spinning wildly, followed by Deston's grunt of pain. He stumbled but kept moving.

Then we were down, both of us skidding through the wet grass, Deston grabbing me at the last minute and yanking me away from the creature's gnashing jaws.

Deston pressed me down into the crushed grass and

rolled on top of me, pinning me to the ground. "Don't move," he warned. "Keep your arms tucked in tight." His body shook under an impact, and my heart froze.

Then I heard the sound.

A wet and horrible tearing, and I knew, even before I smelled blood, that those claws were cutting into him. Then he was ripped away.

I scuttled backwards, seconds before a huge claw scraped the dirt barely a foot from my face. I rolled, landing against Deston, who was on his side, breathing heavily. Blood soaked through his shirt, one of his sleeves was dripping.

Holy shit.

He couldn't dematerialize, and I didn't know how.

There were—I counted swiftly—five revenants circling. *Hungry revenants* since Viktor didn't feed them. We were stuck here, and I knew from experience we'd never outrun them.

No, I'd watched them overtake Mom, then slaughter her right in front of me.

Our only option was to fight.

Out of the entire pack, one was more aggressive. The leading revenant was a huge male, his skin dry and scaly; he looked ancient. I crawled away, trying to put as much distance between me and that thing as possible. Trying to draw it away from Deston lying in the grass, blood pouring out of him at an alarming rate.

Then, impossibly, he staggered to his feet, waving his arms and screaming at the drooling pack. They tracked him like prey, heads held low, ready to charge. He was drawing them away, but holy hell, they were going to slaughter him right in front of me.

As if they'd heard my thoughts, the monster swung his

clawed hand, slicing through Deston's arm as if it wasn't made of flesh and bone.

Deston dodged away, but too slowly, and the revenant caught him again. His arm dangled uselessly; his chest heaved beneath his shredded shirt. Every inch of him was bathed in blood. The ancient revenant crept forward as if to make his final attack, and I caught a glint of gold when the beast struck once again.

Something was fused into the creature's paw—hand— and then I remembered, they had once been vampires.

"Deston," I screamed as the creature lunged. "Watch out."

But he, too, was staring at the ring—because that's what the glint was. An ornate ring, set with a glittering black stone.

"It cannot be." Deston lurched forward, straight into the path of the enormous revenant, his face stiff with shock while I watched in horror.

He's going to die.

Deston was about to die, and I was going to watch it happen.

My panic got the better of me, and shadows spurted from my fingers. I cursed my awful nervous habit and forced myself to find my real magic, yank the molten power out, bypass the dampening spell that obviously made our power completely useless in here.

Heat rattled through me, jittering, as if my magic didn't quite work right.

Well, I didn't need it to work right.

I just needed enough to crush everything around us.

The revenant leapt at Deston, covering the ten feet between them before my magic knocked it out of the air. The thing climbed to its feet, and this time, I didn't miss.

Ash rained down on Deston, and the other revenants retreated, growling. He frantically searched the torn-up ground, and then I watched him slip the ring onto his finger. He limped back to me, then stood, so we were back-to-back.

"We will have to fight our way out," he warned in a low voice. "And I'm injured too badly to be of much help."

"Yeah, no shit." He couldn't use his magic, but mine... now that I'd finally unleashed it, power thrummed inside me, anxious to break free.

I went to my knees and shoved my hands through the thick grass until my palms hit dirt, pushing every ounce of my magic into the ground. If I could use my necromancer magic to raise the dead, if there were any bodies buried beneath this ground, I'd have an army at my fingertips.

Literally.

Power flowed through my palms, heated the ground around my hands, but nothing happened. One of the revenants circled closer, those backwards legs flexing obscenely. I flinched away, but he lunged and caught my shoulder. I gasped as the curved claw sliced in deep.

"What are you doing, Seraphina?" Deston yanked me out of the path of another strike. I tried again, shoving my magic into the cold ground, but nothing was happening. Maybe there was nothing dead in the ground.

Tired of waiting, another revenant sprang toward me, mouth agape.

I pulled my hands from the ground, but I was too slow. Just before his jaws closed around me, cold magic enveloped me, and the creature bounced away, tumbling backwards through the grass.

"That's what I took from Lyra." Deston collapsed to the ground beside me. "I've erected a temporary ward, which will hold for a moment, no more. Get moving, Seraphina. Now." He pushed me away, then rolled in front of the creature. Before it reached him, I raised my hands and sent a burst of magic toward it.

Ash rained down on us like dirty snowflakes.

"Run, my Queen." He gripped my arm, fingers digging in. "You can make it to the ward. Use your magic to break through, all you have to do is..."

"I'm not running. I just need my goddamned magic to work the way it's supposed to."

Five more revenants crested the hill, heads held high.

I incinerated two more, but an entire pack of them streamed from the forest, more than I could count, picking up speed.

Deston was white, his normally perfect hair wild, his eyes glowing orange-black, like embers in a dying fire. "My Queen... Seraphina, my love, you must run. Go now. Use your magic carefully, short bursts only. Only enough to keep them at bay. You *will* make it back to the castle. You *will* survive." His hand gripped my arm, then his finger loosened, fell away.

"Luthor and Cyrus..." His head lolled to the side, "they will make sure of it."

Chapter 23
Deston

My heart slowed; my body stiffened with a hollow chill. I'd already lost too much blood, the remainder was draining into the dirt. If my mate would stop being so goddamned stubborn, if she'd only listen to me, just this once...

Seraphina threw back her head and laughed.

My Queen... *my mate... laughed* at the pack of night-marish creatures charging our way, then crouched in front of me like some avenging angel, burying her hands in the grass.

"Come and get me, you ugly bastards." Her challenge floated across the field, urging them faster. "Let's see how many of you I can barbeque."

The first revenant bore down on us, easily ten feet tall, disjointed legs flying in that odd gait, before the thing jerked to a stop, as if caught in an invisible bear trap. It thrashed madly, churning up turf in a cloud of dirt.

"That's right, you fuckers." She rose, stepped in front of me, and raised her hands. A coil of power turned the air molten, racing across the field. Several of them turned into shadowy clouds, then dissipated. "I can do more than ash you. I can summon dead things."

She scrunched her face up in concentration and plunged her hands down, into the broken dirt. I watched skeleton hands burst up out of the earth, yank the creatures flat to the ground, shredding flesh from bone.

"You can't dematerialize, Deston, but my magic seems to work just fine." She grinned down at me, as if she was truly enjoying this. "My little zombie army will keep the revenants busy long enough for us to make it to the ward, but you have to lead the way."

"*Mon Dieu.*" I whispered as the field filled up with skeletons and half-rotted corpses slaughtering revenants. The undead made quick work of Viktor's monsters, which had gone from being apex predators to fighting for survival.

Seraphina held out her hand to me. I shook my head, torn between sorrow and admiration.

"You will be a formidable queen. I wish I could have seen..." I punched my lips together.

"And you will be my slightly shady advisor."

"I can't go with you, Seraphina. You have to leave me behind."

"No, I have to have my steaks cooked medium well. I don't have to leave you here." She offered her hand again, and I grasped it, managing to rise to my knees, then her eyes widened when she realized how much blood I'd lost.

"Oh, you are *so* not dying on me after all that."

"Leave me. Use your magic to blow a hole in the ward. Once you're through, keep moving. Luthor will find you."

"No deal." She bit her wrist, beads of blood blooming against the white skin. My mouth watered. Half dead, and I hungered for her, like I'd never hungered before. "You will live, be my advisor, and we'll fight over stupid shit, just like always." She pulled me into her lap, pressed the punctures firmly against my mouth.

I went rigid the second my mouth fastened on Seraphina's wrist, her flowery taste flooding my mouth. Rich, seductive, life changing.

I couldn't stop the mewling noises coming out of my mouth, knowing that—despite four hundred years of life—this was the most intimate thing I'd ever done. Her blood wasn't saving me, I was being remade, flesh and bone knitting back together, heat and power roaring through me as my entire world ignited.

Seraphina had gone perfectly still, my lips pressed against her soft skin, her delicate hand cradled in mine as I drank and drank.

Far more than I should have, less than I wanted to.

If I had my way, this moment would have lasted forever. But then I took one last swallow and withdrew my fangs, laved my tongue over her perfect, pale skin to get every final drop.

"Thank you, my Queen." My lips lingered for a second longer than proper before I let her hand slip away. She rubbed her wrist on her thigh, as if trying to wipe away the feel of my mouth.

I couldn't say I blamed her.

I'd failed her completely by underestimating the palace's defenses, as blinded as she by the lure of the key and the secret behind the locked door. Had Seraphina been a proper Darkfell queen, I'd be nailed to the Hall of Mirrors stone wall, right beside the other unfortunates.

The remaining revenants were retreating toward the wood when I climbed to my feet and surveyed the gut-strewn field. "Let's get to the ward. Then we'll find our way back to the castle together."

The second we were through, I gathered her in my arms just long enough to dematerialize.

This time, my magic worked.

Despite his injuries, Deston managed to drop us within walking distance of Ravenswood.

My body was still heated from his lips on my wrist, the sensual way his body felt, curled around me as he fed.

We would not be doing that again. I kept telling myself I'd only fed him because he was dying, and I needed him to help me with my magic.

No other reason.

"There, you see?" I said cheerfully, careful to keep a foot of distance between us as we waded through the swamp, crossed through his ward and stepped onto the grounds. "It all worked out."

I was waiting for his pithy reply when, out of nowhere, Luthor hit Deston with a full body tackle that took him to the ground, his still-healing arm flopping uselessly. Blood splattered as Luthor's enormous fist connected, opening up a huge gash on Deston's cheek, snapping his head sideways.

"You fucking bastard, I am going to kill you."

I tugged at Luthor with all my might, but he was too damn strong. "Luthor, stop." His fist struck again, and again, every dull, meaty thud turning my stomach.

"Please listen to me. This is not his fault, and he's already hurt."

Whap. Whap. Whap.

I grabbed Luthor's bloodied fist with both hands, my fingers barely encircling his thick wrist. I dug in my heels and *yanked*, stopping his next blow. Very slowly, Luthor raised his head, his rage fading to disbelief.

"He nearly killed you and you want me to stop?" He growled, his eyes the color of aquamarines. "Not that long ago, I pulled you off him, Seraphina. Now you're defending this bastard?"

"This whole thing was my idea," I explained quickly. "I was the one who talked Deston into sneaking me out of here tonight, and whatever the consequences are, I should be the one paying them."

Luthor's eyes narrowed dangerously. "Bullshit, Seraphina."

"No bullshit." I pulled the key from around my neck. "Mom left me this. It opened a door in the palace..."

"You were at the fucking palace?" Luthor's entire body shook, his voice so quiet I could barely hear him.

"Is this true?" His eyes ignited when he glared down at the vampire pinned beneath him. "You took our Queen to the palace and put her in danger?" His hands wrapped around Deston's throat and bore down. "Fucking hell. I should have ended you weeks ago."

"Luthor." I reached through our bond, whispering calming words, begging him to understand. *Please, please, just listen, just listen...* His big body stilled, but his hands never left Deston's neck.

"You have to listen to what I'm saying. This was my idea. *My fault.* I...threatened to go by myself. Deston only went along to keep me safe, so you should really be thanking him."

"You have a bad fucking temper, Fontaine." Deston

started coughing, blood and spit splattering up Luthor's front. "Just...give her a chance to explain."

Luthor's dark, penetrating glare sent goosebumps exploding on my arms. He'd never looked at me like that before, and something inside me shriveled down to nothing when he focused on the key.

"That's one of the palace's royal keys. Only the Knightsguard commander and the current liege has access to those keys."

"And yet, my mother hid this in the back of the painting. She left this to me, along with a note. Come inside and I'll explain everything."

I traded a glance with Deston, praying he'd keep his mouth shut. Somehow, I couldn't tell Luthor about Lyra just yet. He'd guarded her for nearly half his life. He may have been in love with her. How could I tell him her fate, when it was so horribly fresh?

"Deston only went along because I threatened to sneak off to the palace." I took a steadying breath. "Alone."

Luthor went even more still.

"That was dangerous, Seraphina." Cyrus stepped out from the shadows, his silver flecked gaze fixed on me, turning savage when he turned to Deston, his lip lifting to show some fang. "You were supposed to come to us for help, not him. You could have told us, you know." Then his face gentled, "We would have understood."

"I know. I fucked up." I rubbed my face, feeling utterly miserable.

"But Deston figured out what I was up to and offered to take me himself. He's spent two days making sure Viktor would be out of the way. We chose tonight because the palace was empty."

"Not entirely empty," Cyrus pointed out, nodding to

Deston's bloody shirt. His eyes were glowing with a silvery light, far brighter than I'd ever seen. I had to tread lightly, or this whole night would go badly for all of us.

"No," Deston said. "Not completely. Revenants abound on the palace grounds. Though fewer than when we arrived." He quirked a brow at Luthor, as if egging him on.

"Stop it," I warned him. Both of my males were powder kegs ready to blow, and I wasn't risking an all-out war. I was tired and confused, and I needed to sort out my feelings right now, not watch them brawl.

"I haven't decided whether to kill you or not," Luthor warned, Cyrus stepping closer to his side. "What you did... Seraphina is all that matters. She could have died, she could have been *captured*."

"I'm not nearly as indecisive," Cyrus said, his tone deadly. "Let's kill him now, so it's done."

"Stop it," I cautioned, plenty tired of death and killing and blood. "There'll be no killing tonight, certainly not among allies."

Luthor froze. "So Deston is considered an ally now?"

"He is," I said angrily, unsure of how tonight had gone so far off the rails. "For now. And get off him. He's hurt."

"Ally, my ass," Cyrus muttered. "Watch your back, *cousin*."

Luthor rose, then sniffed the air when Deston stood and brushed himself off, acting the injured party to perfection.

Luthor's furious gaze swung over to me, his expression going from volatile to frigid. He inhaled a deep gulp of air and then growled. *At me.* I was shocked into stillness before I remembered. My blood was inside Deston. *A lot* of my blood.

We'd agreed this would just be the three of us, and I'd

broken that promise, along with about a hundred others tonight.

With one final scathing look, and Luthor turned on his heel and stalked off.

"*Goddamn it.*" Even though Deston and my exchange had been perfectly innocent—and completely necessary—I understood how Luthor would feel betrayed. *Hell, I didn't know how to feel about the experience.*

"He's not the only one," Cyrus muttered, and I squeezed my eyes closed. All I'd wanted to do was find mom. Now everything was falling apart, right in front of my eyes.

"You still have me, Seraphina." With a victorious grin at his cousin, Deston offered me his arm.

Frowning, I stepped away from him. "This isn't some pissing contest, and I'm not some sort of consolation prize. You didn't *win* anything tonight. We have a problem," I shot Deston a hard look. "A problem that's bigger than the four of us, so don't fucking push your luck. We survived, but that's the only good news."

I was twice as angry now, seeing him leverage Luthor's jealousy to his benefit. "Don't make me regret saving your life. And don't you ever try playing Cyrus and Luthor against each other again." I jabbed my finger into Deston's chest before taking Cyrus' hand.

"You have some serious explaining to do, Seraphina," Cyrus murmured. He wasn't angry, but then, he never was, not at me. Sad and disappointed was more like it, and my guilt grew exponentially larger.

"I didn't do anything other than feed him." I explained softly. "I couldn't leave him to die, and we had to get out of there. It was a friend helping a friend sort of thing."

But Cyrus's silence was condemnation enough. I knew

I'd spend the night arguing my innocence until I was blue in the face and probably wouldn't even be able to convince myself.

Chapter 25
Luthor Fontaine

I stayed long enough to watch Cyrus escort Seraphina through the front doors and didn't breathe easily until they were through. Deston followed them inside, and I hoped the bastard was so weakened by blood loss, his face stayed bruised for days.

I limped into the woods, heading for the bayou. My knuckles were raw, my bad leg twisted as I struggled across the uneven ground, but I welcomed the pain. I was finally thinking clearly. After Seraphina became queen, after Cyrus became commander, after I found her well-trained males for her Knightsguard, I would leave.

I hadn't even noticed she was gone, until it was too late.

Fast asleep in bed, thinking we were safe, full of wine and food, I had utterly failed her.

My instincts were failing me, and the stakes were ramping up higher.

I'd already decided where to go. A small clan in the Highlands, just a handful of old, broken-down vampires, well past their prime. I'd fit right in, and life would be quiet.

Massaging my healing knuckles, I regretted not killing Deston de Rayne months ago when I had the chance, but now it was too late.

She'd fed him.

However it happened, whatever the circumstances, Deston had Seraphina's blood inside of him and nothing would change that. Clearly, he'd used their connection— and the situation—to manipulate her. Every instinct told me he would end up hurting her, and I couldn't allow that to happen.

But I couldn't undo what happened tonight.

And every time I pictured Deston's mouth on Seraphina, my feet started moving back toward the castle, my vision turning the color of spilled blood. *Deston's blood.*

I wasn't angry with Seraphina. Far from it.

She was a newly minted vampire and didn't understand the games our kind played. But Deston did, and he was playing her.

The bastard didn't have a protective bone in his body, which meant he only took her to the palace tonight for his own gain. Leverage, maybe, against the King. Some was to seek the revenge for his dead family, or to gain back the power he'd lost.

My knees went weak at the thought. Deston had traded Seraphina's life away to Viktor once before; nothing stopped him from doing it again. Only this time... I hadn't even known she was missing until she'd been gone for hours.

And that key...

I'd come out here to get my head straight before I charged upstairs and said something I'd regret. Shout at her, demand she tell me what in the *fucking hell she'd been thinking*. My Queen—vulnerable and untrained—had been inside the royal palace, had crossed the wide-open field where she was an easy target for the revenants.

My God, she was reckless.

I knew why she'd hidden this from both myself and Cyrus—she damn well knew we'd have stopped her.

But that key...

Despite all my years spent in the palace, I'd seldom seen the royal keys. They were carefully guarded secrets, and one of the few things I knew next to nothing about.

There were several in existence, but only one was gold, set with emeralds.

That key went to a holding room protected by an ancient spell, created by the very first Darkfell queen. The chamber was only used to contain the most dangerous prisoners—powerful elder vampires, werewolves, and occasionally, Fae.

Over fifty years as the Queen's Commander, and I'd never used that key myself.

I was waist deep in the bayou by now, well outside Deston's protective wards. I tilted my head back and tested the air. Maybe a pack of revenants would come charging out of the dark because I needed to tear something apart. But only the deep quiet of a gloomy Louisiana winter answered my anger.

The last male to open that room had been my old commander—Sebastian Blackwell—and he'd used the very key that now hung around Seraphina's neck.

Right before he'd disappeared into thin air, a good ten years before Viktor slaughtered Lyra.

How she possessed that key... *why* she had such a valuable relic only brought up more questions in my mind, questions I didn't like the answers to.

Like why she'd left Cyrus and me out of that equation.

Then decided, after everything he'd done, to trust Deston de Rayne.

And *that* was the question I really didn't like the answer to.

I'd been pacing back and forth for hours by the time Luthor finally appeared, wet, cold, and still pissed off.

Not that I blamed him. I could have handled this whole situation better, I could have—should have told him the truth from the beginning. Not to mention, I'd disobeyed his only rule, which was to stay inside the wards.

Somehow, I knew I should minimize Deston's role in this debacle, if only to save him another beating. Besides being a nervous wreck, I was shaking, my hands trembling. Cyrus said I'd expelled too much magic, too quickly. He might be right, since my palms were red and blistered.

The second the bedroom door closed behind Luthor, I started talking.

"I'm sorry I snuck out, and I know I should have told you about the key, but Deston was with me the entire time. We got in and out of the palace with no issues at all, and I don't think I was in real danger, at least, not until his magic stopped working."

I winced. So much for minimizing his participation.

In the hours before Luthor appeared, I'd told Cyrus pretty much everything, sans Lyra and the fact their previous queen was trapped in a coma in a secret room in the palace, being used as a magic battery by Viktor.

I didn't know how to tell them the truth.

I didn't *want* to tell them because once they knew their

real queen was still alive, I was afraid they'd fly off to the palace, rescue her, and toss me to the side. Because who was I, really?

A nobody. Not even an experienced vampire, but a liability.

"Still, as incursions go, I suppose tonight could have gone worse."

"Like you ending up dead, torn apart by revenants?" Luthor asked softly. I winced. He was right of course, and now that the experience was over, I hardly remembered why I'd been so fired up to go in the first place.

Cyrus was poised on the bed just behind me, ready to get between us if he had to, but Luthor's anger didn't feel hot. No, it felt cold, immovable, like an iceberg frozen into an endless sea.

"That didn't happen," I told him flatly, reminding him, "and aren't you the one who always says not to focus on what *could* have happened?"

His lips tightened. "If you are done trying to manipulate me, Seraphina, I have some questions."

I shifted uncomfortably because, yeah, that's exactly what I was trying to do.

"Go ahead." I scooted closer to Cyrus and folded my hands in my lap. I still had dried blood beneath my finger-nails, splattered on my clothes, probably on my face, but I hadn't looked in the mirror since our return. I'd been in full damage-control mode, and so far, it wasn't working.

"Let me see the key." He held out his hand, and I drew the chain over my head, placed it in his open palm. His bruised knuckles were covered in dried blood, but healing.

"Let me clean you up, at least," I sighed, getting a wash-cloth from the bathroom, making sure the water was cold, before I wrung it out.

He was still frowning down at the key. "Tell me how you got this and don't leave anything out."

I sat beside him, took his free hand, and gently wiped away the blood. "Mom left me the key and a note." Cyrus handed him the curled paper, which we'd already dissected, word by word.

"That's all I know. I found the key and that note in the back of her painting." I inspected Luthor's other hand, cleaning off his knuckles, inspecting a particularly deep gash, wondering if one of his knuckles might be broken. "It's probably been hidden there the whole time."

Luthor pulled his hand away, scanned the note, his eyes flying over the words.

"No clue how Isabelle ended up with the key, but it's clear she knew what it was for, the secret it would unlock. I have to wonder how she knew."

The secret it would unlock... My chest tightened. *Holy shit, did he know about Lyra?*

"I've seen this key before, when I first joined the ranks of the Knightsguard. There's a holding cell at the palace, only used for the most dangerous prisoners." His steady gaze fixed on me. "Did you open that door, Fina?"

I worried the edge of the rust-stained cloth. "I... I didn't, but Deston did. First, he did something with the magic that sealed the chamber shut, then he used the key, and unlocked the actual door."

Some things in life are inevitable, and you ending up with the key is one of them. That's what Mom said, right before she said the secret will *bring Viktor to his knees.*

But the secret was only tearing my whole world apart.

"What was behind the door, Seraphina?" Luthor asked, his gentle, coaxing tone impossible to resist. My hands twisted helplessly in my lap. "What's this secret your mother talks about?"

Once they knew Lyra was alive...I swallowed. They would leave me. This fairytale of ours would be over and I'd be alone again. Even so, I would have tried to explain, but everything went dark, then Deston burst into the room.

Lit only by a flickering candle, he was still blood splattered from head to toe, his face unnaturally drawn.

"Viktor's here. And he's brought his witch, which means he'll be through the wards in a matter of minutes."

Chapter 27
Seraphina

I snatched the key back from Luthor and hung it around my neck, tucking the chain beneath my filthy clothes. Now I wished I'd taken a shower.

Or better yet, not gone to the palace in the first place.

Luthor and Cyrus instantly went into protective mode, but Deston reached me first, pulling me into his arms and dematerializing us both downstairs. Luthor's roar shook the bones of the castle, and I stepped away, searching Deston's face.

"I wanted to... *Non, ce n'est pas le moment*," he muttered angrily, his eyes searching my face, true fear written all over his. Then he drew a shuddering breath. "I left my cane behind, that's how they knew where to look. Stupid of me, I know, but I cannot fix my mistake now," he swiftly explained, his hand still around my wrist.

"I have enough magic to keep you hidden, long enough to convince Viktor you're far, far away from here."

"And where does that leave you, exactly?"

"When his search produces no results, I expect he will have questions about why I was on palace grounds tonight." Deston shrugged. "I will not answer, he will take me back to the palace for questioning. Luthor and Cyrus will whisk you away to safety."

"Nobody's *whisking me* anywhere. You're not giving yourself up." I looked to the stairs, where Luthor and

Cyrus's heavy footsteps were getting closer. "There's four of us. We'll fight our way out."

"You are not nearly ready, *ma cherie*, especially not after you expended so much magic mere hours ago." He turned my hand over and, to my shock, pressed a kiss to my blistered palm. A small circle of new, pink skin formed, then spread across the rest of my hand, the blisters fading away. "As for myself, I can pull residual power from the house, so I shall manage this one final trick."

He tugged me close enough to whisper in my ear, "Listen to Luthor and Cyrus. They will take you somewhere safe, once Viktor is gone. This castle will stand, at least, until I am dead. Until then, *cherie*, know that I will never betray you. Stay quiet, no matter what you hear, and for the love of God, do not interfere." His lips brushed my mouth.

I stayed frozen, even when his lips moved desperately on mine.

A swirl of air at my back told me Luthor and Cyrus had arrived, and Deston pushed me into Luthor's waiting arms. "Guard her with your fucking lives, or I'll come back from the dead and haunt you both."

His snarled command echoed in my ears as Luthor's arms closed around me and dragged me backwards into the shadows of the library. The room went as dark as the rest of the castle as he smothered the fire with his shadows. "Stay quiet," Deston snapped at us. "They will not find you unless you make noise."

I had no idea what Deston meant until he disappeared behind a wavy illusion that quickly turned solid. I reached out a shaking hand to test the newly erected barrier. The stone wall felt damp and cold—I leaned closer—it even *smelled* like the castle. Woodsmoke and limestone, like these stones had been here forever.

My fingers touched my still-burning lips as Luthor pressed me tightly against the bookshelves. "Viktor won't be able to see us through the glamour. But you must remain still, Fina. They'll smell you if you move around too much."

"Smell me?" I whispered.

"The revenants. Even through the magic, their sense of smell is keen."

"But Deston said..." I sucked in a quick breath. "Deston said this place is protected from revenants. That they'll turn to ash if they step inside."

"Not if Viktor brought a witch." Luthor growled. "Witch magic will shield them, allow them inside. We have to rely on Deston's glamour to hide us, and his lies to convince Viktor we're gone."

I didn't see how hiding would save us, nor did the idea of Deston's sacrifice sit well with me. "We should be out there," I murmured. "We should fight."

Quiet. Luthor forced the order into my head. *Viktor will kill you if he finds us.*

I struggled to stay under control, especially when Viktor's voice—muffled and otherworldly—floated through the magic barrier.

"De Rayne," the king gloated. "Quite the mess you left for me. Imagine my surprise when I was called back to the palace because magic—*necromancer magic*—was expended within the wards."

I couldn't hear Deston's quiet answer, but I assumed it was clever.

"No, you didn't, did you? I suppose you'll make me work for the answer. I've never trusted you, but neither did I think you'd be stupid enough to leave something behind. I've been looking for a good reason to get rid of you, and you just sealed your own fate."

This was my fault. Tonight would end like before, at Gram's. I'd be forced to listen silently while Viktor killed Deston. But I wasn't a weak human anymore, nor a newborn vampire.

I had magic. *Powerful* magic. I fought against Cyrus's hold, desperate to get out there.

An overwhelming, almost primitive *need* overtook me, to defend Deston against the king. I wasn't sure where the strange compulsion came from, or why I felt this protective urge so deeply, but I struggled against Cyrus's hold, trying to get out there.

We engaged in a quiet tug of war until Luthor crushed me against him, effectively pinning me between them.

Stop fighting us, Seraphina. If they discover us, we all die tonight. His commanding voice echoed in my head. *Once Viktor captures Deston, we will have time to escape. After that, we figure out how to get him back. We won't leave him to his fate, we'll save him.*

For some reason, that simple assurance satisfied my chaotic brain.

He lost his cane. That's how Viktor knew. I thought back to Luthor, desperate to make him understand. *In the revenant attack, he lost his cane because he ordered me to run. I couldn't leave him behind.*

"I know they're here in this castle of cards you built. I want all three of them. Give them to me and I won't kill you."

"Will you turn me into a monster, then, Viktor, as you did my family?" Deston's voice was loud, he had to be right on the other side of the barrier. "No, thank you. I'd rather die."

Calm, Seraphina. Stay calm. Cyrus's hands swept up my sides, grasped my shoulders, and I swayed as the full force of his power swept through me. His magic was a drug, filling me with a foggy sedation.

"Give me the girl, or I'll burn this place down around them," Viktor said, his words almost drowned out by the scrape-scrape of claws. The dirty-bog mustiness of the revenants seeped through the wall, and I stopped moving. Stopped breathing. It was true, the magic didn't mask scent or sound. I closed my eyes, praying my heart wasn't beating too loudly.

Five revenants, big ones, I thought to Luthor and Cyrus, my cotton-stuffed head spinning.

"You can try," Deston said lightly. "But you'll find my magic does not burn."

There were low growls from the revenants, then the light, clicking sound of heels approaching.

"This is Adora Blaire," Viktor said. The pungency of ozone seeped through the wall, stung my nose, and I heard an electric crackle. I remembered how Marie's magic had coated the walls of Gram's house with glowing, protective energy.

Adora's magic wasn't protective at all. Bolts of red crackled over the floors and walls, crawling like angry red veins, heating the air around us. She meant to burn this place down.

"Now we'll see how well your illusions hold up, de Rayne," Viktor said, and I heard a male grunt of pain. "I shouldn't think they'll give Adora much trouble."

God, I wished I could see through the barrier, especially when there was another sound, guttural this time, raspy and terrible. Someone grunted, then gasped for breath. The crackling grew louder and louder until I pressed my hands over my ears.

"That's... that's all I have," said a shaking female voice.

"I tried, my King, but I couldn't undo the illusion. Give me time, and I will break through it, I swear."

"Worthless witch," Viktor snarled, and the revenant's growls grew hungrier. I heard a squeak of pain, like a mouse's death shriek, then nothing.

Cyrus fed magic into me in a steady stream, keeping me almost drugged. My head was screaming at me to get out there, to protect Deston, to shove my magic into Viktor until I had nothing left. But my arms and legs were too lethargic.

I heard indistinct cursing, laughter, far-off shouting.

The growl of the revenants drew closer, and I realized they were sniffing along the false wall. Luthor wrapped his shadows around us and cut everything off. I couldn't see, I couldn't hear, even the wet-mud stench of the creatures disappeared.

But if I couldn't sense them, then they wouldn't sense us, and after countless minutes, Luthor dropped his shadows. We emerged into an eerie emptiness, but the barrier was still solid.

"There's a series of passages through here," Cyrus whispered, pushing the end of the bookcase, which swung open —books and all—like an enormous door. "This way."

He guided me, Luthor pressed tight against my back until we emerged into the foyer. Without Cyrus's magic, my head cleared, my senses coming back online.

From the silence, we were the only living things in the structure; the witch's corpse sprawled out on the rug, her limbs grotesquely bent.

"I've heard of this one." Luthor crouched down beside the body. "She's the witch Viktor's been using to reinforce the protective ward around the palace."

"If she's dead, what happens to the ward around the

palace?" I asked, remembering Deston's final warning to me. *This castle will stand, at least, until I am dead.*

The castle was intact, which meant Deston was still alive.

Then the back of my neck prickled, my shadows already wrapping the three of us in darkness. The barest sound—a scrape, little more than a sandpaper hiss broke the silence, and I knew I'd been wrong.

We were not alone.

Chapter 28
Deston

Tf only I hadn't left my cane behind.

If I wasn't so weak after the revenant attack.

If, if, if.

Change one thing over the past twelve hours, and I'd be in bed right now, stroking myself as I dreamed about Seraphina. Debating my next move. Picturing her sweet, red lips wrapped around me. Plotting to end Viktor's reign and take his life.

Now I was fucked, because of a simple, avoidable mistake.

If I lived through this—which I highly doubted—I'd never hear the end of it.

"Put him in my office, we'll interrogate him there." At Viktor's order, the guards dragged me into his pathetic, mediocre library and threw me into a cracked leather chair. I sniffed the rarified air. A lot of blood had been spilled here recently.

I knew why Viktor had brought me here and not the dungeons, but perhaps he'd kill me before we reached the uncivilized part of this process.

Viktor kept me waiting—probably debating the wisdom of killing the witch—before his sneering face was in mine. His red eyes were duller than usual, and I realized the aura of power normally surrounding him had diminished. "I left my revenants patrolling your beloved castle.

They'll flush out the false queen and the traitors and I imagine they won't leave much behind except bones and teeth."

I tried to calculate how weak he really was. "My castle is more than stone and wood. You'll find your creations... will not fare so well as you think once they are inside."

"These will fare well enough."

Viktor straddled the chair opposite me, crossed his arms on the back with an insipid smile.

"They've had a bit of your blood since you left enough of it strewn around. Blood magic, de Rayne, outmatches transmutation any day of the week."

A thrill of fear went through me.

My mind raced, weighing the truth and finding he might be right. If those creatures tasted my blood, my magic wouldn't work against them. My wards would fail, including the one hiding my mate.

Still, Seraphina had Luthor's strength and Cyrus's wits at her disposal. She had her magic if her hands were not too damaged to wield it.

"We shall see. I, for one, am betting on the house." I only had to hold Viktor's attention long enough for them to escape the bayou, find refuge with the one family who would harbor them. "What do you plan to do with me, Viktor? You know I have powerful allies. Eliminating me will only weaken your already tenuous hold on the royals."

He snorted, but doubt flashed across his face, faster than he could hide it.

"You will be made an example, just as Lord Simon Emmett was."

I'd killed poor Simon a week ago, had joked about it with Seraphina. It wasn't so funny now. At least Simon had been dead when they nailed him to the wall. I had a feeling I wouldn't be so lucky.

Viktor leaned in. "Give me the girl. I find your loyalty curious, given you've never cared one way or another about anyone but yourself."

"Go find her yourself, since my advisory duties have been suspended. Or perhaps your revenants will kill her and save you the trouble." Every word tasted bitter while I tried not to picture the hell Seraphina was enduring right now.

Luthor and Cyrus would give their lives to keep her safe.

"Perhaps they will," Viktor mused. "How did you kill those revenants, de Rayne? Nearly fifty of them, torn limb from limb, and the undead were still animated when I returned. I expended a considerable amount of magic to put them back in the ground." His red-tinted eyes were dim, and I realized my earlier suspicion was correct. Viktor's magic was depleted.

"You're no necromancer."

"Are you sure about that? I have many gifts." My gaze drilled into his. "Ask yourself if killing me is strategically your best move. As I've counseled in the past, your position of power is tenuous, at best. There are those who are—at this very moment—working to orchestrate your downfall. You are making it easy for them."

"I don't need you, Deston. I never did."

"Be sure, Viktor," I said smoothly. "Be very sure about that because the smallest mistake will lead to your downfall."

He flipped my cane up, pointed end flashing. "You were careless this time. You left something behind." His gaze narrowed suspiciously. "You don't usually make mistakes."

"No, I do not."

Let him think I was setting him up. Let the bastard second guess his every move, his every decision. Doubt would buy Seraphina more time to escape.

With a raspy hiss, he drew my long rapier from the outer sheath and pressed the point into my cheek. The blade cut easily, sharpened by magic to a razor edge. "Why did you leave this behind, Deston?" he asked, more forcefully this time. "Are you slipping, or are you cleverer than ever?"

"Let us pretend it's the latter." I didn't so much as blink when he pushed the point in until it hit bone. This was only the beginning, and I might as well numb myself to the pain now, since this would only get worse.

He pulled the blade away, doubt blending with anger. "If you won't talk, then you're of no use to me. Every inch of that bayou is crawling with guards, and I've put out a five-million-dollar bounty on the girl's head. Good luck securing allies from the royal houses, they answer to me."

"Of course, they do. You're the King, after all," I said breezily. Luthor should have Seraphina out by now, even if they had to fight their way through. He, like me, would give his life to keep our Queen safe. Viktor would never command that level of loyalty.

Nor would he grasp how determined Seraphina was.

He'd grown soft, his blond hair unkempt, a double chin protruding over the collar of his shirt. He had a gut, evidence of his constant indulgences. I imagined there was constant friction between Viktor and his sire. Vane Carpathian put Viktor on the throne, but even Vane answered to a master— an ancient queen who lived across the ocean.

I'd often wondered why they'd never replaced Viktor with a stronger puppet, but there were advantages to manipulating a weak pawn. Viktor was still king, but he wouldn't be much longer. Lyra's crypt was right down the hall. Barely fifty yards from where I sat.

I only needed a moment, and Viktor's days of kinghood would be no more.

"I imagine your sire heard of last evening's debacle," I commented. "Infiltration of the palace. A revenant massacre. And where were you? Off on a wild goose chase. You're getting sloppy, Viktor, and Vane knows it."

"Father trusts me with the kingdom." Viktor sniffed.

"That's not what I've heard." I crossed my legs, the heavy gold ring on my finger flashing. "I think Vane Carpathian will fly back here, quicker than a bird, to make sure the kingdom is not slipping through your fingers. Or perhaps *she'll* come."

He blanched at that, and I prayed I was wrong.

Viktor's gaze went to the ring, set with a glittering black diamond, which had been in my family for a thousand years.

"Ah yes, I have regained the family heirloom." I lifted my hand. "It seems my sire didn't need this anymore." The moment I'd seen this ring fused into that ancient revenant's paw, I knew who he'd once been. My sire had survived as a monster for too long, and his death...I would like to think his death had been a mercy.

"I'm the last of my bloodline now." The words tasted foul in my mouth, but it was all part of the act. Disinterest was my best armor at the moment.

Viktor would never know how much I hated him for what he'd done to my family. I'd never give him the satisfaction. I leaned back in the chair and grinned at the way his narrowed eyes glowed red in anticipation.

"Nail the traitor up," he instructed the guards. "Put him next to Emmett, let's see how long he lasts."

Chapter 29
Deston

I couldn't describe exactly how I knew the revenants were still in the castle, but I did.

Maybe it was the primal fear tensing up my body.

Or maybe it was because Luthor and Cyrus had me crushed so tightly between them, I could hardly even breathe. "Let me out," I muttered against Cyrus's chest, and I wiggled free and tested the air, trying to get a fix on the intruders.

I could wield my magic—if I had to—since one of my palms had healed. The one Deston had pressed his warm lips to, leaving me all confused and conflicted.

Almost immediately I got a fix on them, nodded to Luthor, and raised four fingers. I pointed upstairs, then down the hallway to the kitchen where the bog-water smell of revenants was the strongest.

Luthor acknowledged me tersely and flashed away. I'd seen both Luthor and Cyrus dismantle revenants with their bare hands, and still, my heart thumped a mile a minute. They were all I had right now, and I couldn't lose either of them.

Something crashed upstairs, and I stepped away from Cyrus toward the staircase. "Not a chance, Seraphina." He pulled me back against him. "Luthor can take care of himself, let him work."

I tested the air again. "Five of them now," I whispered. "Four inside, one outside, in front."

Tell that to Luthor, Cyrus said in my head. *He'll want to know.*

Five total. I thought hard to Luthor. *There are two upstairs, two in the kitchen, one outside, guarding the back exit.*

Only one left upstairs. Luthor sounded so calm, even as the thudding of heavy steps, accompanied by the scrape of claws, sounded above our heads. *I'll take care of the last one up here. Cyrus? Take care of the ones in the kitchen. I'm on it.*

I'm going with you, I thought hard at Cyrus, daring him to refuse. As much as I feared the revenants, I didn't feel comfortable waiting by myself.

Of course, you are. His green eyes laughed as he waved me ahead. *Ladies first.*

Take care of her and don't let her get hurt. Luthor growled in my head. When he didn't get an immediate response, he added, *Do I have to come down there?*

She's got more magic in her little finger than either of us, and she's itching to use it. Let her have some fun.

I'm not sure this is what I'd call fun, I put in, mostly because I was done with excitement for tonight. Hell, for the rest of my life, to be honest.

Cyrus shook his head, a snort of laughter escaping. *You love this shit, admit it.*

The bog water smell grew closer, and along with it came that horrible sound of claws dragging over stone. *Here they come,* I thought at Cyrus, my courage whittling away the closer the claws got.

This is not fun, I thought-yelled at Cyrus. *Not one bit.*

Tell me that when it's over. He inched closer, grinning. *Don't worry, I've got your back.*

The scents changed again. They'd split off.

The dull scraping came from two sides, their breathing getting louder. The tension in the air mounted before they closed in, hoping to trap us between them. I gathered my magic, readied myself to cast it when Cyrus wrapped his arms around me, and we disappeared.

We reappeared in the demolished kitchen where cupboards were ripped from the walls and the stench of revenant was nearly unbearable.

"Whew. This place stinks. It will take them a minute to get their bearings," he whispered. "Luthor's about finished clearing the upstairs. Once he's done, I'll transport you up there so you can pack your book bag. You'll have to make it quick," he warned sternly, his gaze flew over my head to where something big and heavy crashed upstairs.

"Dare I ask where we are going?"

The revenants were already on their way back toward us, taking out the walls as they scrambled down the narrow hallway. I cringed as plaster fell, a chandelier crashed, precious paintings tumbled to the ground. They snapped viciously at each other in the narrow space, the tangle of gray legs and arms making them indistinguishable as they fought for better position.

"Friends. Somewhere safe," Cyrus said, measuring the distance between us and the claws and teeth heading our way.

Thankfully, the leading revenant got stuck in the narrow kitchen door, its wide shoulders jammed against the door frame, and for a second, I got my closest look at one so far. Their eyes were tiny, no bigger than marbles, the mouth was a huge maw filled with gnashing, pointed teeth. Two huge slits in the leathery skin served as its nose, and as I watched, they flared open, then slapped shut with that disgusting moist sound, like a wet towel being dropped to the floor. *Repeatedly*.

But it was no wonder the beasts were such good trackers. Their heads were nothing but scent-filters, their tiny brains programmed to follow a target, then tear it to shreds with those teeth.

These two creatures had once been vampires. Alive. Powerful.

Now they were monsters controlled by an even bigger monster. Once I destroyed Viktor, I'd destroy every last revenant and forbid anyone from ever creating anything like this again.

They struggled to reach us, then one side of the doorway gave way, splintering apart with a deafening crash. Once again, Cyrus transported me away, and we reappeared in the bedroom, the bed still rumpled from last night. He tossed my old backpack to me.

"Pack quickly, Seraphina," he warned. "As soon as Luthor kills the second one up here, we'll be on our way." He pulled a heavy black bag from beneath the bed.

"My go-bag," he explained with a wink. "Like, I'm all ready to go? Get it?"

He frowned at the clothes I had strewn all over the bed. "Only grab what you need."

I sighed and started stuffing clothing into the tiny pack. I didn't have a go-bag, even though Luthor had repeatedly urged me to be prepared for this day. Of course, since they never allowed me out in the real world, how was I supposed to do that? Besides, I'd felt safe enough here.

How wrong I'd been.

Cyrus searched my face and tipped my lips up to his, then gave me a soft kiss. "Everything will be okay, Fina.

We'll be out of here in less than a minute and on our way to a safe place."

"This place was supposed to be safe, remember?"

"And it was, until you..." His voice trailed off, but I knew what he was about to say. *Until you jeopardized everything.* And he was right.

If I hadn't gotten cocky and decided to hunt down the key's secret, then none of this would have happened. If I hadn't decided to go rogue and not include them in my decision, which they'd surely have talked me out of it.

"I know, and you're right, and I shouldn't have. If I could change what happened tonight, I would."

"I didn't say that," he said quickly. "I would have done the same. Look, I get it. If you... or Luthor left me a cryptic note, I would have pursued it until I uncovered the truth."

"Really?" I blinked up at him. I hadn't known how badly I'd needed someone to understand my decision. I'd been so full of doubt lately, maybe I'd just been looking for a way to prove myself.

"Of course, I would have taken backup and not led the enemy straight back to our door, but none of us are perfect." He pinched my cheek with a grin. "Rookie mistake, we all make them."

"You're pretty up to date on the current lingo, Mr. I've-Been-Imprisoned-For-A-Hundred-Years."

He waggled his eyebrows. "It's the interweb. Did you know nearly everyone has a cat and posts pictures of them online? I even have a Facebook page." He hefted the military-style bag.

"Where do you think I got this?" The contents clinked loudly, and I wondered how many weapons were inside. "You can find anything you want on Amazon." He knelt and pulled out an even bigger one that I assumed was Luthor's.

I grabbed a sweater, some leggings, a sports bra and stuffed them into the tiny pack. I left the high-end lingerie, most of it still in the bags. I glanced toward the bathroom but figured I didn't have time for toiletries. A shame because I loved all of them.

I picked up the heavy book—History of the Darkfell Queens—and wiggled it inside the pack. The zipper would only half-close, but at least I had reading material, no matter where we ended up.

"Oh my God, I almost forgot." I snagged the painting from the dresser, wedged it in with the ridiculously huge book.

From outside the bedroom door, I heard a strangled roar, a high-pitched squeal, then the dry crack of bones. "That's the last one," Cyrus said, as if Luthor had just killed a mouse. "Do you have everything you need?"

I nodded and glanced at the door, as a howl rent the air, and I remembered the two revenants still downstairs, plus the one waiting outside.

Would we have to fight our way through? I honestly didn't think I had it in me.

Luthor burst in and smashed me into his chest. I barely had time to tighten my grip on the backpack before freezing air rushed across my face as we flew, the castle and gardens blurring beneath us, the last revenant throwing his head up in a keening howl.

A moment later, my feet sank into the mud, and in one breath I knew exactly where we were—near Lake Pontchartrain.

The lake didn't have anything on the smell of revenants.

Chapter 30
Seraphina

I hugged my arms around myself, trying to fend off the freezing cold. Eventually, I pulled a fluffy pink sweater out of my backpack and pulled it on, feeling slightly ridiculous and no warmer.

"This is too exposed. We shouldn't wait here long," Luthor said, shooting a stern look at Cyrus. "Go and confirm Hugh is expecting us. We can't afford any unwelcome surprises."

Cyrus hefted the two footlocker-sized bags he carried. "Got it. I'll drop these off and be back in a minute." He dematerialized in an instant, bags and all.

"Who is Hugh?" I asked curiously. "I thought you didn't have any contacts in this world anymore?" Nor did I like the thought of relying, once more, on the kindness of strangers.

"In the late 1800s, Hugh Cormier served as Queen Lyra's advisor before Deston forced him out. He's a good male with a solid reputation. We can trust him."

I sighed. We'd been bouncing from place to place since he'd freed me from the prison, and the thought of yet another temporary home took me back to my childhood. I didn't do well with impermanence, and I suddenly realized that Deston's ridiculous castle had felt more like home to me than anywhere else ever had.

"Are you sure we'll be safe?" I asked nervously. "I mean, Viktor has a lot of power, and if they sell us out..."

"Hugh won't sell us out, Seraphina." Luthor pulled me into his arms for a tight hug. "I'd never put you in danger. Deston set this up with Hugh, months ago. Cyrus and I confirmed he'd give us sanctuary, in case Viktor figured out that Deston was hiding us. We'll be okay, I promise."

The only vampires I knew were Luthor, Cyrus, Deston, and Viktor. I'd been part of the vampire world for three months, and I knew exactly four of them.

Two, I trusted with my life.

One I didn't know how to feel about, and the other kept trying to kill me. Not a great track record.

"If it makes you feel better, Hugh Cormier was a close friend of Queen Lyra. He most likely knew your grandmother, as well. He's currently at odds with Viktor over his daughter Contessa. Deston assured us he will not only keep us safe but can get us out of the country if needed."

"And we're going to take Deston's word on this?" I asked. I trusted Deston more than I ever had, but I couldn't get rid of the doubts. He'd sold us out before. He'd sold out everyone before, even Lyra.

"Which is why Cyrus went in first. If it's clear, he'll give me the go-ahead."

"And if it's not?"

His face grew grim. "Then we go back to the Fontaine crypt in the graveyard and figure out what our next step is."

"Okay," I said, my shoulders sagging. "I don't much like that plan, but I agree." The last place I wanted to go was a zombie-filled graveyard, but I didn't have a better option.

Luthor kept his arms around me as we waited for Cyrus's reappearance, and I agonized over what Viktor was doing to Deston. As I thought of a million horrible variations, my stomach tightened. I couldn't explain why I kept having these involuntary reactions every time Deston was in danger.

I mean, maybe he *was* starting to grow on me, but this was more like...

"We'll be safe here, Seraphina." Luthor kissed the top of my head, and I sank into him, exhaustion getting the better of me. "I swear to you, you can trust Hugh," Luthor counseled gently. "There is a long history of Marvelle-Cormier alliances stretching back a thousand years. You'll see when you meet him. Hugh is one of the good ones."

"What about Deston?" I asked softly, then swallowed before I voiced my worst fear. "Do you think Viktor's already turned him?"

"Viktor will keep Deston alive as long as he's useful," Luthor said with no hesitation. "Deston knows too much and has too many allies for Viktor to waste by turning him into a revenant or killing him out of hand. Once we speak to Hugh, we will strategize a plan to get him back."

My aching chest relaxed somewhat. "Really? I thought maybe..." Tears sprang to my eyes before I could stop them. "I thought you hated him, and this might be your chance to get rid of him."

"Oh, I do, but he means something to you, Seraphina," Luthor explained gently. "I don't like that fact, but I'll accept it." He hesitated, before adding, "There's nothing that Viktor can dish out that Deston can't take." But I heard the doubt in his voice. The same doubt I felt every time I thought of Viktor and his endless cruelties.

"It's my fault he's Viktor's prisoner," I pointed out, even though this aching feeling felt deeper than remorse. "If I hadn't threatened to go by myself to the palace, he never would have offered to sneak me in."

"De Rayne should never have taken you outside the

safety of the wards. That was our arrangement." Luthor growled softly, his chest rumbling beneath my head. "He violated our agreement when he put you in danger, which I can never forgive. He knew the risks and yet chose to take them. Even worse, he took you along, and for that..."

His voice trailed off, so I finished it for him. "He deserves everything he gets? Is that what you were going to say?"

I sighed. I felt as though I had the weight of the world on my shoulders and my knees were about to give out. "For the last time, I threatened to go to the palace by myself. Deston is the only reason I am still alive right now."

"Both of you lied to me. You could have come to me with the truth, yet you made a different choice." I squeezed my eyes closed at Luthor's cold tone, even though he had every right to be angry. "You, I readily forgive. Deston however... given his history... Yes, you are correct. He deserves everything he gets."

"No, he does not," I argued softly. "He never would've done it, Luthor, if I hadn't threatened to go by myself. I manipulated him into taking me, even when he argued against it."

"Well, it worked, didn't it?" Luthor snapped. "You got what you wanted."

Tears pricked my eyes. "I'm sorry, Luthor. I am. If I could do it over again, I would have made a different choice, but...I messed up." he turned away, his jaw clenched tight.

I had to tell him the truth about Lyra. Luthor deserved to know what we'd discovered. Part of me feared he'd leave me behind, but part of me hoped maybe we could still save her, despite what Deston had said.

"There's something I have to tell you." I sucked in a

breath, my lungs tight. "We found something in the palace that..."

But Luthor cut me off. "What I want to know is this. Why did you fucking feed him in the first place, Seraphina?" This time, there was heat in his rough growl. "And don't pretend you don't know what's going on with Deston."

"I..." I snapped my mouth shut. "What do you mean, what's going on?"

"Now that your blood is inside him, you cannot take that back. He can hear your thoughts. Did you think of that?"

I bristled at the flat, bitter judgement in Luthor's voice, as if I'd committed some terrible sin.

"He'd be dead if I hadn't." *And Deston had always been able to hear my thoughts. I'd never analyzed his intrusions into my mind before, but now I wondered why we had that connection.*

"Which would've been a good thing."

"So, you expect me to live the rest of my life with Deston's death on my hands? That's not fair, Luthor." I pulled away; my hands clenched. "I wish I'd never found the key in the first place. That none of this ever happened."

Luthor snorted. "Are you really going to pretend that you don't know..."

"I can hear you two from a mile away," Cyrus scolded, reappearing before us. "It's all clear. Hugh said there's an old entrance we can use to access the basement. No one will see us, just in case there is anyone watching."

His fangs dropped lower. "*Or listening.* You're not usually this careless, Luthor."

Cyrus looked between us—me, with my hands clenched into fists, Luthor, rigid with anger.

"Whatever you're fighting about will have to wait. Let's get inside where it's safe."

I picked up my backpack. "We're done here, anyways," I told him, though this didn't feel nearly done. What did Luthor mean about me pretending?

"Tell me a little more about the Cormier's. I don't want to say the wrong thing and offend anyone."

Cyrus offered an uneasy smile, his gaze shooting over to Luthor. "Lord Hugh Cormier is not only powerful, he is also one of the most well-respected members of the clan. He stays on good terms with the other houses, even the Gauthiers. He has strong ties to the old European clans as well, which will come in handy when you take the throne."

Cyrus pulled the heavy bookbag off my shoulder and glared at Luthor, who had the decency to look abashed. "Girls tend to run in the Cormier family, which means they're at Viktor's mercy." He wrapped his arm around me, and the next thing I knew, we were in the middle of a formal garden, not unlike Deston's.

"How does having girls put the Cormiers at Viktor's mercy?" I asked, then realized how ridiculous the question was. I'd spent enough time in the dungeons to know how cruel Viktor was to humans. He probably wasn't any less so to vampires.

"You know Viktor's biggest fear is being replaced by a new queen?"

I nodded. "Yeah, that's why he rounded up me and those other, poor girls on Reaping Night."

I shivered at the memory, and Luthor's hand slid down my arm before he twined his fingers with mine. Some of his anger leached away, and I knew he, too, was remembering that horrific night in the prison.

"I'm sorry, Seraphina," he murmured, and I took his

hand in mine, relishing the contact. "I overreacted. When I realized you were gone... I think I lost my mind for a few hours."

"I understand. I made some bad choices tonight myself. Let's not make any more, okay?"

He nodded, his tight face relaxing just enough that I knew while we weren't finished discussing this, we were going to move on.

"Since you have finally stopped being ridiculous and made up"—Cyrus looked at Luthor pointedly—"I'll explain the situation to our queen. If you are unlucky enough to be born a female in the Darkfell clan, Viktor has ways of controlling you."

We ducked into a garden shed along a high stone wall.

"Through here," Cyrus led the way. "This leads straight to the lower level of the house."

"I don't like sneaking around like I'm a criminal," I muttered.

"Nor do I," Cyrus agreed, "but it's necessary. This will be the first place Viktor searches once he realizes we escaped his revenants. Better that no one sees us enter, that will make our presence easier for Hugh to hide."

"Why is he willing to take this sort of risk for us?"

"He's taking the risk for you, Seraphina, not us." Cyrus held open the small door hidden in the back of the shed, then we headed down a flight of steps that led to a long, dimly lit corridor, a passageway running beneath the gardens.

"Hugh said no one uses this except family. So, there will be no prying eyes, no witnesses for Viktor to interrogate." Despite his assurance, Luthor kept a hand on my arm, ready to whisk me away at the first sign of danger.

"Okay, so back to the Cormiers," I whispered. "Please

tell me that Viktor did not kill their daughters." Because of course, that's where my mind immediately went, considering what he did to all those girls he'd captured on Reaping Night. What he would have done to me if it weren't for Luthor and Cyrus.

"No." Luthor's tense whisper grew quieter. "It's something worse, according to our sources."

Luthor hesitated and my heart sank, wondering what new horrors Viktor was capable of. I didn't want to know, but I had to know, so I could stop him. I nodded, and he finally went on. "When a female vampire of royal blood reaches eighteen, Viktor soul-binds them."

"That sounds awful."

"A soul-bound female—actually, anyone who is soul-bound by an older vampire—cannot betray the vampire they are bound to. Their master controls them completely, right down to their thoughts and actions. It is essentially slavery. Soul-bonding is an archaic custom that started in Moldavia, by..."

"A toxic, sociopathic bitch who should be dead," Cyrus cut in.

"A queen who takes great pleasure in causing pain," Luthor course corrected, although by his tone, he totally agreed with Cyrus. "The tradition of Reaping Night began there as well, where it should have died out." Luthor lowered his voice. "Viktor resurrected two unspeakable traditions that all modern, respectable clans left behind centuries ago. For most vampires, such slavery is distasteful."

"Viktor's using the soul bond to prevent any potential rivals from rising and keep the throne." I was working his motives out in my head and growing more disgusted by the minute. "He sounds as barbaric as this Moldavian queen."

"He's every bit as brutish because they're related," Cyrus grumbled. "The apple doesn't fall far from the tree." He leaned in closer. "Fina, there's another side to Viktor's tortures. I heard that if any female refuses the bond, he..."

"That's enough, Cyrus," Luthor interrupted forcefully. "Let's focus on the problem at hand."

Cyrus drew an audible breath. "You're right. She doesn't need to hear this now. But she'll have to, eventually."

I frowned at them. What the hell could be worse than being controlled completely?

"It appears there's a lot I don't know about this world. And just like Viktor to use fear to control the girls, and by extension, their families." *Was there no end to the King's depravities*? "Even more reason for us to stop him."

Cyrus nodded in agreement. "His depravities have been going on for too long. According to Hugh, his eldest daughter barely escaped that fate a couple months ago."

"Good for her," I said forcefully. "I hope she left a mark before she got away."

"You can ask her sire in a few minutes." Luthor's voice dropped as we approached the end of the corridor. "Contessa was set to become Viktor's next bride," he explained quietly while I repressed my disgusted shudder. "When Tessa and her males defied him, Viktor nearly killed them all."

"Her men?" I looked up at him curiously. "Are they like... us?"

"Exactly like us," Luthor answered. "I've heard two of them, Silas and Caden, are combat trained. I'm hoping they might be candidates for the Knightsguard." He paused. "Hugh got them all out of the country. I'm hoping he'll allow me to contact them and bring them back, once Viktor is gone."

I would have liked to meet Tessa. I'd been by myself in this world for too long. A friend, *a girlfriend*, would be nice. Especially someone in a relationship like mine.

"Deston hoped that Hugh would become your strongest ally," Cyrus added. "If the story about his daughter is accurate, then he has every reason to want Viktor dead. Let's hope Deston was right."

"We need all the allies we can get right now." Cyrus stopped suddenly, opening a door that led to a set of steps.

"Any enemy of Viktor's is a friend of mine, isn't that how I should look at this?"

"It is, though most of the royals would just as soon stab you in the back as vow allegiance to you. Every house has its own designs on the throne, Seraphina. Don't ever forget that," Luthor warned, setting his hand on the small of my back as we climbed the stairs.

"How can I when you keep reminding me?" I sighed. "But seriously, I've been thinking a lot about how I want our court to be, you know, if we actually manage to kill Viktor."

"And what did you decide?"

We stopped in front of the ornate door that must lead into the main house, my already frayed nerves making my knees weak as Cyrus swung it open.

"I want good people," I told them firmly. "Good men and women who know what's right and are willing to help us change the toxic nature of Viktor's reign. I want to change *everything*. None of this soul-bonding bullshit, or raids in the middle of the night, or turning people into revenants."

I took a breath and stepped over the threshold. "That shit is over."

"I'm glad to hear that, my Queen," a calm soothing voice said as I turned to the slender, unassuming male waiting for us. He dipped into a deep bow. "Welcome to my home, Queen Seraphina. I am Lord Hugh Cormier." He gestured to the gorgeous blonde woman beside him, already halfway into a curtsy. "This is my wife, Lady Lilliana."

"Oh please," I said, "Please don't... do that." Panic tightened my chest like a steel band. "That kind of stuff makes me nervous."

"Of course, my Queen." Hugh Cormier straightened with a warm, kind smile. "We are grateful you found your way here safely." His gaze slid over to Luthor and offered his hand. "Commander Fontaine. It has been years."

"Hugh, thank you for offering us sanctuary," Luthor said gruffly. "We weren't followed," Luthor assured him. "But to make sure, Cyrus will circle back to Ravenswood and make sure none of Viktor's creatures picked up our trail."

"A wise decision." Hugh let go of Luthor's hand. "This has been a trying night for you, my Queen."

"Please, call me Seraphina," I said, unsure what the proper protocols were. Maybe they didn't want to call me by my name? "Besides, I'm not a queen."

"Not yet," Luthor pointed out more forcefully than necessary.

"Of course," Hugh said neutrally. Dressed in well-cut clothing, he exuded a calm sense of command, a male used to being in charge, yet not flaunting his power. "My wife and I will show you to your suite, and please do not hesitate to let us know what else you may require."

Hugh offered me his arm. "Lilliana has put you in the west wing. The wards are the strongest there, and should

Viktor attack, we will hold him off and allow you time to escape."

"Let's hope that's not necessary," I told him, my heart skipping a beat at the thought of these people—perfect strangers—willing to sacrifice themselves for me. "I'm sorry. I hate that we are putting you at risk." I looked to Luthor.

"Worry not, my Queen." Hugh patted my arm. I was too tired to correct him again. "Just the fact that you are alive gives me hope for a better future."

We headed toward a winding staircase, and I wondered if every vampire house was made of money. I mean, first Deston, with his ridiculous castle, now the Cormiers with this place. We passed a painting of Hugh and Lilliana, the gardens in the background, three little girls at their feet.

"You have three daughters?" I asked quietly, unsure how to broach the subject of his eldest daughter's situation... *Contessa, Luthor had said.*

"We do," he said proudly, gesturing to the painting as we passed. "Contessa, Adalia, and Madison. The great joys of our life." His tone stayed light, but his wife lowered her head, her lips flattened into a tight line.

"I took the liberty of laying out some of Tessa's clothing for you, my Queen," Lilliana's voice was flat and muted. "You are nearly the same size, and I know you left your previous residence in a hurry."

"Thank you."

As we passed a grand banquet hall, I noted the deep scratches still carved into the floor, half-hidden by a rug. I well knew what made those marks; I'd seen them enough times. Viktor had been here, terrorizing these poor people.

"Luthor said that you knew Queen Lyra?"

"I did. She was one of my dearest childhood friends.

Lyra asked for my counsel at times, after she took the throne."

"Hugh is being modest, my Queen," Luthor volunteered from behind us. "I believe your counsel meant more to the Queen than any of her advisors." His voice turned hard. "Especially her last advisor."

I winced. If they only knew of Deston's final betrayal, Luthor would hunt him down and gut him like a pig.

"Deston de Rayne did have a habit of serving himself first and the court second," Hugh said amiably, a touch of humor in his voice. "I tried never to steer the queen wrong, although I did make mistakes."

I glanced up at Hugh, his lined, yet kind face, his obvious pride in his family, and his fondness for Lyra. This was exactly the sort of person I'd hoped to find for my new court. Someone who put people first and agenda second.

"If you were friends with Lyra, I wonder if you knew Claire Marvelle?"

Hugh stopped in his tracks. "Claire Marvelle. I haven't heard that name in years. I'd heard rumors she survived the coup, of course. But that's all they ever were. Rumors."

"She survived. Claire was my grandmother." I shot him a shy smile, wondering how well he'd known Gram. His pale gaze missed nothing, scanning my face, my hair, finally settling on my eyes.

"Ah. I see the resemblance now. You look very much like Lyra, right before she died."

My mind flashed back to the withered body displayed on the altar, the long hair dragging to the floor. The ends had been dark and curly, like mine. I couldn't describe the feeling that swept through me. Like a reckoning was coming our way, and there was no avoiding it.

"Deston hinted you were descended from House

Marvelle," Hugh murmured. "But de Rayne claimed many things, over the years, so I had my doubts. But... it will be good to see a Marvelle seated on the throne once more, my Queen."

I inclined my head, "We have a long way to go before that day, I'm afraid."

"Who is your sire?" he asked curiously. "Was he from one of the royal houses?"

"I don't know." I'd been wondering this myself, lately. "Gram and Mom never talked about him."

"How did you survive for so long?" Lilliana asked softly. "Without Viktor finding you?"

"Gram and Mom moved us around a lot, to stay ahead of his search parties. And it worked." The words tasted like ash on my tongue. "Until the night it didn't."

It was hard to say the words, but I did. "We were in Ohio when a pack of revenants found us." I drew a steadying breath. "They killed Mom, and Viktor almost caught Gram and me that night. Then we disappeared into the wilds of Maine, and stayed there for years."

"I'm sorry," Lilliana murmured. "We heard you'd been in hiding all this time, but we had no idea you'd been through so much. Lost so much." She appraised me again, this time with approval. "However did you end up here?"

"I was...a student. Viktor kidnapped me off the streets of New Orleans during the Winter Reaping. Gram died a few months ago, at Viktor's hand," I told them, hardly believing it had been that long. "I'm well acquainted with Viktor's methods. And his monsters."

I leaned a bit closer, making sure she saw I meant what I said. "I'll make sure Viktor never touches your daughters again."

Chapter 31
Deston

"The illustrious Lord Deston de Rayne, strung up like a traitor on the King's wall. May wonders never cease."

My already shallow breath shuddered out of my lungs. She could not possibly be here. *This could not be happening. Of all the possible developments in this shitty situation, this was the worst.*

That rich, sensual voice belonged to Queen Katarina and if she was here, things were about to get worse for all of us.

"My Queen." My mocking chuckle was little more than a whisper of sound. "I'd bow, but it seems my legs are not working at the moment."

"It's good to see you haven't lost your sense of humor, Deston," she said, eyeing the blood pooled below me. "Though I'm a bit surprised Viktor has not yet turned you into one of his pets." Her dark eyes glittered. "Think of it. You could be reunited with the rest of your family."

Katarina was a relic from the Dark Ages, when creatures like her were worshiped as gods. She was one of the few vampires on the planet older than myself and answered to no one. Rumor had it, she was one of the original two, from when we were cursed into existence.

I didn't put much stock in folklore, but she was the most powerful vampire alive, as well as the most corrupt queen to ever live. While I could normally hold my own, I was currently nailed to a wall and at somewhat of a disadvantage.

"How is Romania this time of year?"

"Hideously cold and dreary." She swiped her foot through my blood, painting a wide, red smear on the floor. "Though Louisiana is not much better. I expected it to be warmer."

"We're in the middle of a cold snap." This time, I did laugh. "Which thankfully keeps the smell down."

"I do miss our little chats, Deston," she called, disappearing into the hallway beneath me. "We will talk more when I return."

"I cannot fucking wait."

I looked over into Emmett's eyes, which were actually empty sockets since his actual eyeballs had melted away long ago.

"I am royally fucked, aren't I?"

Emmett, of course, didn't answer.

If Katarina was here, she already knew about Seraphina. Nothing else was important enough to bring that evil hag across the ocean. Hell, she hadn't shown her face after Lyra was killed, and that event had shaken our entire society to the core.

But a new queen rising out of nowhere? She'd be curious.

And a curious Katarina was the most dangerous thing of all.

Chapter 32
Seraphina

Hugh wasn't kidding.

Our suite, as he called it, was bigger than any house I'd ever lived in. Three bedrooms, an enormous living area, and floor-to-ceiling windows that looked out over the gardens.

We were surrounded by the trappings of wealth.

Unlimited wealth, from the looks of it. But as beautiful and luxurious as these rooms were, they still weren't home, no matter how grand the trappings. One day, I decided—one day I wanted somewhere to call my own.

A home nobody could take away or make me leave.

My body sagged with exhaustion when Luthor finally stepped in and closed the door behind him.

He took a long time before he turned to face me. I didn't know if he was still mad at me; I didn't know if I was still mad at him. I was too busy being happy we were safe.

"I sent Cyrus back out to cover our tracks and check on Ravenswood."

"To see if the revenants are still there?"

"No, to make sure the castle still is."

It took me a second to remember why. *The castle would stand so long as Deston lived.*

"And if it's still standing, what then?" I asked carefully. "You said we would get him out. Is that still true?"

"Of course, it is," Luthor said forcefully. "I already spoke to Hugh, and he's making some inquiries. He thinks there's a good chance that Deston is being held at the palace, and it seems Viktor may have him on his... *wall*."

I blanched the second the words were out of Luthor's mouth.

He lifted my hands, inspected my palms, frowned when he saw one was covered in angry, red blisters. "By your reaction, I assume you've seen it?" he asked quietly.

"Yeah." I pulled my hands away before he saw them tremble. "I've seen it."

Good God, what if he had Deston up on that wall? Nails in his legs. Nails in his arms. Nails in his hands. "Seraphina. Seraphina look at me. *Look at me.*" Luthor gripped my arms. He was shaking me, and I hadn't even noticed.

"We'll get him back. I swear to you that we will get him back, but you have to calm down."

First, I smelled the smoke. When I looked down at my feet, I found I'd burned an almost-perfect hole around myself, ruining the rug and the wood floor beneath it.

"Oh my God." Tears sprang to my eyes. "Oh, look what I did. We just got here, and I'm already wrecking everything." Somehow, I doubted Hugh would be able to snap his fingers and magically repair the damage.

"You're exhausted," Luthor soothed. "After the palace and what happened with Viktor, it's no wonder you have no control over your magic." He stroked my back, his big hands tracing my spine. "Everything will be okay. You need to sleep, you need to rest."

It had been a hellacious day, but even that was no excuse.

I plopped onto the bed. "I ruined everything," I admitted miserably. "I pushed Deston into something he knew was wrong. I manipulated him, Luthor, and I was proud of how well I did it. I convinced myself that what I wanted outweighed everything else. And now we're on the run again."

"You let curiosity get the better of you."

"No. It's more than that." He settled beside me. "I lost sight of who I am. *Who I want to be.* I don't want to be the sort of person who tricks people into doing things. I always thought I was better than that."

I couldn't even look him in the face. "But I wasn't better tonight, Luthor. I'm not queen material. I'm just...not."

He slid a finger beneath my chin, tipped my face up until I looked straight into his eyes. I nearly came undone. I was ashamed of what I'd done tonight, the way I'd manipulated Deston. After all my fancy speeches about building a better court, I'd stooped to the very tactics I despised.

Ever since I'd met him, Luthor held me in such high esteem. He didn't always agree with me, but he did respect me.

How could he respect me now, when I didn't even respect myself?

His face changed, his eyes softening, the blue glow turning warmer. I wanted to trace the scar running down the side of his face, but I was afraid he'd pull away. When he pressed a soft kiss to my cheek, the tears I'd been holding back spilled down my face.

"Thank you for letting me in." A smile curved his mouth. "I don't expect you to be perfect. I expect you to do your best, and if you fail, then to try again. You've never disappointed me. Not once. And showing me your real self, Seraphina, doesn't make me love you any less. In fact, it only makes me love you more." His gentle understanding only made me feel worse.

"And you are exactly the right person to be queen. If you didn't have regrets, if you didn't recognize your own failings, you'd be exactly like Viktor. That's not you. It's never been you." He kissed my tears away. "Nor will it ever be you."

"Okay." My voice went shaky. "Okay, I love you too."

This was no time for me to lose it. I had to keep it together.

There was nothing but concern in Luthor's eyes when he pushed my hair back. "*This is not your fault.* Viktor won't have Deston for much longer. Hugh has contacts, people he can call in a situation like this."

"Are we sure we want to involve him? I mean, he has a wife and three kids." I gestured at our surroundings. "He has a lot to lose, Luthor. Everything, as a matter of fact." He'd already lost one daughter, was it fair to ask for more? "What we're doing..."

"It's one thing for us to take the risk. But I won't ask anyone else to put their lives on the line for me."

"You won't do the asking, I will," he said firmly. "And once we have de Rayne back..." His voice trailed off at the same time his gaze slid sway. "Then we'll discuss our new arrangement."

"I don't want a new arrangement." I gripped his forearms and brought him closer, laying my head on his chest. "It will be me, you, and Cyrus, just like always. I won't let anything change that."

My heart felt dull, as if it knew I was lying.

Except I wasn't. This whole thing between me and Deston was nothing but a business deal. Except the more I told myself that, the more that didn't feel like the truth.

No, something had changed between me and Deston. Things were different.

We were different.

And while things between us were changing—*had changed*—I was determined not to lose Luthor, who had been my rock for months and months. Or Cyrus, who made me laugh at every turn and never, ever would betray me.

I had everything I needed. The truth was, I didn't want things to be different. I knew where all the males in my life belonged.

I put my arms around Luthor's neck, laced my fingers through his hair, tugged him down to me. Brushed a soft kiss on his mouth. I would not jeopardize what we had together. We'd made promises that I would keep, because that's who I was.

Because despite my mistakes tonight, I was someone who kept her word.

I would push this bullshit between me and Deston to the side.

"It's the three of us remember? Just like we promised," I told him firmly. "That's what we decided, and that's how things will be from now on."

Luthor splayed his hand on my face, tipped my face back. He kissed me slowly and thoroughly, as if reminding himself of what I tasted like. And when he pulled back, I wished I could erase the worry from his eyes.

"As you wish, my Queen."

I STRIPPED DOWN, got in the shower, and stayed in just long enough to rinse most of the dirt and blood off. I fell face-first into bed and passed out before I even pulled the covers up.

Hours later, I woke up with Cyrus pressed into my front

and Luthor behind me, his heavy arm pulling me in tight. They were both fast asleep, and for a moment, I savored the absolute luxury of being warm, safe, and with two males I loved more than anything.

They were my shield against this dark new world, my protection against the evil I didn't yet understand. They were everything I needed, and even more than that, they were everything I'd ever wanted. I was safe with them.

I should have been happy to bask in this dreamy feeling, but curiosity got the better of me.

"You're back," I whispered, poking Cyrus in the side. "What did you find? Is Deston's castle still there?"

"Every miserable inch of it." My heart leapt. He wasn't dead. "Now let me get some sleep. It's been a hellaciously long night."

If the light streaming in through the curtains was any indication, it was daytime.

I didn't know how long I'd slept, but at least a couple of hours. Luthor grumbled when I slid out from underneath his heavy arm, and I kissed his cheek. "Stay here and sleep. I'm hungry, and I bet you are too. I'll bring us back a plate of food."

In truth, I wanted to scope this place out, get a better feel for Hugh and Lilliana Cormier, and yeah, I was *starving*.

Lilliana had left me an assortment of clothes, and Tessa and I were about the same size, as it turned out. I pulled on a featherlight sweater and a pair of soft black leggings before I padded downstairs.

I stopped briefly to inspect the grooves cut into the floor, as if to assure myself that they were real before I continued toward the back of the house, where I hoped the kitchen was. I didn't know the layout of the house, but I smelled food. Cookies, I decided, my nose held high in the air. *Chocolate chip* cookies if I wasn't mistaken.

I stopped in the kitchen doorway, caught between hunger and curiosity.

Two young girls were fishing a finger full of creamy dough into their mouths. The kitchen counter was covered in flour, utensils, and dirty mixing bowls, and there were cookies *everywhere*.

Cooling racks filled with every kind of cookie I can imagine.

"You're up. *Finally*," the younger girl said, finger halfway to her mouth. She looked like a doll, nearly white-blond hair pulled back, showing off clear blue eyes rimmed with impossibly long lashes.

"We thought you'd sleep for a few more hours," the older girl said. She was a slightly older version of her sister, with dark blond hair that fell in a long straight sheath down her back, but her eyes were every bit as crystal clear.

"I'm Adalia," the older girl said, "and this is my sister Madison."

"Maddie," the young girl corrected sternly, helping herself to a generous double-fingered scoop of cookie dough.

I dove in as well, my finger cutting a groove into the creamy brown batter. When I popped it into my mouth... well, this had to be what heaven tasted like.

"You didn't get any chocolate chips," Madison pointed out. "You have to have chocolate chips."

"I actually like the dough better than the chocolate chips if you can believe it."

"Oh, I can believe it," Adalia said. "The batter's the best part. Maddie's the opposite, though. She loves the chips."

"Tessa used to sneak whole bags of chocolate chips into

my room. Just so I'd have a snack," Maddie said before her face fell. "But now she's gone."

"Maybe we can figure out a way to bring her back," I offered, savoring the salty sweet dough melting in my mouth. *Real butter, that had to be the secret.* "Maybe we can bring her back *and* stop Viktor, what would you think about that?"

Adalia regarded me for a long moment before she spoke. "There are others who have tried to stop Viktor, you know. And remember what happened to them."

"What?"

I shrugged at their confused expressions. "I'm brand new, still learning the ropes, so to speak. Heck, I just got my fangs barely three months ago."

"Oh, let me see them." Madison leaned forward with an eager expression. "Tessa got hers early, and Adalia should get hers any day now. I'm hoping mine come in before I'm fifteen."

I lifted my lip and pushed them down. The sensation as they popped free of my gums always felt foreign but was even stranger now that I was on display in front of an audience. Kind of like performance anxiety.

"Oh, they look so sharp," Madison said, wiggling on her chair. "Do you ever bite your tongue?"

"All the time, and it's horrible. It hurts worse than you'd think."

"Maddie you're being rude," Adalia said. "Father and Mother said that we needed to be nice to our guests. Not treat them like animals in a zoo."

"It's okay," I said, laughing. "All of this is new to me too. I don't know how to act and what to say or even what's right."

"I went to human school for two years," Adelia said.

"They're pretty much like us except they don't drink blood, and don't have to worry about being eaten by revenants all the time."

"Is that really what it's like? All the time?" I asked softly.

She thought about it. "It might be easier if you're a boy." Adalia frowned. "But being a girl is risky. That's what Mom says, anyway. Tessa's the only one who's gotten away from Viktor."

"Ever?" I asked.

"*Ever*." Adalia said firmly. "But now she's gone."

"So are Markus and Rafael," Madison added. "And Caden and Silas too. They all left after the night King Viktor brought the revenants to our dinner party. But Father said when it's safe, they'll come home."

"We'll figure out a way to get them all back," I told them. "We'll get them back, and we'll fix this. No more revenants, no more Viktor, no more fear."

"Don't make promises that you can't keep." Adalia fixed me with the level stare of someone much older. "Father always said to make sure you can back up your words with actions."

"Well, that's a good point." I nodded. "How about this? I'll do my very best to make that happen. I want to stop all the bad things Viktor does for good."

"Adelia. Maddie." Lilliana soft voice was sharp with warning. "Remember what we talked about? Caution in everything we say?"

The slight woman swept into the room, put herself between me and her two children. I didn't blame her one bit; in fact, I admired her. Living in this world, being female... I shuddered to think of the constant fear she must feel.

"I apologize." Lilliana inclined her head, keeping an eye

on me the whole time. "They know better than to lecture an elder, especially a queen." Lilliana might be china-doll beautiful, but beneath her fragile exterior was the strength of a lioness.

"Actually, they did me a big favor," I explained. "I don't know anything about your world. I don't know anything about being a vampire. I don't know much of anything, in fact." I offered her a tentative smile. "I just learned more in five minutes than I have in three months."

Part of me wondered if I was doing the right thing, but I had to trust someone.

"I've been running from Viktor my entire life. Ever since I was a kid, younger than Maddie. All I ever had was my mom, and my gram. And while I don't know what it's like to live under Viktor's rule, I'm well acquainted with how he deals out pain and punishment. I mean to put an end to all of this."

Lilliana started wiping handfuls of flour into her hands. But I didn't miss the way they trembled when she tossed it into the sink.

"We are honored that you are here, my Queen." Her words were cautious, measured. *Careful.* "But there are many who tried to defeat Viktor in the past. They've all died."

She fixed me with a contemplative look. "Perhaps it would be better to go into hiding. There are places across the Atlantic where Viktor would never find you. Hugh could make some arrangements."

"That's a tempting offer," I said, even while I knew it would be impossible. Viktor would search for me, no matter how far away I went, and would eventually find me. People would die. Plus, I knew human—vampire—nature. There would always be someone willing to sell me out for the right price. "But I've been running my entire life. I've decided it is time to stop."

Lilliana paused her cleaning long enough to look at me. "You remind me of Contessa," she said, wiping the last of the flour off the counter. "She fights for what she believes in. And while she may be a bit unconventional, she has a good heart."

"I'd like to meet her someday," I told her, "She sounds like someone I could be friends with, if my life ever stops being a complete disaster."

Lilliana ran her hands over Madison's head. "Perhaps someday you will, if we are lucky."

Adalia popped another cookie into her mouth, eying me curiously.

"You really don't know anything about the Darkfell Clan?"

"I know a little about the royal houses, and that the Marvelles and Fontaines were wiped out in the coup. But not much more." I perched my butt on a bar stool and helped myself to more cookie dough. I'd regret eating all this sugar, I just knew it. I should be hydrating and eating healthy. But cookie dough did things for my soul that lettuce and water wouldn't.

"You don't know *all* the houses?" Maddie asked incredulously.

I smiled down at her. "Well, now I know about the Cormiers." I nodded gratefully to Lilliana. "And I'm a Marvelle, Luthor is a Fontaine, which means technically, those houses still exist. And Cyrus is from House Rayne."

Maddie waved her hand in the air. "None of those houses even *matter*," Maddie said so matter-of-factly while her mother looked like she might collapse from embarrassment.

I felt like the new kid in school, anxious to show that I wasn't a complete idiot. "Oh, I know about the Carpathians too. Viktor's house."

"There is also House Dubois, House Gauthier and House Bouderaux." Maddie said, counting them off on her fingers.

Deston would like her, I decided, they had similar means of making their arguments.

"Okay, then tell me about House Dubois," I urged. "I may have heard Luthor mention them, but other than the name, I don't know anything about them."

"Oh, they're the scary ones," Madison said, moving from chocolate chips to what looked like sugar cookies. She slid one across the counter to me, and I took a bite. Still warm, crystalized sugar on top, the edges crispy. It was perfect, or maybe I was just hungry.

"Octavio and Brooks Dubois, they're twins, right, Mother?"

Lilliana nodded faintly.

"They're spies, like the ones on human TV shows. Father calls them the spiders, and with their long arms, they kind of look like it. They are perfectly awful, if you ask me."

Lilliana mussed up her daughter's hair affectionately. "The Queen doesn't want to hear about our boring lives, Maddie. She's tired, she's hungry, and she has bigger things to worry about."

"On the contrary, I've been trying to figure out how everything works around here, so this is very helpful." I nodded to Madison. "Go on, Octavio and Brooks, the twins that look like spiders?"

"Madison is correct," Lilliana said, though she looked troubled. "Dubois House is headed by two twin brothers, Octavio and Brooks. They... provide information to the king. Among other services," Lilliana said with an uneasy glance at her daughters. There was obviously more she wanted to say about the Dubois, and if she didn't want her girls to hear, I was sure I didn't want them to hear it, either.

"What's the next house?" I helped myself to another cookie. They really were perfect.

"That would be House Gauthier. *Might makes right*," Adalia mimed in a mock deep voice. "They're an army. Or at least, their sire runs the army."

"And what are they like?" I asked, keeping my gaze on Lilliana.

"Oh, they're big and loud and they come to all the royal banquets. They have four sons, Gunner, Justice, Crew and Caden." Her face fell. "I liked Caden the best, but he's been gone a long time. I think he..."

Noticing Lilliana's barely perceptible head shake, I decided to move on.

"What about House Bouderaux?"

"Oh, that's the easy one. They're the richest." Lilliana's slight wince made Maddie giggle. "They are, Mother. They have so much money. What does Father call them, Mother? The Bank?"

Lilliana sighed, looking at her daughter with a long-suffering expression. "Madison is correct. House Bouderaux funds the throne, pays for Viktor's mercenaries, and collects the taxes."

"There are vampire taxes?" I asked, then decided it was kind of an obvious question. Of course, they had taxes. Like the human world, vampires would need a source of income to keep the government going.

Taxes were *always* the answer.

"There are, and House Bouderaux sets the yearly rate.

For instance, the rate for the current year is forty-eight percent."

"But that's...half of your earnings." That was a staggering amount, and while the royal houses may be able to afford it, I doubted a regular family could. "It must be difficult for most people to get by on what's left."

"It is yet another way Viktor controls us. If you can't afford your taxes..." Her voice dropped so only I could hear it. "Viktor claims your children for his servants."

"That's indentured servitude."

"Except it never ends," Lilliana murmured. "Once he has you, he never lets you go."

I sat back, my appetite long gone. "So, we have the bank, the military, and the spies? Is that all of them?"

"Just like the human world," Lilliana said. "Except in our world, everyone gets a seat at the table. It's just that some of those seats are bigger than others."

"I understand," I told her, starting to piece things together. "I have some more questions, Lilliana." I kept my voice light and easy. "I wondered if you might have five minutes to spare? Girls, would you mind if I steal your mom for a little while?"

Her eyes—the exact same shade as both her daughter's —flew open in surprise. "Girls, it's time to start your schoolwork. I'll be up to check on you in a moment."

I rubbed my forehead. "They have school? What day is it? I've completely lost track."

"It's a Tuesday," she said kindly, putting some cookies on a plate and sliding it over to me before she poured me a cup of coffee.

"After what you've gone through, keeping track of time shouldn't be a priority."

"No, it sure isn't," I said quietly. "Staying alive has been all I can manage these last few months."

"How did you end up here?" She laughed nervously when I began to answer. "No, that's the wrong question. I'm just curious how you got to where you are. No one has seen the Marvelle family in a century, and I have to admit... nothing about you is what I expected."

"Well, I think that's a good thing." I chewed on a cookie. "I have to say, my experience with other vampires hasn't been reassuring. Seeing all of this..." I indicated the cheery kitchen, the piles of cookies. "This seems so normal, especially after living at Deston's."

Her face tightened up again. "Deston de Rayne is not a stellar example of our kind."

"I sure hope not." I blew on the coffee. "But he does have his charms." *Why was I defending him?* "Meeting you, and your family... gives me hope for the future. There are a lot of things I mean to change if I ever become Queen."

"I'll take that as a great compliment." Lilliana steepled her fingers, setting her chin on them.

"House Dubois is the one you have to watch out for. Octavio and Brooks are ruthless. Completely willing to betray anyone for the right price. They are an integral part of the King's inner court and lurk around in the shadows, looking for anything they can use to their benefit. Personally, I don't let my children within fifty feet of them."

"Which means they aren't possible allies. What about the Gauthiers? How strong are their ties to Viktor?"

"Renard Gauthier is a bit older than Vane Carpathian, Viktor's sire, but I hear there is a strong bond between the two males. My daughter..." Her gaze drifted off as she weighed how much to tell me.

"Caden Gauthier is... one of Tessa's lovers. We can trust

him. But Lord Renard? I just don't know. He's served Viktor for many years and has done terrible things in the name of the crown."

"If we could bring Renard over to our side," I reasoned, "then perhaps we could exert some control over Viktor's army."

"Mercenaries," Lilliana corrected. "In addition to the Knightsguard, Viktor uses paid mercenaries, arranged by Renard."

"Okay, attacked by mercenaries, which sounds even worse."

I did a Deston and counted off on my fingers. "So House Dubois is out, House Gauthier is a tentative maybe. That leaves us House Bouderaux. Where do they stand?"

"To make a lot of money if Viktor stays in power." Her face fell. "If they hear your speech about making changes, if they have any inkling they'll lose money if you take power, they'll do everything they can to prevent you ascending the throne."

"Good point. No speeches, got it."

"You are so different from anyone I've ever met before."

"God," I said, taking a gulp of coffee, feeling the caffeine jolt my brain into working properly, "I sure hope so, given the vampires I've met so far."

"Tessa had a run-in with Viktor two months ago. He almost..." Her hand shook when she picked up her cup, and she took a long sip. "Tessa and her males stood up against him and nearly lost their lives. She escaped but now she's in hiding, and Viktor's offered a large reward for her capture. Hugh and I... we'd like to help you, we really would."

She glanced at the ceiling. "But we have two other daughters to worry about. I can't allow anything to happen to them." I understood that note of sheer desperation in her voice. I'd heard too many late night arguments between Mom and Gram that had that same grave urgency.

"I appreciate you allowing me to stay here. As soon as we find another place to go, I will be out of your hair."

"I wish..." Her mouth trembled, then firmed. "I wish I could do more, but Viktor already has his sights on Adalia. I'm sorry, my Queen, I can't put my child in his direct path. I just can't."

Chapter 33
Deston

Tiresome.

That's what torture was, tiresome.

I was beyond tired of hearing the dripping of my own blood.

Tired of expending precious energy healing my wounds while my weight pulled against the nails holding me to the wall, my flesh tearing with every shallow breath.

So far, I stayed ahead of the damage, and normally, this would be a little more than a nuisance. But I was still weak from the fight with the revenants, from not feeding regularly, from too many things to count.

I did have the family ring back on my finger, though I hoped it didn't end up in a revenant's stomach. Or on a revenant's front paw, like my sire's. Wouldn't *that* be a waste.

Three days, I told myself.

Survive for three days, long enough for Hugh to get Seraphina to get out of the country and to safety, and then I could let go. Go into the Pale and be done with this useless life.

"So, tell me what you did to end up on Viktor's bad side?"

I stared down at Queen Katarina in her finery. She turned slightly, checked her ass in one of the mirrors.

Viktor couldn't have come up with a worse torture himself.

"Oh, you know, the usual. Murder and mayhem, with a bit of breaking and entering thrown in for good measure." My voice remained light and playful, but inside...

Inside I felt an emotion I'd long become inured to. Fear.

"Viktor seems to think that you found a new queen to replace him."

She forgot about me for a moment as she ordered a Knightsguard to fetch a chair, which she strategically placed just so, where she could see herself in the mirrors, the dim lighting complimenting her pale complexion. By the time the guard left, the table groaned under the weight of fruit and meats and wine beside her. She filled a crystal glass, sniffed, then took a sip.

"You look comfortable."

"And why shouldn't I be?" she asked. "I wasn't foolish enough to cross Viktor. You know how vindictive he is, Deston. You should have stayed on his good side. That's what I do."

"You just got here," I observed. "Give it some time. I'm sure by tonight there's a good chance you'll be up here beside me." I shuddered at the thought.

"Oh, Deston, you are quite the jester. As if I would allow myself to be trapped by my own blood." Katarina slowly poured another glass of wine, her glittering eyes scanning the empty chamber behind her before she turned back to me.

"I'm curious about this new queen. My guess is, she's young and naïve. Am I right?"

"And you said you knew Viktor?" I asked, careful to keep my voice neutral. "He sees conspiracies in the shadows. If I had a new queen waiting in the wings, don't you think she'd be on the throne already?"

"Not untrained," she pointed out, sipping her wine. "If she's young and untrained, you wouldn't take the chance. You'd make sure she was at her strongest before she faced Viktor." Her smile showed a wine-stained fang.

"Come now, Deston, let's not pretend we are strangers. You and I spent enough time together. You have no secrets from me. You've been working to replace Viktor for years now. My gut tells me... you're close."

There was good reason Katarina was the unchallenged Queen of the Brasov Clan.

She was ruthless, corrupt to the core, and completely without morals. She'd killed her true mate and replaced him with someone even more ruthless than herself. Once that male served his purpose, his head decorated her castle keep until the skull turned to dust.

By killing her mate, she'd become the most powerful vampire in the world.

Good thing I was a clever bastard, even back then.

I'd killed the male, negotiated my freedom, and moved here, as far away as I could get from Romania. If I ever went back to that hellhole, she would break me.

"I wish all of that were true," I admitted. "But I'll repeat myself. There is no new queen, there hasn't been in a hundred years. Viktor wastes his time hunting down rumors, when he should be focused on running the kingdom."

Her smile turned even more serpentine.

"Let's forget about this queen business at the moment and turn to the real reason for my visit." She shook her head. "It pains me, seeing you up on that wall. I would like to make you an offer."

Here it comes, I thought to myself. *She thinks this is her big chance to get me to do her bidding. When I'd sooner die up here than work for the desiccated old crone.*

"You shall come back with me to Romania. Serve at my side." Her poisonous gaze flicked up my battered body as quickly as her tongue flicked out to wet her lips. "You know what I want, Deston. Stop fighting me and just give in."

"Romania is too cold. Besides, I'm perfectly happy here in the States. Starbucks on every corner, high-speed internet, Taco Tuesdays. Tell me you're not jealous?"

"I know you miss France," she said, running her finger along the edge of the glass, a faint ringing filling the air. It made the iron running through my body quiver, sending shivers of pain through me. But I shut that down. Pain was something to endure at this point. I couldn't let anything cloud my head while this viper was so close.

"Come to Romania, and I will let your young queen live." She looked up at me with those glittering black eyes, and there wasn't a shred of mercy in her face. "What was her name again?" She licked her lips.

"Ah yes. Seraphina Marvelle."

My heart stopped beating completely when that obscene mouth spoke my true mate's name.

"Seraphina, correct?" Her smile turned predatory. "Claire Marvelle's granddaughter, I believe. *If* my sources are correct, and they always are."

"The Marvelle line died out a long time ago, as you well know, Katarina. As did the Fontaines. Viktor made sure of that."

"Viktor's made mistakes in the past." A ghost of a smile flitted across her face. "I trust my source. *Explicitly.*"

My mind raced. There were only a handful of people that knew Seraphina existed, and none of them would betray her. How the ancient Queen had gotten this information I didn't know, but I had to talk her out of it, and fast.

"It's a beautiful name, though," I mused. "Lyra would've liked it, had she lived long enough to have children. Too bad that didn't happen, though I suppose one of her lovers might have fathered a secret child."

One thing about Katarina, she hated Lyra with the strength of a hundred suns. Bringing her name up should change the direction of this conversation.

"Lyra Marvelle was a weak, pathetic excuse for a queen, with a narrow vision for the future," Katarina snapped. "She deserved to die. You should know since you were the one who stepped aside and allowed Viktor to take the throne."

Fuck.

"That's right, my love. Don't forget, I know all your dirty little secrets. If you are under the impression that you will install a new queen on the throne and stand at her side as her trusted advisor, know this." She took her time pouring her next glass.

"Banish that fantasy from your thoughts. Should you attempt to replace Viktor on the Darkfell throne, I will make sure every vampire alive—including the High Council Elders—know about your role in Lyra's downfall."

Everything inside me went deathly still at her threat.

"Every. Dirty. Detail." She tapped her nails on the table for effect.

She raised her glass in a toast. "You looked the other way. You gave Viktor the opening he needed. Which means ultimately, *you* put Viktor on the throne that day." She took another delicate sip.

"Don't be so foolish to think that you can convince a

young, naïve female that you are some sort of hero, when we both know you will stab her in the back at your first opportunity." She raised her glass again. "I should know. Like recognizes like, doesn't it, my love?"

"What do you want from me, Katarina? Fly back to Romania and torture your own doomed court. As you can see, I have a full plate at the moment."

"Oh, there's definitely something to be said about having a captive audience." She swirled the wine in her glass.

"Let me tell you what I think. You found the next Dark-fell Queen. She is young and untried and naïve to the point of being useless. I think you were in the process of training her when Viktor flushed you out, and now she's on the run, alone and scared." Katarina stood, smoothing down her dress.

"I think if I could find this... *Seraphina Marvelle*, it wouldn't take much for me to convince her I was her ally, that I could help her rescue you from Viktor's evil grasp. If I know you at all, the poor thing's already more than a little in love with you. In fact, she is positively *fascinated* by your dark, brooding personality. Maybe she even thinks she can save you."

It was nearly impossible to stop my shaking. Everything she said was true, including the part where she could convince Seraphina. Seraphina's soft heart compelled her to trust nearly everyone, and when the most powerful Queen in the world got hold of her, she'd be putty in her hands.

"You look worried Deston, did I hit a nerve?"

"I'm not worried Katarina, I'm amused. If you think I'd risk keeping a newborn queen in close proximity to the king she's looking to replace, you have more faith in my ability than I do."

She threw back the last of her wine and set the glass on the table with a loud click.

"You're lying, friend."

Her audible breath was a dull echo in the empty room.

"You, Deston, are the source of my information. And your innermost thoughts never, ever lie to me because I know your heart, every bit as well as I do my own."

That was impossible, I would never...

"The bond, Deston, my darling. Did you forget about our soul bond, the holiest of all bonds?"

"You broke the bond yourself, after I did your dirty work, Katarina." Not only had she broken it, I'd had Marie confirm the damn thing was gone. *She had to be lying.* Surely, I'd know if I was still soul-bound to this monstrous female.

"Did I, now?" Her predatory smile promised me not only how wrong I was, but I'd be paying for my impudence. "Do you truly think I would allow you to escape me? It amused me to watch you serve Darkfell queen after Darkfell queen, when all the while I stripped information from your unknowing mind."

Her face grew hard while horror consumed me. "It amused me, knowing you betrayed Lyra, then existed in disgraced isolation, a prisoner of your own guilt and anger. Imagine my surprise when I discovered that dismal period of your life had ended."

She wrapped her coat around her. "When Viktor told me you had returned to the fold, had traded your precious cousin's life for a human girl and Luthor Fontaine, I called him a liar. It pains me to discover he was, in fact, telling the truth."

I kept quiet. There was no good way to play this, except wait to see what she planned to do.

Then stop her.

"You were always mine, Deston. *Always*. I allowed you a hint of freedom, and look what you did with my generosity? Betrayed my kin. *Betrayed me*."

Numbly, I noted her dark red coat perfectly matched her lips.

Both of them, the color of blood.

"Knowing the Darkfells like I do, your young queen has only two potential allies. I believe I shall begin with the Cormiers. I heard their eldest recently disappeared, but they have two young daughters left."

Her predatory smile was the sort you'd see on a circling vulture. "I wonder if they'll be willing to trade your queen for the lives of their own children?"

Chapter 34
Seraphina

Luthor, Cyrus, and I were sprawled across the bed, the empty plate of cookie crumbs between us.

"You two look more tired than me," I told them, which was almost kind given we all looked terrible. On the positive side of things, both my hands were healed, which meant I was back in the magic business.

"We were up until dawn talking with Hugh," Luthor yawned. "He had some interesting suggestions for freeing Deston from the palace."

My heart leapt, higher than it should have. "Do you care to share your plans?" I smiled teasingly. "Or will you be leaving me out of the planning stages, per usual?"

They shared a glance, one that didn't include me. "Let's find out where he's at with his arrangements. Then we'll tell you what we're thinking."

"You're really leaving me out of this?" I'd been joking and was seriously offended they were not telling me what they were up to. "Come on, Luthor. What are you three working on?"

"Hugh is organizing more manpower." Luthor evaded. "Let's just leave it at that for now. I don't want to get your hopes up in case this doesn't work out."

"Fair enough." Really though, there was nothing fair about being left in the dark.

"Since you don't want to include me, I'll go practice." All those cookies made me jittery, not to mention my head hurt from the sugar buzz. I might as well do something with all my nervous energy.

"Practice? Magic?" Cyrus's grin took up his entire face. "Don't forget, my cousin's not here to clean up after you."

Just hearing him say that out loud sent a stab of pain through my heart. "I'm well aware of that, and I'll try my best to make my magic behave."

"Take care, Seraphina," Luthor said gravely. "Don't stray too far from the house. Hugh assured me that this place is well warded, and Cyrus confirmed that last night, but we're out in the open now. We have to be careful."

"When am I not careful?" I teased, tousling his hair, then kissing his nose for good measure.

"Maybe you should stay inside," Cyrus suggested. "Just until we get a feel for the situation."

"No," I said softly. "I have to learn to control my magic while I still have time to practice." I shrugged off their obvious concern and decided to come clean. "Deston was right. I really haven't been trying all that hard these past few months."

"Don't say that, Seraphina," Cyrus argued. "You've been..."

"No. I'm telling you that he was right. Deep down inside..."

I might as well just tell them. "I didn't want to be a queen. I didn't want the responsibility. I didn't think I was ready. Subconsciously, I've been dragging my feet."

Luthor looked at me for a long moment before he spoke. "And now? What's changed?"

"Everything." I looked out the window for a moment,

trying to organize my thoughts. "Viktor's got Deston. But more than that, I realized the stakes are higher than just us. Viktor's ruining families, everyone lives in fear. Before last night, this whole fight seemed so far off, but..."

I rubbed my forehead, trying to get the ache to go away. "Now it's real. Viktor's coming for me, and if I'm not ready..."

I couldn't say the words out loud. I couldn't say that if I wasn't ready, Viktor would kill all of us. I couldn't say that if I wasn't ready, Hugh and Lilliana and their daughters would die.

"I have to be prepared. I have to figure out my magic, and I have to be ready the next time Viktor attacks. But first, let's get Deston back." Everything hinged on that. I wasn't sure why, but every instinct told me his welfare was most important.

Luthor's face changed. Actually, the atmosphere in the room changed, becoming colder, charged with tension.

"Once we get him back, then what?

"I don't know. But one thing's for sure. Viktor will come after us, so I can't afford to be the weakest link anymore."

Luthor, ever the gentleman, started to protest, and I shook my head, stopping him. "It's true, and you know it. You and Cyrus have been doing all the heavy lifting to give me time to get my bearings. Deston did his best to walk me through the magic part.

"I didn't take advantage of the time we had, and now I don't have a choice. I have to figure this out." I took Luthor's hand and gave it a squeeze. "I'll keep practicing while you two find us allies." I managed a weak smile.

"If we get Deston back, then he can go back to doing whatever he does."

"Even if we manage that, we've lost our inside access to

the royal court," Cyrus pointed out. "Which leaves us blind."

Luthor pulled his hand out of mine. "And when Deston's back, what then?"

"If you're worried about Deston..." My heart felt heavy because, of course, Luthor was worried. Despite how strong my feelings were for Deston, my resolve to keep my word was stronger. This was an impossible situation, but I knew what I had with Luthor and Cyrus.

I wasn't going to mess that up.

"Don't be. I won't deny something's changed between us. Maybe because he fed from me, maybe there's more, but bottom line, I still don't trust him enough to let him into our partnership."

"Fina, we can sort this all out later," Cyrus said gently. "Let's see if Hugh comes through on his promise and get my cousin out of prison. If we're all still alive after that, we can sort out personal shit."

"No, we get this settled now, before we go to the palace. I can't go another day with this weighing on me. and on you." I ran my hand up Luthor's stiff arm.

"I made you both a promise, and I mean to keep my word. I cannot imagine my life without you. Either of you. I will not jeopardize what we have, not for a second, not even for Deston. I'm sorry I lied to you. My decision had nothing to do with how much I trust you, it was just..."

"You knew I'd stop you?" Luthor tensed beneath my fingers, and I slid my hand down, grasped his, then reached out to Cyrus. "You are the most important people in my life. I can't stand the thought of making either of you unhappy or disappointed."

Cyrus grabbed my hand, squeezed hard, giving me a lopsided grin.

"Yes, I knew you'd stop me. But that wasn't the whole reason."

Luthor hadn't pulled away from me yet, so I kept on going.

"I just wanted to have my way on this *one thing*. I've spent the last three months—my entire time as a vampire —doing what everyone else tells me to do. I guess I just thought it would be nice to do something by myself for once."

"I... I never looked at it that way." Luthor looked thoughtful, then touched my face. "I thought you didn't trust me, Seraphina. I thought you didn't trust us." He looked at Cyrus, and after a second's hesitation, Cyrus nodded.

"Maybe that's what this looked like, but that's not what this was about. I just..." I clasped my hands in my lap. "Ever since Viktor snatched me off the streets, my life has been completely out of my control. Mind you, I didn't have a lot of control over my life before, but now I don't have control over anything."

I steeled myself and looked up at Luthor, his blue eyes drilling through me.

"I know I made a bad decision, a huge mistake, in convincing Deston to take me to the palace. But I knew neither of you would let me go, and I had to find out what Mom's big secret was." I choked off my laugh. "Little did I know..."

My voice trailed off as I realized I still hadn't told them about Lyra.

I should tell them. I had to tell them.

They should know Lyra was still alive, but after keeping her existence a secret for this long, I didn't even know how to begin explaining.

"I understand," Luthor admitted in a hushed voice. "We should have realized we were smothering you. We certainly saw how frustrated you were. If practicing will make you feel better, then you should practice," Luthor said quietly. "At least with Deston gone, you won't have anyone swearing at you in French."

"Huge bonus, for sure," I joked, even though my heart cracked open a little wider, every time someone mentioned his name. I had to figure out how to compartmentalize my conflicted feelings for him. Once I managed that, he'd stop being a distraction.

"You go practice." Luthor kissed my hand. "As soon as we have a concrete plan, we'll let you know what the next step is. Deal?"

"Deal," I said, feeling him relax beneath my touch. We were making progress, but I'd done serious damage to the trust between us when I'd gone behind his back to the palace, damage I still had to mend.

"Okay. Let me see if I can manage to get through a couple of hours without destroying the Cormier's lovely property, and then you can tell me what comes next. Can you at least give me a hint of our plan so I don't look like an idiot if anyone asks me?"

"Let's just say Hugh is arranging backup. If things work out, we'll be ready to roll by tonight."

A thrill of excitement mixed with fear went through me. We were finally going to get Deston back, after hours of just talking about it.

"Look at you, Cyrus. Scanning the internet has really paid off."

"I know, right? There's this thing called tick-tock, like the clock..."

"Let's stay focused, Cyrus," Luthor said. "We have a

long way to go before you have any more free time on your hands to scroll the interweb."

Twenty minutes later, I was alone in the middle of the woods. I'd trudged through one perfectly manicured garden after the next and realized I just didn't have the heart to destroy any of them.

I didn't have Deston here to fix things for me, and as much as I liked to speechify about taking care of myself, I had to face facts.

I needed my males to do some stuff for me.

At least until I could figure out how to do that stuff myself.

"Alrighty then, let's see if I can manage to cast magic without causing a forest fire."

I gathered a small ball of magic in my hand, let it grow, lifted it over the tops of the trees, and dropped back down. Aside from a few leaves that drifted down, I'd managed to not destroy a single thing.

An hour later, I was weaving streams of magic through the massive tree trunks, threading them through sliver-like openings and, so far, hadn't even singed the bark.

Maybe not having an audience was the key.

Or maybe, as much as I hated to admit the truth, Deston had been right. The problem had been me all along. I didn't know what had changed, but I almost felt like I was getting the hang of this vampire queen shit.

"Very good."

I spun around and found Lilliana watching me.

At least it *looked* like Lilliana, right down to her straight, blonde hair. I couldn't quite pinpoint what exactly was different about her, but I knew to my bones that this was not Maddie and Adalia's mother.

In a second, I raised every single protection I had, shuttering my mind, drawing Luthor's power to me, readied my magic, hoping this would all be enough.

"Thanks." I kept my hands loose at my side, just in case whoever this was decided to take a run at me.

"It's a lot harder than it looks, isn't it?" Not-Lilliana took a step closer. Every nerve in my body constricted. Fight or flight took over as I realized I was reacting to the power that drifted off her in sheets. I knew I'd never met anyone this powerful, not Viktor.

Not even Deston.

I double checked the shield around my mind, frantically going through everything Cyrus had taught me. She stood between me and the house, and I knew without a doubt that I'd never make it past her.

"I thought you went to the store?" I asked curiously. "Are you back already?"

After the briefest hesitation, she smiled. Her face changed, became something else entirely, especially paired with the odd tilt of her head. "I'm back, it only took a minute." She took a step forward, the leaves crunching beneath her feet.

I held my ground. If her intention was to herd me deeper into the forest, then she'd kill me the second I lost sight of the house. Or rather, the house lost sight of me.

"I suppose you're out here to finish up that chat we had started earlier?"

"Yes, that's exactly why I'm here." Another brief hesitation. "Seraphina."

This woman—whoever she was—knew my name. That meant none of us were safe.

I had no idea how to play this. If Viktor sent this woman—and there was no doubt in my mind he had—implicating the Cormiers would be a death penalty for the family, if they were even still alive. If they were dead, then I was next.

If they were alive, then I couldn't implicate Lilliana or Hugh in any way. Nor could I let her know about Luthor and Cyrus.

"I have to thank you again for helping me last night. But after my car broke down, I didn't know what else to do. I appreciate you letting me stay here until it gets fixed."

The smallest hint of surprise crossed her face. "Ah yes, the broken-down car. And where were you heading again?"

"Ohio. Cleveland, actually. I have family there. After I lost my job, it was the only place I could think to go. But I expect the garage will call any minute and tell me my car's done." I shrugged my shoulders. "Then I'll be headed north."

"Perhaps you should stay here, with your own kind?" Not-Lilliana said. "We have lots of room."

There it was.

This woman knew my name, knew I was a vampire. Viktor had sent her to kill me, and nobody was here to save me this time.

I bounced nervously on the balls of my feet, leaves crackling merrily beneath my boots. "I appreciate the offer, but I have family waiting for me up there."

"Seraphina, you know you're welcome here." The woman offered me her hand, and I eyed it doubtfully. "We are friends, after all."

If I touched her, what would happen? Could she read my mind? Even with my mental barrier? Would she dematerialize me away?

I tucked my hand away. Her eyes flashed dangerously, and something dark and cold crept through my head, like scuttling spiders or scraping revenant claws, poking, trying to cut their way in. I threw everything I had into protecting my mind from her invasion.

After a moment, frustration crinkled the corners of her mouth. A swell of relief poured through me, and I forced myself to smile up at her. Forced myself to speak the lies she expected to hear.

"I don't know what I would've done without your help. It's hard, especially..." I let my voice trail off helplessly. "Especially being a vampire."

"All by yourself with nowhere to go," she mused. "You're so lucky to have found us. Even so far from the city. And everyone else." Off by the house I heard voices, and the stranger's mouth tightened.

"It is far," I admitted. "But this is where my GPS took me, and I'm hopeless without it. I was lucky to be close to your house when my car died, don't you think?"

In a blink, she'd linked her arm with mine.

I tried to shake her off, but her grip was like iron and just as unbreakable. I couldn't stop the shudder that went through me, nor the ripple of fear in its wake. Power rolled off her, more power than I'd ever felt before, and behind Lilliana's pale blue eyes something evil glittered.

"Now that you're here, I'm loath to let you out of my sight. It's not every day one meets someone of your stature. A queen doesn't come along every day."

Fuck. She knew exactly who I was.

This close, it was easy to spot the difference. Even wearing Lilliana's gentle mask didn't hide the predatory gleam in her eyes, the craven curve of her too-red lips, the way hunger seeped from her expression, like she was thinking of taking a bite.

She dragged me deeper into the woods, toward the edge of the property.

With a flick of a finger, I shot a burst of power towards the biggest, closest tree. The trunk splintered apart with a crack that echoed through the forest, hopefully all the way up to the house.

As luck would have it, the tree fell straight toward us.

I leapt away as Lilliana lost her grip on my arm. In that instant, I wrapped Luthor's shadows around me. Between one second and the next, I was crouched beside the ruined trunk, praying she hadn't heard the leaves crunching when I sprinted to my hiding spot. The woman spun in an angry circle, searching for me.

"You sneaky little bitch. Not quite as helpless as I thought you'd be," she crooned in that rich, velvet voice. "You can dream of queenhood, girl, but you'll never be willing to make the sacrifices needed to truly access the depths of your magic."

A cruel smile curved her face. "Killing the one who makes you weak is the only way to ensure a true rise to power. Lyra couldn't do it."

This woman, whoever she was... *was another queen.*

"I, on the other hand, was perfectly willing to kill my true mate in order to garner more power. And to make this even more delicious, I had help."

I closed my eyes, praying she didn't say his name.

"Deston de Rayne, your mentor. *Your friend.*" She looked down her nose at where she assumed I was. "I fail to see why he'd bother to help you. Though he does have a history of choosing the weak ones. Like Lyra, you're insignificant, unfit for the throne."

I balled my hands into fists, forced my denial back down my throat and kept my mouth shut.

She cast a wide net of magic, glittering in the cold air

like black fairy dust. The edge of that beautiful, deathly cloud never reached me, and I curled in tighter.

"You want to play games? I like games." Her shrewd gaze scanned the woods, the fallen tree before her gaze flicked back to the house. "I know where Deston is. As a matter fact, I spent most of last night watching him suffer while I enjoyed a bottle of rather mediocre wine. How he writhed, up on Viktor's wall."

I bent over as pain ripped through me, from just the idea of Deston suffering. She stepped toward my hiding spot. "If you want to see him alive again, you'll do exactly what I say."

Beneath my protective shadows, my hands shook because, yes, that's exactly what I wanted. Except Deston didn't mean a thing to me, *he didn't*. We were nearly enemies, at most, uneasy friends.

So why did her words rip my insides apart?

One thing was for sure, I didn't have time for a poorly timed existential crisis. I had to get past this evil creature and back to the house to warn the others.

Crouched down beside the tree, I remained still long enough for her to search the woods, the loud crunching of leaves a constant reminder that I couldn't take so much as a step without her discovering me.

I went weak with relief when I heard my name being called from the house, a pause, then Luthor's voice echoed through the trees once more.

With an angry scream she dematerialized but not before I glimpsed what she really looked like.

Dark hair, glittering black eyes, blood-red lips.

I'd remember that face forever and promised myself that, whoever she was, she'd pay for hurting Deston. It took me a minute to learn to breathe again, another to trudge out of the trees and toward the house. Even so, I kept Luthor's shadows wrapped tightly around me, just in case she wasn't really gone.

"There you are…"

Cyrus met me halfway, his grin disappearing when I dropped my shadows and he saw my face. "What's wrong? What's happened?"

"We have a major problem."

Chapter 35
Deston

Katarina tossed her coat in the chair on her way to the open wine bottle. Dispensing with the glass, she raised it to her lips and took a long swig.

"It appears I was right," she said when she was done. "She is young. And quite naïve."

She'd found Seraphina? How close had this venomous witch gotten to my mate? Was she still alive? I vibrated with fear induced rage. How could I have mucked everything up so badly? It was one thing for me to be here, paying for my mistakes. It was another thing for Seraphina to be pulled into Katarina and my fucked-up relationship.

"Young and naïve and beautiful." Her sing song voice rattled off the stone walls. "If I didn't know she'd be dead soon, I might be jealous."

"You were never jealous, Katarina. Jealously requires a heart, and we both know spiders don't have one."

My cruel words bounced off her tough hide.

"Better spider than sacrifice, I always say." She took another swig, her back to me. "Once I tell Viktor where she is, Seraphina Marvelle shall make a lovely revenant, don't you think?"

Anger smoldered like fire through my veins.

I would fix this. There had to be a way to save Seraphina; I just wasn't seeing it yet. Some way for me to tear myself off this wall, to crawl the fucking Seraphina and warn her.

"Oh, and the poor, desperate Cormiers." She pulled the chair across the stone floor with a hideous screech. "Once Viktor finds out they've betrayed him, he'll have that lovely wife and her two daughters nailed up there beside you."

"What do you want, Katarina?" All of this was only a game to her. She was after something big, perhaps something even bigger than Seraphina. What happened on this side of the Atlantic rarely caused any interest on her part. But something had pulled her away from her corrupt court.

"What I always want. Power. Money..." Her dark gaze raked over me. "Sex."

"I'm sure you have plenty of candidates at home. Why come here?"

"They are all willing, eager, to share my bed. But you Deston... You've fought me at every turn. Even when you were young, you were so deliciously defiant. There's something about resistance, don't you think, that makes domination taste all that much sweeter?"

"I know you're not talking about me, Katarina. You tired of me, remember? You threw me away."

"I never tired of you. I put you to good use."

"Yes, by killing your mate and getting you all the power that you ever desired," I reminded her. "You never wanted me. I was just someone to do your dirty work."

"And you did. Willingly, as I remember."

I hadn't been willing; I'd been desperate. Desperate to get out from her clutches, desperate to get away from that poisonous court and their games, and back to my family. So, I'd done what I had to do, to get free.

"I discovered after you left, that court life was lacking a

certain panache, shall we say? I want you back, Deston. And I shall have you, one way or another."

"I'm not going back. I thought I'd made that clear. Viktor can kill me or turn me into a monster, it matters not, but one thing is for sure, you will never touch me again." For one long moment we traded glares, then she looked away.

"Surely, you don't mean that, Deston."

"I would rather die than go anywhere with you, you poisonous bitch."

She sprang from the chair. "You fucking bastard. I offer you the world and you throw it back in my face."

"Don't be so dramatic. You offered me a prison, and I chose freedom. It doesn't matter what you give me, Katarina. I was done with you then, and I'm done with you now."

"And what about your young queen? Are you done with her?"

I should've made some dismissive comment, told her that Seraphina meant nothing to me, but my body betrayed me. Instead, I hesitated, hate glowing in my eyes.

"Ah," her voice softened. "The young queen has stolen the traitor's heart. I could've killed her today, Deston." She snapped her fingers, the sound echoing around the room.

"I could've crushed her as easily as a bird, but I think I'll give her to Viktor, instead." I knew that look on her face. She'd do everything she just mentioned. More, if she had the opportunity, since Katarina did so enjoy breaking things.

"He has such interesting things planned for her. I believe he spoke of making her his for a time, before he adds her to his collection of Carved Women. I cannot wait to see what he does to her face. I am sure she will be...unrecognizable."

My heartbeat accelerated, panic skyrocketing through me.

"He'll have to catch her first," I countered. "My guess is she's already on the move."

"Your guess is correct." She walked around to the other table and popped a grape into her mouth, the juices sliding down her chin before she fell into the chair. "I can give Seraphina to Viktor. Hand her over like the virginal sacrifice she is. And I will. Unless you give me what I want." She leaned in.

"I told her exactly where you were, Deston. My guess is, that sweet young thing is on her way to the palace as we speak. Right where I'll be waiting for her."

"What is it the humans say?" I paused. "Ah yes. You can go fuck yourself, Katarina."

She crossed her legs, resolve written all over her face.

"I wanted to give you a chance, you know," she mused. "Free will and all that nonsense. But you are as stubborn as ever." Interest quickened the air. "This is how things will be. I will assert the bond once more. You will obey, like before."

Her smile grew wider. "And sweet, sweet little Seraphina will become Viktor's."

The edges of my vision darkened, and though I fought with everything I had, the claws of the soul bond gripped me like a prison I'd never escape

Chapter 36
Seraphina

O nce we were safely inside the house, I tugged out of Cyrus's firm hold.

"I just had a little talk with somebody in the woods, someone disguised as Lilliana. I think she was a queen, *another* queen, I mean."

I ran the confrontation down as concisely as I could, leaving out my conflicted feelings for Deston, which didn't matter right now. Hugh finally interrupted me.

"That could be Katarina Cozma from the Brasov Clan. She fits the description you just gave, and if that's the case, then we don't have much time." Hugh shoved his chair back. "It's a good thing reinforcements are almost here. I'll send Lilliana and the girls somewhere safe."

"How long before their plane lands?" Luthor was already armed to the gills; the Kevlar vest was a nice touch I appreciated. "We should be moving in the next half an hour to stay ahead of Viktor."

Hugh checked his watch. "Any moment now. I also called in a favor to an old friend, but it will take him another day to arrive. He'll miss this fight, but if there is another, he will be at your disposal. Baz is a good fighter, he will be a valuable asset to your court."

I wanted to tell him I was in no position to be building a court, then decided I wasn't in a position to turn down any help he could give us.

"At least Katarina confirmed Deston is at the palace." Cyrus was just as heavily armed, and fear skittered through my veins, wondering if weapons were enough against magic. "We can move ahead with our plan."

"Viktor killed the witch who reinforced his wards." I remined them. "The wards will be at their weakest right now, but once we're through, we need to worry about the revenants."

"My Queen, perhaps you should stay here..." Hugh offered hesitantly at the same time Cyrus laughed.

"I can't wait to see you turn them to ash, my Queen. I hope you turn that entire place into a smoking ruin."

"Trust me, she's going with us." Luthor gave me a curt nod. "One thing about our Queen, she refuses to be left behind."

"As you wish." Hugh sounded doubtful. "Although I am a bit curious how you know about the wards and the revenants. I thought you said Claire kept you out of our world?"

"Chalk it up to recent experience," I muttered, unwilling to share how my mistake had landed us in this spot in the first place.

"Needless to say, there will be guards, and recent intelligence tells me that Viktor is currently in residence," Hugh pointed out.

"Katarina is there as well." When all eyes swung to me, I explained, "She said that she'd seen Deston." My throat constricted enough that my next words came out strangled. "Up on the wall. she was pretty...graphic with her description."

Everyone went silent for a moment.

"House Carpathian originated in what is now Romania," Cyrus mused. "Since Viktor is a far-off relation of hers, it makes sense they've joined forces to keep him on the throne. What I'd like to know is how Katarina knew about you?"

"It's obvious, Deston told her," Luthor snapped. "How else would she know?"

"She could've found out from Viktor," I offered, hoping that was true. There was always the chance that Deston had sold us out again, but that logic felt wrong. *He wouldn't do that.*

"Either way, they know you're here. It's only a matter of time before they come. I'm sending Lilliana and the girls away. I already sent the staff home, and our backup should be arriving within the hour."

"I hope they're bringing an army." We needed one. "Something that seemed odd—well, odder than usual—Katarina's visit seemed more personal than anything. Even though she pretended to know a lot about me, I think she was mostly guessing. she didn't know much beyond my name."

"Don't give de Rayne more credit than is due," Cyrus cautioned. "I've known my cousin far longer than you. Trust me, he always makes sure he comes out on top, no matter who gets sacrificed along the way."

My thoughts went back to Katarina's odd claim, the one about killing your true mate. Why would she have divulged that information, unless she was trying to goad me. Or make a point?

I mulled this over as Hugh made more phone calls. Cyrus and Luthor dematerialized to reinforce the wards. But I doubted their magic could keep someone like Katarina out. Not as strong as she'd been.

I managed a hot shower and changed into something comfortable. Black jeans, a dark t-shirt, leather jacket, heavy boots. I wasn't going to war, or on the run, unprepared again. This time, I'd be ready.

Somewhere downstairs, a door slammed loudly. Heavy boot—a lot of them—pounded across the floor beneath me, and my heart leapt into my throat. Then I heard Hugh's calm voice and relaxed.

Reinforcements had arrived.

Luthor appeared next to me and caught my hands in his own. "Backup's here, Seraphina. Keep your magic tamped down. You'll need it later." He surveyed my sensible outfit with approval, then kissed me quickly. "I'll let you handle the revenants, but remember, we're there to get Deston out, nothing more."

"Let's just hope he's still alive." I stifled the sudden urge to see if his castle still stood.

Luthor tugged me toward the door. "Let's go down and meet your team."

"I have a team now, huh?" A shadow flitted across his face, and I wondered why, just before I was inserted into an introvert's worst nightmare.

"Seraphina, this is Markus, Silas, Caden, and Rafael." I recognized those names. Tessa's four men—all of them fully dressed for combat—inclined their heads politely. Caden was the biggest, Silas looked to be the deadliest, going by the assortment of knives sticking out all over his complicated-looking gear.

Markus was the only one who bowed, then kissed my hand. "It's an honor to finally meet you, my Queen."

"Don't mind him." Rafael elbowed him away. "He's got the manners of a royal but the cold heart of a lawyer." His grin was sincere. "Tessa's been talking about you for the entire flight." He leaned in, dark hair flopping over his fore-head and nodded toward the blond woman embracing Hugh, her face buried in his chest, her shoulders shaking. "She cannot wait to meet you."

"This way, gentlemen." Cyrus ushered them into the dining room. "We'll run down what we know." I waited outside while they disappeared, all of them appearing deadly and perfectly capable, and hope flared a little brighter. *We had an army.*

"This is my daughter Contessa." Hugh led the woman over and squeezed her arm affectionately as he surveyed her outfit of jeans, boots, and a leather jacket.

I was dressed nearly the same, with my favorite hoodie underneath my jacket. "You're wearing my clothes. I'm glad they fit." Tessa grabbed both of my hands, a huge smile on her face.

"I've been dreaming my whole life of seeing a new queen take the throne. The fact that you're here..." Her voice trailed off, tears gathering in her eyes while I shifted uncomfortably. "Sorry, but it's hard for me to believe the rumors were true."

"Rumors?" I asked curiously.

"We all heard about you. Viktor was holding us at the palace, he was about to..." She shook her head. "Never mind, what's important was someone had sighted you, and just that bit of information rattled him. His anger was a lovely sight to see."

She grinned. "I hate that bastard, obviously."

"I heard you were next in line to be soul-bound to him?"

I felt her shudder of revulsion through our clasped hands. "I was. Having that hanging over my head was like a death sentence. But then you appeared and, long story short, distracted him long enough for us to get away."

"I'm glad I could be of service," I joked, sketching a little bow.

"As am I." She curtseyed deeply, and I stopped her, embarrassed.

"Okay, we don't do that stuff."

"You will, once you take the throne. I can teach you if you'd like," she offered, linking arms with me. "If there's anything you want to know about the clan, just ask. I've spent the better part of my life learning about archaic social customs and outdated, misogynistic practices." She winked. "One might say I'm an expert snob."

God, I liked her already.

I wanted to ask her everything. How did she manage four men, when I could barely manage two? How did she escape Viktor, when no one else ever had? But it was Katarina's taunt that kept bothering me.

"I have a question. Just a curiosity, really. What do you know about mates?"

"Like true mates?"

I nodded. *That had to be what Katarina had been talking about.*

"You know those archaic social customs I mentioned? This falls into that category. True mates are a myth, though, kind of like a vampire urban legend if that makes sense?"

"So, there's no such thing?"

Tessa shook her head. "Not that I know of, and I know most of the royal house members, plus a handful of common-born families. I've never seen a true mating."

"In theory, though, what is it?"

"It's when you find your soulmate, and I'm not talking some mushy, romantic notion. From what I know, you would be bound to that person for the rest of your life." She pursed her lips, thinking. "You would deeply feel that person's presence, in your soul, as long as they were alive."

"And if they died?"

"The connection would be severed. Which, I imagine, would be quite unpleasant."

"And if I were the one who killed them?"

Her face clouded over. "My Queen, perhaps we shouldn't..."

"If I killed them, what would happen then?" Tessa dropped my hands, a suspicious tilt to her head as she stepped away, putting some distance between us.

"As a vampire queen, it's said you would be blessed with endless power."

"Katarina told me she'd killed her mate. I just wondered what she was talking about."

Her face cleared, and she shot me a relieved smile. "Okay, you had me worried there for a minute. First of all, I doubt that old hag ever had a true mate, and secondly, it's just a superstition passed down through the generations."

"Are you sure it's just a superstition?"

She shrugged. "It's more like a fairytale. You know the kind." She lowered her voice and did a good imitation of Vincent Price. "The evil queen on the throne who was willing to do anything for more power, including sacrificing her mate." She waved her hand in the air. "Like everything else in this world, it's just another way to make the females look bad. Or keep us in line."

"Stepping out of line needs to be a thing, if I manage to remove Viktor from the equation."

"Stepping out of line is kind of what I do best." Tessa laughed, linking arms with me. "Come on, Markus just sent me a message through the bond. We're leaving."

"You're going with us?" I asked. For all my arguing to be

included in the dangerous stuff, somehow, I wanted to convince Tessa to stay here.

Which, I realized, made me a total hypocrite.

"Are you kidding?" She grinned. "I wouldn't miss seeing you kick Viktor's ass for the world. Besides, I've been to so many formal balls, I know every inch of that hideous palace, which might come in handy."

Cyrus transported me to the outskirts of the king's territory while Luthor kept us all wrapped in his shadows. We were nine strong, and these guys came prepared.

Going in with actual backup was a new experience, and I didn't know how I felt about it. On one hand, I was more confident; on the other hand, there was an enormous responsibility to keep them all safe.

Tessa, especially, who was even younger than me.

Luthor drew me aside as everyone made a show of checking their weapons. He hesitated, went to speak, changed his mind, staring over my head, eyes narrowed.

"Just say what you're thinking, Luthor."

"My Queen, before we go in, you must prepare yourself for the possibility Deston may not be alive."

Pure dread rippled through me like poison. That idea had surfaced, but I'd pushed the prospect right back down. *Deston was alive. He had to be.* "I've considered the likelihood, and if he is, then we get everyone back out in one piece."

I managed a wan smile. "I'm banking on his smart mouth keeping him alive."

"It's more likely Viktor cut his tongue out," Luthor said, snapping his mouth shut at the look on my face. "I apologize, my Queen, that was..."

"Probably true," I muttered. "And please, call me by my name, not my title, Luthor. These next hours will be difficult enough. I'm tired of you putting distance between us."

"Seraphina." His voice was tinged with hesitation and something that sounded a lot like guilt. "There's something you need to know about Deston, something you should know about all vampires. I overheard what you asked Tessa earlier, about true mates and..."

Markus tapped Luthor's shoulder. "Sire, if you two are ready, we should get on with our invasion of the palace." He nodded at the shimmering ward and the lone figure standing at its base.

"The quicker we breach and assess, the better our chances of coming out of this in one piece," Caden added, brandishing a gun as big as my arm and an even bigger grin.

"We're coming." Luthor squeezed my arm, staying close as we made our way to the ward.

"You were correct, my Queen," Silas told me as I approached. "When we infiltrated the grounds several months ago, Caden's father, Renard, opened the ward for us. The magic is far weaker now." Silas's dark magic ate a hole in the shimmering ward, the magic crackling around the opening, wide enough for us to step through, one at a time. I sucked in a steadying breathe, remembering the last time I was here.

On the other side of this ward was a killing field filled with revenants ready to run us down.

I spooled up my magic, felt ice flow down into my hands.

But the wide-open clearing was empty, still marked with piles of fresh dirt from where my necromanced skeletons had pushed through from below. As a group, we jogged shoulder to shoulder toward the castle, scanning the dark woods for movement.

Luthor wrapped his shadows around the group, thickly enough we wouldn't be spotted. My necromancer magic curled around the ends of my fingers, ready to be shoved deep into the ground, to raise an army to protect us.

But we made it across the wide-open field without incident.

Whoever these guys were, they were good. Aside from the occasional rattle of equipment and the hush-hush whisper of footsteps in the deep grass, we were nearly silent as we crept up to the palace walls.

"We can use the servant's entrance down there." Tessa nodded to the western end of the building. "That wing has been closed down for years."

"The guards on the roof haven't spotted us yet." Silas indicated the central structure of the palace to our right. "And the perimeter guards are sticking close to the front doors."

"They must think we're amateurs." Caden chuckled before Luthor punched his shoulder. "Sorry, that was the adrenaline talking, Sire."

Tessa led us toward a broken-down door. "This door dumps into the cellar. There's a main corridor that leads up to the main floor and into the foyer opposite the throne room. That's our most direct route."

"And you know this, how?" Rafael whispered, and I was grateful, because I was wondering the same thing.

"Do you really think I attended all those royal balls for the monotonous conversation and shitty food?" She shook her head. "I know this place like the back of my hand. Figured the knowledge might come in handy one day, and look, here we are." Something scraped overhead, and a dark form shifted position on the roof.

"Lots of guards on duty tonight. He's expecting trouble," Luthor observed coolly, drawing a gun out of his holster and holding it barrel-down.

"He is," Silas agreed quietly. "But he hasn't sensed us yet, and I'd like to keep things that way." He indicated the broken-down door sealing the entrance. "This will be a problem. Nobody's been through here in years."

"I'm on it." Luthor murmured. "Once we're through, remember Lady Contessa's directions. You take point, Cy and I will bring up the rear. Everyone keep their eyes open, Viktor's bound to have more guards posted inside."

Luthor's shadows curled up like a billowing wall, forming a solid barrier between us and the rest of the palace grounds. Caden, nearly as broad as Luthor, shoved open the door with a dull metallic groan. While I winced at the horrid sound, with Luthor's shadows in place, no one else would hear.

Once through, we down the narrow staircase into an ancient cellar with rough stone walls dripping in mildew and mold, the dusty stair treads clogged with debris. Luthor was right. No one had been through here in years.

We kept moving until Silas held up a hand.

Two sets of stairs led to the upper floors. Cyrus, Caden, and Markus broke off to the left, while Luthor, myself, Tessa, Hugh, and Rafael went right.

"Standard pincer move," Luthor murmured, his mouth pressed tight to my ear. "We attack from both sides, trap the guards between us. You and Tessa will stay out of the fighting." He laid his finger across my lips. "This is nonnegotiable, Seraphina. Cyrus and Caden will get Deston down from the wall. Once he's secured, we exit straight out the front doors."

He came closer, laying his warm cheek against mine. "I only ask one thing. Do not get separated from me, Seraphina. I mean it. I don't care what you see. I do not care who is there when we get upstairs. This is *not* the time to take on Viktor."

"But what if..."

No." His expression went flat. "We fight, you keep your head down. Promise me."

"I promise to stay out of the fighting unless I have no other choice." I muttered, and Luthor's blue eyes lifted over my head, tracking movement, but his lips finally twitched.

"Fine, I suppose that's as good of a guarantee as I'll ever get."

Once the people allowed to do the *actual* fighting crested the top of the stairs, there was shouting. Gunfire. The grunting and crashing of vicious hand-to-hand fighting. Rafael looked miserable as he kept me and an equally frustrated Tessa cordoned in the small alcove until the sounds of the scuffle faded.

It wasn't until Tessa pushed past him that I got a good look at what happened.

Bodies of guards were strewn through the foyer area, and the only ones still on their feet were our people.

I stepped forward, but this time, it was Tessa who stopped me. "Wait for just a second, my Queen, you...might not want to see what's in the Hall of Mirrors." She bit her lip. "Caden and Cyrus will bring Lord de Rayne down. I'll tell you when it's..."

I shoved past her. If Deston was in there, I *had* to see what Viktor had done to him. I wanted to know everything he'd endured. Because while I didn't understand the reasons, some deep, primal part of me needed to suffer right along with him.

In five more steps I discovered why Cyrus and Caden had halted in the doorway, because over their shoulders, I saw what stopped them. The glittering black eyes and blood-red lips of a wild looking Katarina.

"You're too late, little girl." She grinned down at a

blood-covered Deston crumpled at her feet. "He's all mine." Her satisfied gaze went over my head, where the pounding of military boots thundered at us from all directions.

"And you, I believe, are the little newborn queen who belongs to Viktor. Honestly, I cannot wait to see what he does with you."

I didn't think.

I just acted. Call this instinct, or muscle memory, but my magic roared harmlessly past Luthor and the others, striking the oncoming guards like an onslaught of deadly, shadowy spears, thrown with unerring accuracy.

There was a clatter, a few errant bullets ricocheting harmlessly off the stone walls as the guards fell in bloody heaps. Katarina's lip lifted off white fangs, eyes glowing. Red, like Viktor's revenants. Red, like Viktor himself.

I stepped towards her, gathering my power. Deep, delicious hatred bubbled up and I embraced that vicious surge of darkness, *welcomed* the vile intense need to hurt her. I'd tear this bitch's heart out, then I'd paint the room red with her blood.

One glance showed Deston was still not moving, and his outstretched hand...oh God...his fingernails were...gone.

My vision ruptured into a haze of black, every thought vanishing except the need to inflict the same kind of pain on *this bitch*. I'd never experienced such extreme loathing before, but the rush of emotion made me feel strong. *Invincible.*

"That's it, youngling, come for me with all that fire in your heart. I'll kill you quick, no need to draw this out." Like me, power glittered at her finger, then a whip of magic black as night cut through the air.

Before her magic found its mark, Deston pushed up off the floor, wrapped his arms around Katarina's middle and tackled her. That burst of darkness brushed by me, but there was a low groan of pain behind me.

I stalked forward, not missing a step. I was seriously going to kill this woman, and I was going to enjoy every minute of it.

She and Deston rolled across the floor, and she came out on top, then pressed her clawed hand against Deston's throat, that black magic wrapping around his neck like a noose. His eyes found mine, everything he'd never said written in them so clearly.

Regret, shame, desperation.

"I'll kill him." Katarina hissed. "One more step, girl, and I'll cut his head clean off."

I stopped, fingers twitching at my sides.

My mind urged me forward, but my body had locked up, as if I had no control over my own muscles. My magic shuddered inside of me, then quieted, going from hot and fiery to heavy as lead in a second.

Katarina drew a nail across Deston's throat, filling the air with the rich scent of Deston's blood.

All I could do was watch her mutilate his neck, my eyes locked with his. I couldn't explain what was happening. This was like being turned to stone. I pushed my body, urging myself to *fucking move*, but my feet were fused in place, my stiff hands helpless to channel my magic.

Blood spurted when her fingers pushed in deeper, flooding the floor around them.

"Stop hurting him." I begged. "Please, please stop." I didn't recognize the weak, pathetic plea coming out of my mouth.

Then she laughed.

This craven bitch *laughed*, and whatever spell held me captive, finally broke.

I spooled up everything I had, every last bit of dark power and screamed when I sent it roaring across the room, a scream filled with the force of all the rage and pain I felt, remembering the regret and shame in Deston's eyes. *Because fuck her.*

My magic hit Katarina square in the chest, lifted her entirely off Deston, tossing her against the opposite wall like a weightless doll. From the cracking sound, I hoped every bone in her body was broken.

Deston, my beautiful, ruined, traitorous Deston, was crawling across the floor to reach me, leaving a trail of crimson in his wake. He would bleed to death, right in front of my eyes.

Then I was on my knees, futilely trying to stem the flow.

In a second, Tessa was beside me. "He needs blood. Right now. Yours." She grasped my wrist, bit in deeply, then pressed the punctures into Deston's mouth. "Drink, you bastard, drink or die."

I didn't think he would. After everything he'd been through—I couldn't stop glancing up at the bloodstained nails sticking out of the wall above us—I didn't see how he would survive this. His arms and legs were ravaged, from what I could see through his torn clothing, the damage was...horrifying.

Finally, Deston's mouth fastened on my wrist, his weak pulls turning steadier.

Before my eyes, beneath the gleam of blood, his throat healed back together.

"That's the power of Queen's blood," Tessa whispered, sitting back on her heels. "It has more healing powers than any other magic, even a witch's healing elixir. He'll be fine."

He didn't look fine. In fact, he looked a hundred years older than the last time I'd seen him. His hands curled around my arm, and I became transfixed by the sensation of his lips moving against my skin, the way his fingers dented my flesh as he drank.

"That's enough." Luthor ripped Deston away. "Pick him up and get us the hell out of here." Luthor scrubbed his face, then offered me his hand, and pulled me to my feet.

Two of our people were bleeding, Caden was injured, his pantleg blackened from Katarina's errant magic, his shin...broken, from the look of things.

Deston was unceremoniously hoisted up between Silas and Raphael, after trying futilely to hold his own weight. His blood soaked my hands, my clothes, the scent overpowering. It had long since lost its warmth, and I shivered in the freezing chamber.

Katarina's crumpled body at the base of the wall twitched.

"Get her out of here," Luthor ordered. "Get Seraphina moving. *Now.*"

Because I hadn't. I swayed, watching Katarina's body jerk unnaturally as her limbs rearranged themselves back into logical order, the awful popping making me gag. How was that even possible?

"Get moving," Luthor ordered, his hand gripping my arm. "*We have to leave, Seraphina.*"

I knew Luthor was right. I *had* to get out of here before she got back on her feet.

And yet, I couldn't move a muscle. Something was happening to me. Something I didn't understand, something that *hurt.*

My insides were on fire, my chest squeezed by a rubber band, stretching and stretching until the tightness threatened to tear me apart. I doubled over, ripping out of

Luthor's hold, all the air going out of my lungs in a whoosh, something inside me giving way.

As I was torn into pieces, something else slammed into place inside me. The back of my scalp caught fire, and I reached up to rub the pain away, but touching the spot only made my skin burn hotter.

I hesitated, then probed where it hurt. There was something on the back of my neck. Something raised, small and round. *Like I'd been branded.* That pressure in my chest intensified, like someone had hooked me with a giant anchor, and *yanked.*

The pain made me gasp, then my feet began moving of their own accord, following Deston as they dragged him into the hallway. Some instinct urged me to keep him in sight, my heart hammering wildly at the thought of him disappearing.

I couldn't have stopped myself, even if I tried.

Deston was all I wanted. All that mattered. Like the entire universe was pushing me in his direction, and I didn't have a choice in the matter anymore.

W e escaped the palace grounds without seeing Viktor, though I wondered if that was part of the plan.

It would be just like the king to pit Katarina and I against each other, to see who came out on top. I was calling this one a draw, since we were both still breathing, though I wasn't the one piecing myself back together like a broken doll.

By the time we reached the Cormier mansion, Deston was walking under his own power. Staggering, more like it, and only out of sheer stubbornness, because he still looked like shit.

The tight, rubber band feeling at my center hadn't gone away. In fact, the connection was stronger than ever, and by now, I knew exactly who was on the other end of that tether.

"I need to talk to Deston. Alone," I told everyone, as soon as Hugh shut us inside.

"There's a drawing room in the back. You'll have some privacy there," Tessa murmured softly, something like pity on her face. "No one will disturb you, I'll make sure of it."

Her males formed a tight, protective knot around her, and a burst of jealousy went through me at the sight. *That's what I'd always wanted. A family of my own. One that stuck together, no matter what.*

That sinking feeling grew as I reached up again, fingers brushing over that raised mark. Despite my promises, despite my resolve, if my suspicions were correct, what just happened could rip me, Luthor, and Cyrus apart forever.

But I would not allow anything—absolutely nothing—to come between us. I would fight tooth and nail to keep my family together. They were all I had. All I ever wanted, and I wouldn't lose them.

Luthor turned my arm over, frowning at the bite mark on my wrist. "Be careful, Seraphina. We don't know if we can trust him. Or if he talked. He *was* tortured, it wouldn't be unheard of." When he brushed back my hair, my heart broke at the sadness on his face. Like he was already saying goodbye.

"I'll find out. If Deston gave Katarina our location, I'll get an answer for you, and we'll have to decide what to do next."

"We should be in there with you," Cyrus muttered, his tone brittle. "I don't trust that fuck."

"I'll be fine. He'll talk more freely if it's just the two of us."

"We won't be far." Luthor said, "Right here, within earshot. You need us, you just call and we'll be there." He dragged his knuckles down my cheek. "I love you, *Seraphina*. Remember that."

"I know, and I love you both too." I kissed Cyrus, then Luthor, relishing their salty taste. Remembering it, in case this new development broke us. Then Luthor herded everyone away as I walked away down the hall, knowing Deston would follow.

Because of course, he'd follow.

Deston would follow me because he didn't have a choice.

Neither of us had a choice anymore, and I couldn't think of anything more terrible than losing our free will. With every step I took, the burning on the back of my neck grew hotter, and my rubbing wasn't doing anything except making it worse.

I'd run to the palace to free him. He'd been half-dead, yet had crawled across the floor to reach me. We were acting like a couple of lovesick teenagers.

But I couldn't explain the depth of my rage, seeing him crumpled on the floor in front of Katarina.

How deeply emotion swamped me when he drank from me.

There was a chain around my heart now. A chain that led straight to him. He was my anchor, and the more I thought this through, the more I replayed Tessa's words, I couldn't deny the truth.

We were true mates.

I wanted to rage at the universe. How could I be mated to someone *like him*? Why not Luthor, with his endless strength and patience? Why not Cyrus, with his humor and good heart?

Why hadn't Fate marked *them* as worthy?

All these questions rolled around and around in my head as I walked through the door, spun around with my arms crossed over my chest, waiting for Deston to appear.

I deserved to be *happy*, damn it.

Not destroyed, feeling like I was being torn apart.

It took a moment for Deston to step through that empty doorway, and damn if panic didn't riddle my body until he appeared. I would not live like this. He was four hundred years old—certainly, he knew how to break this bond?

He closed the door behind him, and staring across the ten feet that divided us—which might have well been a mile—I rubbed the strange, aching heat on the back of my neck.

"What is this?"

"You know what this is, Seraphina."

Even in this state, broken and battered, nail holes in his hands, the still healing wound on his neck, I'd never seen anything more beautiful than Lord Deston de Rayne. Our connection was divine, profane, impossible because I didn't want any part of this.

With droplets of blood splattered down my arms, his face streaked with gore, I almost laughed at the sheer absurdity of our situation. Fate meddled in our lives, threw us together, impervious to what we wanted, or who else was involved.

I stayed silent, waiting for him to fill the space between us with his endless lies.

"Seraphina." Deston's dark gaze flickered, fastened on my face. "I can explain. But we don't have long, an hour, perhaps, until Katarina heals herself and regains her power."

"I don't give a shit about her," I spat, forcing all emotion from my voice. "How long have you known?"

His mouth tightened into a long, thin line, and I didn't give him an opportunity to spew his endless bullshit. "You know what? Never mind answering. I've heard enough of your lies to last me for the rest of my life."

"I cannot lie to you. Not ever."

"Katarina told me how you killed her mate. To pave her way to the throne. You've betrayed everyone you've ever claimed to love." A manic sort of glee took over, pulling every poisonous word from my lips. "Maybe it's time for you to turn over a new leaf, embrace who you really are, become the villain of your own story, instead of the hero."

I had a purpose now.

I would tear him down to nothing, prove to myself that Deston de Rayne could *never* be my mate. Prove to him that he could *never* have me. "Because that's how you think of yourself, isn't it? As a hero?"

I railed against his silence, filling it with accusations and truth. "You abandoned Lyra to save your family. And yet, you saved neither. You sold me out to Viktor, claiming it was for my own good, when all you did was save your own ass. You will never, ever have me." I licked my cracked lips. "Let me tell you why."

His face turned as hard as mine, looking like a male awaiting his final judgment, which I was more than willing to give it to him.

"You're not a hero. You're a self-serving motherfucker who stands on the shoulders of better males in order to draw his last gasp of air. All you know is emptiness and misery and vengeance, and I hate you with every ounce of my being."

The bond between us turned cold; my vision went fuzzy.

"You cannot mean that. We are mates, Seraphina. *True mates.*" His every word was precise, even, and cut me to the quick. "Our bond cannot be broken, save for death. As they say in the human world, from womb to tomb, this has been ordained."

Deston's face was impassive through his entire speech, so obviously, he wasn't any more enthused about this than me. I prayed he'd just turn around and leave. That would be a fitting ending to our flawed relationship.

Anticlimactic, but fitting.

"And there's a saying in *our* world. Fate is inevitable." His voice was devoid of feeling, every word hammering away at my denial. "Regardless of circumstance, true mates recognize each other across time and space, and while the connection may get tangled over time, it will never be broken."

"That's all well and good, when it comes to things that are *supposed* to be. But what about this?" I gestured between us. "What about mistakes? Can this get fixed, because this is surely the biggest fuck up fate has ever made?"

"You think the Fates made a mistake?" Deston came a step closer. His voice was too calm, his face too blank, to give me the slightest hint of what he was thinking.

"No, I don't *think* this was a mistake." I held my ground as he advanced. "I *know* this was a mistake. I could never be mated to someone like you."

"You believe you deserve better?" Deston asked, his gaze turning remote.

I bit back a curse. "Don't you dare make it sound like I'm some stuck-up, prissy bitch. I was dragged into this world kicking and screaming, remember? I've fought and I've bled and I've worked my ass off to survive. In all that time, I've managed not to betray a single person. Can you say the same?"

Through this unholy bond, I felt his outrage, then his acceptance that what I said was the truth.

"Where you... *you* sell out everybody you claim to serve. Tell me this Deston—should I trust you? Or should I be smart and turn my back on you, like you've turned yours on so many others?"

The bastard took one more step until we were barely

two feet apart, his face as still as a statue, the air between us vibrating with more I wanted to say.

I'd trusted this asshole, bared my soul to him, allowed him to bare his darkness to me. Maybe that was why this betrayal felt so huge, as if the floor was falling beneath my feet, pushed over the edge by the multitude of lies I'd allowed myself to believe.

"You really think so poorly of me?" His question was quiet, his dark eyes missing nothing.

"Of course, I do," I snapped quickly. Because how could I think otherwise? If I let myself sink to his level, accept the things he'd done...

"I told you about Lyra. That day in the garden. You did not condemn me for that."

"That was before I recognized the pattern," I retorted. "Obviously, I should have realized what you were, even back then."

"That was the moment I knew," he murmured softly, and my heart clenched. "That's when I knew what you meant to me. That was when I knew you were my mate, Seraphina. And I've known it every day since." *He was lying. We'd... so much had happened since then.*

"I knew I did not deserve you. That you were too good for me, that I was ruined, and would never be whole. But I was helpless to walk away." His chest rose and fell as he took another step forward. I retreated, my back to the wall.

God, why was he so beautiful? Why did the mere thought of being apart from him rip at my soul? I hated feeling like this, as if I had no choice in my own existence.

"In that moment, I wanted you to know the very worst about me, if only to warn you." Every single word was laced with self-loathing. Every word filled with doubt.

"Well, it didn't scare me off," I told him, "Though it

should have." Did Deston really think that crime was the worst he'd ever committed? Trying to save his family? I could easily list off a dozen more heinous crimes, and I'd only known him a handful of months.

"Yes, it should have." His tone turned curious, his gaze going to my hand, still trying to rub away that painful burning on my neck. "Why didn't you run, Seraphina?" He took another step, his scent wrapping around me until I was drowning in him.

"I... I don't know."

Not only that, I'd kept his dirty little secret, not even telling Luthor or Cyrus.

"Back to my question. Can this mating thing be reversed somehow?"

"No." He was inches away from me, and God help me, I wanted him even closer. There had to be something wrong with me. There was definitely something wrong with these terrifying carnal urges controlling my body.

I wanted to close the space between us and taste him, have him taste me. I want to consume every gorgeous inch of him in a blazing feast of tongues and lips and teeth. Desire became a lush flood, saturating my body, so powerful I could barely contain it.

And then he touched me.

"Let me see, Seraphina." Deston's hands were so gentle as he turned me, his fingers featherlight when he lifted my hair. The hiss that came out of his mouth made my heart race even faster. "The mating mark," he murmured, a second before he pressed his lips to it. "It's beautiful. *You're* beautiful, *mon amour, mon amour le plus précieux*."

His lips nibbled, fangs scraped while he murmured to me in French, and while I didn't understand the words, I felt the emotion behind every single one of them.

Instantly, my body responded, my back arching, driving my ass into his groin, eliciting a heated growl. He pushed a knee between my legs, his hand clamped around the back of my neck, holding me to the wall.

Yes, yes, yes. My body sang, responding to his forbidden touch.

"Deston..." Then I couldn't say another thing as he twisted my head around and kissed me.

He caught my tongue between his teeth, then devoured my lips, like he wanted to possess every angry piece of me and was running out of time. He tasted like darkness and betrayal, and I meant to break the kiss—*I did*—but instead, my traitorous mouth sucked his tongue in deeper, wanting the imprint of him somewhere inside me.

This utter insanity, this heedless hunger for him... this had to be the mating bond at work. Nobody had the right to want another person this badly.

I wanted to consume him.

I wanted him to consume *me*, and I didn't care what was left of me when he was finished.

Heart pounding, lost in sensation, I pushed back against Deston, but he held me in place, releasing my mouth long enough to yank my jeans down, exposing my ass, before pinning me beneath him again. One knee pushed back between my legs, forcing them wider and wider, and delicious heat spiraled through me.

Then he bit me.

Right on the mating mark.

My knees went weak, and I would have collapsed, except for Deston, thrusting up into me, his cock stretching me wide as he drove himself inside. He pulled out, thrust again, my face skidding along the wall with every hard stroke, sweat and my own cum lubricating him as he moved against me.

This was fast and dirty and overwhelming. The slap of his hips against me as he thrust in and out, my nipples so hard they hurt, my hands bracing myself on the wall, and the feel of him so deep my core pulsed around his cock, as if trying to keep him inside.

He reached around, his thumb skimming my clit, over and over as I made inhuman, mewling sounds, trying to find some kind of leverage to push him in deeper than he was. His deep growl sounded like it came from a thousand miles away when my body tensed, just before I came apart.

Deston shoved the meat of his palm into my mouth, and I bit down, muffling my scream, which would have surely been heard around the world, or at least, everyone outside in the Cormier's banquet room.

I was clamped tightly around Deston when he came, his lips on the mating mark, and I felt every light brush of his body against mine, down to the depths of my soul. Then he slid out of me, cold air brushed my nakedness, his seed trickled down the insides of my thighs, and I realized the enormity of what we'd just done.

"Put me down, please."

My head was spinning when Deston set me gently back down on the floor. My knees shook, my body was in shambles, still trembling with aftershocks.

"I... I didn't mean for that to happen," I told him.

"Clearly it was a mistake," Deston agreed. But his fingers trailed slowly down my arm before he finally released me and stepped away. His eyes searched mine, and I saw the sorrow in them, every bit as much as I felt the distance growing between us.

I put my other foot through my jeans and pulled them back up. The rampant lust had fled as quickly as it appeared, and now I just felt dirty. I avoided Deston's gaze as I straightened myself up, taking one shuddering breath after another.

Without thinking, I touched his arm. "I mean it, Deston. This shouldn't have happened. It was a mistake, especially when you take everything into account. Me and you, this would never work. I can't hurt Luthor or Cyrus, and with Viktor and Katarina involved, this whole situation is already a mess. We can't add to that."

"I understand, Seraphina. Believe me, I do." He straightened the lapels of his ripped, bloodstained jacket, his face barren of emotion, and still, his fallen angel beauty made my heart hurt.

"Which will make this next part a bit easier, I believe."

He fastened the front of his pants, tucked his shirt back in. Gone was the male who'd just been inside me, kissing me like I was his lifeline. Gone was the male who'd pushed me to succeed, even when I hadn't believed in myself.

No, that male disappeared, the second Deston smoothed his face back into an unreadable mask.

"What do you mean, this next part?" I asked, quickly glancing at the door. Praying Luthor or Cyrus didn't just walk in.

"You needn't worry about them," Deston assured me calmly. "They'll never know this happened, Seraphina. Isn't that what you want? To keep this secret? To pretend that I haven't tainted you in some way?"

Guilt tasted like battery acid, burning a hole in my stomach. "That's... that's not what I meant." *That was exactly what I meant.* And it left me feeling disgusted with myself.

Looking at him like this—after what we'd just done—I felt for the first time that my eyes were clear when it came to Deston. Maybe I *had* been wrong. Maybe he had been doing everything to keep me safe, to save his family, to make things right.

No, I told myself sternly, *that couldn't be it. He's betrayed everyone he's ever known, and he'll betray me, too, if given the chance. Don't get sucked in by his lies.*

"It's all right, Seraphina." There was no hint of any emotion on his face, his eyes coldly blank. "There was a time when I wanted people to think I was perfect, too. for them to look at me and see only the good parts, while I hid my ugliness away."

I bristled at the implied insult.

"Don't be angry with me, *ma cherie,* you are right. Your

reputation is fragile, right now. You are unsure in this new world, and you're scared." He brushed his hand down my cheek, and I couldn't help leaning into his touch. "If I could take all your fears away, I would. But the only thing I can do right now is protect you from the people who want to hurt you the most."

Deston straightened his bloodied coat, filling the air with the coppery tinge of old blood. "I'll be leaving straightaway." His face remained impassive, but his dark gaze fixed to my face as if committing it to memory. "You'll never see me again, which should make Luthor and Cyrus quite happy."

No, I thought, stepping toward him. *No, you can't just... leave.* He evaded my reach.

"You will make an excellent queen. If you ever think of me, I hope it's with kindness." With every word, our bond strained, as if stretched to its very limit. The mating mark cooled until it felt like ice being pressed to my skin.

"And where, pray tell, are you going?" My tongue felt swollen, the words garbled. He couldn't just leave, could he? He'd been in New Orleans for hundreds of years, why would he leave now?

"Romania. With Katarina. We renewed our soul bond, and as I am now bound to her, she thought it best that we remain together. Forever."

Soul bond...bound to her...forever.

The entire room, our surroundings, melted away until all I saw were his lies. He'd played me again. And I'd fallen for it. "You can't be serious. What kind of game is this, Deston?"

"I am the one who told Katarina about you. I am the one who divulged your location and the reason she found you at the Cormier's." Shock kept me still, my brain turning into sludge. *He had to be lying. I'd trusted him. We were true mates. You couldn't hurt your true mate.*

He offered me a reluctant shrug. "As you pointed out, self-preservation is my main directive. Your heart-of-gold knights will keep you safe, and with the Cormiers' support, you have the beginnings of a decent court. Don't squander this chance, Seraphina. You won't get another opportunity."

In the shadows of the room, his eyes glowed like embers igniting.

"I'm leaving, but I want you to know this. You are right about everything. You might've been dragged into this world, but you're going to be the most powerful Queen the vampire world has ever seen. I would request only one thing."

I couldn't even answer, couldn't so much as formulate a single word.

He reached out and tipped my chin up, forced me to look into his eyes and see every emotion that was there. "Don't ever lose your soft heart, Seraphina. I once thought it was your biggest weakness, but it's the most beautiful thing about you."

I wrapped a sheet of steel around that softness, protecting myself from his crushing words, which threatened to break my barely beating heart. *Break me.*

He ran his fingers down the side of my face, then traced the edges of my cold lips. "You take my breath away, *mon amour.*"

I felt see-through, nothing but bones and air, my feather-light body barely touching the earth. *This couldn't be happening. Ten minutes ago, I was more complete than ever before, now I was being torn apart.*

He'd sold me out to Katarina. He'd betrayed me, just like everyone else.

I'd had the audacity to believe I was different. Better.

But I was just like everyone else, at least to Deston de Rayne.

His face was resolved when he stepped away. "Don't let them steal a single piece of you away. Viktor will come for you now, and you must be ready."

He tugged at the chain around my neck and drew out the key, kissed it. There was a metallic hum from the metal, as if he'd infused it with a bit of his magic.

"You may not believe this, but I remained loyal to you, even while nailed to that wall. In his haste to punish me, Viktor forgot to dampen my magic, my Queen."

His dark eyes flashed. "I removed the wards around Lyra's crypt. All you need is that key, and you can take away all of Viktor's power. Without Lyra to draw from, he can be killed."

"But I can't..."

"Kill a shell that was once filled with life? End the agony of a female I once served and admired? Which of these can't you abide, Seraphina? Ask yourself this." He dropped the key behind my shirt and curled a lock of my hair around his finger.

"If you were suffering on that table, would you want to be responsible for allowing Viktor to ruin everything you had built? To maim and torture and kill the subjects you loved? Or would you welcome the chance to stop him?"

I didn't answer because we both knew the answer to that one.

"Do not attempt to find me. Do not attempt to contact me." Every word drilled into my brain like an ice pick, and on the back of my neck, the mating mark went cold. "My life is with Katarina now. I will forget about you, Seraphina, I will forget everything between us."

His body went translucent. "You'd best do the same."

"Deston..."

But his name hung in the empty air where he'd been standing seconds before, and I realized he was gone.

In the emptiness he left behind, I realized I'd just gotten exactly what I wanted. He was gone, just like I'd hoped. I'd given him nothing, but he'd given me everything in return.

He'd offered me a chance to become everything he thought I could be, and his message was clear enough.

End Lyra's torture and kill the king.

Chapter 41
Seraphina

I double checked myself before I went through the doors, patting my burning cheeks, willing them to cool down.

"Deston's gone," I informed Luthor and Cyrus, keeping my tone easy and uncaring. "It looks like he sold us out all the way around. He's headed back to Romania with Katarina."

I couldn't even believe the words coming out of my mouth.

How had I been fooled so thoroughly?

Because despite my constant jabs at his character, I'd been convinced he'd never betray me.

"He's gone? Are you sure?" Cyrus asked sharply as I tried to pinpoint the pinched expression on his face. His nose flared, then he added quietly, "Are you all right, Seraphina? Let's get you out of those clothes." I pulled away, aware that he was smelling Deston on me.

I squeezed my eyes shut. "Let me go get cleaned up, then we should talk. I have a lot to process, and a lot to tell you, but..." I plucked at my bloodied clothing, then sidled away from him, eager to get the vestiges of Deston washed away.

Which was why I couldn't quite figure out why I stood staring at the running water for twenty minutes. I *liked* smelling like Deston. In fact, I wanted his scent all over me. As crazy as it was, I *wanted* to be mated to him.

But that was the mating bond speaking, not my head.

My head knew what my heart didn't.

Deston could never be trusted; it was in his nature to betray the ones he loved, no matter how deep the bond. Which was why he was headed to Romania right now, his arm around Katarina, her fangs in his neck, his cock in her...my mind went blank.

Renewed their bond. That meant they'd been bonded before.

The mere thought of them together—and I painted that fucking picture in my head, over and over—filled me with inexplicable, white-knuckled rage. Almost like jealousy, but...I wasn't jealous. I *couldn't* be.

I stumbled into the shower. Once I got his scent off me, I could forget what happened in the drawing room. Forget him completely. forget meeting him, forget I had *something branded on the back of my neck.*

Bonded. Deston was...what had he called it? Soul bonded to Katarina, not me.

He'd played me. Just like he always did. Well, never again.

By the time I walked back into the bedroom, a towel wrapped around me, I knew that wasn't going to happen. Between this tightness in my belly and the faint burning on the back of my neck, I knew Deston had stamped himself on to me permanently. I had to get him off. *Out.*

By the time I got downstairs, everyone was in full-blown planning mode. Caden, Silas, and Luthor had an attack plan laid out, down to the last second. Tessa was giving a speech about how she was looking forward to watching me tear Viktor's balls off. And everyone else was laughing uproariously.

Only Cyrus watched my every move, his quicksilver eyes gleaming far too brightly for my liking.

Since avoidance is usually the best policy, I went into the kitchen and made myself a sandwich. I inhaled it. I couldn't even remember the last time I'd eaten anything. Maybe that plate full of cookies that we had in the morning, which seemed like a thousand years ago.

Cyrus wandered in, skimmed his hands down my back, but even his calming magic couldn't take the edge off whatever I was feeling. Panic maybe, anxiety certainly, some misplaced sense of loss, perhaps.

"Do you know why he left, Seraphina?" Cyrus asked, running his hands down my arms this time and frowning when he didn't get the expected result.

"He left because he's a liar and a traitor. He's the one who told that evil witch about me, then he soul-bonded himself to her. So yeah, he's gone, and he couldn't care less about what we do next. That's all I want to say about the matter."

"Soul-bonded to Katarina, huh?" Cyrus asked thoughtfully. "That doesn't sound at all like my cousin."

"Well then, maybe he's lying about that too," I sniped as I slapped together another sandwich. I really was starving.

"Deston wouldn't lie about a soul bond. Those are some serious shit, Seraphina."

I rolled my eyes. "I don't think I'm ever going to get used to you speaking like that. Maybe we should cut back on your screen time. I know there's a setting..."

"I like my screen time, and you're not taking it away." Cyrus poured me a glass of milk, sliding it across the island to me. "Drink that, you need to hydrate."

"Milk is not hydration," I explained patiently. "Water is

hydration, or maybe unsweetened tea. But milk, not so much."

He rounded the island and wrapped his arms around me, as if willing me to feel better. "I don't care what it does, just drink it. You've lost weight, Seraphina, and I don't like seeing those bruises beneath your eyes. Do you want to talk about Deston?"

"No," I said curtly, drinking the milk to placate him. "Shouldn't we be evacuating? I mean, Viktor's going to be coming for us, right?"

"We're not going anywhere," Tessa said defiantly from the kitchen doorway, her hands on her hips. "He's driven me out once before. This is my home, and we're making a stand here. If Viktor wants to come after us, then he has to get through all of our defenses first."

"I appreciate that, but Katarina got through fairly easily," I pointed out uneasily. "I mean, she just *poofed* right in and out."

"Katarina is a two-thousand-year-old Queen. She has ancient power at her disposal. Viktor's, what? Two hundred years at most? He's strong, but he can't penetrate Father's wards, not without some effort, which means we'll have ample warning."

"And if he does get through?"

"Then you have to kill him, Seraphina." Tessa's eyes let off a faint glow of anticipation. "That's what all of this is been about, right? You getting strong enough to kill Viktor."

My fingers skimmed down the chain and curled around the key.

Deston's last words rang in my head. In order for me to kill Viktor, Lyra had to die too.

But what if I could save her and still kill Viktor?

"What are you thinking, Seraphina?" Cyrus murmured

in my ear, his hands massaging my shoulders. "This is a group effort now, which means we work as a team. No going off on your own and doing stupid shit." He squeezed especially hard to make his point.

"Stupid shit is kind of my thing, though," I joked half-heartedly, knowing that statement was truer than it should be.

"I think it's time me, Luthor, and you had a talk. Because to be honest, I don't know what to do next." In fact, my stomach was twisted into knots just thinking about this decision. Tessa turned to go, and I stopped her.

"You should know what's going on. Maybe... maybe you can help."

The reason we were in this mess was because I did exactly the kind of stupid shit that Cyrus had just accused me of. Maybe it was time I gave this *team player* thing a chance.

"Then we'll talk," Cyrus said neutrally, his gaze resting on Tessa. "I'll fetch Luthor. Is there somewhere private we can go?"

"The drawing room..." Tessa began.

"No, not in there." I interrupted. *Dear God, not in there.* "Is there anywhere else?"

"Father's office," she said firmly. "It's the next best place."

Luthor and Cyrus returned, and then Tessa led us to Hugh's office, closing us in together. I pulled the key out from beneath my shirt and placed it on the table between us, Tessa's eyes widening.

"That's a royal key," she whispered, glancing toward the locked door. "There are only five of them, and they remain with the King at all times."

"Not this one. It's mine."

Her eyes widened, and I turned to Luthor and Cyrus, unsure how to approach this. Maybe I'd included Tessa as a buffer, or maybe I'd just wanted some back up because what I had to tell them was momentous.

"I should've said something earlier, but to be fair, I didn't get a chance before Viktor came bursting in and everything went to hell." I cleared my suddenly dry throat. "Deston and I went to the palace to figure out what this key unlocks. Luthor, you straight up asked me what was in the chamber, right before Viktor invaded Ravenswood." His face went still, but Cyrus gave me a small, encouraging smile.

"I never answered you."

I took a deeper breath, which didn't seem to fill my lungs all the way. I feared, deep down inside, that the truth —and my deception—would cost me Luthor, if not Cyrus too.

My voice came out barely more than a whisper.

"Lyra's behind the door. She's still alive, well technically alive. Viktor's been siphoning power off her all these years. That's why he's so strong, how he's *stayed* so strong."

I looked between their stony faces, my determination ebbing by the second. "I should've told you before now. Should've found time, found a way, to tell you everything, but I just...didn't want to break your heart. I kept the truth from you and that's on me."

I squared my shoulders and waited for the inevitable outburst. "She's unconscious, and in some kind of long-term stasis, according to Deston. But we know about him and the truth, so take that with a grain of salt."

"She can't..." Luthor's voice trailed off, and he looked helplessly at Cyrus, who looked just as doubtful.

"We watched her die, Seraphina." Cyrus had absolute

conviction in his voice. "It's been over a hundred years. She can't be alive."

"She's alive... and in this...stasis, is what Deston called it. He couldn't get a read on any brain activity, and even though we were there for almost ten minutes, I never saw her take a breath."

"Stasis doesn't last a hundred years," Tessa said gently. "A few months, maybe a year, tops."

"She's alive," I said forcefully. "I wanted to bring her with us, but we never made it back to the room, like I planned." I shrugged my shoulders, looking Luthor in the eye. "I made a mistake, going alone, not trusting you. If you and Cyrus had been there, I know you would've found a way to get her out."

"If she's been in stasis this long," Cyrus said thoughtfully, "there would be nothing left of the Queen we knew. Her magic would have consumed her." He looked at Luthor, but he was deep in thought, his face inscrutable. I held my breath when he finally spoke.

"That door is warded with ancient magic that only the Queen... or Viktor, can bypass. Even with the key, we can't get to her."

"Normally, that would be true. But Deston claimed he dropped the wards on Lyra's crypt, while being held prisoner in the palace." I didn't want to give them false hope and reminded them gently, "But you know we can't trust him."

"We can on this," Luthor said firmly. "Deston was vested in Lyra's reign, did everything he could to ensure she remained in power and to hold the court together. He might be a cheating bastard, but he never let Lyra down."

I remembered his gentleness when he'd laid her hand

on her chest, pushed her hair back. Or had that all been for show, as well? I could hardly tell anymore.

I was the only one who knew Deston had sold Lyra out, paved the way for the Carpathians to attack the palace that fateful night. If Luthor and Cyrus ever found out the truth, they'd hunt him all the way to Romania and put his head on a spike.

"Even so, we have two options." I nodded at the key. "If she stays alive, Viktor has access to endless power. I'll never defeat him, no matter how much I try, and the only other option is..."

I let my voice trail off. Murdering an innocent woman while she was in a coma was one of the most heinous acts I could ever consider.

"If she's a purmagicae, then there's nothing left of the Lyra we knew," Luthor said quietly. "I'm your commander. I'll do it." But there was enough doubt in his voice, I knew he'd never get over it.

"If Viktor can help himself to her magic, why can't Seraphina?" Tessa asked cautiously. "I mean, if her power is based on Queen's magic, then she and Seraphina's power would be far more compatible."

She talked faster. "Familial magic is usually passed down from generation to generation. It makes sense that Lyra's magic would complement your own." Her eyes flashed. "If you take Lyra's magic before Viktor, you'd be stronger than him, even though he's two centuries older."

I rebelled at the idea. I was no thief, nothing like Viktor.

But this was exactly the kind of information we needed, in order to make smart decisions. I'd included Tessa in this conversation on a hunch, and now I was glad I did.

"We'd still have to get back into the palace. Access her crypt," I pointed out. Though another attack would be harder now, since Deston wasn't around to stage a distraction.

Viktor was probably headed this way, bringing the fight to us. Which could offer a solution to our dilemma. My brain was starting to work again, after that unmentionable escapade in the drawing room. But this would avoid us having to kill Lyra, which no one wanted no matter how much we rationalized it.

"So, we figure out a way into the palace. We did it once, we can do it again," Cyrus said, backing me up in words and by wrapping his arms around my middle. "In the meantime, what do we do about Viktor? You know he's coming."

Panic tightened my chest at the thought of it. Viktor would come, and it was up to me to stop him.

"But if he comes here, he'd bring all his forces, wouldn't he?" I suggested cautiously, "which means there won't be anyone left guarding the palace, will there?"

Chapter 42
Seraphina

Deston was gone and my newly minted mate mark burned like hellfire.

As if the damn thing knew we were separated by thousands of miles.

I arranged my hair, making certain to hide it. I didn't know if this sensation was something I'd have to get used to, or if it would eventually fade with time, but the pain cut through me like a blowtorch set on high.

I glanced over Cyrus's shoulder at the others gathered in the main banquet room, where Luthor was already proposing another palace incursion, Tessa emphatically backing him up, while I hid in the corner and licked my wounds on the couch.

I just couldn't come to terms with the fact Deston had sold me out to Katarina. I knew I hadn't been imagining all those moments we'd shared. And what we'd done together...

No, he hadn't been faking his desire. Nor had I.

Cyrus's hands began working their way toward the mark, and I shifted away, redirecting his hands lower. "I'm okay, just a bit stiff."

"Seraphina, I know." I looked away from those green eyes that seemed to know too much.

"About my shoulders? Well..."

"No, about the mating with Deston." The air whooshed out of me, my body going rigid with shock. Or fear.

"I... I don't know what you're talking about."

I pushed him away, but Cyrus pulled me right back into him, turned us until his body shielded me from the rest of the room. Laid his forehead against mine.

"It's okay, Fina. I know you're scared. I know Deston left, and while I haven't heard the whole story, I do know this. A mating bond can't ever be broken."

"Never?" *What did it make me, when that single word lifted my heart up with hope?*

"Never." He pulled away, his green eyes filled with pity. I hiccupped, then words spilled out of me like a fountain.

"He sold me out, and I trusted him. I trusted him, Cyrus. Do you know how many people I trust?" I held up two fingers. "You and Luthor. That's who. And he wormed his way into my heart, and then he told Katarina I was at the Cormier's. She could have killed someone."

I drew a shaky breath. "He betrayed me. Just like everybody else."

When he wrapped his whole body around me, all my confusion and misery finally took over, and I melted into a puddle. Burning tears spilled down my face; my chest shook with silent sobs. "We'll figure this out together. Everything will be all right, love. I promise."

He lifted my face up. "You planned on keeping this a secret, didn't you?" There was no accusation in his voice, not even when he added, "Didn't you think you could tell me?"

Now that Cyrus knew, and I didn't have to hide anymore, I fell apart.

Pain exploded inside me, made the words tumble out. "Because this hurts us, Cyrus. I lied to you both. And for what? For someone who's already bonded himself to another and flew away to freaking Romania, of all places. I've made a total mess of things." I tried to keep myself tamped down, but my nose was running, my throat raw.

"I'm sorry, Cyrus." I hiccupped. "I am so sorry."

Now they'd leave. And I wouldn't blame them one bit.

But all he did was nod. "I understand why you chose not to tell us. That we're your family. That you don't want to lose us. But you have to tell Luthor. He has to know, Fina, and he has to hear the truth from you."

I'd faced down revenants, Katarina, and Viktor, and none of them made me feel as afraid as I did right now.

"I know." I didn't think my misery could get any worse, but the thought of facing Luthor broke something in me. I couldn't stand hurting him, and this... What if he walked away?

"I can come with?" Cyrus offered gently, and for one wild second, I almost accepted. But I'd made this mess, and I'd face the consequences, without using Cyrus as a crutch, much as I wanted to.

"No. Luthor deserves the truth, and I'll tell him myself. Alone."

"I'll be right here when you get back." Cyrus's hands went back to massaging my sore muscles. "I've been around a long time, Fina." The kneading stopped. "Times like these, when your whole life seems to be slipping away..." He shook his head, his blond hair spilling over his shoulders. "It's not the end. I love you. Luthor loves you. And as much as I fucking hate to admit it, Deston loves you."

He sent another pulse of his magic into me, and my convulsing sobs eased up.

"Clearly, he doesn't." I rubbed my wet cheeks. "Because he's with Katarina. In *Romania*."

"Things aren't always what they seem."

"Seemed pretty clear to me. He told me never to..."

"Fina, think about how soul bonds work. My guess is, Deston never bound himself to Katarina of his own accord. She bound him to her, I expect, a long, long time ago." His fingers squeezed harder. "The one who's bonded cannot hide anything from their master. Not even their thoughts."

Everything inside me just stopped.

If that was even remotely true, then I'd been looking at this the wrong way. Hope curled in my chest. What if he hadn't told Katarina anything? What if she'd...read his thoughts?

"We've figured out how we'll get into the palace," Luthor interrupted. How he'd crept up on us, I didn't know, but one minute we were alone, the next, he was sprawled on the sofa next to me. I drank in the sight of him, memorizing every strong line of his face, the slightly crooked nose, the silver-streaked hair down to his shoulders—just because I liked it that way—when he couldn't care less.

"When Viktor launches his attack, he'll leave the palace mostly unguarded. That's when we go in and you'll take Lyra's magic."

I squirmed. "I'm not sure I'm comfortable with that."

"I've seen magic transfers done before." Tessa plopped down beside Cyrus. "I can help." She tilted her head to the side. "Hey, are you okay? Your eyes look..."

"Seraphina. Are you ill?" There was a note of alarm in Luthor's voice, and I pulled away from his hand massaging my knee. Instead of the usual delicious heat, his touch just made me feel guiltier.

"I'm fine, just heading outside to practice, Luthor." My

fake smile slipped off my face as quickly as it appeared. "I know you're in the middle of... planning. But could you come with me? I need some advice." I pushed off the sofa.

"It's not safe out there, Seraphina," Luthor reminded me, his tone patient. "Better to stay inside and out of sight tonight."

"Maybe, but since Katarina's on her way back to Romania, I don't have to worry about her skanky ass ambushing me in the woods."

"Skanky ass. I like that." Cyrus laughed softly, but I caught the hint of sadness there, too.

"I'll go with you, but we can't stay out long." Luthor's shoulders sagged and I glanced at Cyrus. *Does he already know?*

Cyrus discreetly shook his head.

"We're heading outside," Luthor informed the room, and activity paused for a second before resuming. One last scan of the room had Luthor's eyes glowing intensely, his posture—his entire demeanor the exact opposite of how he'd been acting these last few days.

He had a purpose now; it was clear in the way he held his body, the set of his shoulders, the pride. After months of being my lover, I was finally seeing the real Luthor. Even if he couldn't accept the truth about me and Deston, maybe he'd stay on as my commander.

That way, I could still see him, even if he wasn't mine.

Luthor offered me his hand and I took it, noting how my own disappeared completely into his.

I didn't want to lose him.

I wanted to be happy.

And if I failed at the first, I would never have the second.

"THAT WAS..." When I cast my magic, Luthor's voice trailed off in quiet wonderment. "Thank you for showing me. I've never seen anything like that, Seraphina. Not even with Lyra."

We'd opted not to go into the woods after last time. Instead, we'd compromised on the long, gravel drive, the moss hanging from the live oaks swaying from my last burst of power, but not a single leaf was out of place.

I was every bit as amazed as Luthor.

I didn't know how, but everything had finally clicked. My magic belonged to me, feeling as natural as my body did. There was an ease to using my magic now, and miraculously, this power did exactly what I wanted it to do.

So, I had one thing going for me, at least.

Luthor—biceps bulging beneath his tee—seemed perfectly happy to be out there, settled on the hood of a very expensive car, the cold not bothering him one bit. He looked relaxed, but beneath his mask of ease, he was tense, waiting for me to drop whatever bomb I was about to drop.

And I was dragging this out.

"Luthor, I..."

"When we get to the palace, I want you to stick with Caden. Cy and I will take the lead. Silas assured me he knows the palace like the back of his hand, so he'll bring up the rear."

"Luthor..."

"I thought you wanted to know the plan? Then Caden will—"

I stepped up to him, put my finger over his lips. He closed his eyes and kissed my fingertip gently and something dark and empty tightened my belly. I had to tell him.

"Luthor, I'm mated to Deston." His brow crinkled in confusion, then his eyes narrowed, as if trying to discern if I was joking. From my miserable expression, he decided...I was not.

"Me and Deston are mated."

His whole body went perfectly still. Dread filled me up, erasing all of Cyrus's encouraging words, leaving nothing but me holding my breath while panic crawled through my veins. Luthor tilted his head, the watery sun picking out the silver streaks in his hair. He spoke tonelessly when he was under duress, precisely, cutting off every word like a knife.

"I know, Seraphina. I've known for days, now."

I pulled back, searched his face and found him to be every bit as miserable as I was. "You did, didn't you? That's what you kept trying to tell me, isn't it?" He nodded.

"I...guess I was the only one who *didn't* know what was happening." I sighed.

"So, why are you still here? You should be with him, Seraphina. You should be with your mate." He asked so gently, so sincerely, he broke my damn heart. His shoulders were stiff, his face molded into harsh planes, and still... *he only thought of me.*

"Because I'm right where I belong."

I'd realized something just now, after my little break-down. "I wouldn't have left with Deston, even if he'd asked. I'm staying here. With you and Cyrus. Because you are my family, and I couldn't bear to lose you."

I touched his cold hand, sent a burst of heat from my fingers into his. "We have work to do. A king to kill and a kingdom to save. And we're the only ones who can."

I raised my hands, sent another powerful wave of magic down the driveway, scattering gravel as the force pushed the air out before it. Calling the power back into myself, I thanked my lucky stars that the family cemetery was on the other side of the house.

No sense in causing skeletal mayhem just yet.

"I didn't choose any of this, Luthor. This chose me. The clan, the mating, all of this—is now my life." A thrill of realization shocked through me. *And I'm glad for every bit of it.*

"You should also know there's more between Deston and I than just the mating. I have feelings for him, ones that I don't understand." I wasn't really a queen yet, but I was learning to be. And part of that was honesty and accepting the consequences.

I touched his arm, his face, willing him to forgive me. "I may not have chosen this life, but I did choose you and Cyrus. The thought of losing either of you... I can't even fathom what that would be like, and I won't. All I can do is ask you to stay long enough for us to figure this out. There has to be a way to make this work." I didn't know if Luthor realized I was holding my breath, or how scared I was, or the ten thousand arguments I'd use if he did decide to leave.

"A mating complicates things, Seraphina."

"It does," I agreed. "But if we love each other... Can we make this arrangement work, somehow?"

"What have I told you, Fina?" Luthor tipped my face up to his. Kissed me, as reverently as he had that very first time. Like I was the most precious thing in his world. "All I've ever wanted was to see you happy." He brushed his knuckles down my face, and I leaned into his touch. "We'll make this work."

He chuckled. "Cy already knows, doesn't he?"

"He guessed. I was the only one who was surprised, which shouldn't really be that...surprising, I guess."

"Thank you for trusting me with the truth, my love." He kissed my forehead, and some of my fears settled, hopelessness replaced with a flicker of optimism and the knowledge that I really didn't deserve this male

Luthor's arms tightened, his lips tracing my cheek. "I know how much rests on your shoulders. How hard learning this new world has been for you. But most of all, I know what it cost you to come to me, but all your worries... are for naught. I love you, more than life itself, and nothing will ever change that."

Maybe this would work. I snuggled deeper into his protective embrace, into this feeling of safety and adoration. *Maybe our family would stay intact, and we'd kill Viktor and all my dreams would come true.*

One thing was for sure, while I had my doubts about Deston's motives, I was no longer conflicted about what came next.

Viktor was going down, and his kingdom would be mine.

I shivered and without another word, Luthor ghosted us into the grand foyer, where I draped my thin coat over the end of the carved banister. I was chilled to the bone, my feet numb.

I flexed my stiff fingers, renewing my undying hatred for the cold.

And for winter, in general.

Cyrus grinned when we reappeared and gave me a thumbs-up. I gave him one back, feeling completely ridiculous, even while elation bubbled inside of me like a fountain.

Part of me was whole again, but the other part...

I couldn't lie. There was a physical hole in my center where Deston used to be.

And fuck Katarina for using magic to enslave him. Fuck her for twisting the truth so cleverly, when I should have trusted my own gut. Had I known the full scope of her depravity, I would have stood over her broken body and finished the job.

My legs felt like lead when I trudged upstairs for another shower. Maybe Deston would find a way to break the bond between them and come home. There had to be some way to break such a bond...

I sighed. *I knew the way.*

Katarina had to die. But first, Viktor had to die, so she'd

have to get in line. If I could be two places at once, I'd free my mate and kill a monster, but I was only one person. One thing was for sure, my anger at Deston was gone. Our mating wasn't his fault—it was the universe's, so I should really direct my fury toward the stars.

And, for an hour, I did exactly that, until my skin turned red and pruny, a crazy idea forming. Getting into the palace was our biggest challenge, using precious manpower and putting everyone's lives in danger.

But there was a better way.

A nearly fool-proof means of accomplishing our goal, without expending a single bullet.

I appreciated Tessa and her males, I did.

Hugh's help in getting us reinforcements had been genius. Still, I thought back fondly to when it had only been Luthor and Cyrus and I. Now there were other lives on the line, and I felt the weight of that responsibility like an anvil on my heart.

My job was to protect the most vulnerable among us, both as their Queen and as their friend. If I planned to shoulder all the responsibilities of a queen, I had better start thinking like one.

So, the more I considered my crazy idea, the more this seemed like the right path. If what Deston said was true, I didn't have to unravel the magic wards that guarded Lyra's crypt, I just had to unlock that door.

The door opened, and Luthor walked in, steam parting before him like the Red Sea. "We've got a solid plan for breaching the castle." His gaze slid over my naked body, and heat of a different sort raced through me, especially the way his eyes got all dark and hooded. "When you're ready, come down and we'll fill you in."

I gazed at him longingly through the glass shower door, but didn't invite him in.

I couldn't, not when I still felt guilty of how I'd handled everything these past days.

But soon. soon we'd be together again, once Viktor was dead.

"I know that look on your face, Seraphina." Luthor leaned his shoulder into the doorframe. "You're thinking about going after Viktor by yourself, aren't you?" He shook his head, taking up the entire doorway. "Not going to happen."

"And you'd rather put all these people in harm's way?" I countered hotly, shutting off the water.

"These *people*, as you put it, are your court. They would die for you," Luthor countered, a touch of temper in his voice. But he picked up a towel, held it open.

"You have to see this from their point of view, Seraphina." He wrapped it around me, pushing wet curls out of my face.

"If they thought for one second you'd put yourself in jeopardy because you didn't trust them?" He shook his head emphatically. "Speaking as your commander, you'll never win the loyalty of people you're not willing to trust, Seraphina."

"And I'm not willing to put a bunch of lives at risk, just to get inside the palace, when there's a better way." I stood still while Luthor dried me off, leaning into his familiar touch. Most of the tension was gone between us, leaving a lingering uncertainty. I'd decided I could live with that, for now.

"Then how, pray tell, do we get in?" Luthor's narrowed, suspicious gaze met mine in the mirror.

"The same way Deston did. Viktor will take me there."

Once I was dressed, we headed downstairs.

After Luthor explained my plan, Cyrus laughed for a full minute, while I fidgeted and wished I'd just kept my idea to myself, like usual.

This trusting-other-people-shit wasn't for the faint of heart.

"You must be crazy, if you think either of us would agree to that."

"If we go in there, guns blazing, what's the first thing Viktor will do?" I spread my hands wide. "He'll unleash his guards on us. His revenants. *His magic.* God knows what else. We'll be fighting for our lives, and there will be casualties. What if he turns these people into revenants. I won't live with that on my conscious, *I can't.*"

The room, and the table, were empty, since everyone else had left to get a couple hours of sleep. Silas and Rafael were outside, on watch. It was funny, how easily I'd begun to keep track of people.

"We have a window of opportunity, and we can't let it slip by." I urged softly.

"We launch a full-on attack, before he engages us, he'll siphon off all of Lyra's power. Then he'll resurrect the wards around that impenetrable chamber. Once he does, chances are, I won't be able to kill him, no matter how hard I try."

Luthor slid into the seat next to mine, and Cyrus sat on my other side, his hand resting lightly on my knee.

It felt good to know we were a team again.

"However, if he takes me prisoner and thinks he has the upper hand?" I winced when understanding dawned on their faces. "He won't even think about that chamber, which means all I have to do is incapacitate him long enough to open that door and reach Lyra."

"What if you can't access her magic?" Luthor countered hotly. "Just the fact you're even considering this as a viable option makes me want to pull my hair out."

"Please don't, you have very nice hair." I attempted a smile, but it slid off my face. "Look, if Deston really dropped the wards, all I need is a couple of minutes. I remember where the door is, not far from the Hall of Mirrors where Deston was." I refused to say *nailed to the wall*.

I clenched my hands into fists in my lap.

"If I take all her power, there will be nothing left, and I could end this. Isn't that what you both want?" I looked between them, and finally, they nodded. "Then this is our opportunity. All this talk and posturing about killing Viktor, and here is the way to do it. Cleanly, so nobody gets hurt."

"Except for you, of course," Cyrus observed coolly. "You go in there, and one step of this doesn't work, you're dead, Fina."

He snapped his fingers. "If Viktor finds the key? Dead."

Another *snap*. "If he incapacitates you first? Dead."

"The slightest little mistake? Dead." *Snap.*

"Yeah, I get it. I fuck up and I die. What else is new?"

Luthor and Cyrus traded glances.

"You clearly want to say something," I set my hands on my hips, "So say it. I have the control part down. With Lyra's power...I can kill him. I know it."

"You escaped from him once before." Luthor said quietly. "Viktor won't risk losing you again. He'll kill you quick this time."

"Except he won't kill me, at least not right away. Like Deston, he'll want to gloat because it feeds his ego." I walked myself through the scenario, seeing it from Viktor's perspective.

"He'll keep me alive because I'm a shiny, new toy. Because he's weak and he needs time to guild himself back up. All I need is *one* opportunity. What do you think, Cyrus? If I managed a direct hit, would that give me the time I need to reach the crypt?"

"It could," Cyrus said, while Luthor glowered at us both. "But you're making a lot of assumptions here, Fina. And there's about a hundred things that can go wrong. A frontal assault keeps you out of the fighting and accomplishes the same goal."

"A frontal assault puts twenty people, maybe more, in danger. This way...it's only me."

"And that's supposed to make us feel better?" Luthor snapped, dragging his hand through his hair. "If you think for one second, I'll allow you to put yourself in..."

"She's our Queen, Luthor," Cyrus quietly reminded him. "There is merit to her plan. You saw what she did today. If she had more power, she could kill him."

Luthor shot him a cold, disbelieving look. "And like you said, one tiny mistake, and he kills her."

"What if Viktor managed to catch both of us?" Cyrus suggested, tapping his fingers on the table. "I'd be inside the palace with her, so she wouldn't be alone. I could make sure she got that opening that she needed."

"Neither of you are listening to me." I pushed to my feet, panic already simmering in my veins at the thought of

Cyrus getting hurt. And while I realized how absolutely hypocritical I was being right now, I couldn't stop myself, not when it came to protecting my males.

"I said *alone*. That means *by myself*. That means nobody except for me. I go in, I get this done. Worst-case scenario, I fail." I paused, taking a breath. "But once Viktor discovers that chamber is unprotected, it won't take him long to realize what we're after, and our window has closed for good."

Luthor fixed us both with a steady stare before limping to the door.

"Give me an hour to think this through. On the surface, my Queen, your plan is a clever one. I especially like using Viktor's ego against him. But there has to be another way. Any one of us could take that key and open that door. It doesn't have to be you."

"But according to Tessa, only one of us can access a queen's magic. And that *is* me. Plus, Lyra and I share Marvelle blood, which must account for something. Two minutes, max." I assured him. "I know exactly where Lyra's crypt is. I can do this, Luthor."

"I said, I need to think about this." On his way out, Luthor fixed us both with an ice-cold gaze before adding, "Just because it's a good plan, doesn't mean it will work. And I can tell you from experience, everything that can go wrong, will."

He didn't turn back. "And that's not a risk I'm willing to take."

K atarina slid me a look beneath her lashes, one I was sure, she thought was seductive. I wanted to vomit.

"How long has it been since you've flown, Deston?"

"Under my own power? Or someone else's?"

She indicated the plush cockpit around us. "In a plane. In the sky. Don't be difficult, Deston, just because you didn't get your way."

I gritted my teeth. We were still on US soil, where the painful, insistent tug of the mating bond between Seraphina and me was a constant reminder...*my mate was in grave danger.*

Right now, my only goal was to get Katarina out of the country and away from Seraphina.

The old spider was stronger and faster than the rest of us, and her brain was half-rotted by time.

Between her and Viktor, Katarina posed the bigger threat, and I wanted this monster as far away from my mate as was physically possible. Once we reached Romania, I'd find a way to neutralize the soul bond and kill her without an ounce of remorse. Then I'd come back here and finalize my mating bond with Seraphina.

Because we were not finished. Not even fucking close.

I'd done everything I could to help Seraphina and the others before Katarina activated the soul bond. For the next few weeks, I would have to guard every move I made, every casual thought that floated through my head, because she would know everything if I wasn't careful.

"Ah, thank you for explaining simple aeronautics. When are we taking off?" I asked. "Obviously, I'd like to put some distance between Viktor and I." I flexed my hand, nail holes almost healing, but still flecked with blood.

I had surrounded myself with a thick enough layer of magic, she wouldn't smell Seraphina's scent all over me, and I wouldn't drop it until we were across the ocean. If Katarina had the slightest idea of what Fina meant to me...

Fuck. I couldn't even imagine what she would do.

Dropping the wards on Lyra's crypt was the best advantage I could offer my mate, especially given my miserable situation. Once Seraphina killed Lyra, once Viktor was weakened, she stood a chance.

If she was strong enough to kill Lyra.

Everything hinged on Seraphina doing the wrong thing, when her soft, gentle heart was telling her to do the opposite.

My mating mark, seared into my left side, burned like nothing I'd experienced before. I cringed, knowing Seraphina was enduring the same agony. I resisted reaching down and rubbing it, wouldn't allow my moment of weakness to tip Katarina off.

I knew if I opened up the mating bond, I'd feel Seraphina's confusion, even her fear.

But I closed that thought down, as well. If Katarina ever discovered Seraphina and I were true mates, she'd move heaven and earth to make sure Seraphina died.

"Why are we still on American soil?" I asked peevishly. "I thought you were eager to return to Romania and show off your prize?"

We'd been sitting on the tarmac for hours and hadn't so much as moved. The plane was ready, the small private runway clear. Clearly, Katarina was waiting for something.

"We'll get there soon enough," she said, beckoning a minion over who showed her something on his phone. From the look on her face, the news wasn't what she was expecting.

I had no doubt Katarina hadn't bothered to learn the intricacies of this century's technology. Back when I knew her, she barely understood the mechanics of a horse and cart, so cell phones would be far beyond her patience to master.

But she had weaknesses, ones I could exploit. Ones I *would* exploit.

"I've been summoned back to the palace. It seems Viktor wants to know why you are not languishing on his wall of shame."

"Shall I explain you rescued me?"

"I will tell him the truth." She smiled that red, wicked smile. "Your little pet attempted to save you, so I fought her off and took you for myself." She sighed. "Sweet little Viktor will not argue the point, especially once I deliver this rogue queen to him."

I rose from my seat, my body reacting instinctively to this threat to my mate. Katarina yanked on the soul bond and shoved me back down into my seat. I glared up at her, fighting her stranglehold with everything I had. She smiled, lust kindling in those dead eyes of hers.

"Fight all you want, lover. There's no escape."

She ran a nail up my cheek. "You will stay here, Deston. I will smooth out this little snag, and then we will be on our way. In the end, everyone gets what they want."

Chapter 46
Seraphina

Rushing down main touristy street in the Garden District, I tightened my coat around me, cursing the cold. For whatever reason, this horrid weather didn't affect either Cyrus or Luthor the way it did me.

A light rain fell, and the hushed silence was louder than any screaming crowd could ever be. Several sets of eyes followed our progress, the same ones that had been watching us for nearly ten minutes.

I pretended to scratch my neck, double-checking the chain and key were still securely around my neck and trying to soothe the annoying burning sensation from the mate mark.

Easy, Seraphina, Cyrus gave my arm a reassuring squeeze. *The guards are closing in, but they won't risk an all-out fight in such a public place, not with all these humans around.*

So far, we were on schedule.

Luthor was a dozen yards behind us, hiding in plain sight in front of one of the small, trendy shops that lined Magazine Street. We weren't too far from my old apartment where I'd been abducted and thrust into my new life.

New Orleans was a foreign world now, filled with laughter and cell phones and brightly colored shopping bags. I'd only been away a few months, and now I didn't fit in anymore.

Cyrus hurried me down the street, dodging families finishing up their Christmas shopping, if their packages were any indication.

Christmas.

I wondered if vampires celebrated holidays, or if we had our own?

Keep moving, we should seem nervous to make this more realistic.

I am nervous, I thought back at him. *I don't want anyone to get hurt.* I nodded toward the woman with two little kids standing in front of a window full of animated snowmen.

Once we get to Louisiana Avenue, there will be less foot traffic. They'll ambush us when there are no witnesses. Which means they'll wait.

I knew Luthor was right behind us, wrapped in his shadows, and hoped the Knightsguard wouldn't discover there was a third person in our party.

Don't look up, there's two on the roof.

Got them, I assured him, easily spotting the fast-moving vampires racing through the shadows above our heads.

More coming up behind us. Cyrus sped up until we were almost jogging. *They're more eager than I expected. We need to draw them away from these humans.*

There were screams behind us as a group of young girls tumbled face first to the pavement, packages and purses scattering across the pavement.

They couldn't see the fast-moving trio of uniformed guards that had hit them, racing faster than their human eyes could track. One guard leaned down, grabbed a handful of hair, and snapped at a delicate throat. Another guard yanked him away.

We'll kill that one first, I thought to Cyrus, anticipation rising inside me

My bloodthirsty Queen, I'll take that as a direct command, he responded coolly.

A ripple of relief went through me when we made our right onto Louisiana. Cyrus was right, there were hardly any people here, and half the streetlights were burned out. This place was perfect.

They're going to rough me up, Seraphina, and you're going to let them, Cyrus reminded me sternly, for like the tenth time. *This is no time to deviate from the plan.*

Bullshit If they get too rough, I'm kicking their asses.

No way I would let Cyrus get hurt, just to make this appear more real.

Luthor only agreed to this because you swore that you'd follow his directions to the letter, Cyrus reminded me, hand squeezing my arm. *You promised you'd keep your word, remember?*

Yes, I did say that. But now that we're here... I jogged faster to keep up. *The thought of them putting their hands on you makes me twitchy.*

Twitchy or not, you'll let this play out, understand? They'll rough me up plenty, but nothing I won't heal from.

Luthor's stern warning echoed what Cyrus just told me. *The important thing is getting you both inside that palace in one piece. Outing your magic now won't accomplish that task, Seraphina.*

You never let me have any fun, I thought back at both of them, magic stinging the ends of my fingers.

The more power you show now, the tighter the bonds will be when they bring you in front of Viktor.

Look like a little mouse, and they'll treat you like one. Cyrus smiled down at me wolfishly.

Roar like a dragon, and they'll put you in shackles, and then neither of us are going to get out of this.

Fine. I spooled my magic back in, surveying the nearly empty street. *This looks like as good a place as any, do you agree?*

I do.

I pulled out a borrowed cell phone and pretended I was searching for a location.

After you kill Viktor and become Queen, can I have one of those? Cyrus asked, reminding me of an anxious middle schooler, eager to get his first smart phone.

If you're good and keep your grades up, then yes, you can.

Cyrus nuzzled my neck. *Oh, I intend to keep it up, my Queen, trust me on that.*

My whole body tensed as guardsmen closed in from all sides.

I had to hand it to Viktor, they moved in clean formation, not giving us a clear avenue of escape. Not that we couldn't escape if we wanted to, but still, I was impressed.

Just like Cyrus predicted, they were rough when they tackled him down to the pavement, an oncoming car nearly hitting them, my heart freezing as I watched the tires barely miss Cyrus's head, pinned to the street.

As much as it pained me, I followed directions, limiting myself to one broken nose and a possible fractured arm when they finally got me under control.

I'm right here, Seraphina, Luthor's reassuring voice echoed in my head. *I'll be with you all the way through those palace doors.*

By the time they subdued Cyrus, one of the guards lay dead in the street, and another had his own knife sticking out from his shoulder. Cyrus waggled his brows at me with another wolfish grin before we all dematerialized out of the human world and straight into the vampire one.

The smell of putrification filled my nostrils before we even stopped moving, and I knew exactly where we'd landed.

The room swam into view, Viktor on the throne, Cyrus forced to his knees beside me as I tucked my hands behind my back, hoping if I appeared small and weak enough, they wouldn't think to bind me.

Cyrus hadn't been roughed up too badly, at least from what I could see out of the corner of my eye. But he'd been shackled with those awful magic-dampening manacles, which meant he would be little to no help.

Excitement and panic did their little dance inside of me, leaving me nearly breathless while I mentally ran down my to-do list.

Incapacitate Viktor.

Take care of any guards that stood in my way.

Unlock the door and borrow Lyra's magic.

I was using the word borrow because stealing seemed like a shitty thing to do. And no matter what, I wouldn't kill her. There had to be another way, I just hadn't come up with it yet.

I didn't blink as Viktor fixed that mad, red-eyed stare on me. Time stretched out between us, while everything—the guards, the old, rotting bodies nailed to the wall, even the air itself—faded away.

This asshole had to die.

Outside of that, nothing else mattered.

Viktor's face stretched into something that he probably thought was a smile, then an ashy, maggot-feeling magic filled the room, buffeting me, sending the guards reeling back a step. I squeezed my sweaty palms closed but never dropped my stare.

A raspy hissing sort of sound came out of Viktor's mouth, and it took me a minute to realize he was laughing. After a second, I saw why. Two of the guards had Cyrus face down on the floor, the point of a sword pressed against the back of his neck.

"I've tried cutting his head off before," Viktor said conversationally, "Yet it always grows back. Perhaps this time, it won't, and I can shut him up for good."

Oh, no no no no no.

"I can assure you"—Cyrus growled, even though his face was smashed into the floor—"I'll never give you that satisfaction."

The tip of the spear dug in deeper, and Cyrus's voice rang in my head.

Pull up your power now, Seraphina, before they shackle you.

Two of the guards headed my way, a set of gleaming iron shackles dangling from their hands and a shiver of fear trembled down my spine. Viktor leaned forward on his throne, mouth parted in anticipation.

I let my magic flow freely, reveling in the rush of power, even as the onslaught made my blood heat. But...there was a new strength to my magic now, an untested depth that resonated through me. I didn't know what was different— my magic or me—but this dark power was more attuned to my wishes, as if waiting for my direction.

Darkness wreathed my fingers, and now...now I *swore* I tasted Deston on my tongue, swore I could almost *feel* him carefully guiding my magic, the mating mark glowing with heat.

Could...could this control be a side effect of our mating?

Do it, Seraphina. do it now.

The second I willed my magic to become invisible, an

ephemeral rush of power coated everything in the room, like a shimmering layer of illusion. Candles flickered wildly overhead, the shadows in the corners of the room seemed to shudder.

I twisted my fingers and burned away every residue of Viktor's magic in the room, choking the breath out of the approaching guards, who dropped to the floor, clawing at their throats.

Then I pinned the blond king right where he sat, on his beloved throne.

"Enjoy that throne while you have it, motherfucker, it won't be yours much longer."

I didn't care if he heard me because the floor was riddled with the bodies of writhing, choking guards, while Cyrus was already on his feet, turning his back to me.

With a thought, my magic transformed into a sliver of a key, unlocking the manacles, and the shackles fell from his hands. Together, we turned to face the king.

Captive on his throne, Viktor roared Cyrus's name, cursing both of us as he fought.

In this moment, I still had the advantage, but I was already down to the reserves of my magic. In my haste, I'd drawn too deeply and too quickly. Viktor was fighting me with everything he had, and my grip was failing, as he ripped holes in my magic. If I didn't get to Lyra, and soon, Cyrus and I would both be back on our knees.

I released Viktor, then wrapped every ounce of magic I had around his neck and *squeezed*.

There was something satisfying about watching his red eyes roll back in their sockets and his body go limp. And if I had more magic and more time, I would have finished the job, but the second that he collapsed at the base of the throne, I turned, then raced down the hallway leading to Lyra's crypt.

"Luthor and I will hold off anyone foolish enough to come after you," Cyrus called, but I didn't have time to answer. I had only moments to take Lyra's power for my own, before Viktor recovered.

While I ran, I pulled the key from around my neck. I tentatively reached out to touch the door. If it was still spelled, if Deston had lied, the ward would most likely kill me. My fingers touched plain old, half-rotted wood, and I slid the key into the lock, then watched in bemused wonderment as the gold liquefied and filled the chamber.

I heard the faint click, then the pungent smell of burning pitch hit my nose.

L yra lay on the altar, exactly how Deston and I had
left her.

I pushed my sleeves up to my elbows, walked
over, and held my hands over her still body.

"I'm so sorry, Lyra. I'm sorry about all of this," I
murmured, feeling like *somebody* had to apologize to this
woman for everything that had happened to her. "I wish
my grandmother could've done more, or Luthor and Cyrus.
I wish that everything had turned out differently, that you
were still Queen, and I could've grown up knowing you."

A trickle of magic rose from her body, crackling ozone
burned my nose.

My palms felt like they were pressed against frosty
metal, so intense, they *burned*. A deeper cold pierced me
straight through, something mercurial, heavy, old. Why
wasn't her magic like my fire? Were we really so different?

I calmed my racing heart, forced myself to relax and
accept her magical gift, not fight this awful sensation of
being taken over by something foreign.

Lyra's magic slipped through my veins like quicksilver,
mercurial enough I couldn't get a read on what it did or
even how powerful she was, only that for every drop I took,
Viktor got one less.

By now, my palms were numb, the bone-chilling cold

creeping up my arms, across my chest, spilling into my lungs, making breathing impossible. I assured myself this pain was worth it because every piece of power I took made Viktor weaker.

Frost bubbled up over my face, right before crystals crackled into my mouth, then ice froze my stiffening tongue. This tasted like a Minnesota winter. Bitter, empty, arctic. Nearly painful as her power tangled and twisted with my own.

I tried to blink. couldn't.

Tried to suck in a breath...*couldn't*.

All of a sudden, I felt like a thin, glass lightbulb trying to contain a nuclear explosion. Fragile.

Breakable.

On instinct, I pulled away.

Struggled to yank my hands back, away from the agonizing pain that exploded through my hypothermic body, from my head to my frozen feet. But my body wouldn't respond because my flesh was already *solidifying*.

If I'd been human, I would have already been dead, my skin blue and frost-coated, my rigid arms holding my frozen-solid hands over Lyra's body, as she pushed more and more of her power into me. I searched for my fire, anything to fend off this creeping chill, but my magic was gone, buried beneath an avalanche of ice.

And that's when Lyra finally spoke.

Hello, niece.

Queen Lyra's melodious voice sounded so much like my mother's; tears sprang to my eyes. Then froze on my cheeks.

Only a small piece of me remains amongst the dust, and skin, and magic. Nothing you could even call vampire, anymore. But you will become my vessel. I will fill you with my magic, down to the dregs. The king who steals from me, leaves enough power in the well to replenish. Once I give you everything I have, this will finally end.

Please stop, I begged. *You're killing me.*

Sometimes, killing is a mercy.

Oh God, she was using me to end her suffering. My eyes were wide open, my brain still able to process the maelstrom of magic swirling around the room, the shivering, stabbing pain in my yet-unfrozen flesh, but...

Was I even still alive? Could vampires survive being frozen? I didn't know anymore.

I need you to stop.

No one stopped Viktor. No one came to save me. Except you.

I can't take any more, I pleaded. *Please, please don't make me do this.* My arms were solid now, rock-hard, pain like I'd never felt squeezed through me as muscles went rigid, blood froze in my veins.

Take it all, child, take every last drop. This must end.

I couldn't have stopped her if I'd wanted to. My organs stiffened. If someone tapped a finger against my forehead, I would crack into pieces.

If I took another drop, I'd die.

Almost there, child, just a little more, Lyra's voice commanded obedience, even as she forced the last bits of herself into me. My brain went sluggish, her words turning to sludge as winter wrapped around my brain, turning the gray matter solid.

Suddenly the onslaught stopped, the trickle of frost and starlight ending as quickly as it began.

Please. Someone help me. Don't let me die.

My last bit of consciousness reached for a lifeline, anything that might save me before I disappeared. There was a flicker on the back of my neck, the dying ember of my mating mark, the one that once burned like melted steel in a bellow fire. I latched onto that faint flame and *yanked*, and a faint tendril of warmth curled through my body. Not enough. Not nearly enough, as darkness crept in.

Somewhere, on the other end, someone tugged on the chain around my heart.

Deston.

Hang on, Seraphina. I've got you.

Heat roared through me, melting ice, frost turning to water droplets on my blue-tinged skin, prickles of pain racing through me as my flesh went from solid to supple once more.

In the distance, Luthor was screaming.

Blood bloomed in my mouth, dripped from my nose, and I wondered if I was dying.

Time seemed to stop, or perhaps, sped up, I couldn't tell. I vaguely heard Luthor calling my name while I clawed myself out of death and into life.

By the time my eyes thawed out enough to see, Lyra was gone, her shriveled body boasting a long-handled dagger sticking out of her chest, a faint bloom of red around the hilt where it sunk into her chest between her clawed hands.

A huge, rugged male stepped back, his gaze flicking from Lyra to me, the glimmer of recognition in his amber-gold eyes disappearing the second our gazes connected. Then Luthor stepped in front of me and blocked everything out.

"Seraphina." Luthor swept me up in his arms, hugged my shaking body against his. "You're alive. You were... God, I don't know what you were."

Through the doorway, the sounds of battle echoed, then we ducked as gunfire crackled over our heads, bullets pinging off the stone and rattling around the crypt. Luthor ghosted me to safety against the wall behind the door.

"Fontaine," the stranger ordered, "I don't care how you do it but get her *moving*. The girl has to finish this before Viktor and Katarina kill us all."

I curled desperately into Luthor's big, warm body, absorbing all the heat I could. "How long was I out?" My thick tongue struggled to make words, my still-thawing body prickling with pain, like my flesh had been asleep for years.

My brain finally caught up to what the burly stranger said. *Katarina was here?*

"An hour," Luthor muttered roughly, his arm banded around me like iron.

"An hour?" Anxiety spiked high. "It couldn't have been that long. I just walked in here a couple minutes ago."

"Maybe a couple of minutes to you, but to the rest of us, it's been an eventful hour." He glanced through the open door, then over to the broody stranger. "Caden brought reinforcements, and they're all good soldiers, but they're outnumbered and outgunned."

"Fontaine." The stranger poked his head out the door, then growled. "Get her moving, or this will be over before she gets her chance. They can't hold out much longer."

"Look, strange person who I don't know." My words were a muddied snarl of sound, barely intelligible. "I was frozen into a solid block of ice about five minutes ago. Give me a second to pull myself together here."

"Name's Sebastian Blackwell. Your magic wore off, Viktor is free, Katarina arrived, and the throne room has become a bloody battle ground that's about to get a whole lot bloodier if you don't get moving."

I frowned at his rundown of the past hour's events.

"Katarina's out there?" My thawing brain matter was having a hard time keeping up. "Is Deston with her?

"Deston de Rayne?" The big male snorted. "Haven't spotted that bastard yet, but when I do, this knife will go into his chest next." He yanked the long sword out of Lyra's chest with a wet, sucking sound.

"My secret weapon." He coolly wiped the blood off, then flipped the knife to show me the handle. "Carved out of a cross from Notre Dame." He flipped it again and displayed the blade. "Melted silver communion goblet from the twelfth century."

"Uh, yeah, neither of those things are the least bit sacrilegious." *Who the hell was this guy?*

"Can you use that on Viktor, and would it kill him?" I tried bending my fingers, the dull cracking as the joints loosened up and muscle stretched made me gag. My brain was sludgy, and my eyes wouldn't focus right.

This immortality stuff sure wasn't for the faint of heart.

"Maybe, but I'd never get close enough," he said matter-of-factly. "Katarina's set a warded shield around the King, none of us can penetrate. My guess is, your magic can kill him, but only if you stop dithering about and asking questions that don't matter."

"I'm dithering? Look at you, busy showing off your fancy knife."

"Fuck off, Sebastian. Give her a minute." Luthor's hands were scrubbing my exposed skin, trying to get blood flowing. Everywhere he touched felt like fire, and I wanted to howl.

"In case you haven't looked outside lately, we don't fucking have a minute." He growled.

"Fine. Point me in the right direction, I guess," I muttered sarcastically, blinking away the dark spots in my vision. "Maybe I'll get lucky and hit the right target."

"What does your magic feel like, Seraphina?" Luthor rubbed my arms harder. "Will it even still work?"

I was shivering, pain spiking through me as I adjusted to the renewed blood flow, or maybe I was going into shock, if vampires even experienced shock. I poked around inside myself, locating the flickering flame of my original magic, which was curled into a tight ball against the cold.

Yeah, I know how you feel. I'd like to do the same.

Lyra's magic was like a thick layer of ice, the polar opposite—no pun intended—of my fiery power. The two were *trying* to combine, but every time they did, my fire either went out or hers melted down.

Just my luck, the cosmos decided to give me two things that would never mix.

"Yeah, it's still there, but I'm not sure how to make this work." I shrugged my shoulders, which felt like an overwound rubber band. "Like Knight Templar here said, I have to get out there, or we won't get another chance."

"Lyra's dead. You have all her magic. Better to retreat," Luthor suggested softly. "Reorganize, evaluate." He stopped rubbing the cold away, tipped my chin up so my eyes met his. "Come back when you're ready."

"Except I'll never be ready for this, not really."

"This is a lost cause." Sebastian Blackwell rolled his eyes. "I'm pulling them out, Fontaine."

"*No.* I'm not leaving, just...give me a fucking minute to get caught up." I wasn't quitting now, not when we were so close. "We do this now. We know Viktor's power source has been cut off. There's no guarantee I'll ever be better prepared than I am right now."

Luthor gave me a curt nod, then caught my wrist when I swayed. "Blackwell and I will distract Katarina. She's covering Viktor's flank. With her out of the way, you'll have a clear shot." His firm hands gripped my arms, and we shuffled toward the door together.

Hopefully my poor muscles would loosen up, or this would be a dumpster fire.

He pulled me to the side, trapping me against the wall beside the door. "You know what you have to do, Seraphina." His voice was full of conviction, his blue gaze steady. "You've been practicing for months. Wait for a clear shot, then take it. Do not hesitate, do not second guess yourself. Hit him in the chest or the head."

He ran his knuckles down my cheek. "Once we enter the throne room, do not stop. There will be fighting, don't get distracted. Once you cast your magic, keep the flow going. Do not allow Viktor any time to recover. If he gets up, finish him off."

"I got it." I kissed him, wishing I shared his unshakeable faith. "I know what's at risk, and I won't let you down."

"If it so much as looks as the tide's turning, I'm getting you out of there."

"Not me." I zipped up my coat, cracked my swollen fingers, rolled my neck with a loud pop. "The rest of them. If this goes badly, get everyone out. I'll keep Viktor busy until everyone's safe."

Chapter 49
Seraphina

From the sounds of it, the battle was in full swing.

"What if Viktor and his supporters dematerialize?" It would be just like Viktor to turn tail. "Do we chase them down?"

Since I hadn't mastered that particular skill set, I could only imagine pursuing someone around the world while flying through the air. How did one even navigate? I stepped through the door, and Luthor's hand shot out to stop my admittedly slow progress. A guard flew past, crashed into the wall, then slid down, his neck broken.

"When I arrived, I activated the dampening wards on the entire palace," Luthor explained quickly. "They are a palace defense mechanism, meant to keep anyone from dematerializing in or out of this building. Which will hinder us, but prevent Viktor and Katarina from escaping."

"There's another upside to this situation." I filled my stiff lungs with air, prayed they held. "If Viktor's been fighting, he's been expending magic. Lots of it." My next breath went a little better. "While I'm filled to the brim. Once I hit him with everything I have, he shouldn't get back up."

Revenants roared, the creepy slip-slide of their claws heading straight for us.

Sebastian Blackwell firmed the grip on his unholy weapon and pulled another knife out of his thigh sheaf.

Luthor cocked his gun.

I tried to get my eyes to focus.

"Stay out of the way," I warned them. Revenants would be a good first test for me, if I didn't completely fuck this up. "I have no idea how my new magic will work, but they offer a big enough target. I shouldn't miss." *Theoretically.*

The first one poked its ugly head through the doorway, and I tried raising my leaden arms. I managed to get one halfway up and flicked a ball of magic toward the abomination.

Where my old magic was white hot, tinged with a trace of blue fire, the combined magic looked different. It was glitter and snow, a sea of bluish ice, sparkling with crystalline stars. It even moved differently, flowing like water, not like flames.

The ball wasn't big, barely the size of a marble but, when it struck, created a perfect circle in the thing's head, right between its beady little eyes. At least I was still accurate.

One more step, then the revenant jerked, misshapen legs twitching as though its muscles were going mad, then the whole thing turned inside out. One second it was leathery and gray, the next, shiny and wet. An organ pulsed, deep within the goopy mess. A second later, the red heap crumbled into a pile of black-edged gray dust.

My brain was still trying to process what I'd done when the second one leapt, then landed hard, scattering ash everywhere. Another marble of combined magic, and this one died in the same gruesome fashion, Blackwell's eyes going wide in his grizzled face.

Yeah, my new magic would take some getting used to.

Or therapy.

"Well, there you go," I muttered to Sebastian. "I told you I could do it."

I managed a couple wavering steps, every muscle groaning, the bottoms of my feet aching, like shards of glass were being shoved up into them.

"Remind me never to get frozen solid again," I muttered to Luthor. "This totally sucks."

Taking up position on one side of the wide doorway, Luthor indicated the top of the throne at the end of the Hall of Mirrors, barely visible through the tangle of fighting. "We'll get you close to Viktor. Sebastian and I will distract Katarina, but Viktor's sticking close to the throne, using the high ground to his advantage. We'll get you a clean shot, Seraphina. Use it wisely."

"I will," I promised. "If anything happens, get everyone out of here. Swear to me?"

When he didn't answer, I poked him in the chest. "Swear to me, Commander, you'll get everyone out. That's an order, Luthor."

"Yes, my Queen," he muttered, between gritted teeth.

The two males sandwiched me between them as we moved into the room, jostled this way and that from the battle raging all around us. Everywhere I looked fists flew, teeth gnashed, bullets whistled through the air, filled with the sound of clanking metal and screamed orders.

Luthor and Sebastian sheltered me from the worst of the fighting, then, when we approached the dais, they stepped away, and I gave Luthor a confident nod. My position was perfect. Viktor was right in front of me on the raised platform, cowering beside the throne, using the metal as a shield while Silas and Caden kept him pinned down, sparks flashing as their bullets ricocheted off harmlessly.

Viktor's protective shield looked like a giant red soap

bubble, an iridescent shimmer constantly changing as the magic absorbed blow after blow, both magical and metal.

"Any idea on how to get through that?" I asked Luthor, whose gaze was already fixed on Katarina.

"Try using a delicate touch, everything else seems to be bouncing off."

I watched Luthor and Sebastian long enough for them to flank Katarina, who was using a battalion of guards as living shields, then turned back to Viktor, his attention completely focused on Silas and Caden. Silly vampire. He hadn't spotted me.

Cold bit into my skin when I called up my magic, and I forced myself to tolerate the flash of pain, letting it gather, searching for an opening.

Slow. Luthor counseled.

Slow and steady and it'll go right through.

My first try bounced off, like the bullets, but now I had Viktor's attention. He pointed his finger, and I dodged the black magic that he sent roaring toward me. "I'll kill you, girl, then hang you on my wall," he screamed. "You'll stay up there until even your bones rot away."

I really wished he wasn't so loud, because now Katarina had me in her sights as well, her smile promising retribution for escaping her in the woods. And for breaking her apart.

Blackwell made a run for the guards shielding Katarina, took out the two on the right while Luthor dropped another on the left, leaving Katarina practically unprotected. Luthor emptied a full clip in her direction, but his bullets turning to black raven's feathers, drifting harmlessly to the ground.

I was knocked sideways by Rafael grappling with a guard, nearly tripped over a body, then adjusted my position until Viktor couldn't use the throne to his advantage anymore.

I had a clear shot, if I could only access Lyra's icy power. I had no idea what sort of magic this was, except it was old and ancient and really crochety

I stroked that frozen layer at my center, coaxing it to allow me to borrow a drop. My fire licked over the surface, melting it enough to mix its frosty essence with my fire.

The combination trickled through me like heavy metal, and I threaded that weighty mixture down my arms, letting it pool in my hands like quicksilver. As fast as I could, I sent that mercurial ball spinning across the space separating me from Viktor, praying Katarina didn't interfere.

It struck Viktor's shield, not with a crack, but like silly putty on a ceiling, sticking tight. I watched the mercurial goo spread across his shield, turning the shimmer into a hoarfrost-covered mirror, intricate snowflake patterns spreading and spreading until they covered the entire surface, completely obscuring him.

The whole time my magic froze Viktor's protective ward, I staggered toward him, pain shooting up through the soles of my feet. I never stopped putting one foot in front of the other, faster and faster until I reached the now-frozen sphere.

I tapped my fingernail against the paper-thin surface.

The globe shattered into pieces, the tinkling shards hitting the floor like a thousand bells chiming.

The king lunged for me, claw-like hands reaching for my neck, red eyes glowing with hatred. I dodged out of the way and momentum carried him past me, unable to stop in time.

I caught his ankles with my foot on the way by and took him down. It had been a long time since I'd fought hand-to-hand, but I remembered every single one of Mom's lessons. In ten seconds, I'd immobilized the King of the Vampires and had his face pressed to the floor at the base of his throne, my knee firmly in the small of his back, my elbow pressed into the back of his head.

Before I could doubt my decision, I sent a pulse of magic into him, then stepped away.

I didn't know what I expected.

Maybe for his death to be clean and neat?

Tidy, so I could reassure myself later this was for the best.

What I'd done was not tidy. It definitely wasn't neat.

Even worse, he rolled over, so I had to see his face through the entire, gory process.

He'd tortured Luthor and Cyrus for years. Killed Gram, laughing the whole time. Almost turned me into a revenant. This monster had destroyed entire families, scarred young women, and was responsible for countless atrocities I didn't even know about.

But this...my heart paused beating as I watched my magic work.

Viktor's legs and arms jerked and twitched, as if the bones were rearranging themselves beneath his skin. His flesh liquified, congealed, then began to flow, like some twisted, special-effects movie. Behind me, the room had gone mostly quiet. Either everyone was equally horrified, or the fighting was over, but I couldn't tear my gaze away long enough to check.

And those goddamned red, accusing eyes drilled into me the entire time.

Until they turned to jelly and melted out of their sockets.

I lurched away from him, sick to my stomach.

Disgusted, I heaved a mouthful of cold water onto the floor. How could I have done that to another living being? I was no better than Viktor, than Katarina, than the worst monster ever born.

The air in the room changed as the last of Viktor's magic fluttered away, like dust in the air, and my arm began to itch. The sensation was nearly as intense as when I'd almost been turned revenant. Startled, I yanked my sleeve back.

The hideous scar that encircled my arm like a ropey root began receding. The puckered edges faded, the keloid scar evened out, my skin flattening until it was pale and smooth. Seeing the horrible mark disappear, I remembered Marie's prophecy—*once Viktor was dead, our scars would heal.*

Elation pushed me across the floor to where Luthor stood, watching me with such pride, he looked like he might burst.

"Luthor. Let me check your leg." I went to my knees in front of him—in front of everyone—pushed his pant leg up and watched in amazement as his leg straightened, the heavy scarring turned healthy and pink, the deep divots in his leg filling in with smooth muscle.

"Cyrus," I yelled. "Cyrus, your neck." He reached up and ran a hand down it, his eyes widening when he discovered he was healed.

My warriors were whole again—at least on the surface —though I knew they'd always bear the scars of what happened down in the dungeons, as would I.

While we didn't have the visible reminders of our suffering, I knew none of us would forget. No, we'd remember Viktor and what he'd done for the rest of our lives, as well we should.

If only to keep ourselves from making the same mistakes.

"*Seraphina.*"

I heard Cyrus's scream a second before something big and heavy hit me from the side, flattening me to the ground, all the air whooshing out of my lungs. "I'm sorry, my Queen." Sebastian Blackwell muttered in my ear. "But..."

Whatever he was about to say was cut off by a choking cloud of black, glittering magic sweeping in around us. Sebastian clawed at his neck, gasping for air as he collapsed beside me. Then all around me bodies hit the floor, everyone fighting for breath, convulsing.

Katarina.

I winced as Silas went down, along with one of Viktor's guards.

She didn't care who she hurt, she'd cut everyone down, just to reach me.

"Here," I screamed, waving my arms. "Come and get me, Katarina." I sidestepped around bodies and slipped in blood to put some distance between myself and the fighters trying to protect me.

I searched wildly for Deston but didn't see him. *Where was he?*

Katarina glanced down at what remained of Viktor. The look she gave me...a mixture of pity and admiration and I wondered if she could see my deepest thoughts. "Who's the monster now, Seraphina?" She called, her red lips curving as the entire universe narrowed down to her and me.

I hated her.

Hated her in a way I'd never hated anything before.

I could count off a million reasons, but this really came down to just one thing.

Deston.

As I much as I'd lied to myself and everyone else, the mating mark seared into the back of my neck was real. She'd hurt my mate. Controlled him. Invaded his mind. Was planning to take him away from me.

Magic unfurled within me, like a bird coming back to life, and I dipped my finger into the cold well of Lyra's magic and stroked frost onto my fire.

Like sprinkling sugar on strawberries, or salt on popcorn, Lyra's ice made my magic that much better. *Stronger.* More vicious.

Sebastian was down on all fours, spit hanging from his mouth as he fought for air; Silas was crawling away when he collapsed, so still I wondered if he was dead. I couldn't help them. Better to draw Katarina away, and bring her magic with her.

I was breathing harder than I should've been, my still-thawing body heavy and slow, and I stumbled as my feet caught on the floor while I headed for the opposite side of the room. Physically, I might be compromised, but my magic—*oh my magic*—was hungering to get free.

Both of us stopped, separated by a scant ten feet. The fighting was thirty feet behind us, everyone slowly pushing to their feet as they got their breath back. Little possibility of collateral damage. Just her and me.

I was going to kill this bitch.

"You are a blight on the world." I coaxed a bit more of Lyra's magic onto my own. "And you took something that belongs to me."

I didn't even sound like myself.

Hell, I sounded more like Katarina if I were to be honest. But I couldn't think about that right now. All I could think about was killing this female before she hurt anyone else. Before she took Deston away from me.

"And you are a babe in the woods, who's about to discover she's made an enormous mistake."

I cast my magic first, maybe out of fear, maybe because she was right. I *was* new to this, and I didn't have a clue what I was doing. My magic became a thing of beauty, a perfect, undulating wave of blue power tinged with frost.

She shot me a mocking smile, turned diaphanous, and my magic passed straight through her.

"My turn," she said lightly, and the air between us filled with glittering black dust that turned into diamonds, their blackened edges as sharp as razors. They hurtled toward me so fast, I barely erected a pathetic shield in time. None of them hit my vital parts, but they sliced through my arms, one leg, the top of my scalp.

Behind me, someone grunted in pain.

If I didn't stop her, everyone in this room would die.

Blood trickled down my face, soaked through the rags that I had left for clothes. Katarina was virtually untouched, and she checked her hair in a mirror, just to make a point, before her red-painted mouth curved into another serpentine smile.

"Such a baby. You don't deserve the throne. Deston is far better off with me. I can give him what he needs."

My scream of anger pushed my magic out of me, racing straight toward her, before she morphed into a puff of black smoke. When she reappeared, she'd changed places, and I shifted clumsily to parry her next attack.

Get out of there, Seraphina, Luthor urged in my head. *I can't make it there in time, you'll have to run.*

The hell I'm running away, I told him, raising my hands. *I could do this. I could figure out a way around her magic, even if she was older than me. More experienced.*

With a grin, she snapped her fingers and this time, she conjured a sea of black spear heads, filling the air with glowing points coated in vicious, red magic. My stomach churned, recognizing what she was about to do.

Necromancer magic, the kind that would turn everyone in this room to revenants.

Move, Seraphina. Cyrus sounded completely panicked. *You need to move, now.*

She flicked a hand, and the deadly cloud spread wider, large enough to encompass the entire room. To turn everyone here into a monster.

Fear flared as I dug deep for my magic.

They would pierce straight through all of us. Nail us to the walls, just like Viktor did to Deston. We'd be trapped, and then we'd transform, and I would have *failed.*

Everything inside of me rejected that thought.

She grinned and sent one hurtling toward me. I slipped, nearly fell, trying to avoid it. There was another grunt of pain behind me, a thud. Desperate, I yanked Lyra's magic up, forcing that frozen power to do my bidding. Begging the frost to obey, just this once. Ice crackled in blue crystals on my fingertips as Lyra's magic solidified, growing thicker and thicker.

I built a blue, frozen wall between Katarina and I, between her deathly projectiles and *my people*, who I'd sworn to protect. I made my wall thick, and impenetrable, willed the ice to withstand fire and diamonds, and anything else this bitch threw at us.

With a scream, she sent those glowing spears screaming toward me.

Barbs slammed into the wall, their red glow cutting

through the thick ice. Cracks appeared, fissures chinking through the barrier as the barbs wormed their way through, then began winking out as my magic held firm. Katarina's beautiful face became a grotesque mask, disfigured by the now-melting ice sheet. Praying it would hold, I flattened my palm on the barrier.

Frost bit into my fingers like gnawing teeth.

Katarina drew closer until only a few inches separated us.

She reached out, touched her side of the barrier, her fingers brushing the frosted ice.

My breath stuttered in my lungs before she yanked back, screaming, as though she'd been burned. Through the ice melt, I barely made out her blackened claw of a hand, but the hatred in her eyes?

I saw that perfectly.

Out of her good hand, something dark spun towards the nearly clear shield. Ice cracked, spiderwebbing from the point of impact. Mirrors shattered on her side, glass raining down all around her like silvered rain as she screamed in a fury, and then...she was gone.

With a hideous crack, the wall gave way, collapsing in chunks, and air swept across my face as somebody yanked me away from the disintegrating ice. We landed hard, rolling over and over across the stone floor of the palace's grand entrance until we came to a stop at the bottom of a suit of armor.

Chapter 50
Seraphina

I untangled myself from my would-be savior and crawled away on my hands and knees.

"Stop manhandling me, you big oaf." My poor, mangled body couldn't take much more abuse. "This is a war zone, not a gridiron."

"I was stopping you from being crushed. That was an ill-thought-out move, Seraphina." Sebastian Blackwell's amber eyes reiterated that sentiment ten-fold.

"Yeah well, ill-thought out or not, it worked, didn't it?"

Blood dripped from the gashes in my arms, off the ends of my fingertips, was already matted into my hair and on my face. I lifted my forearm, where the deep gouges were starting to heal over, then stepped toward the Hall of Mirrors, intent on helping the injured.

Experimentally, I reached for my magic.

There was nothing there. Or rather, everything was frozen solid, and when I stroked Lyra's magic, this time, that layer of ice didn't thaw. "I can't touch Lyra's magic." I searched for my fire, which was barely an ember, almost out. "Shit, I don't have any magic left."

"You used everything you had erecting that barrier." Blackwell seemed bemused for a moment, then nodded. "But it worked."

"Barely," I acknowledged. I limped toward the throne room, afraid of what I would find.

My wall was nothing but melting hunks of ice.

Half the room was destroyed, shards of mirror mixed with blood and spent bullets across the corpse-scattered floor. Tessa and Hugh were already treating the survivors and I tried to pick familiar faces out of the injured.

Where did Katarina go? I wondered. *She'd been injured, but she'd had me.* Surely, she sensed I was weak enough to kill, and someone like Katarina didn't miss those kinds of chances.

Luthor wiped dirt and gore off his face as he hurried toward me. Cyrus arrived a moment later, skimming his hands over me experimentally. "You're hurt."

"So are you. We'll heal." I scanned the entire room, even the rafters spanning the high, vaulted ceiling. "Where did she go?"

"She dematerialized." Luthor muttered, then bent his head, whispering to Cyrus.

I nearly sank to the floor in relief. "Thank God."

Luthor shook his head. "This isn't good. She shouldn't have been able to. I activated the dampening ward, remember? That ward's ancient, powerful enough to affect all vampires. Even Viktor couldn't leave. But it had no effect on her."

"How did she, then?" I asked. "Is she really that strong?"

"It's not about how strong she is. Katarina shouldn't have been able to override the spell. Period. There's something here we're not seeing." Sebastian's grim expression made me believe every word. "Unless..." He shook his head, as if he'd just had a thought too impossible to believe.

"He's right. It's impossible for her to bypass the wards and dematerialize." Cyrus's face looked every bit as serious as Sebastian's. "But obviously, she did. And her magic was... I've never seen anything like it."

"She's more powerful than I ever gave her credit for." Sebastian used his foot to roll a uniformed guard over. He looked so young. "You were fortunate you managed to hold your own today. Even luckier you managed to survive Lyra's magic. Otherwise, this could have gone poorly."

"Yeah, well, luck is my middle name. So, how did she manage to dematerialize?" I rubbed my face, wishing I knew more about everything worked.

"Only a Darkfell queen could override that spell." Luthor murmured, studying the scene before us. "The magic is keyed specifically to their blood."

"It was almost like she knew the spell itself." Sebastian bent to check another body. "But that's impossible." He indicated our surroundings with a gloved hand. "That spell was created by the founder of this clan, then passed down from queen to queen... and then finally to Viktor."

So how could Katarina—and not Viktor—override the spell?

Luthor didn't let me out of his sight as I hurried toward Caden, lying prone on the floor. Tessa was on her knees, pulling back his flak jacket to reveal a gash on his side. "It's pretty bad, one of those diamonds hit him." I laid my hand over hers, then knelt and examined the wound. While I probed it, Luthor pulled Sebastian to the side. I couldn't hear them, but once Luthor finished speaking, Sebastian glanced over at me and nodded.

Yeah, I could guess what that was all about.

I rocked back on my heels and offered Tessa my very best reassuring smile. "Nothing vital is hit, but it's deep. He'll be fine with some rest."

"How do you know?" Tessa breathed

"Three years of pre-med and advanced physiology classes. Plus, he's a vampire. We heal from freaking *everything*." I tried to keep my smile reassuring.

"I'll mend just fine," Caden bit out, but beads of sweat slid down his pale face.

"No doubt, but you need to stay immobile." I turned to Tessa, who was nearly as white as Caden. "Is there someone we can call to speed the healing process along?"

"We have a family healer. I'll text Mother. She'll arrange it."

I stopped on the threshold, then turned around to find Sebastian dogging my heels. "Don't you dare try to talk me into leaving. Viktor's dead, which means I'm Queen." I reminded him, and he retreated a pace, dipping his head, his hand resting on the hilt of his sword.

"My Queen, I am under strict orders to get you to safety." *Yeah, I could just guess who'd given that order.* "Please allow me to escort you back to..."

"No, I'm staying," I repeated more firmly. "There is work to do and I'm in charge now, right? I won't be escorted off my own damn property because it's *not safe*."

"Please, my Queen." There was a tone of desperation in Sebastian's plea. "If Katarina dematerialized out of this room, she can get back in. Let me return you to the Cormier's."

"Oh, don't worry, she can get in there too." I chewed my lip, watching Luthor hoist Caden onto his feet. "I'm staying here. There are injured people." *My people.* "I want to make sure everyone gets home and has proper medical attention."

"I would be remiss if I didn't warn you against this path." Sebastian looked positively flummoxed that I wasn't following his every command. "This is for your own good."

"Yeah well, people are always warning me against stuff. I usually don't listen. Just ask Luthor, he'll tell you, which is why you're the one trying to convince me to leave, not him."

I surveyed the nearly silent throne room, then made my way over to an injured Silas, who was doing a good job of joking his way through the pain. Cyrus joined me, and I touched his healed throat, barely believing our luck.

"Is anyone else hurt?" I asked softly, wrapping my arms around his waist and laying my cheek against his chest. In all the chaos, it felt so good to just...listen to his heart beating, to feel his arms wrap around me.

"I thought you were supposed to be..." He chuckled, tugging me closer. "Never mind, I told Luthor he was wasting his time, trying to get you to leave."

He lifted my hand, inspected the cuts on my arm. "I think you've already seen the worst of the injuries. Caden caught one of those diamonds in his side. Silas had a bullet in his arm..." When he scanned the room, his mouth tightened into a thin line. "Wait, no. Rafe was hit by that last blast of Katarina's magic."

Hugh was crouched down beside Raphael.

That must have been the scream of pain I'd heard.

"Those barbs were tipped with red magic." I hissed, unable to keep the fear out of my voice. "I recognized that red glow. *Necromancer magic.*"

"We're on it." Cyrus waved Sebastian over. "Blackwell, help get him back to the Cormier's as fast as you can. I heard there's a healer coming, tell them he's been contaminated with necromantic magic. Have them treat Rafael first."

"Okay." *That would have to do for now.* "Let's figure out how to ward this place against Katarina."

Sebastian shook his head. "That won't be possible," he muttered. "Everything you see"—he indicated the room—"all of this was built upon the same basic magic. There's no way to modify the genesis of a magical system. You'd have to start all over again."

"So what...we just remain unprotected forever?"

"It can be done." he said slowly. "But rebuilding a protective ward from scratch leaves the palace, and the Queen, vulnerable." His face brightened, as if he'd just found a solution to his problem. "Which is why you should return to Cormier House, where it is safe, my Queen."

"And as I said, Cormier House is no safer." I dropped my voice. "She found me there, as well. A few days ago."

Sebastian's gaze narrowed, mouth thinning out. "And you survived?" He shook his head, as if he didn't believe me. "Katarina Brasov is the oldest female vampire on earth. How did you manage to escape her? Or...did she let you go?"

I took a good, long look at Sebastian Blackwell. He was a grizzled male who'd seen plenty of action, deep lines spreading out from battle weary eyes, the touch of gray at his temples standing out against his inky black hair.

"Who are you, and how do you know all of this?"

He inclined his head. "I served here for many years, my Queen. I was once commander of the Knightsguard, centuries before Lyra took the throne. When she and I had a disagreement over this very subject, we agreed I could better serve Queen Maeve in Dublin. After that, I became what they call a freelancer."

Just for a second, his amber gaze flit over to Luthor's, and I wondered what the story was there. "Hugh Cormier contacted me two days ago, and I came as fast as I could. As it turns out, my timing could have been better."

I shook my head. "Your timing was good enough to save my life. I appreciate it."

He inclined his head, his amber eyes never leaving my face. "I'm happy to be of service, my Queen." The title rolled off his tongue as if he'd been saying it his entire life, and I wondered if he had.

Hugh and Tessa were organizing getting everyone back to the mansion. I sighed. Despite my little speech, we couldn't stay here. The carcasses of revenants lay where they'd fallen, as did the bodies of the guards who had died defending their king.

I took a deep breath and walked over to where Viktor lay, nothing more than bones in a pool of red liquid. I forced myself to look at him. Forced myself to face what I had done. Forced myself to acknowledge the terrible power of my magic.

It was exactly like all my horrible nightmares, and I had to wonder if somehow, even subconsciously, my magic had made my very dreams come true.

"He's really dead, isn't he?" I asked Cyrus quietly, who'd come to stand beside me. His hand wrapped around mine and squeezed.

I mean, if Cyrus could grow his head back and I could freeze into an ice cube and not die, was it possible that anybody could come back from... *this*?

"He is dead, Seraphina." Cyrus released me for a more thorough inspection; his hands roamed lightly over me, pausing on each wound before weaving through my hair, pausing when he found the mating mark on the back of my neck.

I pulled away, ducking my head. "I'm fine," I told him. "I'm already healing up."

"And your magic?" he asked carefully. "Are you all right,

Fina? That was...I've never seen anything like that. There was no sign of your fire."

"I am... different." I finally settled on, since nothing else seem to fit. "I think Lyra's magic will take some getting used to, just like mine did."

And with Deston gone, I'd be figuring that part out on my own.

Chapter 51
Seraphina

In the end, we all went back to the Cormier's. I didn't have the heart to ask anybody to clean up the mess, not when everybody was battle worn and exhausted.

"Maybe I'll just set fire to the entire thing and start over again," I muttered to Luthor as we made our way into the mansion, where the soft lights glowed and classical music played. This felt like walking into a different world. I stumbled over the threshold, and Cyrus caught me by the arm.

"Easy there, Seraphina. I think we should get you to bed."

"I think that's a grand idea." I didn't even fight him, a testament to how exhausted I was. I eyed the endless staircase with no small amount of loathing. "How many stairs are there again?"

"Thirty-three," Cyrus teased. "I've counted."

"That was a mostly hypothetical question, but thanks for the accuracy."

Tessa and her males were gathered in the banquet room around Rafael and Caden. There was someone with them, the healer, I supposed. Caden had been in the thick of the fighting, right along with Luthor and I heard he'd single-handedly slaughtered three revenants.

"I'd like him to join the Knightsguard," Luthor murmured in my ear. "He and Silas, both."

"What about Markus and Raphael?" I asked curiously. "Can they help us?"

"Markus would make an excellent advisor," Luthor suggested quietly and I knew the source of his hesitation. That was supposed to be Deston's role. A role I'd resented... until he was gone.

Now I'd give anything for him to be here, dissecting what had happened, picking out Katarina's weaknesses, tell me how to best her. He'd know how to ward the palace, and how to protect everyone.

But now...*it was too late*, I realized, bitterly.

"What about Rafael?" The male lay still on a couch, his animated face slack, hair matted to his forehead as Tessa bent over him, speaking to the healer.

"He's common born, my lady," Sebastian offered. "Only those from a royal house can be on the royal court."

I glared at him. "Yeah, we're not doing things like that now. If he's smart and trustworthy, I want him on the court." I willed my feet to keep moving. "Okay then, I have an advisor, and we have the beginnings of the Knights-guard. Viktor's dead, and once we get the palace cleaned up, we can set that place up as our headquarters."

"A solid plan, my Queen. And that is all for tonight, until you get some rest." Luthor tucked a hand beneath my elbow. That support was all that got me up the final seventeen steps.

It wasn't until Luthor shut the door, closing off the rest of the world, that I realized how wobbly my knees were and between the adrenaline crash, the exhaustion, and the pain, I completely broke down. Luthor gathered me against him, Cyrus rubbing my back, and I sobbed until my eyes were dry, my throat raw.

"I can't believe it's really over." I rubbed the tears away.

"I can't believe Viktor's dead. I can't believe that Katarina got the better of me."

"She's over a thousand years old," Luthor reminded me gently. "She has the advantage of experience and time."

"Why didn't you tell me magic can turn into diamonds?" I muttered. "Or poison barbs?"

"She's had years to perfect her craft. I expect there's lots more that she can do. Magic we don't even want to know about." Cyrus peeled off his shirt while I eyed the enormous distance between me and a hot shower.

"Let us help you, Fina." Cyrus cupped my face in his hands and kissed the end of my nose. So simple, and yet, tears sprang to my eyes once more. Together, they stripped off my dirty, bloodstained sweatshirt. The thin tee stuck to my battered body. My tennis shoes and jeans.

"I need to get this blood off me, but I honestly don't have the energy."

Cyrus picked me up and carried me to the bathroom. "How about we pin you between us in the shower, and we all get clean at the same time?" He waggled his eyebrows. The water had been running for a while; the mirrors were already steamed up.

"Clean would be nice." My head spun when he set me down. "But that's about all I have the energy for. I'm not even kidding. I'm about to fall asleep on my feet."

"You almost died today, Seraphina, and we all learned something valuable. Taking another vampire's magic can have dire consequences."

"I thought we'd be compatible because we're family." Now that I said that out loud, it sounded ridiculous. Families weren't compatible; they were oil and water. "I watched Deston do it, and nothing happened to him."

Except that wasn't exactly true. His face had twisted in pain, hadn't it?

"Deston's an abjurist. His body was made to absorb another's magic. You're a necromancer. You manipulate death, not another's power. We should have been more careful."

I mulled that over as Luthor dumped shampoos in one huge hand.

"Who is this Sebastian Blackwell guy? Can we trust him?"

"Sebastian was the commander in Queen Lyra's court when I first came into the Knightsguard. Before that, he served Queen Esme, and before that, Queen Adaline, when the clan was still located in France."

"Which means he's been around forever," Cyrus mused, nudging me under the water. Every drop felt like an icepick digging into my skin. "I expect he knows more about Katarina than both of us combined."

Luthor's fingers worked the shampoo into my hair, massaging my scalp my body going boneless until Cyrus had to brace me up. Eventually, the ice picks turned into little zings of heat, flowing over my cut arms, down my legs. The heat was delicious after being nearly frozen to death.

As much as I didn't want to think or talk about Katarina anymore tonight, I had so many questions. I knew I'd never sleep. "Somehow, I get the feeling that Viktor was never our real enemy."

"You could be right. If Katarina's been involved, she could have been pulling Viktor's strings. He may have been her puppet this whole time."

"Is she really the oldest vampire? You know, in the world, like Sebastian said?"

"There are some even older than she," Luthor told me, gently working his way down over my aching shoulders. "If they are even still alive."

"But they're all far across the ocean, and you don't have to worry about them," Cyrus said soothingly, and even with my eyes shut, I knew they were exchanging that *special look* they had. The one that said *that's enough of that subject.*

While they massaged and scrubbed, I wondered if Deston was with her.

If he even knew about tonight's battle that nearly got us all killed. Somehow, I imagined Katarina hadn't skimped on the details, especially my inability to do a fucking thing to stop her.

Except build an ice wall, which she'd make sound especially pathetic.

"So, Sebastian was essentially your boss, huh?" Now that I was thawing, I motioned for Luthor to turn around and soaped up his enormous back, skimming my hands over the now-smooth skin. Every single scar was gone. "Would it be a smart move to ask him to rejoin the Knights-guard? I mean, would he be willing to work for you, Luthor?"

My hands slipped over silky skin as Luthor shrugged his shoulder. "I'm not sure bringing Sebastian on board would be the best move. He wasn't much of a rule follower, if I remember correctly."

I chuffed out a laugh. "He and I have that in common, at least."

The second we were all reasonably clean, we dropped into bed, hair still wet, and were asleep in seconds.

327

WHEN I WOKE, every single muscle in my body ached. So much so, I spent ten minutes talking myself into sliding out of the warm and comfortable bed.

Gawd, did I rupture every cell in my body yesterday?

"Heading downstairs," I mumbled to my still-sleeping men. "Will bring coffee."

Snores were my only response, and I slipped into the softest, loosest clothing I could find. Katarina's diamonds had left long, thin scars on my arms and I prayed the marks wouldn't be permanent.

The last thing I needed was the constant reminder I'd been bested in my own throne room.

I followed the delicious scent of coffee all the way down all thirty-three steps—Cyrus was right—and into the kitchen, only to find Sebastian's serious amber gaze pinning me down. He was a smart male, not speaking until I poured myself a cup, slid into the chair opposite him, and took my first sip.

"Good morning, my Queen. I shall leave you to your quiet." He inclined his head, then rose, preparing to leave.

"Stay." I waved for him to sit. "Thank you for yesterday. I think... I think if Lyra had poured any more of her magic into me, I wouldn't have survived."

There was something oddly familiar about him, in addition to those whiskey-colored eyes. Maybe it was the smooth way he moved or the tilt of his head. I couldn't put my finger on what, exactly, nagged at me, but I felt like I knew him from somewhere.

"You would be correct, my Queen." His words were so carefully chosen. "I was happy to be of service."

"Are you staying then?" I asked. "Or maybe I should ask, do you *want* to stay?"

"My life is complicated. I've been on the move for a

long time," he answered evasively, looking over my head at the door. "I owed Hugh a favor, and was happy to finally settle that debt. Better that I take my leave today, my Queen."

He was acting so skittish, I checked to make sure my magic had refilled overnight, just in case I had to suddenly defend myself. I'd discovered it wasn't always easy to tell vampire friend from vampire foe, and it would be a shame to survive an epic battle, only to die over my morning coffee.

Still, Luthor and Cyrus both vouched for him.

"I'm a new queen, trying to build my first court. It would be nice to have someone experienced on board."

"Fontaine has plenty experience." He muttered gruffly, edging toward the door. "So does Cyrus Rayne."

"And according to both of them, you have more."

"I'm better off on my own." This time he kept moving, until he was almost through the doorway. I just couldn't shake the feeling I knew him from somewhere.

"Have we ever met?" My question stopped him in his tracks, and his shoulders sagged, ever so slightly. "I know we probably haven't, but you just..." That strange feeling washed through me again, stronger, this time. "Seem so familiar."

"No, Seraphina. We've never met." He took another step, as if he couldn't wait to get away from me. "I knew your grandmother, but that was a long time ago. Luthor told me what Viktor did. My condolences on her passing."

"Thank you," I said, automatically watching him pause in the doorway, his hands clenching at his sides.

Then he reached up and tapped the doorframe with his index finger, as if trying to make his mind up about something. "Her daughter, Isabelle, I heard she died a few years back." His voice was thick, a heaviness there I knew I wasn't imagining. "I'm sorry for that, as well."

"So am I." I almost called him back, grilled him until I got some answers, but Tessa bustled in, stopping when she saw the two of us. "I'm sorry, I was just getting...Oh, I'm interrupting." She began backing out.

"This is your kitchen. Your house," I reminded her firmly. She looked exhausted, and I realized she'd probably been up all night. "Let me make a fresh pot of coffee."

When she started to protest, I pointed to a chair. "Sit down and let me do this for you. It looks like you haven't slept." I filled the coffee maker, started a new pot.

"Rafael's wound won't heal." Her blue eyes swam with tears and she fidgeted with the hem of her shirt. "The healer tried everything they knew, and it won't knit back together. There's something...wrong."

"I'd be willing to take a look at it," Sebastian offered kindly. "I've been known to heal a battle field wound or two in my time."

"That would be wonderful. Silas thinks... Silas said the barb was still glowing when it hit Rafe in the chest." I poured her cup of coffee, which she cradled with shaking hands.

Sebastian smiled kindly down at her. "You drink that, and then the three of us will look at Rafael, together."

"YOUR FRIEND SILAS WAS RIGHT." Sebastian settled back on his heels, all of us staring somberly at Rafael's wound, which had red lines fanning out around it like a spider's web. His deathly gray face was framed by dark, matted hair, his entire body soaked with sweat.

I swallowed. I knew if I lifted his lids, his eyes would glow red.

"It's definitely inside him." Sebastian's worried gaze slid to mine before he smoothed his face back into a serene mask. "Necromancer magic, from the looks of it."

A thrill of fear went through me. That single barb missed me, but had caught Rafael right over his heart, and the transformation was happening fast.

I pulled Sebastian away. "Can you heal this?"

"I don't have the right skills to undo necromancy. What I could do is use a healing spell to draw the magic out of his body," he explained gravely. "But someone has to destroy the magic once it's free, or it could find another host."

He looked me up and down, then frowned. "If I pull the corruption out, perhaps...well, that's where you come in, my Queen. Once I have extracted it, you could burn the magic away to nothing."

I looked around the room. Every eye was pinned on us, every face full of hope, and I nodded, even though I had no earthly idea of how to do any of that.

My magic was a tangled mess of ice and fire this morning, and I sorted through a thousand different threads of power while Sebastian crouched back down and placed his hand on Rafael's chest, just above the wound.

I'd barely managed to grasp the end of my fire magic, to gather enough magic around my fingertips to do *something* when a cloud of red glowing magic rose up from the wound, like a vaporous poison into the air. Rafael's body arched up with a pained groaned.

"Now, my Queen."

Since I didn't know what to do, I fed a tiny burst—no bigger than a puff of smoke—into the red glow. The color and light winked out, turned to ash, then showered down like fine dust.

Cool. Finally, something useful.

"More Seraphina, more," Sebastian urged. "We must destroy every last piece, leaving this corruption roaming free..." He nodded at Tessa, then Luthor, and Cyrus, who'd just joined us, their hair still tousled from sleep. *Probably wondering why I hadn't returned with coffee.*

Because I'm vaporizing evil magic, that's why. I flexed my fingers.

"Got it. Eliminate the evil magic." I was sweating, my brow tight as I concentrated on keeping my magic needle sharp, touching only that thin strip of corruption Sebastian kept pulling out of Rafael.

Finally, the red tendrils turned wispy, then vanished, Sebastian heaving a sigh of relief.

"That's the last of the corruption." His expression turned almost proud. "That was exactly the right way to do this, Seraphina, with a light touch. I couldn't have done it better myself."

Tessa squeezed me into a tight hug. "Thank you."

"I'm glad I could help," I said honestly. "Usually, it seems like everyone else is doing all the work, and I'm just standing around trying to figure things out."

"That was impressive, Fina." Luthor pulled me to my feet, and we headed back to the kitchen. "Quite a start to the day, even for you."

"Not my plan, but I'm glad it worked out." I murmured, running my hand up his arm. "We should head over to the palace," I decided. "If that's going to be our new home, then the sooner we get it cleaned up, the quicker we can settle in. I'm not crazy about going back there, but I can't lie, I'm excited to have my first real home."

"You never had a home?" Sebastian asked curiously, leaning against the wall by the door, as if he was still debating leaving.

"Not really. Gram and Mom and I moved around a lot when I was young. I used to think it was because I had a hard time in school." I laughed softly. "Imagine my surprise when I found out a ruthless vampire king had been hunting us all those years."

Sebastian's mouth thinned into a line. "Viktor knew about you? How?"

"Beats me. But that's how Mom died, protecting me from revenants." I couldn't stop the way the words tumbled out of my mouth, nor the slight tremor in my voice. Maybe one of these days, I'd be able to think about that night without falling apart.

"I did not know," Sebastian muttered, so quietly I barely heard him. "I did not know Izzy died that way."

Every one of my nerves went on high alert.

BLACKWELL USED Mom's nickname so naturally, I knew everything he'd worked so hard to portray—the loyal guardsmen, the experienced knight—had been a cover for something else.

"How did you know her nickname?" I edged closer to Luthor and Cyrus, both of whom had gone perfectly still, like they did when there was danger. Was Sebastian *dangerous*? Is that why Luthor didn't want him on the Queen's guard?

Sebastian rubbed his face, then looked straight at me. "Goddamn it. I knew this was a mistake. I should have left last night." Wariness kindled in his gaze as he looked between us, his mouth thinning out.

"I knew your mother when she lived in Paris. From the second I met her, I loved her."

Chapter 52
Seraphina

I felt like I'd been punched the gut.

"Excuse me?" I heard myself ask through the dull roar in my ears. "What are you talking about? You knew Mom?"

And that was when his comment about him *loving her* finally sunk in.

That meant......

Sebastian wasn't familiar because I'd met him before. Sebastian Blackwell was familiar because I saw some version of that face in the mirror *every single fucking day*.

"You mean to tell me, you're my dad?" My hands clenched into fists.

"I... I must be. I never knew Izzy was pregnant." His voice was halting, as if he was trying to process some terrible revelation. "I never considered I might have a daughter. Not until I saw you standing over Lyra, nearly frozen." He clasped his hands behind his back.

"If I'd known I was your sire, I would have found you, taken care of you, I swear. But Isabelle... she disappeared from my life without a trace. I was never able to pick up her trail, though I tried for years. I thought she tired of me. It never occurred to me that she'd come back to America."

"When was that?"

"Over twenty years ago. I met Isabelle in the city, she

was a painter, living a quiet life. I was looking for the same, I suppose...after Ireland."

I'd been conceived in France. I wondered why she'd returned to the States, when she knew Viktor was hunting her. When she knew the danger.

"I never cared that Isabelle was a null—a vampire with no power." He smiled slightly. "Your mother had a different kind of magic. She could make worlds come alive with a palette of paint and a brush in her hand. In all my years, I'd never seen anything more powerful than that."

"Then how did we end up on the run, and why am I just finding out about this now?"

I was pissed. I believed everything he said—about loving my mother, looking for us—the whole story. But if he'd been with us—a commander of the Knightsguard—Mom might still be alive.

He gave Isabelle the key. Luthor interrupted my furious thoughts. *That's how you ended up with it.*

Luthor's right, Cyrus added. He was pressed tightly into me, one hand clasping mine, ready to whisk me away if Sebastian made the wrong move.

I agree, I thought back to them. *but does that make him a friend or foe?*

Why don't we find out? Luthor asked, shifting closer.

"I mean your Queen no harm." Sebastian held out his palms, looking between the three of us. "If I had known Seraphina was my daughter, I never would've come."

"Well, that's nice," I muttered sarcastically. "You'd rather help a complete stranger, than your own flesh and blood."

"That's not what I meant at all." Desperation rang in Sebastian's voice, but without knowing his motives, I was trusting him less and less.

He nodded to my open shirt, the chain that disappeared beneath it. "Isabelle took something from me before she disappeared. I assumed that was why she vanished. I assume you used the serpent key to open the door?"

He frowned at his own logic. "But that doesn't explain how you got around the wards, they should have been impenetrable."

"I'll tell you how, if you tell us why you had the key in the first place."

"I stole it from the palace, months after Viktor's coup. Lyra was gone, but yet, she was not." He frowned. "I'm sorry, that is not clear. Despite reports that Lyra had been killed shortly after becoming queen, she erected a small chapel near the edge of the woods. She would go there often for solitude and reflection."

I nodded. "I've seen it. If she built it with magic, it should have disappeared when she died."

"Exactly."

"How could you know this, Seraphina?" Luthor stared down at me, confusion and curiosity mixing in his gaze. "That's ancient magic."

"Deston once told me his castle would stand until the day he died. It all makes sense, if that's how magic works. When the person who casts the spell is gone, the magic disappears. I'm surprised Viktor let that slip though."

"I don't think he was that well-versed in the intricacies of magic," Luthor observed. "He was more interested in how he could corrupt power to his own ends."

"Nevertheless, the chapel stood, and I knew Lyra somehow survived the attack. That crypt is the most secure room in the palace, perhaps in the world. If Lyra was alive, she would be there."

"Then why didn't you save her?" I asked bitterly. *Could*

everything had been avoided if Sebastian Blackwell had just followed through?

"I did try," he snapped. "I got as far as the wards around the door and never made it through them. That's why I was in France, looking for the final piece of a spell I could use to get into that room."

"You went to Metz." Luthor's voice turned deadly, menacing. "To see the defector?"

Sebastian shrugged. "I thought he would help, if only to see Viktor's reign end."

"That was foolish," Luthor told his former commander coldly. "Foolish and dangerous."

"Maybe so, but Alaric was my only choice. He's the only one who hates Katarina enough to want to help, and the only one powerful enough to dare defy her."

"And did he?"

"Of course not." Sebastian shook his head. "The bastard's as cold as death. I think he'd love to watch our kind fade away."

I snugged my hoodie tighter, resolving to start buying warmer clothes. I was positioned near the front of the palace, trying to avoid the guards carrying bodies out of the building and loading them into trucks.

But the cold kept the stench down, which meant it was good for something.

"The reek is from burning revenants down by the woods," Luthor told me matter-of-factly. "We searched the woods but didn't find a single one alive."

One of our grislier discoveries of the morning—everything Viktor created with his corrupted magic had perished along with him. In much the same way he'd died.

Good, I was glad everything was gone. Saved me the trouble of killing them myself.

Another wisp of smoke floated by and my stomach twisted, even though I hadn't seen the carnage with my own eyes.

"Hugh received a report today. According to a manifest filed last night, a private plane bound for Romania, with two passengers aboard, left shortly after Katarina disappeared."

Fuck. Deston was really gone. Far beyond my reach.

"I'm sorry, Seraphina. I truly am, I wish..." Luthor's voice gentled. "I wish I could take away your hurt, I wish I could fix this, but I cannot."

I stared across the wide-open field, trying *not* to remember sprinting across it with Deston. The rush of adrenaline. His fangs in my wrist. "And the chapel? Is it still there?" Until that chapel vanished, Lyra still existed, on some plane, even if it wasn't this one.

Luthor drew up short. "I forgot to check. I will go check, then report back."

I was ready to tell him not to bother when Caden strode up. "We've closed down the dungeons and rounded up nearly twenty of Viktor's soldiers, what do you want done with them?" From the coldness in Caden's eyes, he'd already decided.

After what I'd endured down in those cells—at their hands—I tended to agree.

"I'll speak to them. I want to see if any of them have anything vital to offer up before they pay for what they've done. But first, I have to..." Luthor's voice tapered off as he scanned the area for a babysitter. "Don't go anywhere until I find Cyrus. I want someone with you at all times."

"I'll be fine," I assured him with a wave. There were a hundred people in the vicinity, and someone was always in sight, whether it be Hugh, or Lilliana, or Tessa and her men. "Go deal with the soldiers."

But once inside, I milled around helplessly. Everywhere I went, I was in the way. I finally picked a chair in the front hall and sat down, trying to keep tabs on progress while feeling like I was no help at all.

Cyrus finally appeared, then was called away on a minor emergency. Lilliana brought me a sandwich. Tessa gave me a much-needed update on Rafe.

I took the last bite of my now-stale crust.

Katarina was gone, three thousand miles away. So what, exactly, was I afraid of? This was *my* palace, my grounds, *my forest.* A shiver of defiance went through me. If I wanted to go outside, then I would.

"I'm going back outside," I told no one in particular. "I'll stick close to the front doors."

It was clear today, the sky brilliant blue against the column of black smoke rising from the edge of the woods. I squinted but didn't see the chapel. The dilapidated structure had blended into the woods, the roof nearly covered in vines. I reached the edge of the drive, but even squinting through the smoke, I couldn't be sure.

A few minutes later, I was jogging toward the woods, steering clear of the putrid smelling smoke, heading for the empty spot where Lyra's chapel had once been.

One minute, the ankle-high grass was nothing but a sea of brown around me.

Then next, Deston appeared in front of me, his face oddly blank, hands reaching for me.

"Seraphina," his cold, dead tone sounded nothing like his usual, mocking arrogance. "Someone would like a word with you."

I spun away, but the second his hand brushed against me, the mating mark roared, my knees going weak. "Fight it, Deston. Fight her hold on you." I tugged at Lyra's magic, and it turned impervious, as if determined not to be put to use.

Fine, worthless magic, don't save me. I'll save myself.

I backed away, willing my fire magic to work. If Deston took me back to Katarina, I was so, so dead.

He lunged for me. I winced, then punched him in the face, blood splattering everywhere. He wiped his sleeve across his nose and narrowed his gaze, no hint of recognition in his black eyes. This was not the Deston I knew.

This was Deston ensnared by the soul bond, Katarina

controlling his every move. She'd gotten him past the wards, and I realized how foolish I'd been to drop my guard, for even a minute, thinking she was gone.

I turned and ran, my feet pounding through the grass, avoiding clumps of dirt.

I raced for the palace—*how did I get this far away*—and Deston reappeared right in front of me. My feet slid on the grass and I barreled straight into him. He caught me easily, my traitorous body instantly purring as he crushed me against him, the mating mark screaming for me to get away.

Run, run, run, he said. *Do not trust me, mon amore.*

Or maybe that was me.

I fought his hold, but we were already flying.

Chapter 54
Seraphina

We landed in some scrubby little field where I couldn't get my bearings, since there wasn't a landmark in sight.

Except for Katarina in her ludicrous coat and high heels, watching me like she hadn't eaten in a century.

"There," Deston said, stepping back, his hands in his pockets, like he wasn't the biggest traitor ever. "Here is your little imposter. All wrapped up in a pretty bow just for you, my love."

There was nothing familiar about his cold smile. Nothing encouraging about his flat, obsidian gaze. "She can't even dematerialize by herself, so she's all yours."

I couldn't believe I'd been careless enough to get kidnapped. The mating mark was on fire, warning me to get away, and here I was, caught between an impossible-to-reach Deston and Katarina, looking like she'd just received the best Christmas present ever.

"I don't know how I'll thank you." Katarina ran her fingers possessively over Deston's arm and across his shoulders before she dug her fingertips into his neck, twisting his head so his throat was exposed. "But I'm sure I'll think of something." She cupped his cock and squeezed, her gaze never leaving mine.

Everything inside me went taut, fury roaring in my

veins, my heart crashing against my ribs as I imagined ripping her hands right off.

Blinded by jealousy, I might have made a mistake.

I might have actually lunged for her, claws out, hate in my heart, except...pure revulsion rippled down the bond, through the mark, raising goosebumps on my arms.

Deston hated this. *Hated her.*

My mate was still in there somewhere. All I had to do was reach him.

I pulled my sleeves down to cover my involuntary reaction to Deston's disgust. What if Katarina already knew about the mate mark?

No, she couldn't. From the covetous way she treated him, if Katarina knew Deston and I were mated, I'd already be dead.

There'd be no toying with me, no gaudy shows of power, no gloating over little victories.

She'd finish me off, make him watch, then take what she wanted.

If I wanted to survive this, she couldn't find out.

She tossed back her hair, raven-black and perfectly coifed, even out here in this dismal place. "Show me one of those little tricks again. Let's see how your ice wall fares out here in the middle of nowhere." Her mocking laughter rang loudly over the emptiness.

"Deston, I thought we were friends. Please, please take me back to the palace, or she'll kill me." When all he did was tilt his head, horror twined through me. Katarina controlled him completely, a fact that was never as clear as when he sketched her a bow.

"This is all for you, Katarina." He waved at me like I was a fly. "A gift to my true Queen. Once this fraud is gone, you shall rule over the two most powerful clans in the world."

"Hm. That sounds like Katarina speaking, not you," I said tartly, trying to buy some time.

I remembered what Tessa told me about the soul bond, but I'd never imagined Katarina's influence over Deston would be this complete. It was like he didn't even recognize me. Or the bond between us.

Which meant a soul bond was stronger than a mating bond. I had to break her hold over him.

but how could I sever something I couldn't see?

I hugged my arms around me—these thin hoodies seriously needed to go—and Deston subtly shifted position. I realized Katarina was using him as a shield, betting on the fact that I wouldn't hurt him because I was a pushover.

She was right but for the wrong reason.

And while I couldn't see how she kept Deston prisoner, if I could somehow cut off her influence, even for a few seconds, it might be enough for him to get his mind back.

While I didn't have the power reserves I'd had yesterday, I had enough to cause a distraction. If I could give Deston back control of his mind—even for a few seconds—he could get me out of here.

I fixed Deston with a flat stare. "I suppose, this just proves that I was right about you all along." I gathered my magic together, spooling up as much fire as I could manage. "Treachery is in your blood, and you can't help but stab everyone you know in the back."

I shuffled to the side, let frost dust my fingertips. Deston matched my every move until he filled up my vision, close enough I could cast my magic without Katarina noticing.

I kept imagining Viktor. The revenants, that inside-out heart still pumping.

God, please don't let me kill him with my weird magic.

The mating mark flared, then cooled, like he was trying to send me a message.

"You betrayed Lyra, you betrayed me, how long do you think before you betray Katarina too?" I asked loudly, sending a pulse of emotion back down the bond. "It's in your nature, after all, to stab anyone who gets close to you." Something moved behind Deston's dead eyes, a spark of awareness. A rejection of what I said.

"How soon, Katarina, before he gets tired of you? How soon before he starts looking for a way out?"

I closed my eyes and sent a burst of emotions through the mating mark—begging him to come back to me—and Deston's entire body jerked, like he'd been hit with an electrical current

That's it. Fight this. I know you're in there somewhere.

"I am going to so enjoy watching him kill you." Katarina waved her hand, and Deston stepped toward me, his jaw clenching. "And after you're dead, I'll enjoy releasing him from the bond and watching him relive your death over and over again. I might actually be able to break him, this time."

I backed away as he pursued me, slowly, while Katarina taunted me with all the ways she'd torture him, once I was dead. One thing was for sure. She had a good imagination.

Deston's hand snapped out, reaching for my neck, but I anticipated the move and dodged out of the way. He grabbed my arm instead, squeezing so tightly my bones ground together.

"I'm really sorry about this, Deston," I apologized, right before I slammed my knee up into his groin. I was the one who winced when I made contact. Katarina's laugh rolled across the open field.

His fingers dug deeper into my arm. I threw a punch. He blocked me with his forearm. We grappled, legs twisting together, before momentum took us flying and dry grass crunched beneath us.

When we finally stopped rolling, Deston was wrapped in a web of my magic while I prayed I didn't flay my own mate alive.

Katarina was already bearing down on me, black, glittering magic gathering at her fingertips, murder in her eyes, tottering on her heels.

Time spun out as I threw up a shield, but my magic was no match for two millennia of power, and she sliced straight through it. I crawled away, she caught me by the hair, yanked me back.

This is it. I'm dying in this shitty field because I didn't listen to Luthor and Cyrus, and now this evil bitch is going to kill me.

There was a burst of light, the smell of ozone, and suddenly, I was free.

I sat up in the gravel-strewn grass to see Deston covered in a glowing shimmer of power. My magic, cutting him off from Katarina, had given my mate back his free will.

He was back, my beautiful fallen angel, and he roared at Katarina, his rage-driven magic knocking me back onto my ass. He was free, and Katarina threw her hands up in front of her face.

She was cut off mid-scream, blown across the field, shredding her precious coat and leaving dry grass and dirt sticking out of her tangled hair. *Served the bitch right.*

Missing a shoe, Katarina staggered to her feet, shrieked, then threw a wall of those razor-sharp diamonds at us, clearly her signature move. I curled up as small as I could, expecting the slice of pain.

They'd almost reached us when Deston's arms wrapped me up, and we were in the wind, streaking through the air. I didn't care where we were going. We landed back at his castle, still standing, the shriveled gardens drifted over in dead leaves, the trees sagging in the cold.

One more quick jump and we were in one of the beautiful rooms, still torn apart from Viktor's incursion...had that really been weeks ago now?

It felt like a hundred years since I'd last seen him, a lifetime spent thinking I'd never see him again. I ran my hands over every inch of skin, only to discover he was still completely encased in my magic.

"Are you... really you?" I reached up and ran my thumb down his cheek. My magic turned phosphorescent, leaving a glowing trail everywhere I touched him. He closed his eyes and leaned into my touch, sighing in pleasure. I hadn't known how much I'd missed him until right now, and I hugged him closer, the mate mark purring in approval.

"I am, and I will be, so long as your magic is protecting me." He nuzzled against my cheek, and I kissed his throat, blood racing through the artery just below my hungry lips. "And my wards, of course."

"Is that why you built this place?" I wondered aloud. "Because she couldn't get through?" If that was true, then he'd been protecting me from the very beginning, my seeming imprisonment something else entirely.

"Yes." His hands were warm and gentle through the thin material as they raked up and down my back. "She couldn't sense you here, so long as you remained on the grounds."

"You should have told me," I murmured. "You should have told me everything from the very beginning. Everything could have been different. We could have had more time."

"I didn't know... *I couldn't*, Seraphina. I'm bound by her will, a side effect of the soul bond. I cannot speak of her secrets nor can I betray her." My throat tightened at the pain in his voice. "I truly thought she'd freed me from the bond and forgotten about me. I didn't know she was using me to spy on Lyra's court and the ones that came before."

He released me, but I followed, pressing myself into him again, feeling complete and safe.

"I should have, though," he added softly. "She's the one who taught me everything about court politics. I should have known she'd been using me the entire time, especially after Lyra was dethroned. She even bragged she was the one who instructed Viktor to imprison my family, knowing I'd do anything to save them."

"Is she really capable of that long a game?" I asked.

"Vampires live forever, mon très cher amour. We have nothing *but* time." He cupped my face in his hands.

"Katarina wants total control over the vampire world, both here and in the Old Country. She's been laying the groundwork for this for over a thousand years, since she was exiled. She's old," he said quietly. "Older than anyone knows."

"Sebastian told me," I said absently, my body responding to being this close to my mate. He smelled delicious, and it had been days since I'd fed.

"Sebastian Blackwell?" Deston's fingertips skimmed over my scalp, sending shivers through me. "Katarina neglected to say he'd made a reappearance."

"I'll bet she did," I said, running my hands up his chest. There were a million things I wanted to tell him, but right now...

"We won't have long." His dark brown eyes were glowing with emotion, and though I felt his rising hunger through our connection, he backed off, putting more distance between us. "She's already searching for us, and once she finds this place, it will no longer be a refuge."

"Is there any way to break the soul bond?" I asked hopefully. "There has to be a way out, right?"

"Only if the Maker breaks the bond. Or dies. Otherwise, it's permanent."

"What about my magic, it's working now, isn't it?" I wrapped another thin layer around him, relishing the power of cutting him completely off from Katarina.

Deston stroked my cheek, his fingers a brush of heat against my face. "Much as I would like to, I can't stay wrapped up in your magic forever, Seraphina. And Katarina will never let me go." He gripped my arms, forced me to look into his face, to acknowledge what he was about to say.

"I will go back to her. You will move on. Forget about me. Stay close to Luthor and Cyrus, build your court, create a kingdom strong enough to stand up to her."

"And what about you?" I asked angrily. "You're willingly selling yourself into servitude?"

"Not willingly, out of necessity." His hands gripped me harder. "If Katarina wants to keep me, she stays across the ocean, thousands of miles away from you. That's the deal I will offer her, and she will agree."

"How can you be so sure?"

"Because if she refuses, I will end my life." My entire body went limp as his voice turned colder, harder. "I will be very convincing. She will acquiesce to my demands."

"You...can't." The back of my neck was screaming, my chest was caving in. *This couldn't be happening, there had to be some way out, some way to fix this.* "That's a bullshit deal for both of us, and you know it."

"It is a deal that keeps you safe and me alive long

enough to figure out how to kill her. Katarina has been alive longer than anyone else. Don't ever underestimate her power. I can't tell you everything, but..." His face tightened, like he was in pain.

"Her magic is the basis of most vampire magic, her influence is so interwoven through our kind that it cannot be separated out. All the spells that guard the palace come from her, which means, if you want the palace to be secure, you'll have to destroy every piece of magic that guards your kingdom and start over again."

"We're already on that," I told him, "I'm not going to tell you how, just in case..."

"Smart."

"I'll figure out how to protect myself and the others. There's no need for you to go back." I raked a hand through my hair. "Why can't we fight her? Why are you so willing to just give up?"

"Because she'll kill you with a snap of her fingers." His head flicked to my face. "I'm not doing this *willingly*. I'm doing this to keep you safe, Seraphina. Once your magic fades, once I step out of these wards, I'll be forced to obey her every whim."

His eyes went dark as night. "I would have *killed* you today, is that what you want?"

"No." The word shuddered out of me. "No, of course not."

"Katarina wanted that, though." My breath went shallow at his bitter, spiteful tone, clearly meant to drive me away. "She would have reveled in watching you die at my hand, then forced me to relive that moment over and over again. Do you know what that would have done to me, Seraphina?"

Now he was the one advancing, and I was retreating,

not wanting to hear another word. I stepped backwards until my back hit something and I had nowhere else to go.

"It would break me." He hissed, gripping my arms as he pressed me to the wall. "And if I break, *I cannot save you*. If I break, *I will be no good to anyone*."

"You are not going to push me away by being horrible, Deston." I put my hands against his chest. "Stop trying to drive a wedge between us, because it won't work. Not this time." I managed a trembling smile. "Never again." His heart thudded against my hand, his chest heaving like a bellow.

"I am going to save you. She is not going to have her way, not this time." I sent another burst of protective magic over Deston, my already drained reserves running dry. But I had to do *something*.

"You cannot keep this up, *ma cherie*," he said gently, trying to peel me away. "You have to let me go."

"Ten minutes, Deston." I wound my hands in his shirt. "Just...I want a little time with you, before she takes you back." My fingers skated over warn, supple skin and a growl rumbled in his chest.

Deston tilted my head up to his, the tips of his fingers heated from my magic.

"Then release me, love." He urged. "Drop your magic, so I can truly touch you, taste your mouth." The glowing shield slowly faded away, leaving Deston's lips just inches away from mine.

I pushed up on my toes, putting every bit of love and desperation into my frantic kiss, telling his with my lips, with my body, all the things we didn't have time to put into words.

I loved him. I loved him and I was only just realizing the truth, even though...I'd felt like this for a long time.

His lips roamed over mine, gently nibbling, as if we had all the time in the world. He explored my mouth with a reverence I never would have thought him capable of, a tenderness so at odds with the cold, heartless vampire I'd first met, a prisoner on this island.

"Upstairs." I told him roughly, tugging his shirt free of his pants. "Your bed. Now."

If this was our last time, I didn't want him to take me here, amongst the ruin and wreckage. I wanted to be in his bed, smelling him all around me, and I wanted both of us naked. I wanted to feel him, taste him, remember every needy sigh and husky groan.

Another rush of cold air, and I looked around a room too beautiful for words. "Holy shit, is this seriously your bedroom?" The space was a pool of shadows with an enormous bed in the center, covered with a comforter the exact color of the night sky.

"It's ours. Or rather, it was *supposed* to be ours." He said apologetically, shrugging out of his jacket, pulling his shirt over his head while he herded me towards the bed, his face so wild, I lost my breath. His body was a goddamned work of art, layered with toned muscle, yet elegant and lean.

Every notion I'd ever had about him—his coldness, aloofness, arrogance—was blown to smithereens when I glimpsed this version of him. Passion burned in his eyes like wicked fire, his face filled with hunger as he stalked closer, intent on devouring every single piece of me, and I would give him everything he wanted.

"After I'm gone, feel free to come sleep here anytime. I can still feel your emotions through the bond, you know," he added with a wicked smile. "I expect you to remember me fondly."

Deston tugged the hoodie over my head, then drew

back, his breathing shallow and fast. He reached out a trembling hand and traced my neck, my collarbone, between my breasts. "I've imagined you countless times, *ma cherie*. But in person...." His pupils dilated as fire took over. "You take my breath away."

Then we were a tangle of hands and hungry, seeking mouths, stripping each other, my hands tracing his smooth muscles, leaner than either Luthor or Cyrus, a beautiful, deadly predator, silky hair falling over his shoulders in inky waves. His own hands were near-reverent as they explored my body, cupped my breasts, traced the curve of my hips.

I would have liked to take forever getting to know his body, finding out how he liked to be touched. I would have worshipped every perfect inch of him, found out what made him moan, or bite his bottom lip, but we didn't have time.

We were mates, but this could be the last time we were together.

A wave of panic rocketed through me, then Deston dipped his head, bit my shoulder, and everything faded away except the pure pleasure of my mate, having his teeth in me.

That's it, this is all that matters, Seraphina. You and me. Us.

His fangs sank in deeper and anticipation turned my entire body loose.

Then he pulled back, his greedy gaze sliding over me, his fingers resting intimately on my mound, then sliding down farther, brushing over my swollen, aching clit before he dragged his finger through my folds. His barely-there touch brought on a rush of need, and I arched to my toes, pressing against him.

Those fingers were seriously talented, and I rocked my hips harder, demanding *more*.

"You are so fucking wet. Such a needy mate. If we only had more time...*fuck*." His growl turned nearly feral, his fingers sliding through my folds, then plunging in deeper, curling inside me as he dragged them slowly back out, my body shivering with need as I rocked my hips, trying to drive him deeper.

He pulled away with a curse and that coiling ache turned to raging fire.

"I'll take that ache away, Seraphina. How I want to lick and bite and suck every inch of your delectable body, but..." He tipped me back onto the bed, his hips falling between my open legs, my hands on his face as we kissed each other, tongues lashing, trying to imprint ourselves onto the other. This was torture and heaven all mixed into one and everything was moving too fast, like time was slipping away.

"Stop, Fina. Look at me." I opened my eyes to find him staring down, face still as death, lips slightly parted, the tips of his fangs showing. "We will have more time together. I swear this, *ma cherie*."

Then he canted his hips and the head of his cock nudged at my entrance. "Keep looking at me. Look at me while I take you. I want to see...*yes, that's it*," he breathed, a whisper of air, as his cock slid in deeper and deeper, filling me full, not stopping until he hit bottom, our hips fused together.

He went still, his heart crashing against my own.

His hands were still cupped around my cheeks, our eyes locked together. Neither of us could have looked away, even if we wanted to. And I didn't want to. I wanted to commit every second of him to memory, to hold these perfect moments in my heart forever.

He moved slowly against me, drawing this precious time out like the threads he'd spoken about before, those connections that would never break, no matter how thinly they were stretched.

"Bite me, Deston. I want..." I wanted so much. I wanted everything, and when his mouth latched onto the tendon in my neck, when he bit down with a pinch of pain, euphoria raced through me, like I was being unmade.

No, like I was being *remade*, crushed beneath this rising pleasure, the deep, unbreakable connection fusing between us, tighter and tighter, as my entire body writhed, the aching, demanding need swamping my senses as he slammed into me, murmuring in French.

"Don't forget about me, Deston," I commanded desperately, my fingers sinking into his shoulders like claws, demanding he obey me. He hissed when I clenched around him, growling when I raked my nails down his back, dug my heels into his clenching, churning ass.

"I mean it. You will remember *all of this*."

"You must remember for the both of us, my love." My eyes burned, my throat closed off as I hung on harder.

No, I don't want to remember for both of us. I want us to remember together.

That is not in the cards, ma cherie. But there will come a day when I will find my way back to you.

He slammed into me hard and, at the same time, pressed his fingers into the mating mark. My entire body —*my magic*—responded to his touch, rising and rising until I felt like I was floating. My hands frantically traced his body, moving like a wave over me, and beneath the finger of my right hand, I found the small, circular mark I was looking for.

He hissed again when I brushed across it, then growled deeply when I pressed down, angling his hips to drive himself into me deeper, harder, the head of his cock dragging up and down inside me. My orgasm started as a sparkle, followed by that coiling tightness as I clamped down on his long, thick length, then finally, finally, I seized up as a shock wave rippled through me.

The world crashed to a halt, leaving me suspended midair, like a soaring bird.

Then I plummeted, a messy tangle of ecstasy and howling heat and consuming fire, swallowed by something so powerful, I didn't even know if I would survive the crash. The world came back slowly, my body quivering, fingers still digging into Deston's shoulders, like I couldn't let him go.

He was staring down at me, and I couldn't describe the look on his face.

Like he was seeing the ocean for the first time.

"How I wish I would remember that look on your face, *mon très cher amour*." He said softly, "Because I've never seen anything more perfect in my entire life."

With a groan, Deston bowed his head and slammed home one last time, emptying himself into me. He collapsed, the weight of his body atop mine the only thing that felt real right now.

"You are mine, now, you belong to me." I whispered, wishing the words were be true as I retraced the mark on his side. "And I will love you, Deston, no matter where you go, no matter if you can't feel it or even know who I am."

"I love you too, ma cherie, forever and always."

I was more connected to him than ever. Every emotion —devotion, dread, regret—were as clear as my own. It was like he awakened a part of myself I hadn't even known existed. I wanted this little bubble of peace to last forever. To be in his arms like this, forever.

Around us, the castle creaked, as if there was an earth-quake. A shiver of dust fell from the ceiling.

Katarina.

Deston sprang from the bed, waved a hand over both of us, and all remnants of what we'd just done disappeared, as if our lovemaking had never happened. He dressed quickly, yanking his jacket over his loose shirt. "Stay inside the wards until Luthor and Cyrus come for you. I have already sent word. They know where you are."

I covered myself up, listening numbly while he dressed, his instructions desperately urgent.

"Listen to them, Seraphina. Listen to them and learn everything you can. Your stubbornness is your worst enemy, but you must be clever now. The time for games is over. You are Queen, you must take charge, mold the kingdom to your vision." His dark gaze raked over me, a mix of regret and desire.

There will be those who wish to harm you. Destroy them before they get the chance. Keep those you trust close, and don't ever come looking for me." His eyes narrowed, then he crossed the room, leaned down.

"I'll find a way to get free. Don't you *dare* come after me, Seraphina. Swear it."

"No," I said sweetly, crossing my arms over my chest. "I won't swear to anything because I'm not letting you go without a fight." Anger swirled up and threatened to swallow me whole as his physical form began to fade.

"Deston. No." I moaned.

Do. Not. Come. After. Me.

Deston's final command hung on the wind, long after he disappeared.

Chapter 55
Seraphina

I 'd barely dressed when I sensed Luthor and Cyrus's arrival.

They must have dematerialized the second Deston contacted them and now they waited downstairs, which gave me time to get myself together.

Not that time would help me right now.

I wasn't together—I might never be together again. I didn't have a clue how to deal with the fallout of my actions. While both Luthor and Cyrus knew we were mated, Deston was also a traitor and a liar and had done despicable things.

I sensed plenty of jealousy, seeping up from downstairs.

Not for the first time, I wished I wasn't an emotionally stunted woman who'd spent most of her life on the run. What would I have been like if I'd actually developed healthy coping mechanisms? Probably not standing up here, scared to death to face the two people I loved more than anything.

"Seraphina?" Cyrus must have gotten tired of waiting. "We should get moving. You're not safe here."

Why, then, did I feel safer here than anywhere else?

I smoothed down my jeans. "Coming."

Luthor's relief pulsed through our bond when I started down the stairs and some of my panic ebbed away. The three of us might have a different connection than what I shared with Deston, but ours was familiar and comforting. They were my home, and I was theirs, no matter the circumstances. Once I worked this out in my head, I raced toward them, my tennis shoes skimming quickly down the stairs.

At the bottom, doubts got the better of me and I paused, my heart pounding in my throat, then Luthor opened his arms wide. I blinked to clear my vision as my heart started beating normally again.

They were my family. My loves. And they always would be.

I threw myself into them, the tears coming so fast, words hiccupping out of me until they became a steady stream of misery. "He's gone. It was awful. Katarina tried to make him kill me, but he didn't, then he brought me back here where I'd be safe because of the wards. I think she used the bond to call him back, and now I don't know if I'll ever see him again."

Luthor kissed the top of my head. "If there's a way, we'll get Deston back, Seraphina," he promised, without a shred of hesitation.

"Really?" I pulled away, searched his face, then Cyrus's. "You mean that?"

"Of course," Cyrus promised with quiet conviction. "Why wouldn't we?"

Luthor brushed my hair back. "We could never be angry with you, not for being who you are. Your happiness is the most important thing in the world to us. I've told you that, over and over. Why can't you believe me?"

"You did, but...." *He had. Many times.* "This means there's someone else now. Being mated... I'm afraid it will change how we feel toward each other."

"It only changes the arrangement, not our feelings,"

Luthor insisted, Cyrus nodding in agreement. "I can say I wish this was someone other than de Rayne, but I can't say I'm shocked." He ran his finger down my cheek, a slight smile forming on his lips. "You're full of surprises, my Queen. Is there anything else you'd like to drop on us, before we head home?"

"Not much. Except I'm killing Katarina, the second I'm able."

Luthor handed me off to Cyrus, his soothing magic flowing into me like a sedative. "I think my cousin's rubbing off on you," Cyrus said, not letting me go as he prepared to dematerialize. "But please, don't take on any of his odious personality defects. I don't think I can stand it. And I thought you were supposed to stick by the house?"

"I'm just sorry... I shouldn't have wandered off today. I thought with Katarina gone we were out of danger. I should have known it was a ruse."

"We should have double-checked Hugh's intel. In the future, we will." Cyrus sounded like he was going to make that his mission in life.

"I have been hiding something from you, Seraphina." Luthor shifted his feet as Cyrus nodded encouragingly. "Before I got the use of my leg back, I... I thought I was not strong enough to serve you, as a proper commander should. I'd been...planning to leave, as soon as I arranged sufficient troops for the Knightsguard."

My mouth dropped open. "You were going to leave me?" I repeated, hurt and a fair amount of anger surging through my veins. "When?"

"After you killed Viktor and I knew the threat had been eliminated."

"That's why..." My words trailed off. "That's why you've been so distant lately. That's why you've seemed so distracted. Because you knew you wouldn't be around much longer." I glared up at him.

"Well, I don't fucking accept your resignation. You are everything I need in a commander, Luthor. If you so much as try to leave, I will hunt you down, I swear I will."

"But I'm not..."

"We should get moving." Cyrus urged, scanning the damaged walls. "This isn't safe any longer."

"I'm serious, Luthor. You're not going anywhere." I glared at Cyrus, for good measure. "And for the record, neither are you. I'm your queen, so consider this a lifetime appointment for you both."

"Why are you dragging me into this?" Cyrus spun me into his arms. "But a lifetime appointment works for me." He was still grinning when we dematerialized, landing in our bedroom at the Cormier's. *Not the palace.* I looked around, bemused.

"We're still cleaning trash out of the palace," Cyrus explained matter-of-factly. "And we thought we'd let you pick out our suite." His green eyes twinkled with humor as he hip-bumped me. "We know this will be your first real home, Seraphina. You should get to choose."

"Okay." A rush of emotion leached any remaining energy from me, and I leaned my forehead against his chest. "I can do that." But inside, I was a mess. In the past few days, I'd killed a king, defeated a queen, gained a mate, then lost him.

"Everything will be okay, you have to give yourself time, Fina."

Cyrus's light, clever fingers skimmed up my back, lifting my shirt over my head. I pulled it back down, embarrassed. He kissed my cheek, trailing a finger where his lips had just been.

"I just want to get you out of these clothes. We're starting slow, my Queen. Think of this as a new beginning for all of us."

A thrill of relief went through me, followed by disappointment. But maybe this was part of the learning process, getting comfortable with each other all over again.

"You need to rest. Heal. So for the time being, sleep and nothing else." But his nose flared slightly when he looked down my body.

"And when you're ready for more, remember this." Luthor leaned closer, wrapping his arms around me, and I lost myself in the feel of them, in the wonderful warmth of their love. A smile tugged at my mouth when Luthor finished, "I'm always ready to serve."

As it turned out, I couldn't sleep.

Not yet.

Luthor and Cyrus were dead to the world when I unwedged my backpack out from beneath the bed, jimmied the huge book free. The embossed letters—History of the Darkfell Queens—mocked me as I read the very first page.

Queen Katarina Cozma, of Brasov, Romania (born c. 61*, Katarina Kobus in Moselle, France) is a founding elder of vampire society, along with Caine. Through time, she has ruled the Darkfell Clan (exiled c. 1088), the Cherven clan (now defunct), before founding the Brasov clan in 1191.

From her line are descended the following royal families:

House Carpathian (US), House Flauvian (Denmark), House Usora (Bulgaria), and all French lines, including House Valois, Aquitaine, and Provence.

Once considered the most powerful witch in the world, her magic serves as the foundation for all vampire magic.

*rumours persist Katarina was born prior to year zero, though no records support this.

I squeezed my eyes closed. Why did I not read this weeks ago?

Deston, bound by the soul bond, had been incapable of warning me against Katarina. But Deston's magic, capable of creating wondrous things, had written down the truth, right here, for me to see.

My mate had given me the only gift he could, and I'd never taken the time to look.

Maybe if I'd seen this earlier, things would have turned out differently. Maybe Deston and I would be together, and the four of us would be figuring out our new dynamic. Maybe...

I traced the passage about her magic.

This was why Katarina had asked me to show her one of my tricks. Because that's all my magic would ever be to her, a parlor trick. My magic was derived from hers, which meant she'd always be more powerful than me.

Until I figured out another way to defeat her.

Chapter 56
Seraphina

The back of my neck tingled, and out of habit, I reached up, pressed my finger in gently, wondering if I was sending a message back.

It had been weeks since I'd last seen Deston. In the interim, I'd learned to trust the mark, to trust my instincts, and to think before I spoke.

Like right now.

"My advice would be to forget de Rayne altogether. It's clear he's chosen his side, the fucking traitor. Focus on building your court. More applicants arrived this morning and would like to speak with you."

I frowned at Sebastian... Blackwell... *Dad*? Sire? Hell, I didn't know what to call him, so I didn't call him anything, just yet.

The company line was Deston had betrayed us and defected to Katarina's court. Luthor, Cyrus, and I also decided nobody could ever know we were mated. Which meant I wouldn't exactly explain why *forgetting about de Rayne* was not an option.

"Show them in," I said instead, dreading this latest onslaught of horrible people I had to deal with. The royal houses, and just like Maddie said—they were perfectly awful.

A group of immaculately dressed vampires glided in—

three males, two women—their clothing and jewelry taste-fully expensive, dark eyes sparkling with cunning.

So far, they'd all been like this.

Horrible, treacherous creatures, looking to climb the social ladder.

The five of them stopped dead in their tracks when they saw me.

I'd have liked to say it was because of the fearsome power I possessed, but no, it was because I looked like a dirty street urchin in my hoodie and tennis shoes. That's what Tessa called me, anyways, but I wasn't about to dress up for these people. If they thought I was trash, then fine, I wasn't about to become someone else just because I had some fancy title.

"Octavio and Brooks Dubois, their advisor, Markus, and wives, Corvina and Lila."

I had no idea who went with who, but it didn't matter. They'd served the Carpathians, and now they wanted to serve me. And coincidently, they were the *perfectly awful* vampires Maddie had been describing.

"My Queen." One of them, dark-haired and lean, his long arms tucked behind his back, stepped forward and did the customary bow and flourish. The blonde woman followed his every movement approvingly before her blank gaze settled on me. "Allow me to present myself for service. I am Octavio Dubois. My brother Brooks and I are eager to offer our assistance in this time of need."

"I wasn't aware I needed your assistance," I said lightly. *They did look like spiders.* "But since you're here, what do you bring to the table?"

I was sure there was a whole polite song and dance I was supposed to be doing, but seriously, who had the time? These snakes would sooner wrap their coils around my throat and squeeze, than help me build a better world.

So really, *fuck them*.

The leader—Octavio—bared his teeth in a parody of a smile. "We bring eons of experience to your newborn court. You are still young, my Queen, and do not yet understand court politics. We can guide you, help you...."

"Help me what? Understand how you provided the intel to the Carpathians as they coordinated a coup against Lyra?" By now, my fangs were down, and instinct told me to keep them that way. "Or know that you were the one who suggested reinstating Reaping Nights ninety years ago, in order to prevent another queen from rising?"

I leaned back on the throne, my body relaxed and in control, my anger anything but.

"Perhaps I should thank you," I said dismissively. "If not for you, I'd still be human, traipsing through life, completely blind to this world, while you wove your web of deceit around Viktor."

I fixed my gaze on Octavio, well aware my eyes glowed gold. "But I'm not, am I?" I clicked my tongue. "As a matter of fact, I'm sitting up here, and you're down there." I let a tendril of frost-tipped power trickle down the steps, wrap around their ankles. They stilled, like vermin in a trap.

Clearly, they'd heard what my magic could do. We'd spread some rumors, specifically for instances like this. Being flayed alive, it seemed, gave even the most treacherous vampires pause.

I was tempted to do more, but Luthor had warned me last night.

No killing. Fine.

"This is how things will be from here on out." I stood, winding my shadows around me like a cloak. "If I hear the vaguest rumor you are planning another coup, if a single hair is harmed on an innocent head, I will come for you. I will wipe your entire house from the face of this Earth, and nobody in this clan will even remember your names by the next morning."

The brothers didn't so much as blink, but their advisor paled.

"I wouldn't allow you to corrupt *my* court with your poison." My shadows reached for them, and they backed away as I stalked toward them. "Go back to whatever nest you crawled out of and don't ever set foot in the palace again."

They skittered off like rats, probably to find another ship to infest.

"That was a refreshing change from the usual court politics. More efficient too." Luthor appeared beside me, a dazzling smile on his face. I refrained from jumping into his arms because that didn't seem very queenlike. *But I wanted to.*

"That was cleaning house," I replied. I couldn't stop looking at him. He'd assumed command as effortlessly as he did everything else, his movements confident and strong, a rigid set to his shoulders, his spine held in rigid tautness. Even better, no more thinking he wasn't good enough.

Ridiculous male.

I love you too, Seraphina.

"That was a beautiful thing to see." Luthor clasped his hands behind his back. "Renard Gauthier is next. I wish to be present when you spoke to him."

"You don't trust me to handle him?"

"I don't trust *him*," Luthor said flatly. "Caden vouched for his sire, but Renard provided the soldiers that overthrew

Lyra during the coup. Let's just say, I'm not entirely convinced."

"Understood." I couldn't help it. I squeezed his hand. "I like you being here. You're nice to look at." He frowned at the compliment, and I jabbed him playfully in the side. "What? You can be handsome *and* useful *and* terrifying at the same time, just so you know."

"Oh, I know," he said slyly, waggling his eyebrows at me. My throat burned from the tears threatening to burst free. *We were a team again.* No secrets between us, just like we'd first promised, and my heart soared.

"I love you too," I told him softly.

"Likewise, Seraphina, likewise."

"Renard Gauthier, my Queen." Sebastian shot me a warning look, and I nodded back. I already distrusted this guy, and I'd never even met him.

Renard was burly, wide-shouldered, and densely muscled, and he moved confidently, owning the room as he made his way toward me. "My Queen." There wasn't a hint of deference in his tone, his clever eyes scanning every inch of the room before they settled on me.

If he was part of Lyra's murder, I should kill him right now and be done with this charade.

Listen to what he has to say, Seraphina, Luthor counseled gently. Renard moved the same way as Caden—sharing the same dark hair and bottle-green eyes—but he lacked Caden's easy grace. This man bulldozed his way through life.

"I have been waiting to meet you for some time." Renard's tone was imperious, not ingratiating. I respected that, after all these kiss-asses I'd had to endure. "When I heard of your existence, I was quite encouraged."

"Encouraged enough to hunt me down and try to kill me."

His face clouded. "Yes. I did send Viktor to Albita Springs. I knew you'd escape him, given Fontaine and Rayne were with you. Which you did."

"Barely. Only because my grandmother bought us time to get away."

"*Et pour cela, je m'excuse humblement.*" Renard bowed his head, and the contrition in his voice seemed real enough. "I was only trying to save my son, his friends, and the woman he loved."

That explanation lined up with what Tessa had told me. Viktor had captured them, brought them to the palace, and nearly fed them to the revenants. Renard had not only saved their lives but covered up their trail so effectively, Viktor never even discovered they'd escaped.

I could use someone like that.

He'd done terrible things. We all had.

No doubt, we'd do even more terrible things before this was over.

I was also stepping over the straight line I'd laid down for myself. The one separating good and evil. Between black and white. If I filled the court with too much gray, I'd end up with the same problems as before. A court bloated with the morally compromised. I planned to create something different.

"Would you do the same to me?" I was trying hard to read him, but Renard's inscrutable gaze gave nothing away.

"Save you, my Queen?" There was a wrinkle of confusion between his brows.

"No. Would you betray me to save your son?"

Renard hesitated. Enough that I knew his next words were a lie. "I would remain loyal to you."

"Is that really true, though?" I asked pointedly, holding his stare. "Doesn't blood always win out?"

He inclined his head until I couldn't read his face. "You put me in an impossible position, my Queen."

"I'm putting you in a position you've found yourself in before. All I'm asking for is the truth, and it's pretty simple. If you were forced to make the choice, would you choose your son over me? Your own blood over the crown?"

This time when he raised his head, his defiant green eyes were unblinking when he answered. "Yes, my Queen, I would. Every single time. My family is everything to me, and I would die to protect them." Beside me, Luthor's hand went to his weapon, Sebastian closed ranks, and I sensed Cyrus nearby, ready to join them if this interview went south.

"That was all I was looking for. The truth." I could use this male. He brought a lot to the table, and with Houses Dubois and the Bouderaux firmly on the other side, I needed allies. Badly.

"If you can speak the truth, every time, then you belong in this court. If you cannot, then take your leave."

"Clever and fair. I should have expected it, being Claire raised you. You shall do well in the Darkfell clan." His smile turned frighteningly cunning. "Very well, indeed."

But he still hadn't said yes. "Your answer?"

"I shall serve you, my Queen." For such a big man, he dropped gracefully to one knee, crossed his arms, and bowed his head. I would never get used to this. Even though all eyes were on him, I felt like the spotlight was on me.

Luthor stepped up. "Say the words, Renard."

"I swear fealty to Queen Seraphina, her house, her

court, and to this kingdom. I shall keep her from harm and shall be faithful to her cause. May her reign be long."

Renard rose in one, smooth movement. The hint of defiance was gone, the lines on his face relaxed. He was relieved. I was, too, just a little.

One step at a time, I'd build my court. I'd make the best decisions I could, and I'd rely on Luthor and Cyrus to steer me when I didn't know the way.

"Thank you, Lord Gauthier. I expect we shall have a long working relationship."

Epilogue
Deston

Romania was odious, as I knew it would be.

During my rare periods of lucidity, I tried to recall what Seraphina smelled like, tasted like, before those memories were stolen away by the soul bond.

I'd wake with bloodstained hands, the stench of death hanging around me like a pall, and know Katarina had used me to carry out some heinous execution, most likely in public, for all to see.

She made me into a monster, and I couldn't even remember why.

This was one of those times. I'd already washed dried blood from my family ring, dressed myself in the beautiful clothes Katarina provided—she did hate me looking shabby—and went for a walk. Brasov castle sat high on a craggy outcropping, the foundations built into the granite, the entire mountain saturated with Katarina's corrupted magic.

Nothing grew here, nothing natural anyway, although I caught the furtive movements of revenants skulking from shadow to shadow. I hated this place. I'd thought never to return.

Yet here I was, staring out over the same ghostly landscape I'd once escaped.

I'd been a fool to believe I'd be able to kill Katarina. For weeks, I'd clung to that hope, as desperately as I'd wanted to stay with my mate. But my moments of clarity were rare, and here, on her mountain where a thousand years of magic imbued every stone, she was invincible.

No, I'd never escape because she already had everything she wanted.

There was no mate to kill, no kingdom to infiltrate, just a host of enemies to be eradicated, like so many rats. I was little more than her exterminator.

One shaky exhale while I considered what *little more* meant.

The soul bond was good for one thing. I didn't have to remember the press of her flesh against mine, her tongue in my mouth, her teeth in my neck. Yes, I woke up well used and bloody, but thank the gods—I suppressed my shudder —I didn't remember any of it.

I still remembered the horrifying day when she'd bound me to her—nearly two hundred years ago now when she'd set me free—although that, too was a lie.

I took a deep breath and touched my finger to the mating mark. On the other end, I sensed Seraphina's emotions as clearly as if she was right in front of me. Determination tinged with a bit of annoyance, which meant she was safe and things were normal.

I'd sent Fontaine one final message before Katarina recalled me to her side, and I expected he'd honor it.

Do not allow her to find me. Ever.

The directive would both keep Seraphina safe and Fontaine happy, I expected, as he and my cousin would have no rival for her affections.

I breathed in the oily scent of shale and old blood, the dirty stench of revenants, the desperation in the air. This was my present. My future.

I'd die here, and I deserved this fate.

I was at peace with that ending because, for the first time in my existence, there was something I wanted more than my own survival.

Across the ocean, my mate would live a full life. She would be happy. Love others, who would love her back. I expected a stab of jealousy with that thought, but there was none. Something to think on, the next time I had my mind back.

Seraphina would rule a kingdom, the greatest in the world.

And someday, when her powers truly matured, she would rise and become something this world had never seen.

I only wished I'd be there to watch her soar.

**Seraphina's story continues with
Lost Kingdom!**

www.ingramcontent.com/pod-product-compliance
Lightning Source LLC
Chambersburg PA
CBHW060222030726
47499CB00004B/1160